FLOWERS STAINED WITH MOONLIGHT

Four years have passed since Cambridge schoolmistress Vanessa Duncan, defying the social conventions of the 1880s, turned detective to prove the innocence of a friend wrongly accused of murder. Now she is being called on again. It seems that Mrs Bryce-Fortescue's daughter Sylvia is suspected of killing her husband in the grounds of their manor home, but could the weak and apparently vulnerable Sylvia be capable of such a crime? Vanessa's investigations take her from the English countryside to the bright lights of Paris, but can she save the day again?

FLOWERS STAINED WITH MOONLIGHT

Flowers Stained With Moonlight

by

Catherine Shaw

Magna Large Print Books
Long Preston, North Yorkshire,
BD23 4ND, England.

British Library Cataloguing in Publication Data.

Shaw, Catherine
    Flowers stained with moonlight.

    A catalogue record of this book is
    available from the British Library

    ISBN   0-7505-2408-1

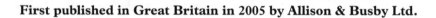

First published in Great Britain in 2005 by Allison & Busby Ltd.

Copyright © 2005 Catherine Shaw

Cover illustration © Old Tin Dog

The moral right of the author has been asserted

Published in Large Print 2005 by arrangement with
Allison & Busby Ltd.

Magna Large Print is an imprint of Library Magna Books Ltd.

Printed and bound in Great Britain by
T.J. (International) Ltd., Cornwall, PL28 8RW

To my eldest daughter,
always my first and best reader.

I dreamed I stood upon a little hill,
And at my feet there lay a ground, that seemed
Like a waste garden, flowering at its will
With buds and blossoms. There were
pools that dreamed
Black and unruffled; there were white lilies
A few, and crocuses, and violets
Purple or pale, snake-like fritillaries
Scarce seen for the rank grass,
and through green nets
Blue eyes of shy peryenche winked in the sun.
And there were curious flowers, before unknown,
Flowers that were stained with moonlight,
or with shades
Of Nature's willful moods...

Lord Alfred Douglas, 1894

Cambridge, Monday, June 6, 1892

My dearest Dora,

Please forgive me for not having written before; several days at least must have passed since I last wrote, but oh dear, the days sometimes seem to resemble each other so, that I quite lose count. Only today – today is the sixth of June, and that date will always be the most unforgettable one of my life! It was four years ago today that I invaded the Courts of Justice, confronted the Judge, and confounded the whole of a stolid British jury. How well I remember it all, and also the days that followed! Borne upon a cloud, I envisioned myself plunging into the adventure of turning my little school into a daring and audacious experiment, while my heart was overflowing with the joy of being engaged to be married. How happy I was! The prospect before me enchanted me so, that I believed myself content to wait any length of time before taking the next step and discovering the secrets of the wedded state.

Today, looking back, I begin to realise that *four full years* have come and gone since those days, four years that sometimes seem to weigh heavily upon me. Do you not ever feel so, Dora, you who have been waiting just as long for your betrothed to return from overseas? You never speak of impatience, you always seem tranquil and full of joy, but in your heart of hearts, do you not feel with a pang that we are getting older, Dora, you and I? Why, we will be twenty-five in just a few more months! Here I spend all my days with children, and have none of my own – and I long for them more with every passing hour. The very sweetness of my little pupils makes me ache all the more. They are so delightful, and it is so rejoicing to see all their big eyes fixed seriously upon me as I read to them of goblins, or explain the ins and the outs, the ups and the downs, of the many marriages of Henry VIII. I have come so far in these last four years; read so much, studied so hard, working each night by candlelight, that I sometimes feel like a different person from the ignorant girl I was when I first arrived in Cambridge – I am certainly a much better teacher than I used to be!

And yet, I am not altogether different after all. Rereading now what I have just written, I do seem to perceive some traces of the old impatience which used to seize me whenever life seemed to advance too slowly for my rushing blood.

Oh – a knock at the door! Who could it be?

Dora, how strange! A small boy has just delivered a message from a lady called Mrs Bryce-Fortescue; the name is perfectly unknown to me. It says that she wishes to know when she can call upon me for a matter of discretion and import-ance. Goodness – whatever can it mean? I have told the boy that I will be at her service tomorrow evening.

Perhaps it has something to do with the school. Yet why would discretion be necessary for that? I do hope it will be something more mysterious and exciting! Oh dear. I sound quite childish. Do I really deserve to become a respectable married lady?

Your very intrigued sister,

Vanessa

Cambridge, Wednesday, June 8, 1892

My dear sister,

I am sure you are wondering about the mysterious Mrs Bryce-Fortescue, and what she could possibly have wanted with humble me!

I certainly wondered greatly myself, but I could not rid myself of the dampening idea that she simply must be a lady, perhaps newly arrived in Cambridge, who had heard of my school and was considering enrolling a daughter or even a son there. A pleasing prospect, but not one liable to set the heart beating. Still, the idea that the reputation of my little school should be spreading was a flattering, not to say inspiring one, and I put a great deal of energy into the day's teaching. The children will very soon be free as birds for the remainder of the summer, and in the (probably vain) hope that they will not immediately forget all that they have learned, I multiplied the tasks I set them, so that they became increasingly nervous, especially in view of the warm sunshine and blue sky which beckoned them so invitingly out-of-doors.

The day finally came to an end, I shooed the children outside, bid goodbye to Mrs Burke-Jones and Annabel, who was helping her tinier charges into their summery wraps, and hastened home more quickly than usual, eager in spite of myself for a little novelty.

I bustled about my rooms, vaguely trying to occupy myself, but lending a tense ear to the goings-on outside my door the while, until finally I heard a ring, then a rather decided voice speaking to the landlady, and finally a sharp knock on my own door. I opened it speedily.

There stood a lady. Tall, forceful, with black eyes in a sharp yet handsome face, dark hair very slightly streaked with grey, gathered into a fashionable knot, and clothes most beautiful in every detail, if not absolutely fashionable nor absolutely new. Something strong-willed in her forehead and nose gave her a faint resemblance to an eagle.

This lady remained silent for a long moment, fixing me with her eyes as though guessing and analysing my thoughts. I waited for her to speak, but as she did not, I quelled a faint feeling of dismay, and proceeded to emit some welcoming noises.

'You must be Mrs Bryce-Fortescue,' I stammered, 'I was expecting you. Please do come in and sit down.'

She did so, with a sweep of her skirts, closed the door behind her firmly, motioned me to sit in front of her, and began once again to stare at me closely and alarmingly.

16

'Yes, you are as I remembered you,' was her first, unexpected remark.

'Why, have we met before?' I queried, surprised.

'No, we have not met, but I have seen you before,' she answered. 'I saw you in Court, four years ago, when you presented your evidence to the Judge and boldly rescued a certain rather wilted young gentleman from a most disagreeable and apparently quite undeserved fate. Such cases interest me, and I come into town purposely to follow them on occasion, although I do not live very near. I live well off the beaten track, in the countryside, in a manor that has belonged to my family for many generations. Ahem–' and she broke off suddenly, as though she had meant to say more, but hesitated.

'Oh!' I said, enlightened but greatly embarrassed by this speech. Dear me, how bold and unladylike and *visible* it made me sound! I felt quite like the Hottentot Venus, poor girl, brought thousands of miles from her native Africa to be gaped at in wonder as some sort of extraordinary phenomenon.

'But what has brought you here today, after so many years?' I asked after a moment of awkward silence.

'It is a long story,' she said, and then, after another hesitation, she amended, 'Or no, not such a long one, but a complicated one, and more than anything, it is a story requiring the greatest of discretion and delicacy. I need help, and I need a certain kind of help, and I could not think of anyone who could afford me the exact

17

kind of help I need. Someone who could be both daring and discreet, and also understanding of ... of good taste. I could not bear a scandal.'

She paused, waiting for my response. Clearly the service she had in mind to ask of me had nothing to do with enrolling a new student in my class. My spirits began to rise.

'Please, do tell me exactly how I can be of help to you,' I encouraged her politely.

'Yes, I shall tell you,' she answered, her tone suddenly firm. Sitting rigidly, she spent a few moments choosing her words.

'I must get to the point immediately. There is no sense in beating about the bush. No matter how unpleasant it is for me to recount the facts, obviously it must be done.' She stopped briefly, and seemed to brace herself somewhat. I had the impression that she was rehearsing a speech prepared beforehand.

'I am here to ask you, Miss Duncan, if you would be willing, in an entirely private capacity, to undertake an investigation for me. Namely, to investigate the death – no, the murder – of my son-in-law, Mr George Burton Granger. He was found shot dead just three days ago; that is, last Sunday. His body was discovered in the early afternoon, lying in a grove of trees bordering his estate, where he was in the habit of taking a daily constitutional. The police appear to be foolish enough to suspect my daughter of the crime, which is perfectly ridiculous. Sylvia is of a weak and fragile nature; quite incapable of murdering anybody. However, I perceive that the police suspect her, and I am greatly afraid that they will harass her and accuse her, and perhaps even browbeat her into making all kinds of foolish declarations. I do not know who killed Geo – Mr Granger, but I am perfectly certain that it was not Sylvia, and unimaginably anxious that she should not undergo the experience of an arrest, let alone the public shame, scandal and agony of a trial, whatever the outcome. It is not only the harrowing nature of such an experience, which she is but ill-equipped to endure, that I fear. No, worse – I see that the primary wish of the police is to arrest and convict a culprit as quickly as possible, so as to preserve their reputation of efficiency, as you well know from your own experience. They have not yet arrested Sylvia, but I feel impending disaster in the way they treat her; indeed, I believe that only the fact that I insisted on being present the first time they interviewed her prevented them from accusing and even arresting her at once! It hangs over us like a Damocles' sword, and this situation simply cannot go on; a stop must be put to it immediately. I am asking you to come and stay with us, and to employ your particular talents in order to exculpate my daughter once and for all.'

'I!' I gasped, truly startled by what could, after all, however well-controlled, still be termed an outburst. 'I am not a detective! I should have no idea what to do.'

'I am aware that you are not a professional detective. I should not have come if you had been. I am simply asking you to try to do for me exactly what you did four years ago; apply your mind and your efforts to seek for the truth. I cannot count on your success, I can only ask you to do your best for me, if you are willing to try. My idea is to invite you to stay with us, ostensibly in the capacity of a friend, of course, or perhaps a daughter of friends. As far as financial considerations are concerned, if you succeed, no reward would be sufficient to express my gratitude! But in any event, I would undertake to cover all expenses you might incur, should you need to travel.

'I realise that you are surprised and taken aback by my offer, and I see plainly from your expression that you are filled with doubts. But I have seen and known many people in my life, and I recognise something in you that is enterprising and trustworthy. I cannot trust the police, and I have not the means nor the necessary indiscretion to have recourse to a private detective – I need someone who, appearing as a friend of Sylvia's, can gain the trust of everyone connected with my son-in-law. I am at my wits' end, and I cannot see what can be lost by asking for your help. Anyone who knows my daughter can see that the mere idea of her shooting anyone is plainly absurd, but the police do not see things in the same light, and we are threatened by the horrific danger of her being arrested and tried. I am not beyond believing that it could end in an unjustified conviction! And even if it did not, it would bring down a most unendurable scandal upon us all. Do try to recall exactly how you felt four years ago, and I am sure you will wish to help us.'

'Oh, I do wish to help you!' I exclaimed. 'But I am so worried that I shall not be *able* to do it.'

'Let us simply begin at the beginning, then, by

20

having you come to us for a week or two. You will meet Sylvia, who has returned home, as naturally she could not bear to continue on in her husband's house after what happened. She has a friend down to keep her company, and that is the extent of our small household at the moment. You will learn what you can from them, and can easily travel back and forth to Haverhill, the village where my son-in-law resided, if you should find that to be useful. Come to us and see what you can do, and if in the end you come to feel that you cannot make any progress, we shall terminate the arrangement and bend our heads to endure the storm as we may.'

'Yes, I shall come,' I said, deciding it suddenly and completely. 'Only, I must wait for the end of this week, as my teaching duties continue until then.'

'But today is only Wednesday! I am afraid to wait; every moment is important. When is the soonest that you can come – must you teach until Friday? Can I send a carriage for you on Saturday morning, then? I shall count the days.'

I felt dismayed, distressed, worried, incapable, incompetent and certain to fail and disappoint such expectations, but at the same time, a wave of eager excitement impelled me to give a resounding assent to this proposition. Although I will surely turn out to be hopelessly unable to unearth the slightest piece of useful information, still, I do not seem to be able to prevent my mind from being invaded by heroic visions of astounding success, rescuing of maidens in distress and so on. And then ... deep down, my darling twin, in those

21

recesses of the mind that only you can understand, there is another feeling. Perhaps she is not wrong, perhaps I have some ability, some talent, some special perspicacity which remains sleeping and unused within me, and which longs only to be awakened, once again, after so long – awakened and employed, so that I might fly with my own wings...

I feel humble and also guilty about the secret excitement within me, as though I were profiting somehow from *murder*, and from its accessory, *suffering*. Yet, if only the energy in the excitement can be converted into a meaningful search for the truth, it will be worth it, I believe.

Your confused, worried, distressed yet hopeful

Vanessa

Cambridge, Thursday, June 9, 1892

My dearest sister,

Oh, I was bursting with my news today, as I joined Annabel, Emily and Charles after lessons for our weekly tea together. How difficult it was, at least at first, to say nothing! But I was determined not to, for it was only right that Arthur should be the first to know, and I was not to see him until he should come to fetch me and walk me home.

Fortunately, my secret seething was quite smothered – and I myself quite distracted – by Emily's news.

'Oh, Miss Duncan!' she cried, seizing me by the sleeve the moment I entered the room, after having seen the last fluttering ribbon of my departing pupils disappear down the street.

'Guess what – no, you'll never guess – never! I'm to take the examinations to enter Girton College! I'm to take them this very September, a year before I even thought any such thing was possible. I am so excited, but so frightened, I shall do nothing but study like a mad thing for the whole of the summer.'

'Is such a thing possible?' I exclaimed. 'So many difficulties to overcome – so much to learn, and your mother to be convinced as well!'

'Oh, that was thanks to you, or rather to your good advice. You were so right, long ago, when you told me that with mother, the best way was to keep silent and wait rather than ever insist on anything I dreadfully wanted. I have been keeping silent and waiting for ages, but Mother knew perfectly well the whole time, of course. She would! I know she was against it at first, but without a word ever being said, I came to feel that something in the air was changing. At any rate, we've told her, and all she said was "So the time has come. You will have to work very hard." Well, there's certainly no doubt about that!'

'And what has made you decide to try it out so very soon?'

'Ah, that was me,' interposed her uncle radiantly. 'I'm very confident in my star pupil – I know what those examinations are like, and she's ripe and ready for them!'

Emily exhausted my own humble store of

mathematical knowledge long ago, and her uncle has been teaching her privately for the last two years.

'Uncle Charles says I'm ready for them, but I can hardly believe it myself – there are so dreadfully many things I don't know! And then, I've never sat for an exam. before, well, not a real one, anyway. What if I'm paralysed and can't think at all! And what is even worse, I've got to pass an oral exam. That means I've got to do a problem right up at the blackboard in front of a professor who will listen to me make a frightful mess! Uncle Charles has been making me practice, and it's simply awful – either I have no idea what to say, and fail miserably, or else I keep wanting to laugh! Last time he put on a false beard so I could imagine he was a real professor (oh, I'm so sorry, Uncle Charles. You *are* a real professor, of course! But you know what I mean) and it was worse than ever. What *shall* I do if I want to laugh during the examination? The more I think about it, the more I'm sure I will.'

'Oh, my dear girl,' said Annabel a little sadly, 'I have a solution to that problem, at least. Self-control can be learned through hard practice, and I have many exercises to suggest. You have talent, for look at the way you were able to keep silent about your ambitions for so long.'

'Oh, but I wasn't really! Only to Mother. I'd have died if I hadn't been able to talk about things with you, and Uncle Charles, and Miss Duncan!'

'Well, let me train you a little over the summer, and you will be astonished at the results.'

'Poor Miss Forsythe,' said Emily, glancing at her governess with some surprise, 'have you had to practice so very much self-control in your life? What for? How does one do it?'

'*Il faut d'un vain amour étouffer la pensée...*' murmured Annabel, so softly that I hardly caught the words and Charles not at all. Emily, however, who was all ears, flushed suddenly.

'That's from *Phèdre,*' she stammered, 'really, I – do you mean–'

'Oh, I mean nothing,' Annabel said, with a tiny smile. 'The words came to my mind; Phèdre betrayed a singular lack of self-control, didn't she, in spite of all the efforts of her poor Oenone. But not everyone can afford the luxury of dishonour and death.'

'Dishonour and death – a luxury?'

'Well, not in themselves, but considered as the price paid for the luxury of declaiming aloud what the world would prefer hidden.'

There was a long, rather embarrassing silence. Even Charles, who had begun to pay attention to the conversation, seemed wordless.

'It sounds like you're talking about my father,' said Emily after a while, breaking the silence.

'My dear child, no! I didn't mean to. Please, forgive me, and forget everything I said! I meant only to give a literary reference to the evils of self-indulgence.'

'Well, I shall draw a lesson from it, I believe,' mused Emily. 'The very next time I feel like laughing at Uncle Charles, this conversation will come back to me and wipe it away at once.'

Everybody smiled, even Annabel.

'Come now,' intervened Charles, with the tone of one who is determined to be cheerful in the face of adversity, 'a little laughter is not harmful, and I'm sure you need not be worried either about making a fool of yourself at the exam., or failing it. Why, you've had an easy time of it altogether, preparing for your university studies! I'm sure all the girls in history who've ever felt a yen for mathematics should be envious of you. We were talking about just such a one the other day.'

'Who do you mean, "we"?' enquired his niece with interest.

'Why, I was talking with this fellow Korneck. He's an odd one; I'm not sure what he is or does. He bobbed up in our department one day and he's so overflowing with eagerness that I'm positively tired sometimes, after talking with him!'

'Bobbed up? How so? Where from?'

'From Prussia, I believe, but he seems to be some kind of amateur; well, I'm not quite sure. But the man certainly knows a lot of mathematics, at least in his own topic. He's gone and resurrected an old, well-nigh forgotten problem – Fermat's Last Theorem, they used to call it. It's ridiculously simple to state, yet so diabolically difficult that everyone's given up working on it for donkey's years. It used to be all the rage forty or fifty years ago. The history of the problem is chock full of stories, what with secret identities, sealed manuscripts and so forth. Unfortunately, it was all but killed by the birth of modern number theory; considered to be uninteresting, or impossible, although my new friend Korneck seems to devote his life to seeking a solution.'

'Sealed manuscripts!' I exclaimed. 'I have seen enough of those to last me a lifetime, I believe. They can do so much harm, the foolish things – whatever *do* mathematicians keep wanting with them?'

'Always the same thing, Vanessa,' Charles replied, glancing at me meaningfully. 'Capturing the glory and keeping it for oneself – you know that as well as anyone, I should think!'

'Oh, you're talking about that old three-body problem again,' interrupted Emily. 'What *I* want to know about is the secret identities! What use could *that* be to a mathematician, I wonder?'

'Ah, I'll tell you,' replied her uncle. 'To start with, you have to imagine someone who loved mathematics, and wanted to study them more than anything, but who was prevented from attending university by law.'

'Prevented from attending university by law? Why, that doesn't make sense – what kind of law could that be?'

'You ought to know, you silly goose! Don't you realise that if you were just a few years older than you are, you'd be the one who was prevented! Imagine not realising that.'

'Well, but that's because I'm a girl. Oh! I see what you mean – you must *be* talking about a girl! All right, I am silly. But do tell about her! Did she have to disguise herself to go to university? How exciting! What did she do? Who was she? When was it?'

'Oh well, I'll tell you, even though it's all rather old hat for us mathematicians. We all hear her story sooner or later; in fact the tale was actually written and published by some officious family friend or other. Well, the name of this enterprising creature was Sophie Germain, and she lived in France at the end of the last century and the beginning of this. She must have been just about your age during the French revolution. Probably didn't get to spend a lot of time out of doors as a young thing, I'll bet, what with the *sans-culottes* bloodthirstily overrunning the streets and all. At any rate, not being an aristocrat, she preserved her head, and after it was all over, Napoleon arrived and took over the world (more or less), and among his many activities he also found time to create a glorious brand new university to train glorious French military men in the glorious sciences. It was the Ecole Polytechnique in Paris, and of course there was no question of anyone but men being allowed to attend. However, the mathematics courses were taught by the most famous mathematicians in Paris, and poor Sophie, who had gotten interested in mathematics while spending all her time indoors, longed to take them, so here's what she did. She didn't actually disguise herself, but as I imagine it, she must have started frequenting the cafés around the school, trying to get to know the students who had their coffee there, all dressed up in their fancy military garb with their swords hanging at their sides, and trying to impress the girls. I imagine her trying to get them to tell her about what they learned in their classes. Eventu-

28

ally, by a stroke of luck, she came to hear about one student, Monsieur Auguste Le Blanc, whose name has gone down in history simply for being such a mediocre student that he ended up dropping out of the school altogether. He went off somewhere, but the lecture notes and problem sets that were printed and distributed to all the students weekly kept on coming for him, and as he didn't take them, they just sat in his mailbox until some kind soul took to picking them up and delivering them to Mademoiselle Sophie. She then proceeded to solve all the problems under the name of Monsieur Le Blanc, and posted them in every week to be corrected by the eminent professor who taught the course. She made tremendous progress and everything was going beautifully until one fine day, the professor came to ask himself what on earth had happened to the idiotic M. Le Blanc, to make him so brilliant all of a sudden! And he dashes off a letter which he includes with the next problem set, requesting the reformed student to pay him an urgent visit. Poor Sophie! She must have been frightened out of her wits, and so upset about the risk to her lovely arrangement. Nonetheless, off she went to confront the professor, and discovered that although the governing bodies may have been dead set against girls in universities, a real mathematician cares nothing for such rules and prejudices, and looks right past it all to what is important. He was pleased as Punch, and let her go on as before, and she finished her studies and went on to original research. Her alternate identity came in useful there, again, when she used it to submit some of her results to Gauss, the greatest mathematician of the day. He received them with enthusiasm, but then found out the truth, when she arranged to have him specially protected during Napoleon's invasion of Germany in 1806; he became curious about who was behind the elegant treatment he was receiving at the hands of the French generals and began to make enquiries. "Mademoiselle Sophie Germain specially recommended you to my protection, sir." "Mademoiselle Sophie Germain? Never heard of her – who the devil is she?" "A young lady fiercely interested in mathematics, sir. She has apparently been in correspondence with you upon the subject." "Has she really? I wasn't aware of it! I must get to the bottom of this. Can you oblige me with her postal address, please?" Well, you get the picture.'

'So, did he write?'

'He most certainly did, and she answered, telling him the truth.'

'And was he furious to find out that she was a woman?'

'Not at all – he was simply delighted! I'm ashamed to say it, but it seems that the worst country in Europe for prejudices about the higher education of women is the one you have the poor luck to find yourself in this instant! Why, Girton College is still struggling to have its students awarded degrees, even those who pass the Cambridge Tripos as brilliantly as any man. It's probably a good thing for old Sophie that she wasn't here in England. Still, let us count our blessings: times are changing, even here. Professor

Whitehead teaches at Girton now; he's a great champion of the feminine cause.'

'Well, you seem to be a fine champion too, Uncle Charles.'

'Oh no, I'm not really. I mean, I'm all for it, but I don't actually *do* anything about it, you know.'

'Well, you taught me.'

'Ah, but that had absolutely nothing to do with any cause, or theory or principle of any kind! I'll teach anyone as talented and interested as you are, my dear, whether boy, girl, dog, or cat. It's a simple matter of pleasure.'

Emily turned pink.

'Well, that's even better,' she said happily. 'That puts you on a par with the French and the German professors who helped Sophie Germain. I'm proud of you, Uncle. Now if only I can do proper justice to your teaching, and manage to pass the entrance exams.! It would be so wonderful to study enough to be able to work on problems that no one else has ever managed to solve – just like being the first to walk on new-fallen snow!'

'Yes, it *is* extraordinary. I'm glad you understand that. Sophie certainly thought so; she studied and worked day and night, though her parents tried everything to stop her. They tried depriving the poor girl of heat and candles, in the naïve hopes, I suppose, that she would employ the wee hours to get a little sleep, but it was no use. She *would* huddle over calculations in the dead of night, wrapped in blankets, until she wore them down and they gave up and let her work to her heart's content. And she never stopped right through to the end of her life.'

'She never stopped,' repeated Emily dreamily, pouring tea into her cup until it overflowed.

'I didn't say she never stopped *pouring tea!*' laughed her uncle, mopping up the puddle with a cloth. 'Who's knocking?– Ah, that must be Arthur, come to pick up Vanessa.'

My heart jumped inside me, for believe it or not, I had positively forgotten about my own news. It flowed back into my mind, and it suddenly struck me that telling Arthur about it might not turn out to be as easy as I had supposed.

As soon as I had put on my shawl, and Arthur and I had taken our leave, shut the door behind us and walked down the path in the balmy evening air, I turned to him, and fearing that if I did not begin immediately, I might never get up the courage to address the subject, I blurted out–

'Arthur, I must tell you something very surprising that happened to me.'

'Really?' he said, raising his eyebrows slightly.

'Yes, a – a lady came to visit me, and – oh dear, this does sound quite unreal – she asked me to help her find out who has murdered her son-in-law! And,' I continued hastily, as some instinct told me that I had better get the worst out at once, 'she has invited me to go down and stay with her starting Saturday.'

'S-stay with her? Saturday?' said Arthur, with his slight stammer, which was the more endearing as it has all but disappeared in the last years, and recurs only in moments of distress, of which, indeed, it is often the only sign.

'Yes,' I answered a little meekly.

32

'But what for?'

'Well,' I mumbled uncomfortably, 'she ... well, I don't know why, but she seems to think I can help her – she wants me to prove that her – that her daughter is innocent of the crime. Arthur, I don't know why she came to me – I really don't know. She – she knew about four years ago, and she seemed so very certain I could do something now as I did then, and she tried so hard to convince me to come that I ... that I said I would.'

There was a silence, while Arthur digested this information.

'But Vanessa,' he said thoughtfully after a while, 'it doesn't sound like much of a good thing. Not at all.'

'Oh dear,' I sighed, not so much because of his opinion, which was much what I had expected, but because of the unpleasant necessity of arguing and defending my decision, which in any case – I admit it – was already firmly taken.

'I mean to say, what do we know about this lady?' he continued. 'Who is she? What do you know of her? What does she know of you?'

'I only know what she told me,' I said humbly. 'She says her son-in-law was shot last Sunday in a woods. His name was George Burton Granger.'

'Ah, George Burton Granger. Well, that rings a bell at any rate; I read about that in the paper. This lady must be the mother of the wife then, of Mrs Granger, I mean. But Vanessa – here you are meaning to rush off to stay with perfectly strange people, and furthermore, you're trying to get mixed up in a murder – a *murder*, Vanessa! And what if this Mrs Granger really is the murderer, whatever her mother may believe? Mothers have been mistaken about their children before! And if you start finding out about it, what'll happen to you? No, you mustn't go – it's unthinkable! Whatever *can* this lady mean by coming to you?'

'She – she was, well, there, four years ago, you know,' I stammered. It is never easy to evoke the memory of that difficult time, least of all with Arthur.

'What do you mean, "there"? Ah, at the trial.'

There was a long and awkward silence. I didn't know how to break it. But Arthur did not seem disturbed at the resurgence of old and painful memories; he appeared to be considering the situation, or mulling, perhaps, over the best arguments to dissuade me.

'Vanessa, think about what you're getting into!' he said, suddenly emerging. 'Have you forgotten what it was like, to know that someone around you was a murderer – a murderer! a killer – and that you might be the next victim? Have you forgotten how frightened you were?'

Dora, I had forgotten it. I remembered only my desperate fear for him, and the rush of conviction when I finally felt that I understood what had really happened! But his words brought something else back: the moments of blind terror and frantic suspicion, moments when I trusted nobody, moments when I thought I was being stalked and hunted, moments when noises in the night caused my hair to rise upon my head. And the darkest moment of all, when it was suddenly borne in upon me what it meant for one human being to have dealt out death to another. All these things

34

had receded into the background of my mind, blotted out by the happier memories of the subsequent events. They came back to me as he spoke, and I realised with some horror that I had not properly reflected about what I was going to do.

'And then – how can you tell if this lady is really sincere?' continued Arthur, a wrinkle of worry between his brows. 'It's very strange for her to come to you – what does she really want? What if she wants to *use* you in some way that we cannot conceive of? Why can she not simply let the police do their job?'

'Oh, Arthur,' I cried, reacting only to the last sentence, 'how can you ask that? She – she thinks they suspect her daughter, and she *knows*, like a mother would, that her daughter is innocent, but of course she is terrified that the police will be so eager to show results that they'll hurry to take the easiest step, and arrest her.'

Again there was a silence. Who better than Arthur should know that such a fear is perfectly justified?

'I'm afraid too, Vanessa,' he said softly. 'Afraid for you. I don't want you to go. Think! You'll be far away from me, alone there with a strange family, a dead man, and someone who killed him, and the more you seek to discover, the more you'll be risking your life. No, I can't let you go. You mustn't. Vanessa, p-please! How can I stay here and wait for you?'

He reached for my hand. I gave it to him, and answered slowly.

'Oh, Arthur, perhaps I've been silly and

precipitate. But what you say makes me feel more than ever that I must go. I shall be careful. I'm not going as a "detective", of course, how could I? I'm no such thing. I'm simply going as a friend. Apart from Mrs Bryce-Fortescue, no one will have any idea of what I'm really doing. But you ... what you're saying is making me realise that a life may be at stake here; a real, human life. I cannot stand by, now that I have been called to act! I don't know why I've been called, but I can't ignore it. I can't stand aside and do nothing. I can't even wait, for Mrs Bryce-Fortescue says that the police may arrest her daughter at any moment.'

We had reached our own front door, and stood at the entrance, hesitating to enter and separate, each to our own rooms, as Mrs Fitzwilliam would never tolerate any other behaviour from her lodgers, even if they are respectably engaged. Arthur looked down at me, and his brown eyes were troubled.

'To change your mind would be like changing yourself,' he said softly. 'I wouldn't want you any different, and yet...'

'Good night,' I said quickly before he could continue, reached up to kiss him, and slipped quickly into my room. I have not convinced Arthur that I am right to go, of course, but ... in fact, he has convinced me that I am right! Before speaking to him, I merely thought that I *would* go, and now I feel that I *must* go. Before, I saw it as it as a kind of strange chance or opportunity, but now, it appears to me more like a manifestation of destiny. As for the danger, I cannot, now, perceive it as a serious threat. I do hope I am right!

Your loving sister,

Vanessa

Maidstone Hall, Saturday, June 11, 1892

My dearest Dora,

I have come – I am here – I have arrived! At this very moment, I am settled in a bedroom in which a certain chill and unused look persists, in spite of the family's best efforts to cheer it up for me with lamps and candles, and fresh sheets and a pretty spread upon the iron bedstead. The day has been long, and I have been impatient for some time already to find myself alone. I must reflect on what I have seen and learned (little though it is for the moment!) and look over my newspaper clippings once again.

The clippings are the work of Arthur. He woke me, early this morning, by tapping gently on my window, and by the time I had drawn the curtain and peeked sleepily out into the garden, he was beckoning to me from the garden table, where he was to be seen casually installed in a ray of sunshine filtering between the leaves, which quivered gaily in the light summer breeze. In front of him stood a lovely steaming teapot, a basket of rolls, sundry pots of jam and a large sheaf of newspapers. It would be difficult to conceive of a more tempting prospect; breakfast in the garden is a rare treat, as one does not, generally, have the courage to beg the use of her personal table from Mrs Fitzwilliam (and this in spite of the fact that she never sits at it herself). Arthur had gone to a special effort for me, and I made haste to dress and join him, wondering within me what turn his thoughts had taken over the night, and how he would address the burning issue which still lay unresolved between us.

'What a lovely breakfast,' I said, as I took my place across from him and reached for the teapot. 'But why all the newspapers?'

'The newspapers are for you, Vanessa,' he responded, looking at me with a restrained twinkle in his eye. 'I picked up the whole week's worth from college, where they lie about on the coffee table. What you are undertaking is anything but amusing, but the way you go about it is another story! Are you going to dash off into the middle of things without even finding out what it's all about? Don't you think you ought to try and learn at least the basic facts before being served up the local version of the story?'

I was all ready to feel properly indignant at these remarks, but it occurred to me that, after all, he was right enough, and more, his very words carried a gentle indication of a decision to renounce any attempt to change my intentions. His tone was almost light, but I felt the weight of his unspoken thoughts. Still, if his easy manner did not fool me as to the difficulties he may have felt in forcing himself to adopt it, it certainly smoothed some away for me! I accepted his speech like a gift, therefore, and answered laughing,

'Yes, of course – I meant to! Well, all right, Arthur, I didn't mean to, but simply because I hadn't thought of it. I should have if I had. But I don't suppose the newspapers are really likely to contain anything more than what I shall soon learn, and even less that they are accurate or trustworthy! Still, let us have a look.'

'I already have, actually,' he said, laying aside several pages. 'There is only one article of real interest, frankly. It dates from Monday, the day after the murder, and appears to contain the main facts with less sensationalism than the others.' And he handed me the page containing the clipping which I enclose for your perusal.

Murder Strikes the Quiet Countryside

George Burton Granger of Haverhill Manor in Lower Haverhill, on the outskirts of Cambridge, was found shot dead yesterday in a grove of trees on his estate. A self-proclaimed country squire hailing from Manchester, possessor of a respectable fortune from dealings in the City, Mr Granger acquired Haverhill Manor two years ago from Miss Emmeline Haverhill, last remnant of the Haverhill family who built the manor in the sixteenth century. 'It was a sad day for me when I had to move out,' said Miss Haverhill, 87, when asked to describe the new proprietor of her ancestral home. 'Mr Granger had money, to be sure, and he transferred a sizeable quantity of it to me on the day he bought my house, but I don't think he quite realised that no buying of houses can change who you are and where you come from. If you'll allow me to say so, the man was not to the manor born. I expect all the old homes in England will pass to such people sooner or later. Birth no longer has the rights and privileges it used to. I don't know what the country is coming to, I'm sure. Mr Granger talked all kinds of nonsense about central heating and bath rooms. Why, make life too easy, and you lose all the force of it, and the hardships that sculpt people into what they are! What kind of a person expects to be *warm* while dining! A proper dining room is large enough to seat at least forty; it's silly to want to heat such a place, you might as well heat the garden. Why, that's what the wine and spirits are served for! Little did he know, that Mr Granger. He thought that the things we did were things a person can learn. Riding and hunting, for instance. He actually *learned* those things. What's the point of that? Anyone can see that you've learned it, that you weren't born to it, from a mile off. It isn't the same thing in the least. Installing a groom and all, thinking he was doing the same as my dear father, never realising how silly he looked, poor man. But he *would* go hunting. Well, it all caught up with him in the end, didn't it? Here he's gone and gotten himself shot. Dear, dear.'

Mr Granger's body was actually discovered by the very gamekeeper referred to above, who was crossing the grounds on his morning rounds. He is not available for interviewing as the police have forbidden him to discuss the case because of the importance of his testimony as a witness in a possible forthcoming murder trial. However, this journalist has succeeded in learning from the police that Mr Granger was shot in the chest at quite close range, by a very small foreign firearm which has not been found anywhere on the premises. The lack of any particular expression of fear on the face of the deceased, and the position of his body, quite as though he had been shot in the middle of an ordinary conversation, have led the police to believe that the person who accosted him was a familiar. The police have a theory, and a very simple one, but are presently engaged in collecting testimonies from every person who can possibly have been within hearing distance at the time of the crime.

Mr Granger leaves a widow, Mrs Sylvia Granger née Bryce-Fortescue.

'What a peculiar article,' I mused. 'I almost feel like laughing! What nasty things old Miss Haverhill says about poor Mr Granger – she really seems to feel he was killed because he was the wrong kind of person for her house! Yet I can understand how sad it must be to have to give up one's old home. I expect one simply *must* exercise a little irony to put up with such a loss. Still, fancy wanting all those remarks to be published in a newspaper! And I wonder if he really has learned all that he hints from the police. Do they really talk so much to journalists about their private theories, or is he just making it up? I wonder who he is; the article is signed merely 'PO'. Do you think there's any way one could find out?'

'I have a little theory about that, actually,'

41

replied Arthur. 'I had occasion to meet a journalist on the paper last year, during a mathematical event of note; his name was Patrick O'Sullivan, and he was a freckled Irishman of the purest sort – dashing all over the place, talking and asking questions till your head ached! He had a bit of a strange sense of humour. I shouldn't be surprised at all to find he was the author of this piece. If you like, I could try to locate him.'

'Oh yes!' I cried, 'I'm sure that would be good. He seems to know what the police are doing, at least he hints so, although perhaps that's just for the glory of it. But if I met him, maybe I could find out what he really knows. And how useful it might turn out to be, if he had some real information. Look, Arthur, at what it says about a "simple theory". It seems clear enough that it *is* Mrs Granger who is hinted at! And that, of course, is exactly what poor Mrs Bryce-Fortescue most fears. So she is not inventing it.'

'It does sound like that's what is meant, with that last sentence,' he admitted. 'But Vanessa, don't forget this: *the police might be right*. Listen, I'll try to look out Pat, and I'll write you if I succeed. I shall write you anyway, and you must write to me as often as they carry the post – if you write to me half as often as you do to your sister, I shall be content. Now you had better finish packing your things, for they'll be coming to fetch you quite soon, and I must go to work.'

He rose and kissed me rather solemnly. The kiss was quite intense enough to clearly communicate the disproportion between his feelings and his words.

'Oh Arthur, I am grateful,' I murmured into his ear.

'It would be harder if ... if I didn't feel that you are trying to do something which may, which must surely be a good and necessary thing, however ... disturbing and even frightening it is to me to see you mixed up in such things. I thought last night about the first time you came to me in prison – it seemed wrong then, to me, for you to have come. A wrong place for you to be. And yet in the end it was right, and you could have done nothing better. So how should I presume to judge? Still, I cannot help feeling very worried. You're too d-daring, Vanessa. I wish you were more easily afraid. Remember Laertes: *be wary then; best safety lies in fear.*'

And he turned from me and went into the house rather more quickly than necessary, leaving me to carry the crockery in to Mrs Fitzwilliam.

I returned to my rooms and prepared a small suitcase. I did not know how much to take nor exactly how long I should be away, but I decided that surely I should return to Cambridge no later than next Saturday, even if just for a night, to see Arthur. So I packed economically, and then sat down rather tremblingly to wait for Mrs Bryce-Fortescue and her carriage.

I did exactly nothing but wait, straining my ears, for a good half-an-hour, yet so startled was I when the knock finally came at my door, that I leaped out of my seat, heart pounding! I hastened to the door, was greeted and invited to depart with no further delay.

'If I had known, I would have put this off until tomorrow,' she told me as soon as we were seated within. 'The police are sending their inspector over this afternoon, yet again, to speak with Sylvia. I cannot think of allowing them to see her alone, and am quite worried that they may come whilst we are still on our way, although in principle they should not be at the house before four o'clock. Sylvia is under strict instructions to say that she has a headache and cannot see them until I am home. Make haste, please, Peter!' she added in a slightly louder voice, addressing herself to the red-headed driver, whom I now observed for the first time.

He made a peculiar impression upon me. I would not, somehow, have expected Mrs Bryce-Fortescue to have this style of servant. Tall and young, with immensely long legs stretched before him, he leaned back in his seat, a straw between his teeth, and drove the horses with a *je-ne-sais-quoi* attitude; it sounds ridiculous to say this, but it was quite as though they belonged to him. He did nothing wrong or impolite, to be sure, and yet his whole bearing and expression radiated a certain calm and cheerful ease which nearly verged on disrespect! Definitely not a youth from the country, it was easy to see, in spite of his familiarity with the horses. I could not resist putting a delicate question to Mrs Bryce-Fortescue.

'Has your coachman been with you long?' I said lightly. 'He doesn't look like someone from these parts.'

'No indeed,' she replied with a very slight touch of asperity. 'I may as well tell you, since you are bound to learn a great deal about my family, and it will surely be necessary for you to ask a certain number of questions, some of which may be disagreeable, that my financial situation is really not one which could permit me to keep my own carriage and driver. In any case, you will easily be able to observe our train of living, once you arrive at the house. Peter Middleman and this carriage belonged to – to Sylvia's husband. I – it is most disagreeable for me to speak of these things, but I realise that I myself have begged you to come, and I truly believe you may be able to help us, and I really do not know where else to turn, so I simply must force myself to do what does not come naturally to me. In a word, you must know that as long as the police enquiry is going on, my daughter cannot – her inheritance is blocked. Not only is she not yet the legal owner of her husband's estate, but she is not even allowed to set foot there, which I suppose is normal enough, given that the house and grounds are being searched and studied for clues. However, the police have deigned to allow Peter to drive her to my home in her own carriage, and to stay with us until the – difficulties – shall be resolved. He is a peculiar young man, I agree, and I cannot say that I feel comfortable with him. I believe that he also comes from Manchester, and became acquainted with Geo – with Mr Granger there.'

'Mr Granger was from Manchester, then?' I knew it already, of course, from the newspaper article, but it seemed expedient to let Mrs Bryce-Fortescue tell me everything she could or would in her own way.

'Yes, he was born there and lived there for many years before moving to this part of the country,' she answered soberly.

'It is embarrassing to ask questions – it does seem like prying,' I said with some hesitation, 'but I will certainly need to know as much as I can about Mr Granger's background. Could you – could I know how old he was?'

'I quite understand your hesitations, but we must both of us understand once and for all that such considerations will be nothing but a handicap. We had better leave them aside entirely,' she answered, with a rather forced smile. 'With me, at least, you can and should feel free to pry. With the others, that is to say, my daughter and her friend Camilla, and the servants, and perhaps Mr Granger's servants – with them you will of course need to exercise a little more delicacy, as naturally none of these people have the slightest idea of your purpose in coming. Indeed, it is necessary for you to know that I have told them that you are the daughter of old friends, and that as you have come to live in Cambridge, they asked me to befriend you. If you find yourself obliged to invent any further details, please have the kindness to let me know. Now, about Mr Granger. What did you ask?'

'How old was he,' I insisted awkwardly. I felt rather than thought that she disliked the question, and wondered vaguely why.

'Ah. Yes. He was … let me see, I do not know his exact age.'

'But roughly?'

'Roughly speaking, he must have been nearing

46

– near fifty years old.'

'Oh!' My exclamation was not very discreet, but the information surprised me. As the husband of her daughter, I had naturally imagined a much younger man. Why, Mrs Bryce-Fortescue herself did not look so much.

'Yes,' she replied calmly. 'You seem surprised. I suppose you expected my daughter to be married to a man closer to her own age.'

'Yes, but it was a foolish prejudice,' I answered humbly, disliking to have my thoughts read, even if they were very silly and obvious thoughts. 'Can you tell me how Mr Granger became acquainted with your daughter?'

There was a faint pause. She seemed to be recollecting, or collecting, her thoughts.

'He met her through me,' she said. 'I met Mr Granger at the home of some mutual friends, some seven or eight years ago. I was intrigued by him, for he was very unlike the men I was used to meeting. He had a strong and dominating personality, the kind of personality which leads a man to success no matter what his background. He had done far more, with far less advantages, than any other man of my acquaintance, and I felt a certain ... admiration for him. He became a frequent caller at our house; Sylvia was then a girl of fifteen or sixteen. She was not in the least bit interested in him, but she was a very lovely girl, and I see now that he may have been ... fond of her from the beginning, although he said nothing about it for many years. Indeed, he never said or hinted a word of any such thing until two years ago – all at once, and most unexpectedly.' She flushed.

47

'What happened then?'

'Then he asked to marry her,' she responded drily.

'Was she pleased? How did she feel about it?'

'I do not wish to speak for my daughter,' she replied with a shade of coolness. 'Naturally, she was pleased, as she accepted the proposal. The age difference certainly did not constitute an insurmountable obstacle. But I cannot give you any details about her feelings or about the marriage. Neither my daughter nor I are given to the expression of transports of feeling. You must see if you can learn directly from her what you wish to know.'

There was something curious in her attitude; something strange, contradictory. She seemed to wish to enlighten me, and yet something blocked the flow of information, as though there were something about her daughter's marriage, or about private affairs in general, that she seemed to feel and yet to be unable to pronounce, maybe even to herself. Perhaps she was simply obeying the impulse of discretion and the need to present a certain face to the world.

At any rate, one thing appears clear: Mrs Bryce-Fortescue is not going to drown me in a spate of worldly chatter. She will put her house at my disposal, and answer factual questions to the best of her ability, but I do not think she is sincerely capable of doing more. Her character forbids it.

At length, and after a good deal of mutual silence, the carriage drew up in front of Mrs Bryce-Fortescue's imposing home. The house is indescribably full of charm; summer roses fall in clusters over the low, projecting southern wing, and the warm stone of an unusual rosy hue, bringing to mind the 'Maidstone' of the house's name, peeps through them in the sunshine. Light glints on the casements and large trees cast shade over a wild little garden surrounded by a low, moss-covered wall, with a gate giving onto the vast fields and lanes beyond. I stopped, delighted, and stared about me.

'Here we are: welcome to Maidstone Hall. I am afraid that it is in rather a sorry state,' said Mrs Bryce-Fortescue, leading me up the somewhat overgrown garden path. 'I have not been able to keep it up as it deserves, since my husband died.'

'But it's lovely!' I exclaimed. 'It's one of the loveliest houses I've ever seen!' The sun glanced over its irregular stone surface, burnished by time and enlivened by wild flowers and grasses spilling out of the many nooks and crannies.

'Lovely, but rotting slowly from within,' she replied sadly. 'The entire part of the roof over the west wing leaks, and that part of the house cannot be used. We have no gardener, and the garden is sadly neglected. Mr Huxtable and I occasionally work in it, but purely for the pleasure that a sunny garden can bring – we are no professionals! Snowdrops in January, crocuses in February, daffodils in March, wisteria in April, and then the roses – all these come by themselves, year after year, through no effort of ours other than a mild pruning. In my grandfather's time, a bevy of servants, workers and gardeners kept the place in order; it is not a very large house, but it is extremely old and has a great deal of history. It has belonged to my family for many generations, and each one has added some dramatic event or another to its story.'

'It is enchanting, just as it is,' I told her. 'It would be almost a pity for it to be kept neat and orderly.'

'It would be a pity if the roof fell in entirely! And the day that will happen may not be so far away,' she responded tartly. 'But the rather small part of the house that we occupy is in good enough condition, fortunately. Please come inside. I shall introduce you to the servants, and take you around.'

We entered the front door, bending our heads slightly to avoid the overhanging bunches of roses, and found ourselves in a cool hallway. A very elderly man stood there, greeting us with smooth politeness. Behind us, Peter had unhitched the horses and was leading them towards the rickety stables that could be seen at some little distance.

'This is Mr Huxtable,' said Mrs Bryce-Fortescue with great formality. 'Mr Huxtable, this is our new guest, Miss Duncan.'

Mr Huxtable welcomed me with great, if slightly doddering, polish, and took my shawl and hat.

'Miss Sylvia and Miss Wright are in the parlour. Luncheon will be served very shortly,' he informed us, before disappearing through a swinging door at the end of the passage into some mysterious nether regions of the house which I immediately determined to investigate at the soonest opportunity.

Apart from the swinging door, three other doors gave onto the hallway where we stood, one on the left and two on the right. Mrs Bryce-Fortescue opened the left-hand one first.

'This is the only room in the west wing we continue to use,' she said, beckoning me to look inside. 'As it is on the ground floor, it is not really in danger from the roof. The chamber above it receives most of the water, and we have bricked and covered the floor very thickly and put in a great many buckets, to protect the ceiling here. It is rather a lot of work to keep the water from leaking through, but we cannot do without our library. The collection is the work of my father and my grandfather. Mr Huxtable keeps it in order. I do not know what I would do without him. He does not have much work to do as a butler, here, when I am so often alone, but I believe he enjoys pottering about the house and garden as a pastime.'

I looked beyond her into a very spacious, high-ceilinged room, entirely lined with books on beautifully built shelves, elegantly carpeted, and furnished with burnished wooden desks with leather surfaces and writing lamps, and a few plump, deep leather armchairs. No fire burned in the vast fireplace, but the room was free of dust, and had a warmly loved and lived in look. A long gallery or balcony ran around three sides of it, well above head level, and many more bookshelves stood upon it.

'It's wonderful!' I exclaimed. 'One could stay here for years, just reading!'

'No one could read all that,' she smiled. 'I have not read one tenth, probably not even one twentieth of it. But I love it just the same. I spent many hours here as a child. Now, let us go into

51

the parlour and meet the girls.'

She closed the door, and opened one of those on the right-hand side of the entrance hall. With a swish of skirts, two young ladies who were seated there rose to greet us. The parlour was a much less imposing room than the library, though very charming. The upholstery was much used and the original prints were almost invisibly pale. The large bay window looked out over the front walk up which we had come a few minutes before. All trace of the horses, the carriage and Peter had now disappeared. I had only time to observe so much before my hand was taken in a weak but nervous gesture by a small, very cool one, and I found myself facing a pretty young lady of near my own age.

'I am Sylvia Granger,' she was saying, and I observed her with great care. She was a pale, eggshell delicate creature with an air of almost painful fragility that was quite touching. Her ash blonde hair was drawn back into a soft, loose round mass on her neck. She was, of course, entirely dressed in mourning, but her dress was not fashionably tight about the waist; its supple fabric and soft, unconstraining lines would delight that contemporary arbiter elegantiarum Oscar Wilde.

'I am very pleased to meet you,' I said. 'Your mother has told me so much about you.' The phrase was awkward, but then, so was the situation. I knew that I was supposed to be a daughter of friends of Mrs Bryce-Fortescue, but this morsel of information was far from sufficient to teach me how to play my part – some elements of character were needed! I quickly decided to play, as much as possible, the part of myself: a poor, hard-working, but enterprising young lady, delighted to be invited to an elegant and friendly house. Not so far from the truth.

'Did she?' responded Sylvia slowly, with a hint of annoyance in her tone. I smiled blandly and e-gagingly, in order to convey the impression that Mrs Bryce-Fortescue had made only the most banal remarks. Which also was not so far from the truth.

'This is my friend Camilla Wright,' said Sylvia, turning to her friend who was coming up to join us. She was quite different from Sylvia; rather taller, a handsome girl, with thick black waves of hair combed back and gathered into a large firm knot held with a net. She stretched out her hand and shook mine rather firmly, then suddenly smiled.

'I'm very glad to meet you,' she said simply. 'It's a lovely place. We walk a great deal; I hope you will join us sometimes for a ramble.'

'Oh, yes, indeed!' I chimed in girlishly, feeling rather foolish, and wondering if she, too, were not playing a role. I hoped she didn't mean to keep me at a distance, and that I should eventually manage to get to know her better, as I thought she could be a precious source of information.

Our small talk was a little strained, as I simply could not feel free in the presence of Mrs Bryce-Fortescue, and was furthermore a little nervous about making some awkward slip. It was a relief when luncheon was finally announced, and we entered the dining room next to the parlour.

The luncheon was served by Mr Huxtable,

together with a rather gaunt person called Sarah. The table was long and the four of us were necessarily rather far apart, which made conversation even more difficult than before. The others seemed used to it; their remarks were all tranquilly banal, and mostly concerned the food. The meal was spare and the ingredients simple: a chop and green beans followed by a fruit pudding, the whole of it, however, beautifully prepared. After it was finished and cleared away, Mrs Bryce-Fortescue sent Mr Huxtable to fetch the cook, for she wished to introduce her to me. We spoke only for a brief moment, standing at the swinging door leading into the servants' quarters, but Mrs Firmin was so friendly and plump, so frankly pleased to have another guest to feed, and so openly and simply eager to discuss the fascinating subject of cooking, that I found myself sighing with the sheer relief of being acquainted with such a person after the social strain I had just endured!

'Do you like spotted dick, dearie?' she was saying pleasantly. 'Lovely – we'll have that tonight, then, after the roast. Just let me know if there's any special thing you'd favour.'

Mr Huxtable, Sarah and Mrs Firmin comprise the entire staff of the household. It seems a small one, yet when I reflect that Mrs Bryce-Fortescue lives most of the time quite alone, I suppose that after all it is probably more than sufficient.

After the culinary conversation, Mrs Bryce-Fortescue showed me upstairs to my room, the farthest of a line of three small chambers next to each other on the left-hand side of the narrow passageway lying directly over the large one below.

'My room is there, and the bathroom is beyond,' she said, gesturing towards the closed doors on the right-hand side of the passage before opening the one leading into the room in which she had placed me. It was a neat little square, with a window looking out over the gardens at the back of the house.

'This other door leads into the chamber over the library,' she told me, indicating a closed door on the opposite side of the room from the one we entered by, with a little dressing table in front of it. 'It is bolted shut, for we no longer enter that room. Not only is there a real danger of tiles or parts of beams falling from the roof into the room, as has already happened several times, but the floor has been inundated with water so deeply and so often that we fear it is quite rotten in parts, under the bricks, and we are afraid it may break open over the library. This room used to be Sylvia's old schoolroom, but we have fitted it out with a bed since then. Camilla is next to you, in the room that was once used by Sylvia's governess, and she herself is in her own bedroom beyond. We have no problems with floors or ceilings in these little rooms; they and the roof above them were strengthened and rebuilt just two years ago.'

'It must be a great job to have the roof mended,' I remarked.

'Yes, it is a difficult job, for the rotten beams must be carefully removed and replaced and the roof tiles also. It was ... it was thanks to the generosity of my son-in-law that I could have it done. He offered to have some of the most urgent work on the house done for me when he married Sylvia, and I – I accepted his offer.'

'That was very kind of him,' I said innocently, although Mr Granger's gift sounded suspiciously like what is known as a bride-price in certain primitive societies. Mrs Bryce-Fortescue did not answer, and I began to have a feeling that Mr Granger was not a simple character. I determined that my first step would be to spare no efforts to find out everything I could about the kind of man he was, and decided that my first source of information should be the coachman Peter. I asked if it would be all right for Peter to take me to the post office tomorrow.

'Oh, there is no need for that,' said Mrs Bryce-Fortescue a little annoyingly, although she meant well, of course. 'Just leave your letters on the hall table; he takes them to the post office himself each day. Now, about this afternoon. I have sent the girls out for a walk until teatime, which we take in the parlour at four o'clock. In principle, that is also when the police inspector is supposed to arrive, and if he arrives unexpectedly early, as he frequently does, Sylvia will not be in. I shall leave you now, if you wish, until four, for I am sure that you wish to repose and refresh yourself. Please ring if you need anything and Sarah will come.'

She left me, and I waited until her footsteps died away in the corridor and I heard the click of a door closing. I waited eagerly, with pounding heart, and as soon as I believed I could not possibly be observed, I stepped silently to the second door of the bedroom, shifted the little table in front of it to one side, and tried to slide the bolt back, for something told me that the large chamber behind my bedroom might be a useful vantage point for many observations. The bolt, however, was firmly stuck. At first I was afraid to push as hard as I could, for fear of making a loud noise, but soon I was pulling and pushing at the knob till my fingers were red, alas with a complete lack of success. I sat down on the iron bedstead, upon which a lovely old spread embroidered with faded flowers covered over something unexpectedly soft and plump, which turned out upon examination to be a snugly agreeable feather eiderdown. Resting my hands, I proceeded to reflect.

After several more attempts, including one with a pen which I broke, I decided that only a few drops of oil could have the slightest chance of success with a bolt which had obviously not been opened in a long time. I considered ringing for Sarah, but I was embarrassed, and even more, worried, at the idea that she might ask me what the oil was needed for, or even offer to do herself whatever I needed doing. Finally, I made up my mind to sneak silently and tensely down to the nether regions and try to slip into the kitchen and ask kind Mrs Firmin for an oily rag, with the excuse of some lock or other of mine. I was afraid that it would all be absurd and unseemly and most suspicious and unrealistic, so I descended the staircase very quietly, still not really certain whether or not I really meant to put my plan into action.

Can you imagine – as I reached the bottom of the stairs, who should I see but Sarah, busily engaged in cleaning the front door! She had shined the brass knob and waxed the panels, and was now polishing them vigorously. On the ground next to her lay a whole panoply of cleaning substances and utensils. My eyes were instantly attracted by a tiny flask.

My dear Dora, I need not go into details on the subject of the daring robbery which I then perpetrated, for there is not much to tell! I stood silently, wondering how I could manage to get a closer look, when Sarah rose creakingly to her feet and disappeared through the swinging door. It was but the work of a moment for me to dart forward and confirm that the tiny flask indeed contained oil. I dared not carry it off altogether, nor borrow one of her rags, lest she note its disappearance, so (I am ashamed to confess) I soaked a tiny region of the hem of my petticoat and rushed back upstairs, where I immediately lifted the oily spot and began to rub and massage the bolt with it, so that the stain soon became black instead of yellowish.

By dint of patience, rubbing, twisting, forcing and pulling, I felt the bolt begin to yield, and after some quarter of an hour, I finally succeeded in loosening it completely. It slid very silently to one side, and I twisted the handle of the door and opened it.

I stood looking into a large, strange space. There was an astonishing contrast between my neat room with its little bed, carefully waxed and polished floor and starched curtains, and this damp ruin with partially crumbling walls, in which pieces of rotting wood and broken bits fraternised with old abandoned furniture and diverse objects. The floor was thickly tiled with bricks, and most of it was also covered over with great sheets of heavy burlap material, but it was easy to see how the water had eaten away at the mortar. Pails and buckets stood here and there, probably under the places of the worst leaks, and various strings and strands of material had been attached to the ceiling to guide the falling water into them. Parts of the ceiling were actually fallen away, revealing the underside of the roof.

I leaned into the room and peered about, noticing that both Camilla's and Sylvia's rooms gave onto it as well as mine. Quite near the wall, the floor appeared to be in reasonably good condition, and I hesitantly and a little nervously took a few steps along it, passing the door leading into Camilla's room and stopping at Sylvia's. My feet made a little scraping noise, and looking about me, I chose a piece of thick material and shifted it quietly, making a path for myself just along the wall, so as to be sure that I would be able to move up and down there in complete silence. Then, feeling I had done enough, I scurried back to my room, darted inside, closed and bolted the door with a sigh of relief, shifted the table, and flinging myself into a chair, I drew pen and ink toward me and began to write this letter.

Here I am just barely arrived, and already I am specifically ignoring the injunctions of my hostess, with the purpose of laying the grounds for an eavesdropping expedition! I feel quite ashamed, but quite adventurous. I only hope that no one is spying on me as I am spying on them, for this letter is not very discreet! I had better hide it with care, until tomorrow when it shall be taken to the post office by Peter's ministrations.

I leave you tenderly, my dear, and will write again very soon

Your loving

Vanessa

Maidstone Hall, Sunday, June 12, 1892

My dearest sister,

I must finish telling you the events of yesterday.

We had barely gathered at tea, the girls with damp foreheads and muddy boots from their long tramp across the fields, when a loud ring came at the front door.

'Oh, that will be the inspector already,' said Mrs Bryce-Fortescue, with an impatient, worried look. 'If not early, he is certainly punctual!'

There was a moment of tension, and she glanced at me. As we heard the front door being opened by Mr Huxtable, I rose and, without haste, carrying in my hand the teacup which she had only just filled, I left the room.

I should tell you that I had had a little talk with Mrs Bryce-Fortescue a few moments earlier, when she had knocked at my door to fetch me down to tea. And she had made a rather peculiar request.

'As you know, the police intend to interrogate Sylvia yet again this afternoon,' she told me. 'It is the fourth time since Geo – since her hus – since my son-in-law was killed. I cannot think what they believe they can still have to learn from her, but I am afraid, very much afraid. They came specially and urgently to make this appointment, and as I cannot think what else it may mean, I very much fear that they may have some new evidence to try and use or turn against her. Now, I intend to insist on remaining with her during her interrogation. I will say that she is in fragile health, and I have instructed her to say the same. Yet I conceive that they will not allow me to do so, and I am desperately worried for Sylvia. She is such a little goose, that if they attempt to trap her into some contradiction, she will certainly fall for it straight away; she would be capable of incriminating herself out of pure foolishness, though I have of course told her again and again to stick quietly to the truth and offer nothing else. You know, of course, that she has an alibi for the time of the murder, for she was at home, and the housekeeper and maid have both stated that Sylvia did not leave the house, and could not have done so without being observed. But if I know anything about the police, they will try every possible way to pick holes in that statement, or frighten Sylvia into believing that they have done so. I simply *must* know what they say to her, otherwise how can we defend ourselves?'

'Sylvia must have a lawyer,' I said quickly. 'You

know that she has the right to one, and that the lawyer would necessarily be allowed to accompany her to all police interrogations.'

'It is impossible – I have not the means to pay for a private lawyer, and the court will not appoint her one as long as she has not been formally accused. Furthermore, it seems to both Sylvia and me, and Camilla agrees, that it would appear to be a sign of guilt on her part to thus defend herself; we believe that she should behave exactly as though her innocence were perfectly clear – as indeed it should be – and she believed the police were questioning her merely in order to advance their researches. At least, that is the plan we put together at first, but I am not at all sure that Sylvia has the strength of character to keep up such an appearance, when in truth she is grievously distressed and frightened. Besides, the inspector is due to arrive very shortly, and we must act immediately. That is why I wish to propose something to you. It is rather daring, but not illegal, and I believe that you are a rather daring person. The police have already visited us and they know who is presently in the house, except for you; they have no idea of your visit, as you arrived only today. I want to ask you, when they ring, to slip into the library and conceal yourself in the gallery. If, as I fear, they refuse to question Sylvia in my presence, I will show them into the library for the interrogation, and if I cannot intervene to assist her, I can at least know the worst from an objective viewpoint, which Sylvia cannot have. Not to mention the fact that there are many things she would not tell me, out of natural reserve, allied with a mistaken but understandable desire to protect me. Now I ask you: can you, will you do this?'

'Certainly,' I replied unhesitatingly. Thus, before we entered the dining room, she quickly showed me into the library and indicated the twisted little carved wooden staircase leading up to the gallery above, which ran right round three sides of the large room, and was almost filled with book-shelves jutting out perpendicularly from the walls, leaving only the smallest passage for the prospective reader to squeeze past the railings.

This explains why, the moment I heard the front door opening, I slipped into the dining room adjoining the parlour where we were taking our tea. As soon as I heard Mr Huxtable introducing the police officers (two of them, it seemed to me) into the parlour, I left my teacup on the sideboard – I had carried it off with me in order to prevent the police from detecting the presence of another person (as well as for the purpose of taking at least one or two comforting sips before starting off upon my adventure) – darted swiftly across the hall, slipped into the library whose door we had left ajar, scurried up the winding staircase and settled myself into a nook, well back between two of the jutting bookshelves. As quietly as I could, I pushed a heap of books in front of me, leaving only a cranny through which I could make out the group of burnished leather armchairs in the centre of the large room below.

I waited for a few minutes, and from across the hall, I heard the tones of slightly raised voices. Then the parlour door opened sharply.

'We're very sorry, madam,' said a stern masculine voice. 'It is absolutely impossible. Mrs Granger appears to be in tolerable health, and we must speak with her alone.'

I heard Mrs Bryce-Fortescue's low tones without making out her words, and the unyielding response.

'You are aware that Mrs Granger can refuse to answer any of our questions, if she wishes. This would naturally produce a very negative impression, but such is her right. It is up to her. Now, let us begin.'

'Let me show you into the library, then,' said Mrs Bryce-Fortescue with an audible sigh, and I knew by the approaching sound of her voice that she was already crossing the hall. The two men followed her, and ushered Sylvia into the room before entering it themselves and shutting the door firmly behind them.

The inspector, the sergeant and Sylvia installed themselves in the armchairs in silence. From my hiding place, I could see Sylvia's face directly; it wore a sulky, rather childish expression of stubbornness mingled with helplessness. The officers addressed her with a certain gentle respectfulness which made me think, at first, that they must, after all, believe her innocent. I realised later that their caressing tones were a mere technique to soothe her or lull her into revealing as much as possible, much as one coaxes an obstinate child, knowing that roughness will only increase its resistance.

'Now, Mrs Granger,' began the inspector, the more important of the two, 'we would like to go over your statement once again.' He shook out

some papers and smoothed them rather osten-
tatiously over his knee.

'I really don't see why we need to, Inspector
Gregory,' said Sylvia in a small, childish voice. 'It's
still quite the same as before. Nothing has
changed in what I can tell you.' I thought that her
main strength must lie in a kind of quiet but
efficacious obstructionism which can be extremely
trying, and that knowing her well, her mother had
probably coached her carefully.

'We need to check with you, because certain
new elements have come up – certain information
which alters some of the factors corroborating
your statement.' He paused for effect, but as she
remained perfectly dumb, he gave a little cough
and took a breath. I thought he would proceed to
tell her what had changed, but instead, he said
silkily,

'Mrs Granger, you know that the medical
evidence places your husband's death very close
to one hour after his luncheon, which by the
evidence of the cook means very close to two-
thirty in the afternoon.'

'Well, of course I know that, I've already been
told it several times,' said Sylvia, without raising
her voice.

'Yes, to be sure. Now, your statement claims
that after luncheon, you retired to your room,
and remained there until six o'clock.'

'That is exactly what I did.'

'Two days ago, we told you that your evidence
as to your movements was corroborated by that
of your housekeeper, who claims that you could
not possibly have left the house without being

65

seen, as the only exits are the main door leading to the entrance lobby, the marble floor of which was being washed by the housemaid for a good two hours starting directly after luncheon, or through the kitchen, which was occupied for the whole time by the cook and the kitchen maid doing the dishes.'

He looked at Sylvia, but she did not feel the need to waste a single word, and sat waiting rather provokingly.

'Sergeant Barker, read Mrs Granger the new pieces of evidence which have come to light since Thursday,' said the inspector, looking rather disgruntled. The sergeant, a thickset, youngish man, took out a pad, licked his finger, and turned a few pages with care. He read slowly, and unlike the inspector, quite expressionlessly, staring all the while down at the page before him.

'Evidence given on the 10th inst. by witnesses remaining anonymous,' he enunciated dutifully. 'Statement of Witness Number One: "It's not difficult to climb down from the balcony that Miss Sylvia's bedroom gives onto. I did it many a time myself as a lad, though it's been a while. Yes, I'm sure I could still do it." The witness then proceeded to give a demonstration, by climbing onto the roof of the veranda at the side of the house, and from there to the first-floor balcony, then down again. The veranda opens onto the side garden which is separated from the woods by a low fence.'

Again Sylvia said nothing, but a faint, rather tense smile appeared on her face. I thought that decidedly, her mother must have given her strict injunctions not to speak unless she was asked specific questions – unless it was in her own nature to be so passive, for the desire to make some sharp response was certainly strong within my breast! The sergeant licked his forefinger again and turned another page.

'Evidence of Witness Number Two,' he read. '"I was walking along the high road which borders the part of the woods that lies on Manor property. The time was about twenty or twenty-five minutes after two o'clock. I know because just about five minutes later I came over the top of the crest and saw the steeple, it comes into sight just at that point, and then I heard the chimes. I saw a figure flitting among the trees, coming away from the direction of the house. I recognised the figure as that of Mrs Granger. I thought nothing of it at the time."'

This time Sylvia stirred, and flushed faintly.

'It's nonsense,' she said, but without excitement. 'Nobody can have seen me when I never left my room.'

It seemed to me that the inspector became faintly annoyed at his failure to shake or frighten her. He began to speak, then stopped and motioned his colleague to continue.

'The evidence from the ballistics experts has arrived,' said Sergeant Barker stolidly. 'The bullet is French-made and very probably French-bought. It was fired from a small French-made gun of a type intended for personal use and defence. Such guns can be bought quite easily in France, but also, although somewhat less easily, in London.'

Now the inspector breathed deeply and beamed the full force of his personality onto Sylvia.

'You spent a large part of last winter in Paris, did you not, Mrs Granger?' he said in a tone of accusation.

'Yes, I did,' she replied calmly.

'Indeed you did. Now, Mrs Granger, I would like you to understand the danger of your position. The police are precise workers. You understand that if you purchased that gun in Paris, the fact will be traced and confirmed – if you left your house by the balcony and the veranda, and went into the woods, that fact will be uncovered and sworn to by witnesses. None of your movements have any chance of remaining hidden, Mrs Granger. Therefore, I urge you to speak up now, and tell us before it is too late if you have anything to add to the statement you already made.'

It is hard for me to express how much pressure and threat the inspector communicated through these words, by his deliberate and intense manner of speech, although taken literally, as I have written them down, they do not in themselves appear to be so dreadfully frightening.

'No,' Sylvia replied, but a strange look had come into her eyes; not fear, but something closer to anguish, as she felt her inclination to reserve being forcibly overcome. 'I bought no gun in Paris, I have never had a gun, I do not know how to shoot a gun. If I had had a gun, I suppose the servants would have known it, so why don't you ask them?'

'If you had had a gun, it would be natural for you to keep it very carefully hidden, wouldn't it?'

said the inspector. His tone was smoothly challenging, as though he were encouraging her to keep on speaking. Once again, to my dismay, she responded.

'Nothing is ever hidden from servants,' she answered, with a sudden bitter animation which boded ill for discretion, and therefore pleased the inspector highly. 'Especially George's. They were always spying on me.'

'Spying on you?' he pounced on her words. 'Do you think your husband asked them to do that?'

'I don't know, perhaps,' she said, growing wary, a little too late.

'Now, why would he have done that? He suspected you of something, maybe? Could that be it?'

'Oh – I don't know! What should he suspect me of? I don't know. He was jealous of my time, I think. He left me very little liberty, and it grew worse after I returned from France. He was greatly displeased when I telegraphed him to tell him that I was extending my stay, and came over without telling me, to fetch me back himself. He appeared at the door of my hotel room one morning, and seemed quite as angry as if ... as if he had something to be angry about! But there was nothing. So he had to bluster around and insist I return with him, and so I went, so he had nothing to be angry about really, but he remained angry anyway. It annoyed me at first, but then I left off thinking about it.'

There was something shocking in Sylvia's words and attitude, although I would be hard put to explain exactly what – some indifference, some detachment that ill-suited her position as bereaved widow, allowing her to speak thus of the dead. The inspector looked more and more like a Cheshire cat who has had cream.

'This is all most interesting, Mrs Granger,' he said silkily. 'Now, come – surely you must have some idea of what bothered Mr Granger so, and made him angry. Can you not think what it might be?'

She hesitated, torn between the conflicting desires of obeying her mother's injunctions, yielding to the inspector's charismatic pressure, and surely influenced also by the idea that refusing to speak would tell against her, whereas speaking too much might lead to the same result...

'I've really no idea,' she said finally. 'I never dreamed of asking him. I thought he was just a ... a jealous husband, you know, as many men are. He was not young and perhaps he was worried ... about me, worried that I should, oh, I don't know. Fall in love, or something. Meet some young, dashing handsome man and run off with him, for instance. But that's all such nonsense, isn't it?'

'Is it? Did you never meet any nice, pleasing young men? Not even in Paris?'

'Not in Paris or anywhere,' she replied coldly. '"Nice, pleasing young men" do not interest me.'

'Well, that's very virtuous, to be sure. And surprising, too, for a lovely young woman like you. The contrary would be most natural and understandable, I assure you. Suppose you tell me more about this trip to Paris. You did not travel alone, I suppose?'

'Of course not. I travelled with my friend Camilla Wright, who is here now. We meant to go for six weeks, but then we enjoyed ourselves so much that we wanted to stay on, but as I said, my husband came and fetched me back.'

'Ah. And Miss Wright remained in Paris?'

'No, she didn't want to remain alone. She bought a ticket and returned to England just after.'

'And what did you and Miss Wright do in Paris which was so very interesting and amusing that you didn't want to return on the date you had planned?'

'Oh, nothing! We were free, that's all – free and far from everything! We went out, to theatres and restaurants and dances. We met interesting families and practised our French. We had café au lait and croissants for breakfast on the rue de Rivoli. We had no household duties. We just enjoyed ourselves!'

'You just enjoyed yourself – far from your elderly, severe and jealous husband.'

The inspector's remark cast a pall over Sylvia's conversation, which had become cheerful, almost frivolous. After an uncomfortable silence, she spoke again, but now her tone was somewhat pinched.

'If you are trying to dig up some secret enmity between my husband and myself, for which I wished to kill him, you are barking up the wrong tree,' she said. I thought, and surely the inspector thought also, that Sylvia's personality was more complex than the innocent, sulky child she so easily played at being. 'There was no conflict between my husband and myself,' she went on. 'When he came over to Paris to fetch me, there was no quarrel, as I quite simply acceded to his request. If I sometimes felt that he and his servants seemed to be observing me, I believed that it was because he was worried, not because he suspected me, and I tried my best to reassure him.'

'Quite so, quite so,' said the inspector in a tone of irony, exchanging glances with the sergeant. 'Well, Mrs Granger, we shall return to the subject when we have learned more. For the moment, I will bid you good day.' I believe that according to his lights, he had succeeded in what he had set out to do, namely to surprise Sylvia out of her initial pose and to jerk her into making some unplanned statements. Seeing his drift, she had now recovered control, and he no doubt thought that he had obtained as much as he needed for one day, and that continuation in the same direction would only encourage her to further harden her present mask. He must certainly have hoped that his threats would contribute to ripen the grain of fear he had sown within her. He arose, and opened the door for her courteously. They took leave of each other in low tones, wasting no words, and I found myself alone.

After a few moments, I returned to the parlour, and found the three ladies together, talking about quite other things. Mrs Bryce-Fortescue asked no questions, of course. I gave her a complete account of all that had occurred later on in the evening, and she exclaimed with anger and annoyance when she heard all that Sylvia had said. 'Drat the girl!' she cried. 'Could she not have the sense to hide George's trip to Paris, or at the very least the fact that he was extremely angry at her not returning?'

I wondered very much if Sylvia would mention the interview during the afternoon, but she volunteered nothing. I suppose that if she spoke about it at all, it would be to Camilla. I dearly wished to know if she would do so, and determined to keep my eye on her carefully for the rest of the day. But as it turned out, there was nothing to keep my eye on, for we remained sociably together, talking and working, until supper, and at supper Mrs Bryce-Fortescue persuaded Sylvia to take a sleeping draught, telling her that she looked quite worn out, as indeed she did. As a result, Sylvia retired before any of us, and I talked with Mrs Bryce-Fortescue as Camilla went out for a turn in the gloaming. I went to bed quite early, and heard Camilla come up into her room and go to bed. I admit that I opened my secret door and listened to hear if the two girls would join each other for a nocturnal talk, but they did not; Sylvia was no doubt deeply asleep. Perhaps they will talk when she awakens; they may not, as Sylvia seems a very introverted type of person, but if they do, I feel I simply must know about it! Which explains why I am up already, well before the arrival of my morning cup of tea (although not so early that the birds have not yet begun their day), sitting in my narrow bed with the cosy quilt drawn all around me, writing on my knees, with my ears pricked up like an eager hound's for any sound from next door. How dreadful – I sound like some pointy-nosed old maid, desperately curious about her neighbours' activities! Ah well, one cannot be a detective (and how much, how sincerely I hope that I *am* a detective, however amateur, and am not merely playing at being a detective) without a dose of natural curiosity. If you do not think me very bad, Dora dear, then it must be all right.

Your loving sister

Vanessa

Maidstone Hall, Monday, June 13, 1892

My darling twin,

I am writing to you by the light of a candle in my room, preparatory to going to nest under my quilt, which has become one of my dearest friends within this household. Another, believe it or not, is – but no. Let me tell you all the news in order.

To begin with, Sylvia did not wake while I was writing to you yesterday morning; she slept late, and I kept close to either her or Camilla till mid-day. After luncheon, the two girls once again declared their intention of going for a ramble around the lake until tea, but Mrs Bryce-Fortescue, forestalling my desires out of politeness, or perhaps because they corresponded to her own purposes, turned to me with great cheerfulness and said,

'How lovely for Vanessa! She has not had a

74

chance to see the grounds yet, and the lake is one of the most delightful spots. Have you a pair of rubber boots, dear? It's safest to wear them about the lake. I'll find some for you.'

The girls made no protest, and perhaps I only imagined a slight sulkiness in Sylvia's mood at first, as the three of us went off together. Camilla behaved most naturally, chatting to me and asking a great many questions about my life and activities. I had to quickly supply some details corresponding to the story Mrs Bryce-Fortescue and I had invented together, but the conversation soon centred about the fascinating subject of my schoolteaching, so that there was no need to dissimulate. I waxed enthusiastic, and both Sylvia and Camilla were deeply interested in every tidbit. Sylvia's mood lightened perceptibly as she listened, and she sighed a little wistfully.

'How exciting it must be to live all alone, in one's very own little rooms, and work for one's living! Can you imagine it, Camilla? You see,' she added, turning to me with a look of real friendliness, 'I grew up here in this big house, and I married two years ago, and went to live in another house, an even bigger one – daughter and wife of a country squire, that's the only life I've ever known. Not that George was really a country squire,' she added as an afterthought. 'But he meant to be.'

'And what has your life been like?' I asked, turning to Camilla. 'Are you also from the country?'

'Worse even than Sylvia's,' she laughed. 'I grew up in my family's castle, Severingham. You can call it a country house if you like, with its two hundred odd rooms. It is a splendid place, but

75

not one where a girl can learn anything about town civilisation or independent work! I was raised to be a chatelaine, but I shall never be a chatelaine after all, for when my father dies Severingham will pass to a male cousin, and out I shall go.' She laughed, but it was easy enough to detect the trace of bitterness in her voice.

'Well,' said Sylvia gaily, 'we always say that if Camilla ever needs to make a living, she could probably manage it by sewing. She's a marvellous seamstress – she made this dress for me! It's better than what Mother's seamstress does.'

I admired her dress, which really was a lovely creation in black silk – with, of all things, a rose pink lining which was not visible until Sylvia lifted up the hem of her skirt to show it to me. A single, large pink silk rose gathered up the skirt on one side.

'You see, I've put on the pink rose today,' she said, showing it to Camilla and turning to me. 'I have a black one, too, as this is a mourning dress ... but...'

'It is really lovely!' I said reassuringly. 'Did you make your own dress, too, Camilla?'

Camilla's dress was of a much simpler cut, in dark blue.

'No. I like making clothes for other people, but for myself, I hate it,' said Camilla. 'I made myself a riding habit once. But it's much easier and more fun to do it for someone else. Easier to modify the pattern when you're doing the fitting onto another person – and also, you get the pleasure of seeing what you've made while it's being worn. Yes, I am good at sewing. It's a silly talent to have, isn't it? I'd much rather be good at something else. But my mother discovered this early on, and then I had to have lessons in London with a professional.'

'Is that how you and Sylvia met?' I asked. This time it was Sylvia who answered.

'Oh, no! I've never taken any lessons of any kind at all,' she said lightly. 'We met through friends. Remember Mr Clemming?' she added, turning to Camilla and smiling. 'He's dead now, and his wife lives in Paris. We saw her last winter. Mrs Clemming's parents used to be close friends with Mother's parents, and Mrs Clemming remained friends with Mother although they saw each other quite rarely. But they wrote; I think they mainly wrote about us children! The Clemmings had a daughter the same age as me. When Mrs Clemming was young, her parents used to invite Mother's parents and Mother to their London house for the season, in fact that's where Mother met Father. Then Mrs Clemming inherited the house and lived there with her husband, and they invited me there when I was eighteen, to come out. I spent two months going to balls and parties. I didn't enjoy it much. I didn't like Mrs Clemming so much then; I think her husband made her life difficult. She's really become a much, much nicer person now that she lives in Paris and does what she likes – and doesn't have to worry about marrying off Helen!'

'You can't imagine how jealous Mrs Clemming used to be of Sylvia,' said Camilla a little truculently. 'Jealous for her own daughter, I mean. I think she invited Sylvia like a poor little country cousin, as a foil for Helen. I can understand it, because Sylvia is pale and fragile, and Helen was a great strong healthy girl with a loud voice and red cheeks. But everywhere they went, everybody was always more interested in Sylvia. Yes, it's true, Syl – don't glare at me! I can't help it if that helpless look of yours drives people – men – mad! All right, I'm just teasing you. But Mrs Clemming wasn't always very nice to you.'

'No, it's true,' admitted Sylvia. 'She seemed tired of having me after just a couple of months, and as I was just as tired of her, I came home.'

'I can't imagine living in London during the season,' I mused. 'It's strange to me that you should view my work as something exciting – though indeed, it is in its own way – but it doesn't have much glamour compared to London parties!'

'London parties for eighteen year old girls are stupid!' exclaimed Sylvia animatedly. 'Perhaps later, when people grow up, they can meet and dance and talk and eat together in a happy, amusing way, like Mrs Clemming does now. But not when you're eighteen – then, all a girl is supposed to do is listen to the advice of her elders on which are the most eligible young bachelors, and spend the evening angling to have a dance or a word with them. Oh, I had no talent for it! I hated them all. I was bored silly, while Helen was always busy. Thank goodness, I met Camilla at one of those parties. Then we arranged to meet again and became friends ... best friends. I was such a failure in every other way! I didn't find a husband there and I wasn't even interested!'

'Yet just two years later, you were married,' I remarked.

We had reached the lake as we spoke, and were following a path along the shore. The sun shone through the merest wisps of clouds, the path was bordered by great bunches of tall grasses among which grew wild flowers of all descriptions, delicate-petalled on long, fragile stems. Bees buzzed happily amongst them, and as we crossed an occasional mud-patch, a small frog was to be seen hopping away hastily towards the water, its tiny body stretching out longer than one would have believed possible. The lake shimmered beyond us, flat and greenish-grey, its glassy surface barely rippled by the almost imperceptible breeze. The air was mild, and the mood was generally uplifted and communicative; otherwise, I think that my remark might have risked sending Sylvia scurrying back into her protective shell of silence. Her expression darkened, but Camilla picked a spray of cornflowers and pulling Sylvia close to her, she tucked them into her hair. Smiling down at her – Sylvia is of normal height, but Camilla is quite tall and very gracious – she said,

'Oh, don't let's talk about marriage now!'

'No, don't let's!' agreed Sylvia, touching the flowers and allowing herself to be cajoled. 'Vanessa, do be careful whom you marry!'

'I shall be,' I laughed. 'As a matter of fact, I am already engaged.' I do not know why I mentioned it, for there was certainly no need and perhaps my maiden state was even a kind of encouragement for Sylvia's confidences. But mentioning

Arthur suddenly seemed to bring him closer to me, and goodness knows how I missed him.

'Engaged! Oh! What is he like?' said Sylvia with a mixture of interest and vexation.

'Oh...' I reflected for a moment without speaking. I found it most difficult to describe Arthur.

'Big? Small? Old? Young? Foolish? Intelligent? Strong? Weak?' Camilla said jokingly.

'In a few words: thoughtful, serious, dreamy and–' I meant to say tender, but felt too shy '–and kind. He is six years older than I am. We have been engaged for four years already, but must wait to be married until he has a better position.'

'Four years! Then you became engaged at twenty, like I did! Ah, how I should have loved four more years of freedom!' cried Sylvia.

'Was it really necessary for you to marry immediately?'

'George and Mother wanted it,' she answered simply. 'As for me...'

'Sylvia,' said Camilla, almost warningly, I thought. And most artfully, she turned the conversation onto other topics, and recounted a thousand anecdotes of her childhood and her travels on the continent, which enthralled us until we had finished the full tour of the lake and returned, hot and slightly muddy, to the house.

We spent an uneventful evening all together, but as soon as bedtime approached, I began once again to itch with the desire to know if Sylvia would tell Camilla, in confidence, about the previous day's interrogation. The three of us came up together, and separated into our rooms with a cordial good night. I prepared myself for bed and

80

slipped under the eiderdown, but did not blow out my candle, for I was determined to see if Sylvia did not mean to talk with her friend in private. I dozed off in spite of the candle, which burned out, but so tense was I that some time later I jumped awake, and immediately became aware of a tiny noise in the corridor, then the softest tapping, almost petting, at the door next to mine. I heard movements in the next room, and Camilla opened her door. There was faint whispering. Then I seemed to hear both girls slip away into Sylvia's room, and a faint click as they shut themselves inside. From my room I could no longer hear the slightest sound, but quick as a wink, I rushed across to my secret door, moved the table, slid the carefully oiled bolt, pushed it open and silently stepped out. Hugging the wall as I had done earlier, I stole silently past the door leading from Camilla's room into the strange large chamber in which I now found myself, and reached Sylvia's. A light shone from underneath it, and as the crack under the door actually measured a good half-an-inch in height, I lay down and applied my eye to it.

I could see only feet; Sylvia was sitting on her bed, and Camilla occupied the dainty chintz-covered armchair. But I could hear them well enough; they spoke in low tones, but did not whisper. To my surprise, however, their conversation did not at first turn upon the subject I had expected.

'You're mad,' Camilla was saying in an anxious whisper. 'Burn it, Sylvia!'

'I can't, I won't!' she answered stubbornly. 'No

81

one can find it – no one, Camilla. I've hidden it in a box with a key. A secret box, in fact. And I've hidden the key. No one can find it, ever. And no one would think to look there anyway.'

'A secret box – what secret box?'

'That,' said Sylvia, with some gesture I could not see. 'It has a secret compartment at the bottom. The jeweller showed me how to use it; it needs a special, very tiny key which I keep in an extra-secret place – you can't even see the keyhole if you don't know where it is. Oh, Camilla, if George never found it, no one ever will – there can't be anybody, not even the police, more suspicious than George! I know he looked over my jewellery many a time, to see if I had any pieces he didn't know about.'

'My God, and you left it there?'

'Well, yes, I did. I know it was a risk – I think I actually liked the risk! Part of me was afraid, but – some other part of me really would have liked him to find it! Can you understand that? Anyway, he never did.'

'You're out of your mind – it's too dangerous! Burn it, Sylvia, please!' begged Camilla in a voice of distress.

'I can't – I love it. It's too beautiful. You don't realise what it means to me. Especially when I'm alone. No one will ever find it, believe me. Don't think about it any more, Camilla. I can't think why you should worry about it when there's something so incredibly much more frightening, and you haven't even given me time to tell you about it! It's the police ... they say they have a witness who saw me running through the woods

82

just before George died!'

'No!' cried Camilla – 'oh, no! Oh, Sylvia, you fool, don't tell me – don't tell me it's true! You really went out that afternoon?'

'No, no, I didn't. Of course not! You know I didn't. Why should I lie to you?'

'I don't know. Out of fear? And perhaps you would be right. Sylvia – is it true?'

'No, it isn't! I didn't go out at all, I tell you! Camilla – don't you believe me? Don't you believe me? You don't think I'm lying to you, do you? It's that witness who's lying. But what shall I do? I'm afraid, Camilla, I'm afraid.'

'No, I know you wouldn't lie to me. At least, I believe so, I hope so, I want it to be so. But you're so elusive, Sylvia. What's truth to you? If you didn't go out, how can someone claim they saw you? It's impossible. Surely the statement can't be proved or used. What did you answer the police when they told you?'

'What could I say? I just told them that it was impossible, since I hadn't left my room.'

There was a moment of silence. Camilla rose and crossed over to the bed. I could not see her gesture, but she leaned close to her friend.

'Oh, Sylvia, tell me, tell me the truth. Look at me. Did you leave your room? It's so important! Tell me!'

'No, I didn't. I told you, Camilla. You can believe me.'

'Swear it?' Camilla said almost in a whisper.

'I swear it on my honour, on anything you want, on our friendship,' said Sylvia ardently. 'You can believe me, Camilla. If I'd gone out, I

83

would tell *you*.' I heard Camilla's sigh of relief and the sound of a kiss.

There was a moment's pause.

'So what can it mean, then? How can anybody claim to have seen you?'

'I keep asking myself. Either they saw George's murderer – and he was a bit far off and half-hidden by trees, and they simply felt certain at the time it must be me in there, or ... or else somebody is lying because ... it's somebody who hates me. Some friend of George's. Oh, I wish, I wish I knew who it was.'

'We will find out, somehow or other!' said Camilla hotly. 'I'll have that person's head, the liar! In the meantime, just go on doing as you are. Say as little as you can, and just keep repeating that you kept to your room.'

'I tried to do just that, but they would keep on and on asking questions about George. Oh, Camilla, they kept on hinting and asking questions about – about our marriage, and how George wasn't happy with me. I had to tell them how he came to Paris.'

'Horrors. But you know, I think they would find that sort of thing out for themselves sooner or later by questioning other people; servants and things. And it would look strange, maybe, if they knew it and you never said it. Perhaps this is for the best. Oh, darling, none of it can constitute evidence against you, as long as you just stand firm. Promise me you will, no matter what happens!'

'I promise, of course I promise,' murmured Sylvia, and her feet left the floor. I heard the sound of her snuggling into her bed.

84

At that precise moment, I received a most horrible, unbelievable shock. From out of the pitch darkness of the far corner of the large chamber, a pair of eyes were staring out at me, glinting and glimmering and reflecting I don't know what minuscule source of light.

My blood rushed into my ears and my heart pounded so horrendously that I was momentarily deafened as though by a waterfall, as well as utterly deprived of breath. My fear was so great that I felt blackness closing in upon me. It was unreasoning, for really, the very worst that could have happened to me (discovery, exposure, disgrace) could not conceivably be bad enough to warrant such terror. But try encountering a pair of gleaming eyes in a pitch dark room, and see if your heart does not pound fit to burst!

With a great effort, I prevented myself from moving or making a sound, and as my reason returned to me, I noted that the yellow irises surrounding the glittering, enormous pupils obviously belonged to a cat. At that same moment, it stunned me again by leaping out of its hiding place with a meowl.

'What's that?' I heard Camilla whisper, with a slight gasp.

'Oh, that's just the cat. It always wanders around in there – it gets in by a hole in the roof,' answered Sylvia, her voice caressing and sleepy. Terrified that they would open the door to capture the animal, I slithered and slunk back to my own door as quickly as possible, mentally requesting the creature, which was now proffering a multiplicity of meows to celebrate my presence, to cover for any noise I might be making. I slipped into my room, pushed out the cat which hopefully tried to accompany me, shot the bolt quietly home and sat on my bed, trembling in every limb. All became dark and silent once again, and after many long minutes, I lay down and was finally able to relax. I began to think back over the conversation I had just heard.

Dora, I am as certain as I can be that Sylvia is to be believed. There was nothing but sincerity in her tone, and she protested neither too much nor too little. She cannot be such a consummate actress as to bring that off in such an intimate situation, in front of a friend who knows her very well. In any case, I was really not able to believe for a moment that such a girl actually took a gun and shot her husband coldly with it, however trying she may have found the married state. And with no plan, furthermore, no real alibi, nothing but a half-lame excuse of having stayed in her room.

Yet she is a strange girl, and there is some mystery about her; something, perhaps, related to the object hidden in the jewellery box. Dear me, what *can* it be? How can I manage to find it out? I have spent all of today in a ferment of discreet spying and intelligent reflection (or at least, some semblance of it), in the hopes of learning more, but have not made the slightest progress.

My one useful act today was to strike up a conversation with the coachman, Peter Middleman; I was able to approach him for the first time since Mrs Bryce-Fortescue unwittingly spoiled my plans by refusing my request to ride with him to the post office. He was waxing the saddles in a sunny patch of green outside the rather ramshackle coach house, and finding myself alone in the late afternoon as the sunshine began to wane and the shadows to lengthen a little, I wandered over to him and began to chat. A real groom from the country would have been a little surprised, a little distant, possibly even a little displeased, but Peter is decidedly not of that species. In less than no time we were on the best of terms, and although he does make a special effort to call me Miss Vanessa rather than the simple 'Vanessa' I see trembling on his lips, he would never dream of calling me simply 'Miss'. In fact, he generally does not use any particular term of address at all in normal conversation. I take this kindly enough, imagining it to be a sign of the light-hearted democracy which reigns among the inhabitants of a city street where all are involved in an equal, and probably equally desperate, struggle to make a living.

I led the conversation quite easily to Mr Granger by asking Peter how he came to be a groom.

'I've always loved horses and animals of all kinds,' he told me cheerfully. 'I had ever so many pets as a child – kept bringing home stray creatures I picked up in the streets. I even brought a rat once – my parents made me throw it back out. My parents had some connection with Mr Granger from a long time ago, when he was still living in Manchester and working in trade and finance. He did a great number of financial things, I guess, though I don't know much about it, but one of the things he did was lending money to people to get them started and then having them pay it back with interest over the years. He helped my parents start their grocery store. A grocery store was perhaps just a little thing for him then, but he took whatever came his way, big or little, and he had a great sense of who could be trusted. My parents were grateful to him for many years.' He paused, and the expression on his face changed slightly. 'I'll tell you something, though: they were bitter, too. It was easy enough to see, even though they never talked about it. But the payments and the interest wore them down and ate away at their profits, so that although the shop was a fine success, we were always somehow right on the edge of poverty. They just could never manage to finish the thing; they were always a little behind, and it always had to go on a little bit longer. Yet my parents always spoke of Mr Granger as their benefactor and nothing else; he was a dangerous man to annoy. My parents are dead now,' he added suddenly, unconsciously wrenching a little twig off a bush and twisting it in his fingers. 'They died a couple of years ago, within three months of each other. My father caught pneumonia, and my mother caught it from him, nursing him. They died in the public hospital. Sometimes I think it wouldn't have happened – they wouldn't have gotten ill, I mean – if they hadn't been worn down to a shadow over the years, with all the work. Well...' He broke off again.

'What happened to the shop?' I asked gently.

'Oh, it was seized by Mr Granger for what my parents still owed him. What do you think? He didn't do it out of meanness, I guess. It's just all business with him. You know, he could be friendly, too. I remember that when I was a boy of twelve or so, he saw how I loved animals, and he told me that it was his dream to buy a country house and live there, and that he'd do it in a few years, and take me with him as a groom if I wanted. I was so happy I couldn't wait! And when he came about the shop a couple of years back and saw me again, he made me the offer. He had just bought Haverhill Manor then. Of course I didn't feel the same about him any more as I had when I was a boy. I understood a lot more about what was happening. But I had no money and no choice, and – well – I liked the job he offered. So I came. I can't believe that he's dead too, now! It was a shock – I still can't believe it! I found him, you know, lying there. I didn't even realise he was dead for the first moment. He looked just – just as usual. Only lying down flat.'

I glanced up at him sharply, but my eyes met his; candid and blue, they stared back at me unwinkingly.

'It must have been a terrible moment for you,' I observed gently.

'It was a strange moment,' he answered. 'I stood there ... staring ... and couldn't make out what had happened, until I saw the bloodstain on his chest. It was just a little stain.'

I asked him what it had been like to work for Mr Granger, and as we chatted on, I gained a certain image of Mr Granger's personality, at least from Peter's personal point of view. I tried, tactfully, to bring up the subject of Mr Granger's marriage, but Peter seemed to have no opinion on the question. He is only nineteen, too young to think about marriages, either his own or other people's. Instead, we found ourselves anxiously discussing the topic of his future. I only wish I had something to suggest, but I don't know many country squires in need of grooms, and indeed, even if I did, I'm not sure that Peter would be found entirely acceptable by most of them, even if he *is* immensely fond of horses (and they of him).

I did not learn much of real interest, all in all, and was just preparing to bring an end to our lengthy chat and return to the house, when all of a sudden he became rather shy and sweet, turned red to the ears, and seemed to wish to express something rather difficult. Immediately, I was all ears.

'I'm going to tea in Haverhill tomorrow,' was what finally emerged. 'In the village, I mean. Mrs Bird – that's Mr Granger's housekeeper as was – she was always fond of me and treated me like a son which she never had. She asked if I could come visit her now and again, since she's out of work, and Mrs Bryce-Fortescue said I could take tomorrow afternoon off. I wonder – do you think you'd like to come with me?'

I burst out laughing at this surprising invitation of a hopeful Jack to his Jill, but quickly, realising that it was really a great stroke of luck, I modified my laughter into burst of delight. Indeed, it cannot but be helpful to meet Mrs Bird and gossip away with her as much as can be. So after my initial surprise, I accepted his offer with alacrity, and rushed off to tell Mrs Bryce-Fortescue about it. I feel that I must report to the poor lady again,

90

for she has learned nothing from me since I told her of the police interview. Certainly, I considered mentioning the mysterious contents of Sylvia's jewel box to her, but in the end I have decided to wait until I know more about it myself. For the thought has occurred to me that if, by any chance – I do not think it likely – but if the secret concerned some indication of Sylvia's guilt, her mother would be certain to destroy it. No, decidedly, I must say nothing for the moment.

As for my own newly firm conviction of Sylvia's innocence, I could hardly report that to Mrs Bryce-Fortescue; I'm sure she would find it most rude were I even to hint that I ever had even the slightest doubt on that score. I rather fear she must think I am happily accepting her hospitality while accomplishing nothing at all. Indeed, dearest Dora, sometimes I actually think so myself, for I worry continually over Sylvia, and yet I have not been able to learn anything, so far, which could seriously be of help to her.

Oh well – perhaps tomorrow will yield something new!

Much tender love,
Vanessa

Maidstone Hall, Tuesday, June 14, 1892

My dearest sister,

I must tell you at once that I have spent a most

interesting and informative afternoon. Yes, at last, at last, I have learned something really surprising, and certainly very important, though I do not yet know what to make of it.

The drive to Haverhill was a very tiny little bit embarrassing. I sat up on the box next to Peter, for I wished to talk, but quite soon I grew tense at having his youthful eyes fixed upon me, calf-like, while he blushed until his neck was almost the colour of his hair. I tried to discourage his ardour by telling him my age, which I thought would seem quite hoary compared to his innocent nineteen, but it had no effect whatsoever, and as for my engagement, I simply could not bring myself to mention it at all, for fear of discouraging him too much and reducing him to sulky silence. I wished to encourage his friendship without encouraging anything else, and I can assure you that it was rather a tiresome business, and I was fortunate that his hands were much taken up with the reins of two very lively and spirited bays, for otherwise I do suspect that he would have tried to slip an arm about my shoulders, and I should have had to be severe.

The situation improved greatly as soon as we reached the village. Peter stopped the carriage in front of the village inn, and arranged, for a modest sum, to have it put away in their stable for the afternoon. He then proudly led me a little way down the main street, till we turned off into a very humble lane, at the far end of which we stopped in front of the most ridiculously pretty cottage imaginable. Rose Cottage was its name; not very original, perhaps, but extremely apt, for these flowers tumbled in profusion over the whitewashed walls, while innumerable other species, blue and yellow, bunched at their foot and bordered the pebbled lane with splashes of colour. Peter tapped the doll-house sized brass knocker, the neatly painted green door popped open, and we were ushered down a little shady hallway into the family drawing room, which was more roomy than one would think seeing the house from the outside, and altogether full of people! Unexpectedly, we had found ourselves the central figures – quite the celebrities, in fact – of a classic village tea party. Indeed, Mrs Bird, a dear old plump lady in an apron, used to live in this absurdly delightful little home with her sister before going up to work in the manor two years ago, and now she has moved back down again. Her proximity to the victim of the most sensational event to take place in Haverhill for a century has made her quite famous round about, and with Peter enjoying similar privileges and our invitation having been made known in the village, afternoon calls had been particularly numerous, and in fact tea-time came without any of the callers having felt the necessity to depart.

I was introduced as a friend of Mrs Granger's, which instantly conferred great prestige upon me. A large silver teapot was set out, and a steady stream of cakes and sandwiches appeared from the direction of the kitchen. Perceiving the situation, Mrs Bird had given hasty directions to her cook to prepare tea for a large party, and dispatched a small and freckled boy to purchase the necessaries from the village grocer and baker.

There was too much for the child to carry back in a single trip, and as tea progressed, we could make him out at regular intervals toiling up the lane with a bag in each hand; I felt quite sorry for him, and once I went out to the kitchen to cheer him on a little, as I saw him coming round the house on the path leading to the kitchen door, but I found that he was being heartily encouraged by the gift of a bit of pastry at each trip, and he did not appear to feel that he had any cause whatsoever for complaint.

To begin with, the company was affected by a certain reticence, due no doubt to the unknown quantity which I represented; unknown quantities have an unpleasant habit of taking umbrage at certain indiscretions, and tongues generally become remarkably bland in their presence. But as I showed myself a most willing, if sadly ignorant, informant, the conversation grew freer, questions and remarks multiplied, and more anecdotes were recounted than I can possibly remember.

What emerged above all, over the course of the afternoon, was what I might call a portrait of a marriage. And such a marriage, Dora – such a marriage as should never exist before God! Some of the ladies present thought ill of Sylvia, and others ill of Mr Granger; not a few thought ill of both, but all were agreed that the marriage was a loveless one, and that after the first few months, every trace even of the most elementary mutual respect had disappeared.

'He was fifty-three if he was a day!' exclaimed a fuzzy-haired old creature who cannot have been less than seventy-five herself. 'Marrying a mere

94

slip of a girl – it's disgraceful!'

'Well,' said a doddering old gentleman, one of the rare representatives of his sex, 'if you want a large and healthy family, you must marry a young 'un, it stands to reason. Where's the harm?'

'Large and healthy family indeed,' said Mrs Bird with a sniff. I really do not think she is the least bit spiteful in nature, but her position as the acknowledged star of the day's proceedings led her to make more of her special knowledge, and reveal more intimate details, than tact and elegance would really have allowed. 'No one can have a large and healthy family, or any family at all, living as they did – angry faces, separate rooms, locked doors! Mrs Granger couldn't stand to be near her husband, it was plain as the day to see. And he had no love for her, either. He never loved her, from the very start; just wanted her, he did, as he would have a pretty object. He bought her, I tell you, for the pride of having a twenty-year old wife to grace his wrinkles. And never had the enjoyment of his prize, either!'

A shocked murmur arose in answer to this diatribe. I felt deeply ashamed for Sylvia, to be thus discussed, and ashamed of myself for listening to it all with such attention. Mrs Bird perceived that she had overstepped the line of decency, and began to justify herself by adding further information.

'Bought, yes, I say bought!' she cried. 'Not that he spent the money on her. She wasn't the spendthrift type, and her dresses were always as simple as simple; she made them with a friend, often enough, rather even than hire a dressmaker.

No, I didn't mean it that way. I didn't mean that he persuaded her to marry him with offers of luxury. I mean that he arranged it all directly with her mother. Yes, he mentioned often enough how he was having his wife's home rebuilt so that her mother would have a safe roof over her head. Oh, that sounds kind? It all depends how you say it! Yes, it could sound kind, I suppose – only it didn't! He rubbed it in, yes, that's what he did. There's a way of speaking that denies dignity to the other person, and that was his way, I don't know exactly how he did it, but he did it right enough. Oh, there was a lot more than plain generosity going on there. And what did Mrs Granger tell me, when my very own niece got married last year? She asked how old she was and I said twenty-five. I told her not everyone got married so young as she was, just a slip of a girl. "You must have been in a hurry," I told her, teasing like. And she just shrugged her shoulders and answered, "Mother was in a hurry. Not me." Just shrugged her shoulders, that's all. Oh, she was a quiet little thing and didn't show much, but she felt plenty. Her husband was a strong man and could be cruel, too, but she was a sly one and had plenty of ways of defending herself. An evil chess game, that's what their marriage was. She was pushing for a draw, that's what Mrs Granger was doing. "Let me alone, and I'll stay," she'd say. "Touch me and I'm gone forever. You have no hold over me." And in a way it was true. Mrs Granger wouldn't have been bound to him by money or by propriety – she didn't care much for such things. But he had moves up his sleeve as well. Mr Granger wasn't a man who would settle for a draw. He was going for a checkmate, and he knew what he was doing – and he'd have succeeded if he'd but had the time, for that's the kind of man he was! He'd have been capable enough of having his way by force, and binding her so that she couldn't escape. He was planning something, I know it for a fact, and it was going to be something terrible.'

'Terrible, terrible,' was the essential content of the murmurs which arose from the assembled company. The word expressed my own sentiments exactly, and I almost felt the prickle of a tear in my eye as I thought of Arthur. One or two ladies rose and took their departures with offended airs. But the elderly gentleman took up the conversation rather eagerly, and said in a hopeful voice,

'Did she shoot him then? Is that what you think really happened?'

Mrs Bird appeared to realise that her discourse could be interpreted as hinting something of the kind, although quite unintentionally. She hastened to deny it indignantly.

'Certainly not!' she cried. 'I do not believe for a single instant that poor Mrs Granger shot her husband. Not for one moment. Unhappy she may have been and was, and sly, perhaps, and stubborn as a mule, but never a murderess! Was she, Peter?'

'Course not,' replied that young man with a sudden energy which surprised me, but then I thought that his protectiveness was probably directed at Mrs Bird rather than at Sylvia herself.

Furthermore, I believe, the idea of Sylvia's guilt seemed doubly impossible to most of the people present, because of her fragile and feminine appearance, and also quite simply because she had lived among them. Still, there were exceptions.

'Who else would have done it, then?' said the old gentleman a little wistfully, as though he almost wished, in the dusk of his life, to feel that he had personally encountered real despair, real hatred, real violence. 'She didn't love her husband, you say; she must have wanted him away then.'

'She was a nasty bit of goods,' said an elderly lady sitting quite near me. She was very bony, and it seemed unlikely that the generous plate of cake and muffins she held in her hand would be able to make any significant alteration in that condition. 'I went up to the manor selling subscriptions, and she wouldn't receive me. "Tell her I'm out," I heard her telling the parlourmaid clear as a bell. Closed the door right in my face, the girl did. I went round and looked in the sitting room window and there was Mrs Granger talking with a friend, as calm as you please. And when I tried to catch her about it down in the village, she said she had no time for such things. Rude, that's what she was, and behaving above her station. I wouldn't be surprised at anything she did. Not anything. Who knows what some people will do?'

'Now, Mrs Munn,' Mrs Bird reproved her with some asperity. 'Nobody here can believe she went as far as murder. Why should she? What good could her husband's death do her? Freedom and independence? Why, Gerald Roberts, that poor girl couldn't use freedom and independence if you handed them to her on a silver platter! That girl has to be protected and taken care of like a child, that's all she's really fit for.'

'There are women who can't abide their husbands,' persisted poor Mr Roberts, meekly but stubbornly, like a child deprived of its bedtime story. 'It's a hard thing when there's no love. Some can't bear it. Anyway, if it wasn't she, who could it have been?'

A slight hush momentarily overtook the company, as each person reflected on what had just been said. At that precise moment, a soft, quavering voice raised itself from an obscure corner of the room and murmured something unintelligible.

'What's that? What are you saying?' said several voices. The quavering voice struck up again, a little more clearly.

'Couldn't it have been that strange young man?' it said.

I raised myself on my seat to identify the speaker amongst all the eager, staring faces, and soon perceived that it belonged to a very old, white-haired lady, bent over in her chair, holding her cup of tea close to her as though to keep warm, and leaning forward onto a knotted cane. 'What young man is that, Martha?' asked Mrs Bird kindly. Peter leaned towards me.

'That's old Martha,' he whispered in my ear. 'She's strange; she spends all day wandering about the streets looking about her. Nobody knows what she lives on, but people invite her over for a cup of tea sometimes. She's sharper than you'd think to see her.'

'The dark young man with the red cloak,' is what the quavering old voice was saying when I transferred my attention back to it. 'I saw him on the day, on the day Mr Granger was killed which the devil knows that he deserved. A tall young man, a quiet young man, a strange young man. He walked up the road towards the Granger woods. I saw him, and it seemed to me that I knew him, even, but I couldn't place him.'

'It's true that Martha saw a strange man – I remember it!' chimed in a voice from the other side of the room, belonging apparently to a woman called Betsey Singer. 'I met her over in Simpson's lane and she told me. Handsome face and gaudy clothes she said he had, and smooth seeming. But it can't have been the very selfsame day that Mr Granger met his death now, can it?'

'Yes, it was, to be sure,' insisted old Martha.

'Surely many strangers come to visit the village, don't they?' I asked Mrs Bird.

'No, not too many, unless they're someone's family,' she answered. 'I didn't see any young man myself. I don't think he can have come into the village proper; some of the people here would have surely noticed him. He must have gone around. Still,' she added a little wistfully, 'I do think I remember Betsey telling me that Martha had seen something.'

'I remember too!' The discussion had become general now, as everybody tried to recall exactly what they might have heard or seen. 'Yes, Betsey mentioned it to me! Didn't you, Betsey? Now, when was it? I was at the grocer's ... buying ... buying raspberries. That was it! I told you I was buying them for tea because my nephew was visiting. And you said "Is your nephew a tall, polite young man with black hair?" And I said "No, he's a little boy of nine." Do you remember?'

'To be sure!' agreed Betsey. 'Martha had told me she'd seen such a one, and I thought it must be your visitor when you mentioned him. Now, what day would that have been?'

'Well, it was the day my little nephew came, so it was Sunday – why yes, it was the Sunday before last, the very one!'

Dora, I won't go on telling you the vagaries of the conversation, for I couldn't possibly remember it; the remarks became wilder and more varied, as an ever greater number of guests came to 'recall' something about the mysterious gentleman. Yet as far as I could ascertain, only Martha appeared certain of having really seen him; it was in the early afternoon, and he was walking away from the village in the direction of Haverhill Manor, on that very same road from which (while coming towards the village) some witness claimed to have seen Sylvia running through the woods.

Old Martha may be the 'strange old lady' of Haverhill, but her testimony was perfectly clear, and it was accepted as gospel truth by the whole of the company. An idea to verify her tale formed itself in the back of my mind.

When everything had been said, repeated and speculated over that possibly could, and not a single crumb of bread or cake nor a drop of tea remained, the party began to show signs of breaking up.

'We'd best be going, Va – Vanessa,' said Peter, masking the last word with a grin and a mumble as he glanced around him self-consciously. 'Otherwise, you'll be late for supper getting back.'

I did not feel as though I should be able to eat any supper at all, but I was in a hurry to depart for reasons of my own. We exchanged warm goodbyes with all present, and above all with kind Mrs Bird, who invited us to return with great hospitality; the dear lady was simply blooming under all the attention! I wonder if her past life has not been particularly monotonous.

Peter brought round the carriage from where he had stabled it at the public house, and I climbed up onto the box beside him.

'Peter, before we start on the road home, there is something I would like to do,' I said. 'That is, if you think it is a good idea,' I added with false deference.

'What's that?' he enquired with interest, eager to please.

'It's about that young man, the one they all said they saw. I'm thinking about Sylvia, Peter; I think she's in trouble with the police, as they seem to suspect her, and there may be an important clue there, don't you think?'

'Could well be. But what can we do about it?'

'Just this one thing. It's little enough. Let's stop at the nearest train station, and ask at the window if anyone remembers a young man of his description getting off the train that Sunday.'

He didn't answer, but clucked up the horses, and we started off at a trot. He seemed to be mulling over things in his mind. After a while, keeping his eyes firmly fixed on the horses' backs, he said to me,

'I think it would be best not to meddle.'

'Perhaps – for other people!' I replied hotly. 'But we – why, we are already meddling, just by being acquainted with Sylvia! I shouldn't leave a stone unturned if I thought it could straighten things out for her with the police.'

'Are you such great friends, then?' he asked, in the tone of one who does not believe a word of it. I felt faintly indignant. Indeed, I have only known Sylvia for a very few days, but there is something ... she has something...

'I've become dearly fond of her since I've been here,' I said, 'but even more importantly, I'm just convinced from the bottom of my heart that she's not the murderer. I hate to see the police barking up the wrong tree after an innocent person, when they could be chasing the real criminal!'

'Why are you so sure of that?'

'Why, aren't you?'

'Well, I don't want to speak ill of anyone.'

'Peter!' I exclaimed. 'Do you suspect Sylvia? You never told me!'

'Well, no,' he said quickly. 'I guess I don't really. Otherwise I'd feel funny living there, if I really thought she was a murderess. Still – there were some funny things.'

'What funny things? Tell me at once!'

He paused to think and gather his words, as inarticulate people often do.

'I haven't much to tell, really. You see, it was like this: I was never particularly close to Mr Granger.'

'Well, I can certainly understand that, after all

that you told me about the stranglehold he had over your parents, that he called helping them. I should think you could never feel really close to him!' I said.

'Well, yes. But still, he had taken me on as groom, which was the job I wanted, and I was making money from him, and things were all right really. And sometimes, as I drove him around here and there, he'd talk to me.'

'He'd talk to you? About Sylvia, you mean?'

'Well, about her and other things. He could be a hard man, I'll say that.

'"I'm used to winning", he'd tell me. "I've spent my life struggling to get what I want, and I generally succeed. I wanted to marry Sylvia and I did it. But marriage is no joke, Peter, just remember that when you start thinking about getting hitched. The girl is pretty and the ceremony romantic, but that's only the beginning. People forget that this is for the rest of your life. For better or for worse, that's what we say in the marriage vows, but that's not my way. I won't have Sylvia for worse; it's got to be for better. She hasn't been what I've wanted her to be since we've been married."

'"She's done nothing wrong," I'd say, to soothe him, for nobody ever saw Sylvia doing the things husbands usually complain of – having lovers or improper friends, or spending too much money.

'"It's not what she does, it's what she doesn't do," he'd answer. "She hasn't learned to want what her husband wants." And lately, he'd been getting angry; he talked about it to me sometimes, almost as though he was talking to himself.

'"I'll teach her," he'd say. "I've been patient up

104

to now. I've been willing to say to myself that she's too young. But I'm getting tired of it. I've given her an ultimatum – she'll satisfy me or else!" It was almost scary, how he talked, Vanessa.' (This time, my name slipped out unawares.) 'I didn't want to ask him questions. I didn't feel it was my business. I didn't want to know anything about his ultimatum. But he let fall a couple of hints. He said something about having her locked away, I don't know what he meant. Still, though, who knows how angry she might have been against him, and what reasons she might have had?'

'What an awful man he seems to have been,' I said, trying to conceal the full force of my indignation and disgust. 'Poor Sylvia! Yes, it's easy to see that she had plenty of reason to be angry with him, perhaps even to hate him, deep down. Yet that doesn't prove that she killed him! If every wife of a nasty husband resorted to murder, there wouldn't necessarily be a lot of men left about, would there! Or women either, as the poor things would all be in prison.'

'Oh, husbands aren't all so bad,' said Peter significantly, looking at me this time. 'Lots are ever so nice to their wives.' But I refused to be drawn into this topic, however interesting it may in reality be!

'Well, I for one still believe it must have been that strange young man that old Martha saw,' I cried, 'and I'm determined to try to find out something!'

'Why don't you just tell the police inspector about it next time he comes to the house, then,' said Peter. 'Rushing about hunting things out for yourself, and asking questions – why, that's not right for a lady like you!'

The young and liberated are often the most prejudiced of all, Dora, do you not find?

'Oh, but I shan't do that, Peter!' I said hastily and soothingly. 'I didn't mean to at all – I meant *you* to go into the station and ask. Won't you do it? Please? For me?'

We were nearing the very station by this time, and although I could see that he would have much preferred to avoid the whole story, Peter could not resist my calculatedly charming appeal (accompanied, I am ashamed to confess, by fluttering eyelashes).

'You stay here and wait, then,' he said firmly, alighting. But this suggestion taxed my tolerance too highly.

'Oh no, I want to watch you do it!' I cried with assumed girlishness. 'I shall stay right away from you, I promise – I shan't even listen. You'll tell me what they say.' I suspected that without my watchful eye, he might not take the job seriously, and I had no intention of allowing that.

In spite of his reticence, Peter wished to please me, so he entered the station and I followed him a short way behind, stopped in a quiet corner, and affected to be waiting. Peter sauntered up to the window, and was soon deep in conversation with the gentleman behind it. There were no other clients in sight, no trains, and only two or three other people quietly standing about, and the man seemed pleased enough at the unexpected chat. He soon called another from the room behind, and all three put their heads together. Chuckling and exclamations were to be heard, gestures were made, a timetable was even taken out and consulted. I was most grievously beset by curiosity, but forced myself to bide my time patiently.

Have you ever noticed, Dora, how men are just incapable of repeating a conversation that they have heard? Women are all past masters at the task; they want to recount the very words that were spoken, and even the intonations, the inflections and the glances that accompany them, and top it all off with a keen analysis, whereas men seem incapable of giving even the merest coherent summary. Arthur is particularly hopeless at it, but Peter, alas, was not much better; after a good quarter of an hour of conversation with the men in the station, after we climbed back up on the box together and started off on our way home, all he found to say was,

'Yep, they saw him right enough.'

This information was enough to greatly excite my thirst for further detail!

'Whatever did you talk about for the whole time,' I asked coaxingly.

'I don't know, nothing really,' was the foolish but typical answer. Still, by dint of much insistence, I elicited from him the fascinating information that not only did the gentlemen, who worked there every day of the week, remember a red-caped young man appearing in the station, but even that he stopped to ask for timetables to plan his return to London that same afternoon.

'And he bought his ticket and took the return train, just as he had planned,' ended Peter. 'Now I think you've learned what you wanted to, and had best just explain the whole thing to the police if you really care to do it – personally, I'd leave it alone, police and all, if I was you!'

Should I tell the police about it, or not? There will always be time to do so; it does not seem necessary to be hasty. On the other hand, they have a great many means to discover much more than I ever could about the mysterious young man; where he came from, where he went and so on. On the third hand, they wouldn't tell me any of it. On the fourth hand, if he is the murderer and they discover him, then there would be no need for me to work further upon the case. I must reflect over all this. Oh, how I should like to talk it over with Arthur! I wonder if I can ask Mrs Bryce-Fortescue to let me go up to Cambridge for a day or two.

Your very own loving

Vanessa

Maidstone Hall, Thursday, June 16, 1892

My dear sister,

It is hardly to be believed, but an extraordinary chance appears to have come my way this morning!

I was devoting myself to considering all that I had heard and learned at Haverhill, and wondering how best to investigate this news and where to begin, and as I wandered about, deep in thought, my steps bent their way automatically to the library, perhaps in search of inspiration, or of the padded silence that reigns there.

Thanks to the thick and luxurious carpets, one can cross the room quite silently. As I did so, I suddenly became aware that I was not alone – Sylvia was fast asleep in one of the large, well-worn leather armchairs. I stood near her for a moment, watching her as her breast rose and fell quietly under her soft dress. Her arm was resting on the arm of the chair, and her hand fell over the side; her two or three bracelets had slipped down to the place where the hand widens from the wrist. One of them was a charm bracelet; a robust little silver chain with large links, from several of which depended little silver ornaments; a heart, a cross, a little bow, a tiny key.

A key! A tiny key! My heart leapt as I perceived it, as the words overheard in the dark of the night, and nearly forgotten, suddenly sprang into my mind. *No one will ever find the key*, Sylvia had said confidently. And indeed, who could possibly guess where she might have hidden it, anywhere in this vast manor whose nooks and crannies she knows as no one else does? It had not even crossed my mind that she could have hidden it upon her person. But now, my eyes fixed with fascination on that carefully worked little key, I became filled with the utmost conviction that this, and no other, must be the key to the secret compartment of her jewellery box. Oh, if only I could get it without waking her! Her secret – I had thought it important, and then I had felt less certain, for it had seemed to me that Camilla seemed more fearful of some scandal than of an accusation of crime. And yet, no stone must be left unturned, and here was a golden opportunity!

I knelt by the armchair, and examined the bracelet. The clasp was a simple one, to be pressed and pulled open, and it hung down free from her wrist. My heart pounding with fear so that I was afraid it must be audible – it always does seem to do that at the most inconvenient moments! – I reached out to touch it, and then, stiffening my hands to control their trembling, I took it between the tips of my fingers and pulled it apart with a gentle, steady little movement. The bracelet hung open now. I stood up, trying to calm the rushing in my ears, and took a few steps away from Sylvia, standing behind the chair where she could not see me if she opened her eyes. I was too afraid to wake her by slipping the hanging chain away from her limp arm, and remained wondering how I could obtain the key, when quite naturally, she sighed in her sleep and stirred. She shifted her arm, throwing it across her lap, and as she did so, the open bracelet slipped and fell off onto the thickly piled Persian carpet. I darted forward silently, snatched it up, backed away precipitately and waited to see if she would awake and perceive the lack. But she did not, and I left the library on cat's paws, my heart wilder than ever, feeling like a thief and a criminal.

Oh Dora, perhaps, just perhaps, I shall now finally be able to discover something which has eluded me thus far; perhaps, after all, this key will be the one to unlock not just the box, but the mystery itself!

Only how, how shall I get at Sylvia's jewellery box? Dare I invade her room? What if she hides the box when she realises that she has lost her bracelet? I must act quickly! What can I do? Shall I tell Mrs Bryce-Fortescue? Maybe she, with the authority of a mother, could enter her daughter's room, take the box, unlock the compartment and look at the contents without shame.

Yes, but what if she chooses to do so alone, and finds evidence that may incriminate her daughter, if not of murder, at least of aiding and abetting it? It is just the reason for which I would not talk about this with her earlier. I believe there is no doubt whatsoever that she would destroy such evidence instantly, and for that matter, she would be quite capable of inventing some seemingly innocent excuse to stop the investigation and send me back to Cambridge post-haste. No, I cannot let that happen – things have gone too far for that, and I feel personally responsible now for what I have undertaken. I must do something else; I shall say that I am unwell, and go to Sylvia's room in one hour, while the others are at luncheon. Until then, I shall remain here in my room, with the door open, writing to you and checking whether or not Sylvia enters her room – if she does, I shall simply have to slip into my secret hiding place and try to get some idea of her actions.

Later, after tea (of which I partook rather copiously ... due to my feelings of distress, as well as the lack of the midday meal!) Oh, my dear Dora, I cannot describe the fear which I suffered during the luncheon hour, when, having excused myself

111

lamely (feeling certain that my subterfuge was utterly transparent) and retired to my room, I counted out several minutes, emerged, and tiptoed down the hallway to Sylvia's door.

It was worse, much worse than in the library, and indeed, I believe there was some cause, for if I were to be caught and captured at the critical moment in which I should be dipping my hands into Sylvia's jewellery box, I do not believe that even Mrs Bryce-Fortescue would be convinced that my efforts were all in the interests of her daughter – and whatever happened then, it could only be for ill! Why, if she believed I was stealing the jewellery, I should be in a fine pickle – in prison, perhaps, my reputation ruined and my future blighted, and even Arthur would have trouble believing that the necessity to examine the contents of Sylvia's jewellery box was absolutely unavoidable! And yet, God knows, rings, necklaces and bracelets held so little attraction for me at that particular moment that they might as well have been made of dust!

A seemingly endlessly varied series of similar such undesirable prospects presented itself to me spontaneously as I pressed the door-handle of Sylvia's room and pushed the door slowly and carefully ajar. But my feverish desire to pursue my task was stronger than all my fears together, and I closed the door silently behind me, and slipped across the room towards the famous box, which sat upon the dresser, announcing its character most openly and unashamedly.

It was a rather large, dark red leather box which opened with a nice little brass key that was innocently thrust into its hole, proclaiming to the world at large that Sylvia was unafraid of any investigation of her box. I turned the key, opened the lid, and began to poke and pry within its layered, pillowed depths to locate the invisible keyhole of the secret compartment.

Without being aware of its existence, no one could ever have guessed that the box contained such a thing. But knowing it gave me a signal advantage. I began by examining the box with care inside and out to locate where some unused portion could lie, and determined that it was necessarily at the very bottom of the box; it could not be otherwise, where every possible corner appeared to be accounted for. I then pried all about that section until, pulling two velvet cushions apart from each other, I spied a tiny hole nestling in the depths between them. I took out the purloined charm bracelet, isolated the tiny key with trembling fingers, and thrust it into the hole. It fit, but would not turn – I began to doubt, and yet felt so sure of myself – my nervousness prevented me from calmly trying one direction and then the other – I jiggled the key and grew more anxious by the second – and then suddenly it turned and clicked.

Yet I still could not discover the compartment. I pulled and pushed gently, but nothing seemed to give. The minutes passed, and I grew more and more terrified. I searched for another way, I gently tugged at the leather tags, I pulled here and there at the cushions, I removed a number of pretty stones and bracelets to examine the box more closely. Oh, Dora, I cannot describe how nervous

113

I became at length, how frightened, how my ears pricked up as attentive to the slightest sound as those of a trapped wild animal, which I would hardly hear anyway, as they were ringing with the banging in my chest. Yet my burning impatience would not let me shut up the box and rush from the room, as I was every moment tempted to do! After what seemed forever, but was perhaps only five minutes – certainly not enough time for the meat course to be over downstairs – I stopped trying to force the box and began to observe it carefully, study its structure, and reflect. It was thus that I finally came to the conclusion that the lid of the hidden lowest section could not in any manner be moved or shifted backwards or forwards, or lifted up vertically or in the manner of an ordinary lid. I finally concluded that it must work via some kind of a twist, and taking a deep breath, I took hold of what must be the top of the section and swivelled it. Something folded and yielded, and suddenly it came away and the secret compartment lay revealed to my eyes!!

It was empty.

Sylvia had changed her mind, and changed her hiding place, after her discussion with her friend.

Dismay swept over me, as I wondered if she had, finally, followed Camilla's advice and burned the evidence, whatever it may have been? I glanced at the grate, but there was no sign of a fire having been lit there recently, as indeed it was not likely there would have been, during a warm and pleasant month of June. Still, that proved nothing – anything that can be burned (I assumed it was papers of some sort) can be

114

burned even at a candle, with enough patience. All my efforts had come to nought.

With leaden hands I returned the upper portion of the jewellery case to its place, worked it snugly downwards, rearranged the disturbed pieces, and closed and locked it. I left the room, not without first opening the door a crack and spying out the hallway, and making my way quietly to the library, I slipped Sylvia's bracelet deep down into the crack between the seat and the armrest of the chair in which she had slept so soundly. I then returned to my room, feeling dreadfully disappointed, and lying down upon my bed, I fell asleep from pure annoyance, and woke up at teatime with a great appetite.

Tea has restored at least a portion of my courage and good humour. I find that as I am making unsatisfactory progress with the inmates of this house, I should decide once and for all to turn my attention fully to the young man spied in Haverhill on the day of the murder. For this, I must begin by returning to Cambridge, at least for a brief visit – for how can I undertake such researches without the help of my friends? I am already laying my plans, and will speak to Mrs Bryce-Fortescue about them tomorrow. The young man exists, therefore he must have an identity and live in some specific place. I shall make it my business to discover all that can be known about him!

Your disappointed but not despairing

Vanessa

Cambridge, Saturday, June 18, 1892

My dearest sister,

Here I am back in Cambridge, writing to you at my very own desk, in my very own dear rooms! How familiar, how consoling and reassuring they seem. And just two weeks ago, I felt quite tired of them, and wished very much that something should happen to take me away from them for a time!

Yesterday morning, I closeted myself with Mrs Bryce-Fortescue, and told her what I had learned about the person I call to myself 'the mysterious young man'. She was greatly impressed by the importance of the discovery, and I told her that in order to pursue my researches, I needed to travel. I needed to try to pick up the traces of his journey, and perhaps to follow or trace him as far as London, or wherever else he had decided to go and lose himself. She grew most excited and worried, above all when I asked her opinion on the subject of the police: should we not inform them of our discovery at once? Could they not trace the gentleman much more efficiently than I should be able to? No, Mrs Bryce-Fortescue did not think so. She was much against speaking to the police at all; she hemmed and hawed, and twisted, and said that they would not listen to us, that their minds were fixed against Sylvia, that they would dismiss our words as so much useless gossip. The reasons she gave did not strike me as being extremely

116

convincing, but she is my employer, after all, and in any case, I felt that nothing should be lost by waiting, and much might be gained. After all, the police could certainly be informed at any time, and besides, what prevented them from finding it out for themselves, instead of proving that Sylvia was somewhere where she wasn't? Why, whoever said they saw her ought to have been seeing a red-caped young man instead!

I told Mrs Bryce-Fortescue that I thought I should visit Cambridge before anything, for the young man had almost certainly stopped there in the train from Haverhill, and I thought I might be able to find out if anyone remembered him alighting. For that matter, I thought that one might be able to trace his voyage to Haverhill as well as that going away, and either way, Cambridge would be the nearest major station.

We decided that Peter should take me to Cambridge today, and he took me to despatch a telegram to Arthur to let him know that I was coming. 'Arthur darling returning Cambridge need your help Vanessa' was as much verbosity as my small change would cover (the second word was perhaps not strictly necessary but did much to alleviate the overcharged state of my feelings).

I set about preparing a few things for my journey, for I could not tell how long I might be away nor what I should find out, and tried to put my thoughts as well as my clothes in order until tea-time, when I sallied downstairs. We had barely settled around the teapot, when the sound of cantering was heard rapidly approaching the house.

'Whatever is Peter doing with the horses?' said

Mrs Bryce-Fortescue, going to the window.

'It isn't Peter,' said Sylvia, getting up also.

A splendid carriage worthy of a fairy tale, pulled by two high-stepping and perfectly white steeds, was approaching at a fast clip.

'Is it some friend of yours, Vanessa?' Sylvia asked.

'No one I know possesses such a superb equipage!' I answered, and we remained all four glued to the window, quite breathless with amazement.

The carriage pulled to a halt in front of the house, and a gentleman alighted from each side of it.

'Why, that *is* a friend of mine,' I cried, astonished. 'It's a mathematician of my acquaintance, Mr Morrison! But I don't know the man who was driving.'

The gentlemen saw us plainly, gathered together in the window as we were, and they smiled gaily, but went ceremoniously to ring the bell. Charles' friend, the proprietor of the carriage, was a distinguished although somewhat portly person of fifty or so, with an ample and carefully tended greying moustache. I waited with ill-contained impatience until Mr Huxtable had opened the door, taken the gentlemen's coats and ushered them formally into our presence.

'Did you get our telegram?' were Charles' first words. 'We did send one to say we were coming – you haven't had it yet? I'm so very sorry! We got here before it; it'll come any moment, I dare say. Please do forgive us. We didn't mean to interrupt your tea! Vanessa – Miss Duncan – telegraphed that she was meaning to come up to Cambridge,

118

and my friend Korneck and I thought it would be simpler for everyone if we just came down and fetched her ourselves, as Korneck has the most terrific horses and they were really in need of exercise. Please let me introduce myself,' he added with the debonair manner which had its usual effect of irresistible charm on everyone around him. (Charles is really a dear.) 'I'm Charles Morrison, mathematician, Trinity College in fact, and this is my friend Mr Gerhard Korneck, an amateur mathematician from Prussia, presently also of Cambridge.'

'From the region of Posen, old Poznània, I come. I am enchanted, enchanted to make your acquaintance, dear lady,' said Mr Korneck punctiliously, in fluent English with a marked Germanic accent, addressing himself uniquely to the lady of the house. As she kindly extended her hand to welcome him, he took it and kissed it in a most continental manner! 'I ask a thousand pardons for our so sudden, so ridiculous arrival not announced by telegram.'

'Oh, please do not worry about it,' said Mrs Bryce-Fortescue courteously. 'We were just sitting down to tea, and should be most pleased and honoured if you two gentlemen would like to join us.'

Indeed we were pleased (and perhaps even honoured – who can tell?); the presence of a couple of gentlemen in a society of ladies enlivens the mood remarkably, and witty remarks soon began to fly among the members of the younger generation, while Mr Korneck continued to address himself admiringly to Mrs Bryce-Fortescue, praising her house, her roses, her tea, her cakes and her delightful hospitality. Indeed, he seemed greatly taken by the adventure, and continued to repeat lovingly,

'It is all so very British, so very British,' as though he could not get over this plain and simple fact.

We had a lovely tea (Charles' telegram was delivered in the middle of it, 'Coming to fetch Vanessa this afternoon please excuse suddenness Morrison'). Afterwards, I collected my things, bid farewell to Mrs Bryce-Fortescue, promising to return as soon as I should have some positive information, or to write her if necessary, and took my departure with Charles and Mr Korneck.

Once comfortably installed upon the plush cushions of the most luxurious vehicle I have ever had the good fortune to enter, I scolded Charles vigorously.

'I might have been in the middle of important detection! It might have been necessary for me to stay the night! I might have really wanted Peter to take me into Cambridge – it might have been urgent for me to talk to him!'

'Oh no,' he exclaimed with meek dismay. 'I never thought of all that – I do hope we haven't spoiled your plans! Anyway, you must blame Arthur, not me; it was mostly his idea. In fact, it's all your fault, Vanessa, when it comes to that. It was that "darling" in your telegram that did it. Arthur got all het up when he read that, and here was Korneck with his horses just pawing the ground with eagerness to get going somewhere, and I suddenly had this stroke of genius about how to satisfy everybody at once! I tried awfully to get Arthur to come, but he had to teach his very last class of the year this afternoon. I tried, I did, Vanessa. I told him the students would be delighted to get early vacation, but he just couldn't bring himself to do it.' He shook his head with mock sorrow. 'Poor old Arthur. There's a man who'll never take a walk on the wild side.'

'I'd just as well he didn't,' I answered smartly. 'I prefer him steady and reliable. He was in enough danger once to last anyone a lifetime, if you ask me!'

'That was different,' said Charles; 'it was danger, right enough, but it wasn't courted, any more than the pedestrian on the sidewalk is courting the danger of the brick which all unknowingly bonks him upon the head. It wasn't a consequence of taking risks and living to the hilt!'

'But why should a person court danger? It comes only too often when it isn't wanted, don't you think?'

'Not to me, it doesn't,' sighed Charles a little wistfully. 'It's different for you; here you are in the thick of it.'

'Rubbish, I'm not in any danger!' I snapped, feeling slightly annoyed at Charles' indiscretion, for I didn't want Mr Korneck to know anything about my detecting activities. But it turned out to be much too late for such worries, for that gentleman said cheerfully,

'Yes, yes, I have heard that you undertake a dangerous task, a most dangerous task.'

'Charles!' I cried in dismay. 'You haven't told!'

'Not a thing, not a thing! I only said that you

were hunting down a murderer, that's all. I just told him in the carriage, coming over. No details, I promise.'

'You are impossible!' I was beginning.

'He told me no details at all,' said Mr Korneck hastily, then added with a wink, 'None were needed. I read the daily papers. But reassure yourself, my dear young lady. I will be the soul of silence, I will be the tomb. I am deeply shocked to hear of a young lady engaged in such activities. I do not wish to hinder or increase the danger in any way. I will be of discreet help if possible, nothing more. You may count on me. Your ... *Verlobter*, your fiancé is very good, a very fine man. But if you need further help, please do not hesitate to depend upon me.'

'I haven't introduced you to Korneck properly yet,' said Charles, quickly redirecting the conversation into channels less immediately connected with his own foolish indiscretion. 'You remember I mentioned him last week; he's the one who's working on Fermat's Last Theorem, the lost and forgotten problem.'

'Ah, so beautiful!' Mr Korneck showed a great disposition to be distracted from my doings, and hold forth upon what was obviously his pet topic. 'Do you know the problem, Miss Duncan? Are you a lover of mathematics?'

'I am sadly ignorant,' I smiled, 'but always greatly interested in listening to the conversation of my many mathematical friends. I have heard so much over the past years that the language has a welcome, familiar sound to me, and I feel quite happily at home surrounded by talk of quaternions, matrices, or vectors, even if I cannot participate.'

'But Fermat's last theorem is something different. It is, I believe, much easier to explain than those objects you have just mentioned. You are a teacher of children, Miss Duncan, so perhaps you have already encountered this simple question: can you think of three ordinary numbers, not zero, of course, such that the square of the first plus the square of the second is equal to the square of the third?'

'Well, certainly; that's Pythagoras' theorem on right triangles,' I answered; 'three squared plus four squared equals five squared, for example.'

'Very good, very good! Nine and sixteen make twenty-five,' he nodded approvingly. 'And there are many, many more; an infinite number, in fact. If you seek you will easily find a great many more. Thirty-six plus sixty-four equals one hundred – did you ever notice that? A delightful equation – such beautiful numbers. But now – now for the great mystery of Fermat. Can you think of three numbers such that the cube of the first plus the cube of the second is equal to the cube of the third?'

'Let me see,' I hesitated. 'One cubed plus two cubed is nine – no, that's a square. Two cubed plus...'

'Do not try, do not try any longer, for it is impossible! No such numbers exist, none at all, and this was proved long ago, some say by Fermat himself, although his argument appears to contain an error, which was rectified over a century ago by the great Leonhard Euler. Fermat

123

also left a proof for the fourth powers, a beautiful and astute argument. But he asserted that much more was true. Indeed, his famous so-called "theorem" states that one cannot find three numbers such that the n-th power of the first plus the n-th powers of the second is equal to the n-th power of the third, for any ordinary number n greater than 2. You see, this is what you cannot have,' and he scribbled:

$$x^n + y^n = z^n$$

onto a bit of paper and showed it to me.

'Really? You can never have that for any ordinary numbers x, y and z?' I said, surprised, for the equation has nothing so very startling and improbable in its appearance.

'That is the mystery! For Fermat himself wrote that he *had* proved that you cannot, but his proof was never found. He noted the formula on a page of his copy of *Diophantus*, saying that he had found a most marvellous proof, but that the margin was too narrow to contain it – *cuius rei demonstrationem mirabilem sane detexi. Hanc marginis exiguitas non caperet.*'

'So you think he wrote it down elsewhere? And it has really never been found or rediscovered?'

'Never, although some progress was made towards rediscovery at least. The greatest step of all was taken by a member of your sex, the great, great Sophie Germain, my inspirer and my muse in all things. Ah, the sublime beauty, the unspeakable wisdom of her method! She worked with prime numbers, certain very special prime numbers, the Germain primes. You know that a prime number, p, is a number which is not divisible by any other, save the number one, and itself, of course. Five, seven, eleven, these are primes. But the Germain primes are very special, for not only is p itself prime, but $2p + 1$. Five is a prime number and so is twice five plus one – eleven, so five is a Germain prime! Seven is prime, but twice seven plus one is fifteen, not prime. So seven is not a Germain prime. The notion is so beautiful, so mysterious, so admirable. Inspired by this, I try and attempt to go even farther than she did!'

'And what did she do, exactly? What did she use these Germain primes for?'

'Very nearly, she proved that Fermat's equation is impossible when n is one of them – you cannot have $x^P + y^P = z^P$ for a Germain prime p. Well, I exaggerate. She proved this in the case that x, y and z are not divisible by p. But no one has come close to proving anything so important in the subject, excluding the great Kummer of course, but that is something else, for his techniques are entirely modern and different, whereas hers could have been those of Fermat himself. Such purity, such simplicity! And she sent her beautiful theorem to the greatest mathematician of the day, Carl Friedrich Gauss, but she wrote under the identity of a man, for she feared that her sex might cause her discovery to be despised and rejected because of the prejudices of her time.'

'Yes,' I cried happily, recalling the story, 'Monsieur Le Blanc! Charles told us how she assumed his identity in order to attend the Ecole Polytechnique in Paris.'

125

'Yes, and she used the same name to write to Gauss. But Gauss found out the truth, and contrary to what she had feared, he was filled with admiration. "A *taste for the abstract sciences in general*", 'quoted Mr Korneck in a tone filled with reverence, '"*and above all for the mysteries of numbers, is excessively rare: one is not astonished at it: the enchanting charms of this sublime science are revealed only to those who have the courage to study them deeply*." That is what he wrote to her; the sentence has been like a luminous guide to me. And he went on to tell her that if a woman was able to surmount all the difficulties and obstacles that customs and prejudices put in her way to study these mysteries, then, indeed, she must be a woman of superior genius. Such a man! Such understanding! If I could only write to him, but it is too late, for he died nearly forty years ago. I try to prove something similar to Germain, but even simpler and even more general, something that would work in all cases, something so surprising and beautiful that it may even be the secret proof of Fermat himself! I am working on it, working day and night. It does not quite succeed yet, but I feel that I am nearing the goal.'

'Then you will be famous indeed,' smiled Charles. 'For great minds have worked hard over this problem and given up.'

'Yes, yes, it has been so. But perhaps they tried too hard. Euler, Kummer – geniuses! They poured such a wealth of techniques and ideas into the problem as could not possibly have existed in Fermat's mind. Something different is needed, something simpler; an illumination of perfection

126

and simplicity. Ah, I dream of finding it – and I hope to live my dream! I am no distinguished professor of mathematics such as your honoured friends, Miss Duncan. I am a mere amateur; a lover of mathematics. I have not attended university nor written an erudite thesis. I come from beautiful Posen and grew up helping my father in the running of our family's great horse farm, the raising of the most beautiful and powerful of Prussian steeds. These horses of mine come from our stables,' he added with proud tenderness, shaking the reins over the backs of the white horses whose fresh trot was pulling us along smartly and effortlessly, and who answered his caress by tossing their heads and shaking their manes without breaking their rhythm in the slightest. 'But I came upon the love of mathematics by myself,' he continued, 'although my passion was not so pleasing to my father, and have read the works of Fermat and Pascal and their followers in later generations, and now that I have reached an age at which the stables belong to me and are run by trustworthy men more able than I, and I find myself free to follow my dreams and inclinations, I devote myself to study. I spent many of the recent years in Paris, attending courses of the great mathematicians there, but decided some months ago to spend a year in Cambridge, for it is here that the greatest exponents of the subject of algebra are to be found.'

'I hope you succeed,' I cried enthusiastically. Poor Mr Korneck, he seemed very happy, but I detected a trace of bitterness in his words, as though he felt, in spite of all he had said, that his origins made him into a perpetual outsider in the world of mathematics that he loved. I forgave Charles all of his misdeeds in view of his kindness to the eager amateur, and resolved to restrain myself from upbraiding him more severely in private, as I had meant to do, with the intention of compelling him to greater discretion in the future.

Oh, how pleased I was when the carriage pulled into Cambridge, and we went trotting along the familiar streets! Oh, the delight when we started along the Chesterton Road, and Mrs Fitzpatrick's house came into view! And how my heart beat as the door flew open and Arthur dashed out with uncharacteristic speed to welcome us home! Charles and Mr Korneck left us till the morrow, and I spent a blissful evening pouring out my heart in a great mixture of facts, thoughts, feelings and emotions into Arthur's most receptive ears. Together we analysed, discussed and reflected until there seemed quite nothing left to say – or perhaps, until silence seemed better to express what we wished to say than any words could do.

'I have a surprise for you tomorrow,' he told me finally, as at a late hour, he bid me good night. 'It may be useful, and will certainly be interesting. No, I shan't tell you more!' And with twinkling eyes, he turned down the corridor and climbed up the stairs to his rooms.

I was tickled, and my first thought upon awakening this morning was that I should soon find out what Arthur had in store for me. He remained secretive throughout the morning, but at the approach of midday, he took my arm, and together we walked into the centre of town.

Stopping in front of a pleasant restaurant, he looked inside, and then said, turning to me,

'Ah, here is the person I wanted you to meet. He wants to meet you even more, so he's bright and early!'

In we went, and sat down at a table already occupied by a very red-haired, freckled personage. I wondered greatly who he could be, and why it should be such a surprise for me to thus make his acquaintance, but I beamed upon him cheerfully, out of general feelings of bliss and human kindness that welled up in me purely from the pleasure of being with Arthur.

'I am delighted, delighted to meet you, Miss Duncan!' began the freckled young man, with a very pretty and musical (and perhaps even slightly exaggerated) Irish brogue. 'Will you do the honours, Weatherburn, or must I introduce myself?'

'Vanessa, this is Mr Patrick O'Sullivan,' smiled Arthur, and he watched me carefully to see my reaction. It was a blank one for only the merest second.

'Why, of *course*,' I cried. 'The journalist! I read your article on the murder of Mr Granger.'

'Ah, that's nothing, if you only knew!' he said proudly. 'How many articles I could write if I only could. I hear you're involved in the case, Miss Duncan.'

'Yes, I am interested,' I answered, glancing at Arthur.

'No need for euphemisms,' he said seriously. 'Vanessa has been hired to privately investigate the murder, as you well know. We needn't mince words; Vanessa needs information, and you are

129

certainly in possession of some of that indispensable commodity. I believe you should work together, for the sooner the whole story reaches its conclusion, the better.'

'I need information too, yes I do indeed, it's all part of my job. I'm looking for a scoop for my paper and for my reputation. I'm ready to consider a fair exchange, Miss Duncan: my information for yours.'

'Oh – but I can't really do that – I can't give things I'm not even certain of, or which may not even have anything to do with the murder, to be published in a newspaper! Why, that is exactly why poor Mrs Bryce-Fortescue wants me to investigate – just exactly so that nothing may get into the papers!'

'Well, that's a forlorn hope, it's ridiculous, it is, how many murders do we get about here that we should restrain ourselves from offering them up to our readers as a little delicacy?'

Arthur winced, and I glared at the tactless individual, but little wrinkles of laughter appeared at the corners of his eyes, so that it was difficult to feel seriously angry. I had opened my mouth to remonstrate, but closed it again. Was he so wrong? Did one not read such things in the papers with no more than a mild feeling of faint shock mingled with curiosity, when they did not concern oneself? I felt ashamed, remembering from my single past experience of such things, how much fear and bitter suffering was hidden between the lines of the articles the readers chatted about with casual interest before lightly flipping over the page.

'Come now,' said Mr O'Sullivan encouragingly.

'Are you sure that your Mrs Bryce-Fortescue really wants to keep everything out of the papers altogether? Isn't she just trying to protect her own family pride? It's a funny thing, it is – some people'd kill to be in the papers–' I glared '–oh, sorry – well, some people'd do just about anything to be in the papers, then, and others'd do as much and more to stay out of them. Odd things, newspapers, how they get the blood up. Love 'em, myself. Couldn't live without 'em. Listen, then, Miss Duncan: here's a bargain. I'll tell you what I know, and you'll understand exactly what's threatening your Mrs Granger. You tell me what you know, and I'll see that if Mrs Granger really is innocent, she stays out of the papers altogether. But you must understand that if she's guilty, or even if she's just arrested, I must put it in.'

'How can you know anything about what is threatening her?' I gasped, hearing only these words among the flood of his remarks.

'Well, the long and short of it is that I've got a brother-in-law in the police force, in homicide, as a matter of fact. There, I've told you. I can find out just about anything the police know, for a promise not to spill any of it till they give me the wink that the time is ripe. But they don't know much yet. That's why I'm hoping you can tell me more. You see, this is how it is. If the police reach a solution, I won't have a scoop, for when they're sure, they'll talk to journalists from all the papers. But if we get there before them, then we win! And if we use a little of their knowledge to help us get there, well, that's all in the game.'

'Oh!' I said. 'Dear me, as far as I personally am

concerned, I don't mind at all if they do solve it, as long as they do a proper job. But I'm not sure they are, for it seems to me that they really suspect Sylvia. You must know, then; is it true? They keep badgering her with threatening questions. Why, they even have a witness who claims that he saw her in the woods near the house just a few minutes before the murder took place, and she herself says it's impossible, as she never left her room even for a moment. I for one believe her, but I think the police don't! Am I right?'

'It's not easy to give a yes or no answer to the question. They suspect her, for certain. They don't have a high opinion of her feeble alibi. There are too many ways to slip out of a house without using the main door. But they also believe she may possibly not have done the shooting herself, but have planned it, or know who did it. Their minds are made up that she either did it or knows who did, and they're determined to get her, by accusing and arresting her without full proof, if necessary. As for their witness who saw her, it's all true enough, except that the identification of Mrs Granger turned out to be pretty tentative. You know what I mean: "As I was passing the Granger estate, I saw Mrs Granger running through the trees." But when the police insist, it becomes: "Well, I certainly saw someone that I thought was Mrs Granger." So they ask her how much she could see, how far the person was, whether it was a man or a woman, how she could tell? And it turns out that the person was barely glimpsed between the leaves and branches. Well, the police believe someone was seen, but they were not so convinced by the identification of Mrs. Granger. They just made out that they were to put the fear of God into her. Tricky, aren't they?'

'Tricky! That ought to be illegal!' I cried indignantly, feeling a violent, irrational desire to protect Sylvia sweep over me. 'Why, they're frightening her half to death! Who was it that said she saw her, anyway? Do you know?'

'Oh, it was some old cat that had her knife into your Sylvia. Spent more time massacring her character to the police and complaining about some occasion when she wouldn't let her into the house, than stating what she actually saw. Her statement isn't very helpful when you peel away everything but the facts. She hardly saw a thing.'

'I know that lady – it's Mrs Munn!' I exclaimed. 'And I wouldn't take her word against Sylvia's for a moment. The police may not either, but they certainly talked to Sylvia quite as though they *did*. It's a shame! Well, they're barking up the wrong tree. Sylvia is innocent.'

'They seem pretty certain she had *something* to do with it,' he said, looking at me closely.

'They're mistaken. Anybody can be wrongly accused and wrongly condemned,' I said furiously. 'How extraordinarily apt people are to forget that!'

'Yes, yes, of course. It can happen. We know that, we know that,' he said hastily, glancing at Arthur. 'All right, so the police can be crude in their ways. I'll tell you the truth, since you ask. The police have it in for Mrs Sylvia Granger, whether or not she actually pulled the trigger. They are certain that she holds the key to the mystery, for the simple, telling reason that she hated her husband

133

– and that she inherits everything he had! That's how the police work: motive above all, and when you've got a love-hate motive and a financial motive all rolled up together, they won't look at anything else. So either she did it, or she had an accomplice of some kind, some lover of hers. Clytemnestra, or whatever. And they're ready to put the pressure on her, frighten her, accuse her, even put her in the dock, to make her talk. It's hard lines, but it's neither here nor there, right now. What *we* want – you and I – is to find out the truth, isn't it? All right, Miss Duncan, I've told you what's happening on the police side, and I see well enough that you don't agree with them. You think she's innocent, don't you? I've played my cards. Aren't you going to play some of yours? What do you know? What makes you believe what you believe?'

He turned a most winning smile upon me, but I resisted its charm, and compelled myself to think clearly about the bargain he proposed. On the favourable side, he clearly knew things of essential importance, and with time, as the police investigation progressed, he would know more. On the assumption that Sylvia was innocent, as I believed, anything we discovered would be likely to help her, and if she turned out to be guilty (even as an accomplice), then my failure could hardly matter. However, I feared his bargain because of his very quality as a journalist. I found it difficult to efface from my mind a distressing vision of Mrs Bryce-Fortescue furiously brandishing vulgar articles filled with the Bryce-Fortescue name in my face, and asking angrily who had provided the newspaper with the intimate details they contained!

After a moment's reflection, I decided that this unpleasant prospect could be avoided with sufficient discretion on my part, and that it would be advisable to proceed.

'I'd like to exchange information with you,' I said, 'if I could trust you not to publish any detail I let slip about Sylvia.'

'You can trust me – why, there's no point in publishing anything except a real breakthrough. What I want is a scoop, the real thing! I shan't spoil things before by letting out little bits.'

'All right, then,' I said, 'it is a bargain.'

'Let's drink to that!' he responded triumphantly, lifting his glass. 'Call me Pat, then! And may I call you Vanessa?'

'Of course,' I responded absently. 'Only there is one thing that might annoy you. It's just this: I really don't know very much at all, and some of it probably isn't even relevant. I'm afraid you'll think I'm very useless.'

'Well, go ahead, spill it all and we'll see.'

'There are two reasons for which I believe Sylvia is innocent. The first one is a conversation I overheard her having with her best friend, in private. She assured her that she really had never left her room that afternoon, promised it, swore it even. I found her totally convincing. After hearing her, I simply cannot believe she is guilty.'

'Ah,' said Pat O'Sullivan, looking ironic and unconvinced. 'Would *you* tell your best friend if you'd committed a murder?'

I looked at Arthur, and thought of you, Dora; beyond a doubt, my two best friends on this earth.

135

'I think I would,' I said thoughtfully. 'But anyway – listen to my second reason. It's more important! I've found out that there was a stranger
seen in Haverhill on the morning of Mr Granger's
murder. I heard it from some ladies at a tea party,
the same one where I met Mrs Munn. One of the
other ladies actually claimed to have seen the man
herself. She observed him fairly closely and could
give some description of his clothes, face and hair.
She described him as wearing a red cape. He
might have been the person Mrs Munn spied
flitting between the trees, if she really did see
anyone at all. Now, this young man was also seen
in the train station both coming and going from
Haverhill, and the lady spotted him on the path
up by the fields going towards the Granger estate,
but it seems nobody saw him in the village itself
at all; he must have crossed through the woods
coming from the train station. He seems to have
avoided the village completely, as well he might if
he were planning a murder – you'd think he
would want to remain unseen. On the other hand,
it seems strange, then, his dressing so noticeably.
At any rate, the main thing is that I was able to
confirm that he was observed in the train station
itself on the day of the murder – and he arrived
before it, and left after!'

'Vanessa, this is capital! Do you realise what
you're saying?' Pat became extremely animated,
and half stood up from his seat. 'Now, this is
definitely something for the police! They'll manage to trace him, all right. That's the kind of thing
they do with the efficiency of ... of machines!
They're capable of tracing every person on every

train, questioning everyone in a dozen stations! Let me tell my brother-in-law about this, Vanessa! Anything they find out, we can also use!'

'I think ... I think you may be right,' I replied after a moment's hesitation. 'I have not told the police about it up to now because first of all, I only just learned about it myself, and secondly, Mrs Bryce-Fortescue was very much against it. She cannot abide the idea of communicating with them at all, and thinks that her daughter needs to remain absolutely silent and closed where they are concerned, as her best defence. But I ... yes, I do believe that you are right. The police should begin at the Haverhill train station, and work from there.'

I purposely avoided the idea of their questioning Martha. I doubted that she would speak openly to the police, and I felt disturbed at the idea of their harassing her ... noticing her, and perhaps carting her off for questioning, or worse, sending her to the workhouse. I thought of her wrinkled face, her mysterious eyes.

'Wait, I've just remembered something else!' I exclaimed suddenly. 'The old lady who saw him – she said – I don't know how trustworthy this is, but I thought she seemed clear enough in her mind. Anyway, she said he looked familiar, only she couldn't place him!'

'She did, did she? Well ... well, we mustn't get our hopes up. It could mean nothing at all, I suppose. A vague old lady mixing things up, or trying to seem important. But on the other hand, can you imagine if it were true, and she suddenly remembered? Why, there'd be no more need to detect, then, would there? Vanessa, you must go and talk to her again!'

'Yes. Yes, I must go back to Haverhill as soon as I can.'

'You do that, and tell me if you discover anything. And I'll set the police on the trail of the young man in the Haverhill station. And I won't leave you in the dark if they trace him!'

'Well,' I said, 'I hope they *do* find him, and prove that he is the murderer, and Sylvia is innocent! But if *they* don't, then *we* shall have to.'

'Shake hands on it!' he cried, and we parted the best of friends.

What mixed feelings this strange person provokes in me, reducing the reality of death and murder to a silly scoop. And yet he is right, he is right in what he told me to do. I had very nearly forgotten old Martha's strange words. I must go back to Haverhill and find out more, if I can. And somehow, I feel that I must also manage to discover Sylvia's secret, for it may not be related to the murder ... but then again, it may! Surely, one of these two trails *must* lead me somewhere.

Your loving but overly busy

Vanessa

Maidstone Hall, Tuesday, June 21, 1892

My very dearest twin,

By the time this letter reaches you, you will

138

perhaps have heard about its contents already –
but I am so amazed that I cannot resist relating
the incredible coincidence to you at once! Dora,
this is a strange thing, and I feel it may even turn
out to be important. I hope this is something
more than wishful thinking, for I am sorely in
need of insight into this tangled mystery. I've
made no progress since I returned on Sunday. I
searched Sylvia's room twice, though but hastily,
I have talked with her but learned absolutely
nothing of interest beyond the power of her
careless charm, and I have planned a new trip to
Haverhill with Peter for Friday (I do not dare to
tell you how I inveigled him into inviting me
again, for I am heartily ashamed of it), but that is
as far as my research has progressed in these last
three days. Until now.

Earlier today, Mrs Bryce-Fortescue came in to
tell me that we were not to have supper together
today, for she and her daughter were invited out
and Camilla should be away. I was to ring as soon
as I desired my evening meal, and Mrs Firmin
would have it sent up to me on a tray. I had no
such intention, however; it seemed to me that
much use could be made of the opportunity, and
as soon as I judged it could rightly be about
supper time, instead of ringing, I proceeded to
wend my way towards the part of the house in
which I had always supposed the kitchen to be
located. Naturally, I never before had an occasion
to visit those regions, and I felt some trepidation
at the idea of being discovered and scolded by
one of those servants who consider it their duty
to uphold civilised behaviour, but I met no one

until I timidly knocked at the large wooden door which appeared to form the entrance to the sacred altar of cooking.

The door was opened from within, and I encountered the round, rather heated face of Mrs Firmin herself.

'Why, Miss Duncan,' she said disapprovingly, 'you was to ring when you wanted supper. I'd have sent it up by Sarah. It's ready now.'

'Oh, I *am* so sorry, Mrs Firmin,' I said warmly, edging my way forward into the welcoming steamy atmosphere, so that she was obliged to take a step back. 'Please do forgive me, and send me away at once if I am disturbing you. But it is so dark out, and it is already starting to storm, and I am so frightened of thunder and I felt so dreadfully lonely altogether – I was going to ask you if I could possibly sit here and take supper together with you.'

She seemed mollified, and indeed more than mollified; I should not go so far as to state that she was delighted, but it seemed as though the prospect of a pleasant chat was not displeasing to her, once she had gotten past the duty of objecting to my behaviour.

'Well, Miss, we downstairs have already had our supper, being as we eat earlier than the family. But I'll sit with you and take a cup of tea if I may. It'll save Sarah carrying the tray, and she can go home. Sit down at the table, Miss, and I'll dish up your chop directly.'

She spoke to the maid who was finishing the dishes in the scullery, and then set the kettle on the hob where it began to boil directly (from which I conclude that pleasant cups of tea had already been in preparation), and very soon provided me with a delightful supper of sliced potatoes *au gratin*, green beans and lamb. When Sarah had dried her hands, bid us good night (not without a stern glance in my direction) and departed, Mrs Firmin sat plumply down opposite me.

'Oh, it is so kind of you to allow me to stay,' I began happily. 'I grew up in a cottage on a farm, you know, and I'm really not used to a big house like this; it can be lonely sometimes, and seems so empty, with just the four of us and all those large rooms.'

'Yes, it is an empty house,' she agreed, 'and even four is a lot for these days. It's not like it was when Mrs B., Miss Eleanor that was, was a child. She was an only daughter, but the house never seemed lonely one minute; friends and acquaintances always about, and Miss Eleanor that loved and pampered, her parents would have liked her to live in paradise. Ah, things was different back then, with candles and lights all about, and meals for ten or twelve as often as not. And when Miss Eleanor got married – wasn't that a celebration! No one could ever have thought that the house would end up so sad. Poor Miss Eleanor. She lost her parents and her husband in the same year, and she's never been the same since then. Not that she was ever a bright, fun-loving creature like her mother, she was always the haughty type, but willing to have a good time nevertheless, at least if someone else would take the trouble to arrange it for her. Very used to having everything done for her, was Miss Eleanor. Then, when her parents went, there was the fear about the house. It was to pass to the nearest male relative, of course. Miss Eleanor had grown up here and knew no other, and she'd have given her eye teeth to keep it, but the lawyers came and told her she'd have to give it up and leave, once they located the rightful heir. Months went by as they looked about all over the world, but in the end it seemed there was no male heir anywhere; Miss Eleanor's parents were both only children, and there turned out to be no cousins or uncles anywhere after all. Months it took, and then, when it finally went to judgement that the house belonged to her, Mr Bryce-Fortescue was thrown from his horse and died, and poor Miss Eleanor found herself a widow with practically no income to keep up the house, and so she nearly lost it a second time. I guess it was only then that I came to realise how much this house meant to her. Mr Bryce-Fortescue had had investments, and they were sold and paid in to her, but it didn't come to so very much. He was a wise one, and kept on taking them out and putting them in again, so that the money seemed to go on making itself, but Miss Eleanor never had any mind for such things, she was just cut out to be a great lady. Alone she remained, with baby Sylvia, and all the servants had to go except for me and Mr Huxtable and the girl Ellen who looked after the baby. We three had been here for so long we'd no desire to leave. Ever since Ellen left we've just had Sarah who comes in for the day but goes off to her home at night – huh! that's not the same thing; there's no loyalty to it, no family sense.

Well, a hundred times I've thought how much easier it would be for Miss Eleanor to sell the house and take a smaller one, maybe in town, but she would never hear of it. This place is her place, and no other. Ah, it's not always easy, with all the memories, but I'm too old to think of moving anywhere else. Nigh on forty years I've been here. I helped bring up little Miss Eleanor, and Miss Sylvia too. Whilst the child still lived here, there seemed some use going on, but since she got married and went away, most every day I cook for Mrs B. alone, and she takes it all by herself at the dining room table, with Mr Huxtable and Sarah in attendance. It's a sad thing. I often think how this house was built for a large family with a great many children, but Miss Eleanor's parents only ever had the one, and then she the same, and as for Miss Sylvia, she's had none at all, and now her husband's gone, who knows when there will ever be children about the place again?'

'Miss Sylvia is very young,' I said, 'perhaps she'll marry again.'

'Not she, I don't think,' responded Mrs Firmin. 'A young lady that unhappy in her marriage I never see. Her mother was never so; haughty and distant, maybe, but fond of her husband, and above all, respected him, thought him a good man. No marriage can work if a wife don't feel respect for her husband.'

'And you think Miss Sylvia didn't?'

'I shouldn't be telling you these things, Miss, I don't know why I'm running on like this. But Miss Sylvia never wanted to marry Mr Granger.

Why, he'd been coming to the house since she was a child; he was more like an uncle than a husband for her. There was a time, everyone thought, hoped even, that Mr Granger was sweet on the mother. It could have been, it might not have been too bad, although he was in commerce and not from any family anyone ever heard of. Vulgar, he was, but he was attached to this family and we all got used to him, and thinking maybe a match would come off, but not the one which came off. It surprised us all, and maybe Miss Sylvia more than any, when we heard two years ago that Mr Granger had asked for her hand. And he so much older than her, and older than her mother even. But then when I thought, I thought it must be because he wanted children of his own, as any man would.'

'And was Mrs Bryce-Fortescue pleased with the marriage?' I enquired.

'Oh, no one can ever tell what that one is thinking. She announced it, and organised it, and an elegant party was had, but nothing like the one she'd had herself, and off went the couple to live in the next county where Mr Granger had bought a house, wanting to lord it like a country squire when he was no such thing.'

'And Miss Sylvia didn't seem happy in her marriage?'

'Well, I can't say. She doesn't show much. But it didn't seem right, somehow. No children and didn't seem to want any, and didn't seem to want to run a house or stay home or even have parties or weekends or suppers, now that she was finally a rich woman, but couldn't think of anything

144

better than getting away from him; coming here to visit home, or running off to the continent with her friends. Well, everybody's different, I suppose; who knows what happiness is made of?'

It was at this very moment, when the conversation appeared to be taking a philosophical turn, that a loud and rather abrupt knocking was heard at the outside door which leads into the scullery. Mrs Firmin jumped.

'Now, who can that be? Could Sarah have forgotten something so important she's had to come back for it?' she said, and heaving herself out of her chair, she bent into the low scullery and opened the door. A gust of stormy wind blew into the kitchen.

'Why, Ellen!' I heard her cry in real amazement. 'Ellen Whitman, I declare, after all these years! What are you doing here?'

The woman who came into the kitchen was a beauty, although no longer very young. Tall and simply dressed, she came into the kitchen and removed the kerchief from her hair, shaking out the drops of water, for it was raining quite heavily. She was about to answer Mrs Firmin, when her glance fell upon me.

Dora, I have never seen anyone stare with such transfixed horror. It was as though she were seeing a ghost! She fixed her eyes upon me and they widened so much I could see the whites all about the iris, while her dark and abundant hair almost seemed to stand upright upon her head. The colour drained from her face completely, and in a forced, raucous voice she cried,

'Where's William?'

145

I felt very distressed, thinking she must be mad. I moved towards her kindly, stretching out my hand, and said gently,

'I am very sorry, but I don't know any William.'

'Don't know William?' Her voice dropped to a whisper of anguish. 'What are you doing here? What has happened? Did you follow me? Where's my baby?'

'I don't know,' I said, glancing at Mrs Firmin, but she seemed quite as shocked and uncomprehending as I was. 'Of course I have not followed you, I have been here the whole evening. Is William your child?'

She walked up to me slowly, and stood leaning towards me, her face barely inches from mine. A sinister look came into her eyes, but then I realised it was actually a look of soul-devouring panic and horror, so severe that it could find no outward expression in cries or fainting. It was as if death itself were staring out at me from her crazed orbs.

'I left him with you,' she said, plunging her eyes into mine as though she would hypnotise me into confessing what I had done with her baby. 'Where is he, Miss Dora? Why are you here?'

'Oh, I understand!' I exclaimed in sudden, incredible relief, for I assure you that I was nearly paralysed by the tension of the scene. 'I am not Dora! You must be acquainted with my twin sister, Dora Duncan. Is that it?'

Her face changed somewhat, as she slowly made sense of my words.

'Twin sister? You're not Miss Dora?'

'No,' I laughed. 'I am Vanessa Duncan, her

sister. I know that we look very much alike. It is easy to mistake one of us for the other. But what an extraordinary coincidence that you know my sister. Is she taking care of your child?'

'Yes, I left little William with her not a few hours ago,' she said, still staring at me rather suspiciously. 'Land sakes, is it possible? I've heard of twins but never seen two people look so much alike. Is everything all right then? You're sure you're not her? I thought William must be dead, and she come to tell me.'

'Now, now,' interposed Mrs Firmin, 'that's enough. You've met a pair of twins for the first time and been all shaken up. But there's no harm done, Ellen; your little boy's in the best of hands and enjoying himself like a king, I've no doubt.'

'Oh, he is, if I know Dora,' I exclaimed encouragingly, still feeling a little unsteady inside.

'Come sit down here, Ellen, the water's still hot; I'll make you a cup of tea and you'll tell us why you've come. It's been how many years we haven't seen or heard anything from you?'

'Seven.' she answered. 'Seven years. I've come to see Mrs Bryce-Fortescue. I've got to see her. I don't know what to do!'

'She's out for the evening, dear. Now don't fret, she'll be back this night, or you can spend the night in your old room and see her in the morning. Sit right down. Have you had your supper? No, I thought not. Now, here you go, have a warm meal and tell us about yourself. So you're a married woman now?'

'Yes – no, he's dead. No – why should I lie to you? I've no husband, Mrs Firmin,' cried Ellen, a little too loudly. 'I've no husband and never have, though I wear a ring and say I'm a widow in Langley Vale, where I live now.'

'Oh!' said Mrs Firmin, taken aback. She did not appear to judge the situation harshly, but rather to be at a loss as to what one could possibly say in the face of such impropriety.

'Well, my dear,' she said finally, but kindly, 'you've been through some hard times, I can see. But perhaps your little one brings you some joy. Who's to say that it isn't better this way, sometimes, than never having any. Is he lovely? How old is he?'

'He's – he's a big boy now,' stammered Ellen uncomfortably, 'ever so beautiful. I don't know what I'd do without him. Miss Dora knows him well, indeed she does, Miss; she's helped me sometimes when he's been ill, and brought him things and sent the doctor to us. It wasn't easy for me at first, in Langley Vale, but she helped me from the beginning. I take in washing now, I wouldn't do any other work, not that would take me out of the house and away from my baby. Yes, Miss Dora is an angel.'

My heart was pleased within me upon hearing these words. I would gladly have continued on the subject of little William, but I felt that Ellen was not happy with it, and wished to move to other topics. Indeed, she seemed very worried and nervous altogether, toying with the food Mrs Firmin had provided her with generously, and perking up every time the slightest noise was heard without.

'It's no use your hoping that's the carriage already,' said Mrs Firmin, 'they won't be back till well after midnight, that's certain, and Mrs B. will be tired and maybe won't be willing to see you then. You'd best settle in for the night and get some rest. Do you have some night things, deary? No, I didn't think so. I'll lend you a chemise, though you'll be lost in the size of it, and it'll just take us a moment to make up your old bed with fresh sheets. It brings back old memories to see you, it does! We did miss you when you left. Do you know, we've never known what happened and why you went! Mrs B. said there'd been a disagreement between you and her, but you know how she is, tight-lipped. We never heard a word more, nor where you'd gone, nor anything. What was it about, then?'

I saw Ellen's face grow darker and darker as Mrs Firmin went on talking cheerfully. But she, moving around as she spoke, washing up the few dishes and poking the fire, noticed nothing, and when upon these last words she turned to Ellen, she was so startled at the closed, desperate expression on her face that she dropped the poker with a clang.

'I don't – I can't talk about it,' said Ellen through clenched teeth.

'Oh, I'm sorry!' responded Mrs Firmin, torn between indignation at so cavalier a response to her kindness, frustrated curiosity, and a natural feeling of protectiveness for someone obviously in great difficulties. She overcame her resentment with an effort, and taking Ellen by the arm, accompanied her to the kitchen door, herding me out by the same gesture.

'You'd better get back upstairs, Miss,' she said,

'Mrs B. won't be back for a while yet, but she'd be right annoyed to find you'd been frequenting here. Sit in bed with a nice book if you're afraid of the thunder, that's right.'

I noticed as she spoke that the storm had begun in earnest, and the distant rumblings were getting progressively louder. They are crashing about the house now, and lightning rents the landscape as I write to you by the light of a candle. As soon as I finish this long letter, I shall seal it up and hop into bed, but not before telling you that I expect a *great deal* of information from you, Dora dear, on the subject of the mysterious Ellen. Why did she leave here seven years ago? Why has she suddenly returned? If anyone can find out and tell me, it is surely you! And it is not simple curiosity, for it cannot be a mere coincidence Ellen's coming here today – it ought to have some bearing on the mystery – don't you think so?

Good night, 'angel' sister!

Vanessa

Maidstone Hall, Wednesday, June 22, 1892

My dearest Dora,

I arose this morning early, and dressing hastily, I slipped downstairs and hid myself in what I considered to be the best possible place: just inside the library door. I thought there was a chance that Mrs Bryce-Fortescue might, upon being told about Ellen's presence, receive her in the library. I thought she might conceivably also refuse to receive her, but dismissed that possibility to be dealt with if it should occur. If she received her in her bedroom, I could not think of anything to do except beg you, Dora, to find out what you could about all these strange goings-on, for I have no vantage point to eavesdrop on Mrs Bryce-Fortescue's bedroom as I have on Sylvia's. But I still hoped and believed that she would receive her in the library, for Mrs Bryce-Fortescue is a person who prefers to surround and protect herself with an aura of formality.

After a short time, I saw Sarah come out and mount the stairs with our early morning tea on a tray. I supposed she would set mine down in my room, thinking merely that I had gone on a ramble in the pink flush of dawn. As I wished I could, indeed, for although it had been most disagreeably difficult for me to compel myself to rise so early, now that I was well awake, I found the lovely tints of the rain-washed sky and the fields far more attractive than the dusty gallery where presently I should probably have to squeeze myself. But I kept myself in hand, and listened to Sarah enter Mrs Bryce-Fortescue's room and exchange some words with her. They spoke too low for me to be able to make out what they said from downstairs, but after a moment I heard Sarah emerge and carry in the tea to Sylvia and Camilla, and then to my room. Then she came down the stairs with the empty tray and disappeared through the baize door back into the kitchen regions.

I waited more breathlessly now, for I was worried that Ellen might enter the hall and mount the stairs, and I should have been most disappointed. But a good quarter of an hour passed, and then suddenly, I heard a door open upstairs. I jumped to attention – Mrs Bryce-Fortescue was descending. My heart in my mouth, I scampered to the staircase leading up to the gallery and swarmed silently up it. I had just time to flatten myself against the wall – no time to arrange a hiding place with books in front of me as I had for the police inspectors – and in came Mrs Bryce-Fortescue, followed, almost simultaneously, by Ellen, wearing a humble and drooping air, but with a desperate flash in her eyes as she glanced upwards. The two women did not sit, but stood facing each other, not like adversaries, but very warily.

'It has been many years, Ellen,' said Mrs Bryce-Fortescue. 'I have had no news of you. I hope that you have managed well.'

'I've just barely managed. Just barely. And now – he's dead and I don't know where to turn. I'm here to ask you for help, madam. I don't know anybody else who could help me now, nor even anybody who would help me if they could, except for Miss Dora.'

'Who is dead? What kind of help are you talking about? What do you want of me?' said Mrs Bryce-Fortescue, and she sounded genuinely confused, but her tone also held the slight tension of someone who fears something – fears, perhaps, being asked for money, or so I thought at first.

'Who is dead? Why, Mr Granger is dead, madam – Mr Granger! How can you ask?'

'Mr Granger! What had you to do with him? What is his death to you?' Now Mrs Bryce-Fortescue's tones held faint overtones of a kind of horror. Perhaps I was witnessing something very subtle, but I thought that any suspicion of scandal might cause her to speak in that tone.

'Don't you know? I thought if anyone would know, it was you. No? You don't know? Really don't? Oh, he was a close one. He was very close. So he never, never told. No, I guess he wouldn't, after all, would he? Then perhaps I must, but before I do, I'd like to ask you a question, if I may.'

'Yes?'

'It's about Mr Granger's will. Have you – do you know what was in it?'

'A will! Why, Mr Granger had not made a will. I am sure that he had no intention of dying and saw no immediate necessity for one.'

'No will, no will!' cried Ellen with an accent of great anguish. 'Oh, it can't be, it can't be! Madam, are you sure? Is it possible?'

'I am perfectly sure, and really cannot discuss the question any further without knowing what business it is of yours!'

'But – but you would know, wouldn't you,' said Ellen desperately, 'if there had been a will and I had been mentioned in it, wouldn't you? You wouldn't lie to me, I know it.'

'My dear Ellen, this is going too far! There is no will, I repeat, and if there had been, I can hardly see why you of all people should be mentioned in it! The very idea is shocking, when I remember why you were obliged to leave my employ. I

153

cannot think what you are after, Ellen.'

'You are sure? Sure there is no way he could have left anything for me, even without a will?' Ellen's voice was dull now.

'I can assure you that if you had inherited anything whatsoever from Mr Granger, you would have been informed of the fact before now by his executors.'

'Oh. But what if–' she paused and reflected for a moment, then brightened a little and said, 'Who inherits when somebody dies without leaving any will?'

'Mrs Granger inherits the whole of her husband's property, naturally.'

'And what about – what about if Mr Granger had a child?'

'Child! Mr Granger had no child!'

'But would he inherit anything if he did? Perhaps the lawyers couldn't find the child and that's why he had nothing...'

'Ellen, I must request you to stop this unseemly discussion at once. I cannot continue discussing these private matters in this way.'

'No, let me explain! Let me explain everything, then!' Ellen seemed terrified of being dismissed without being heard. But yet she hesitated. 'You won't like to hear what I have to tell. Perhaps you won't even believe me.'

Mrs Bryce-Fortescue remained silent. Some force of pride prevented her from asking questions, and also, I believe, fear and dismay at what she was about to hear. For myself, I was all ears, while she instead appeared to be bracing herself wordlessly. Seeing her attitude, Ellen continued.

154

'I left seven years ago because of Mr Granger,' she said, raising her voice and speaking quite loudly, as though steeling herself to say things which would be better whispered, or never mentioned at all. 'He told you ... that I had stolen something from him, and asked you to give me notice immediately. You gave me notice and paid me a month's wages. I never said a word to you then, for I thought that as bad as stealing might be, you would be even angrier if you knew the truth. I thought it would make a great to-do, and spoil things that were better left alone. I thought you could make something of the man, and that you would do it.'

There was a pause. Ellen gathered courage to say more, and Mrs Bryce-Fortescue to hear it.

'I never stole nothing from Mr Granger. I've never stolen a penny from a soul, and I'm sure you knew it. I never stole from you, why should I steal from him? He made it up so that you should send me away, quickly, and he made sure I would never tell you ... that I was pregnant. I was expecting a baby. Yes, his baby; his son that was born just seven months later. His baby – my baby! Oh, I never thought of his father as mine, even when he came to me so eagerly in the nights, even when be promised me – told me all manner of lies! I knew none of it was true. I thought he wanted to marry you, and that's what I would have wanted for him. For he was a strange man with a dark side, but there were times that he was happy, here in this house.

'Anyway, he told me to hold my tongue, or he would never give me a penny of help, so I did it.

155

I thought it was for the best. He found a farm for me to stay at, and paid the people. I had the baby there. Then he bought me a house. He told me I should stay far away from him forever, far away from Cambridge and from here, and that's why he bought me the house. I accepted it. He swore to me that if I left him alone, then he'd remember his son in his will, and make sure he had something so he didn't grow up in poverty! And I believed him. We went to the house – it's just a tiny thing, but it was big enough for my baby and me, and I got work washing, so as to stay home with him. We managed somehow, but William's getting bigger and needing more, and times are so hard for us now. It's getting almost impossible! Sometimes Miss Dora helps; she keeps little Will for a day or two, and I go to do some cleaning in the big houses. But it's been so bad lately, I've been so worried, and so tired I hardly knew how I could go on. And then, suddenly, I heard that he was dead. And I remembered what he said. I've never forgotten it – I've lived on the thought! He swore he'd do it, he swore it, he swore it! What'll we do if he lied to us?'

Her voice was filled with increasing despair, and her speech ended suddenly in a tearful wail. Mrs Bryce-Fortescue stepped forward towards her.

'I didn't know, Ellen. I wish I could help you,' she said softly. 'I never heard a word about this, all these long years. Mr Granger was a man who kept his own counsel.' She paused, and then added abruptly, 'I didn't know about this – and I had no idea that he wished to marry Sylvia, either, until the day he asked. I understood nothing of the man, in fact.'

'No more did I, the liar,' said Ellen bitterly. 'I saw he'd married Sylvia from the papers the day he died – I'd no idea! So he courted us all, did he – the mother, the daughter and the maid?'

Mrs Bryce-Fortescue flinched and seemed to withdraw, as though in the presence of something loathsome and vulgar, and indeed there was something shocking in Ellen's remark, although it appeared to be no more than the unvarnished truth. When she spoke again, her tone was more controlled.

'In any case, Ellen, the difficulty is that we have no money at all ourselves, and we shall have nothing until Mr Granger's murder is solved. As long as there is some suspicion resting on Sylvia, his executors will give us nothing, although Sylvia has inherited all of her husband's estate. I am afraid that ... an illegitimate child cannot inherit unless it is specifically mentioned in a testament, but if I – if we – if Sylvia once obtains her rights, we could help you, and we would do it. Only there is nothing that we can do at this point.'

'Sylvia!' Ellen's tone was bitter. 'Miss Sylvia inherited everything from him, did she? Everything! But why? Why? What did she ever do for him? I bore his child, not she!'

'That is not fair. She is so young, and was married only two years, and knew nothing of all this; how could she?'

'She was never a good wife to him and never would have been. Not Miss Sylvia!' asserted Ellen emphatically.

'What are you saying? You must not say such things!' responded Mrs Bryce-Fortescue sharply.

'Why did he marry her? Why did he marry her?' Ellen continued, a note of hysteria creeping into her voice. 'I was the one who carried his child – and you were the one who welcomed him into this house and tried to tame the beast that was inside him. Oh, I knew how it was with you – he told me. He told me a great many things. I'm easy to talk to; Miss Sylvia talked to me too. I knew that Mr Granger juggled a lot of things in his life. I knew what he wanted of you, and what he wanted of me, but I never, never thought he'd look at Miss Sylvia.'

'You are mistaken,' said Mrs Bryce-Fortescue stiffly, 'there was nothing between Mr Granger and myself.' Her tone was so stuffy that I quite thought, for a moment, that she must be aware that I was in the room and be speaking for my benefit, for what was the use of her lying to Ellen, who clearly knew whatever there was to be known? But I realised after a worried moment that the tight denial was meant to reassure nobody other than herself that nothing amiss had ever occurred in her past life – as though silence could have the power to efface the past reality. How strange people are!

'You forget that Sylvia was just fifteen when you left,' she added more gently. 'She grew into a very lovely young woman, and it was perfectly natural that Mr Granger should learn to be fond of her.'

'But not she of him – that I'll never believe! That monster – fifty if he was a day, wanting to marry a slip of a girl. What did you think, what did you think, when he asked you for her? Your own daughter – after all the years you cared for him so! Did it hurt? Did he hurt you then like he hurt me, when he told me in plain words never to bother him again?'

'Ellen!' The word snapped out coldly, expressing the purest reprobation. But Ellen was not to be stopped.

'Why did Sylvia marry him? What kind of arrangement did you make – what did he offer you? Money? Money for her, no doubt, and money for you, too. But for me, nothing! And for his son, his very own child, nothing!'

'Sylvia's marriage was completely agreed upon by all three of us,' she answered, in the same stiff tone. 'As for your child, I am sincerely sorry that you are in such difficulties at present.'

'Then help us!' cried Ellen. 'I was sent away from here, where I was happy and had a good situation, for something that was none of my fault, but his! Things have been so hard for me lately that I – that I had decided to – to ask him for help. It was a hard decision for me to take, but – William is his son! I thought about it and thought about it, and I prayed ... and I decided to go. And then I heard that he was dead, and I thought that God had answered my prayers! Was it all for nothing – all for nothing?'

The more emotion Ellen showed, the more expressionless Mrs Bryce-Fortescue became.

'Again, I wish I could help you, simply in remembrance of past services,' she said almost drily, 'but there is nothing I can do at present. We must see what we can do when Mr Granger's murder has been solved, and his inheritance becomes available to Sylvia.'

'To Sylvia!' Ellen's tone was furious and despairing, and she half-turned around and raised her eyes to heaven. Quite probably she really meant to address herself to heaven, but instead, alas, her eyes met mine, quite directly, as I had not had time to hide myself, and was simply pressed back against the wall. Dora, darling, I believe I benefited from your good works, for she stared at me, hesitated ... and said nothing. Goodness gracious, if Mrs Bryce-Fortescue had discovered me there, she would have been horrendously angry at the idea that I had heard all that had been said! Perhaps Ellen hopes for my help, and indeed, I wish I could do something for her – anything at all. My dislike of Mr Granger grows by the minute.

Mrs Bryce-Fortescue was already moving towards the door. She held it for Ellen and as she passed out, she said in a tone of dismissal,

'Leave your address with Mrs Firmin, Ellen, please. We will write to you if we have good news. For what happened seven years ago – I knew nothing, but perhaps I should have asked myself. In any case, I promise you, as soon as we are able to help you, we will write to you.'

They went out, and I scuttled downstairs and hung about outside, for I had a great desire to see Ellen alone. But she must have remained with Mrs Firmin, and I could not stay outside forever. I missed her departure.

Dora, Dora, can Ellen have something to do with the murder? It is so strange, her saying that she meant to turn to him and ask him for help, after seven years, just the very week that he died! Did she really mean to turn to him, or did she – did she what? What could she possibly have done, poor woman? What did she mean, when she cried out *'Was it all for nothing?'* Ellen's role in all this worries me. Is it all just an incredible, and terrible, coincidence? You can help me, Dora, and you must!

Your own

Vanessa

Maidstone Hall, Friday, June 24, 1892

Oh, Dora–

I hate to tell you this. Ellen said she never saw Mr Granger in the last seven years – but it was a lie!

She must be home by now, and if you have had my letter, you are perhaps already talking to her. Oh, I feel so tormented by it all that I don't know what to do. I cannot get over the idea that – although I hardly dare write this to you – that *she* may have something to do with Mr Granger's murder – some mysterious connection with the man in the red cape, which I cannot yet fathom! Horrible thought. Oh, what a dreadful thing it is to have asked you for your help, when you are her only friend and confidante. Would you betray her even if you knew the truth? Would you answer me if you could? Oh, Dora, I never meant to put you in such a dreadful, dreadful situation. But what

161

else can I do? I await your answer with fear. Will I know how to read between the lines?

Let me tell you what it is that I have learned, which has increased my fears so intensely. As you know, today was the day I was to return for a visit to Haverhill with Peter Middleman (who to my dismay is becoming increasingly devoted). I was trembling with excitement, for I meant to speak to old Martha, as Pat had encouraged me to do, and I could not repress my hope that perhaps she would have remembered to whom belonged the face that she saw that day. And I could not prevent myself from being filled with a strange, agonising mixture of hope and distress, while my mind spun endlessly over all manner of possibilities.

The forms and customs must be respected, so we began the afternoon by having tea, as before, with Mrs Bird, except that by this time, the excitement of the murder has somewhat worn off in the village and no other guests came to greet us. She was delighted to see Peter, and spoiled him shamefully, feeding him a great quantity more scones and seedcake than he really needed, but conversation now turned entirely upon his temporary life at Mrs Bryce-Fortescue's, and his future prospects. He dropped sundry hints which I tried to ignore supremely, but some of them made me blush; blush doubly, Dora, dear, for not only was I distressed by the simple mention of such things in public, however restricted and benevolent that public might be, but they were all wrong and false, and I felt that I was leading on poor Peter very unkindly, above all by never telling him that I was engaged. This is very bad, and I am using him shamefully, but I need him as he affords me my only possible port of entry into the closed little society of the village of Haverhill. My status as detective is, after all, still as well-kept a secret as ever!

Eventually, with some effort, I managed to lead the conversation around to how pleasant last week's tea had been, and to the subject of Martha.

'Old Martha? Yes, she's the strange lady of the village, isn't she,' said Mrs Bird importantly, speaking as one who is a pillar of society. 'She lives in that run-down hut at the very end of the road that runs out towards the Manor, and won't have it fixed up or mended or the chimney seen to, though Bill or Thomas would be happy enough to do a little carpentry or even just some caulking any time, just out of kindness! But she doesn't want it – she's hardly ever in the place anyway, for she walks as no one walks that I've ever seen! At all hours, from dawn to the small hours of the morning, she can be seen walking with her stick, one slow step after another, up the roads and down the paths and through the fields and round the backs of the houses. There's no place you might not run across her. There's some who say as she might be a witch, but walking, walking, walking's all she ever does that I've seen.'

'That is strange,' I agreed. 'Do you think she wanders about the Manor as well as the village down here?'

'I suppose she does. She likes the houses as much as the wild woods and fields. Many's the time I've seen her face looking right through the kitchen window, it's given me a fair start! She doesn't hesitate to peer in if it looks interesting to her. Some people hate it, some in the village have scolded her or closed up their gates or put up thick curtains just because of her, but most are used to her ways. Anything new, anything that goes on, you can be sure that old Martha knows all about it. But she's very close. She doesn't say much – just enough to whet your appetite, usually, and then shuts up tight as an oyster!'

'She doesn't seem to avoid company, since she was here to tea,' I remarked.

'Oh no, she doesn't avoid company, she likes company, but she likes her own society as well. She's a strange one – times are, she'll talk just like anybody else, and other times, she'll say shocking things in the same tones, or even things that make no sense, that nobody can understand. But as I said, we're all used to her hereabouts.'

'What does she live on? What does she do for food?'

'She has a little money, somehow, for she buys a bit of bread now and again, and grows some vegetables at the back of her hut. She eats this and that, and won't refuse an invitation or even a basket that we put up for her. Once Mr Granger came down with a basket for her and managed to find her when he wanted her – eggs were in it, I remember it well, for they ended up on his head. She flung the whole thing back at him and would have none of it. I asked her why but she would never say anything that meant anything. "He's bad," she'd say. "He's a bad 'un. Pretending to give but meaning to take, take a body's soul away, he would and he does and I know it." I'd have dearly liked to know what she meant but she'd never say anything else.'

I felt more and more that I simply must manage to have a talk with old Martha. I had especially brought out two loaves of bread and a large cabbage, in a bag which Peter insisted, embarrassingly, on carrying for me although I had not told him what was in it. I had hesitated about what to offer; delicacies or even fruits seemed to me to be out of place. The bag had remained in the carriage, but now, as we bid goodbye to Mrs Bird, I told Peter about it, and explained that I wished to find old Martha as I had noticed her sad condition during our last visit and wanted to offer her a trifle. Peter is a young man of simple ideas, and although the whole operation seemed entirely unnecessary to him, he did not object to the idea of a rather lengthy ramble in the late afternoon sunshine, so off we went together to search for Martha.

We began by following the main road down to where it thinned to a wide path just capable of taking a single carriage, and wandered off through the fields towards the Manor at a distance of a mile or so. There was Martha's ramshackle little hut. We knocked, and even opened the door (which was not closed, but merely left ajar) to peer into the dark, littered interior. But she was not there, as indeed we had quite expected. Then we tried to guess where she might be, and for a good three hours, we wandered up hill and down dale; we even went through the famous Granger woods where the murder took place, and Peter showed me exactly where he had come upon the body.

165

'Lying right down on his back, he was, almost smiling. He never expected what happened for a moment, that's clear.'

We strolled at length along the road from which a certain witness had espied a certain person whose description had never been made quite clear, and then leaving the road (since we could see along its entire length for a great distance) we went through the woods and circled around till we had returned to the village. We went up the main street and down some lanes, but all without the slightest success; no trace of Martha was to be seen either by us or by the few people we eventually asked in our weariness.

By this time it was nearing nine o'clock and the light was quite dim. Dusk was coming on apace, shadows lengthened till they filled out all the ground and the streets emptied of people entirely. It was not terribly late, but it seemed late because of the absolute quietness which had taken over the streets. A black cat crossed in front of us and Peter jumped.

'Let's just take the carriage and go back home,' he said. 'You'll be ever so late in.'

'I suppose we must go,' I agreed reluctantly. I did not want to leave, but thought there was no hope of finding old Martha now that we could no longer see any real distance in front of us, and complete darkness would come in another hour. So together we wended our way to the public house where Peter left the carriage when visiting the village. He went to get the stable boy to let out the horses, and I went directly to the carriage house, meaning to climb in and collapse wearily on the cushions which, although not comparable to the plushy mounds decorating the interior of Mr Korneck's luxurious vehicle, were nonetheless highly agreeable. And it must be said that I rarely have occasion to take advantage of them, as I always feel I must sit on the box with Peter when he takes me about.

I opened the door and was about to climb in, when I heard a slight rustling sound, and a soft, whispery voice said almost in my ear,

'Pretty, pretty, ain't they? Soft and pretty, nice for a lady.'

My dear Dora, I reeled and nearly fainted from sheer shock! I stood in the pitch darkness, everything about me stiffened to attention, and waited without moving.

But something in the carriage moved and shifted. The door I had unlatched opened wider, and a pale face surrounded by wispy hair peered out from the interior, barely visible in the gloaming. Realising that my shock was due to no more than some elderly person who had settled for a rest within the carriage, I pulled myself together and addressed the pale face.

'Who are you, please?' I said, suppressing a tremor.

'Why, it's Martha, don't you recognise old Martha?' she whispered, leaning towards me. 'You've been a-looking for me, haven't you?'

I couldn't believe my ears, nor my eyes. I had been searching for her for hours, and here she was – and she knew all about it!

'How could you know we were looking for you?'

'I seen you walk up, I seen you walk down, I seen you in old Martha's hut,' she answered. 'I followed you a long, long way. What did you want old Martha for, then?'

I put my foot on the step of the carriage and leaned towards her.

'I – I brought something for you. A little package – it's in the carriage.'

'I found it, thank you, thank you. A nice cabbage. So it was for old Martha you brought the loaves and cabbage, was it? I thought it might be. And why did you bring them, then? What is it that you want?'

I was afraid that Peter might return at any moment, and Martha seemed so entirely perspicacious that I decided it was pointless to beat about the bush at all.

'I wanted to ask you about the young man you saw on the day Mr Granger was murdered,' I said quickly. 'Do you remember him?'

'Of course, of course. I followed him up, I followed him down, just like I followed you, but he walked too fast for old Martha, and I lost him.'

'Last time, you said that he seemed somehow familiar to you. Do you have any idea of whom he reminded you? Could you possibly have seen him before?'

'Ah, it's strange, very strange. I don't know, I don't know. I knew him, yet didn't know him. His head, his face, his mouth, and especially the way he walked. With a sway. When did I see that face? When did I see that mouth? Something's wrong. Where, where? In Mr Granger's house was it? In

168

Mr Granger's house?'

I seized quickly on this new thread.

'Were you ever in Mr Granger's house?' I asked.

'No, never, never, not one time. Mr Granger was evil. I wouldn't enter his house. Martha wouldn't go in there. He wanted to take my home away from me. He tried, he came to me with fine presents and money. He would have put me in a home to get my house. I threw it all back at him. Martha won't eat the offerings of evil, no, she won't. He hated me then. He wanted my house for himself out of greed, out of greed, to make his big park even bigger. I wouldn't let him, I wouldn't talk to him, I wouldn't go near him.'

'But then, how could you have seen someone inside his house?'

'Through the window, Martha looked through the windows of Mr Granger's house often, often. Sometimes she was seen and Mr Granger sent out a footman to say that Martha would be arrested for trespassing, locked up in jail, sent to a madhouse. So I crept up silently, like a cat.'

'And ... can you not remember if you saw anyone there who reminded you of the young man?' I said again, desperately hoping to jog her memory.

'I saw many things, many things no one was meant to see,' she said, with a soft cackle. 'Mr Granger quarrelled with his wife. She hated him, it was plain to see. He told her he'd have the marriage annulled – she said he'd be a laughing stock. He told her he'd leave her and her mother without a penny in the world. She shrugged. He wrenched her arm and said she'd better think hard, because he meant to have her and he would, he'd waited long enough, he'd be damned if he waited longer. She pulled the bell. She didn't say much ever but I never seen any marriage with so much hate. Maybe she didn't do her duty by her husband, but he was an evil man, devoured by greed. Martha knows it. Martha feels the presence of the devil.'

'Perhaps he was just angry. How do you know that he was evil?'

'I saw the lady that came to him in tears and begged for help. "For our son," she said. He didn't deny it. So he had a son, Mr Granger did, him that was living with his girl-wife in his fine house. "We have nothing," she said to him. "I gave you a house," he said. "But we have nothing to live on. I work day and night but it isn't enough," she said. "I told you never to bother me again. That was the bargain," he said. "But it's for your son, your own little boy – so that he doesn't grow up poor and miserable! Your very own child – he looks like you," she said. "I told you I'll leave him something in my will to make a man of him," he said. "That's enough – stay out of my life now and forever, or you'll find yourself out of your house and on the streets where there are a lot of women no worse than you." "Put there by men like you," she cried. "Put there by their own weakness and stupidity," he said. "This world belongs to those who have the strength to handle it. Now get out." And he rang the bell and called for his coachman to throw her off the grounds.'

'What did the lady look like?' I asked.

'Tall. Dark. Handsome. And sad.'

Oh, Dora, I knew she was talking about Ellen. Ellen must have been to see Mr Granger, it cannot mean anything else! And he had renewed his promise to leave William something in his will! Yet he gave her nothing in her despair, and she must have thought...

At that critical moment, I heard a creak; the door of the carriage house was pushed open, and Peter's face peered around it.

'We have to be going, Miss Vanessa,' he said anxiously, and opening the door to its full extent, he led in the champing, stamping horses and began to harness them. I opened my mouth to cry Wait! – and jumped up into the carriage, but I found the place next to me empty. The other door of the carriage swung open. I darted down and looked about, but she was nowhere to be seen. Perhaps she had slipped out the door like a black cat in the darkness, or perhaps she was quietly waiting, pressed against the wall in the shadows. The bag of cabbage and bread had disappeared.

Dora, what an odious man Mr Granger was – rejecting Ellen so cruelly, and his very own child, and leading her on with lies and promises of things in a will he never made. Oh, I'm not surprised he got himself killed, what with all the nasty things he did to people! Why, if there was no risk of an innocent person's being accused, I would leave him to fate quite happily. "I've left him something", he said – who could blame poor Ellen for believing the will was already made? And she did believe it, we know she did. Oh,

Dora – *what did she do?*

Do help me, Dora, as much as you can bring yourself to!

Your loving sister

Vanessa

Maidstone Hall, Monday, June 27, 1892

Dora darling,

I cannot help jumping whenever the mail is delivered, but I know that you cannot possibly have already received my letter, and talked to Ellen, and answered mine and sent the answer. Yet I cannot rest until I have something from you. I am becoming obsessed with Ellen – but I *must* put her out of my mind until I hear from you, for there is really nothing that I can do! I *must* force myself to adopt the hypothesis of her innocence – would that it should be the right one – and search elsewhere, and as I am here, I have decided to concentrate upon Sylvia and everything I can discover about her. I cannot believe her guilty, but I cannot exclude that she may know something, consciously or unconsciously, or that the murder may be connected with her in some way. And I cannot get that hidden secret out of my mind.

I wanted to be with Sylvia alone. I thought I could get her to speak to me frankly if Camilla was not present. Camilla is a much more decided, less influenceable character, so I hoped to find a moment when she should be away. I can understand her wariness, of course; certainly she sees that her friend is in a dangerous position, and like her mother, she feels she must persuade her that tact and silence is her best defence.

This afternoon, finally, I was lucky: Camilla went to town to purchase sewing materials, and I captured Sylvia mooning about like a lost soul and proposed a ramble with a picnic tea. Mrs Firmin obliged us with a lovely basket, and off we went, Sylvia's sparkling spirits forming a strange contrast to the gloomy airs she had been wearing just a few moments before. She carried the basket, swung it as she walked, proposed to show me some of her favourite haunts, and strolled before me along the narrow path between the tall grasses, her hair escaping and blowing, her skirt swinging jauntily, her hat with its wide ribbon hanging back on her neck. The ribbon and her dress were of mourning black, as usual, but set off with a halo of ravishing smiles and winning ways, they seemed positively bright and pretty.

I soon noticed that her mood was not merely cheerful, but positively effervescent, for reasons which escaped me entirely. She blinked, she fluttered, she laughed, she was witty – if I had been a boy, I should have said she was flirting! I responded quite instinctively with a little flattery. No, flattery is an unkind word; I found her quite adorable, and did not trouble to hide it.

'This place is like an island,' I said, after we had walked and chatted for quite some time, and were beginning to settle into a shady grove to unpack our picnic. 'It is so isolated, so free, so lovely.'

'I wish I could live so forever, far from the outside world,' she answered. 'But I'm afraid, Vanessa – I'm afraid because of what happened to George. And because ... oh, I shouldn't talk about this!'

A sombre expression had suddenly come into her eyes. She stopped speaking, and looked at me quizzically. I found myself swept up in an emotional desire to come to her aid which far outweighed my professional desire to learn anything possible from her. I desperately wanted her to confide in me, but not in order to collect clues. Wordlessly, I took her hand.

'Vanessa, I haven't told anybody about this, not a soul. I feel that it would be no use to speak of this to Mother, or to Camilla; they would just tell me it's rubbish, they wouldn't understand. But I *must* speak of it to someone! I don't know what to do. Oh, Vanessa, what it is, is that I ... I believe the police actually suspect *me*. Do you think so? Oh, it's horrible, it's terrifying! Yes, I'm *sure* they do – they keep hinting it! Oh, how can they, how can they? Why me?'

Her accents were so timidly naïve, her horror and distress so genuine, that my heart was lifted on a great wave of protectiveness. It is an odd thing, really; Sylvia calls out tremendously strong feelings in one, yet I cannot identify any precise reason for it. Everything connected with her seems like fluttering shadows; her very presence is strangely elusive. I feel that I am no longer working for Mrs Bryce-Fortescue – my desire to

174

throw off what I perceive as a terrible net drawing inexorably around a silky butterfly has become more of a personal passion than anything else.

'Even if they do,' I said warmly, 'they are wrong, and surely the truth will emerge sooner or later. What happened to your husband is unspeakably dreadful, but once the truth is known, the horror of it will diminish and you must turn to beginning your life anew.'

'Oh, I wish the whole story would sink into oblivion!' she exclaimed. 'Do you know, I feel I cannot even grieve properly while all this is going on! I wish I could just be alone somewhere and cry, because George is dead, and after all, he did not want to die and he was in the prime of life and very busy and enterprising. And ... I don't think he deserved to die, even though he was a very hard man. I have felt sorrier for him these last days than I ever did while we were married. I would like to be like other widows; just to be alone, and to remember the nicest days I spent with him, and that we did have some friendly moments, and cry. But I can't do it! The police have made it all into a terrifying, grotesque, ugly, sickening farce. Oh, I am afraid, afraid of something frightful and nameless, even though at the same time, I cannot make myself really believe that anything dreadful can actually happen to *me*. The fear is unreal, but it is awful; I cannot sleep nights.'

She flung herself on the grass and covered her face with her hands. Her emotions are so very near the surface. Like a child, she passes easily and instantaneously from one extreme to the other. I settled on the grass near her, meditatively chewing a thick blade of grass with little seeds sprouting from the top of it, and let a moment pass before trying to speak in a calm and distracting manner, belying the tension her words aroused in me.

'There is a true murderer somewhere, and the police will look for him. If they only had some clear idea of where to start,' (an image of the Haverhill station flashed through my mind), 'they would not think about you even for a moment, I am sure. Oh, Sylvia, do you not know anything, anything at all, that might help them in their search? Anything at all that can lead to the truth?'

'*I* don't know anything! And if I did, why should I tell them? I hate them!' she said sulkily.

To save your life, you silly girl, I thought, but did not say it. Instead, I chose to use conventional words of morality and wisdom, which seemed to me to be more reassuring. 'Because you, also, need to know the truth about how your husband died,' I said quietly. 'It's as though it would be necessary to set his spirit at rest. Something would remain angry and unsolved inside you, wouldn't it, if you were never to know?'

'No!' she cried, almost choking with emotion, 'I would prefer it, I think – never, never to know! Oh, Vanessa, I don't want to know! Just think how horrible, if the person is found and ... tried, and *hung.* Oh, I would feel so sick and guilty – I pray that it will never happen!'

This reaction surprised me. I felt a little stab of worry.

'Why guilty?' I asked. 'Perhaps the murderer is

some angry victim of Mr Granger's business practices, or even just some passing tramp.'

'Yes,' she said quickly. 'Yes, of course ... and yet, I would feel guilty of a life ... why? I ... I...' Her voice trailed off, but I felt as though her unspoken words rang in the air: *I wished he were dead.* She withdrew into herself in sulky darkness and became stubbornly silent. I began to chatter in order to tempt her to emerge from her shell. 'It is natural to have such black thoughts in your difficult situation,' I told her reassuringly. 'There is something terribly unsettling about a situation which is neither solved nor unsolved. I say it is not unsolved because somewhere, there is one person who knows the truth. My mathematical friends talked to me lately about a mathematical problem like that. Most mathematical problems are either already solved or not yet solved, but this particular one is special in that it is somehow neither; the seventeenth century originator of the problem claimed in writing that he had a most wonderful solution, but it has been lost, and no one has ever been able to rediscover it.'

'Why, didn't he write it down, the silly man?' she said, lifting her head a little reluctantly.

'The solution struck him while reading a book, and he scribbled the result in the margin – but the margin was too narrow to contain the whole proof! It makes the problem a very odd one, for instead of simply trying to solve it, people are forever trying to discover what the lost proof might have been. I have a friend who is making his life's work out of it – that Mr Korneck who was here a few days ago. I do hope he succeeds.'

'Oh, the ponderous Prussian? He seemed to be rather sweet on Mother, didn't he?' she said, smiling. Then she frowned. 'I used to think George was sweet on Mother when I was a girl. No one could have been more surprised than I was when he asked to marry *me* – except Mother herself, perhaps.'

'What did you think, when that happened?' I asked, a little tentatively, for we seemed to be returning to dangerous ground again – ground involving suffering, and perhaps feelings of shame or humiliation which people will not easily admit to. But the need to speak out, now that she had once begun, appeared to be too strong to resist.

'I thought he was old,' she answered abruptly. 'I thought I was too young, and I didn't want to marry at all. But Mother convinced me that it was a good idea. If I married George, we would have no more worries about money, and about the house. The house was falling into ruin; George helped Mother with it after we married. Mother would be destroyed if she had to abandon the house. I used to love it dearly, too; all the delightful memories of my childhood are here.'

'It is exceptionally lovely and charming,' I agreed. 'Do you not still feel deeply attached to it?'

'No, I have changed. Marriage changed me. I think I came to feel that the price to pay was too great, that no house can be worth such a price, and now I am weary of the whole thing, and would see it sold or even abandoned without much regret. I let Mother convince me at the time – I felt she was staking her whole life on it

178

'... and ... I felt something else, I think. I've never said this to anyone before; not even to myself, perhaps. But I'm sure Mother had thought that George would perhaps some day propose to her. He was always about the house, you know; he was much more with Mother than with me. I don't know if she was disappointed when he asked for me, or surprised – or perhaps, they planned it all together. How little I know her, even now! She knows me much better than I know her. She always seems to obtain what she wants from me. She never said a word to me about the marriage that was not perfectly calm, perfectly reasonable and justified, but thinking back, it's as though I dimly felt an echo of some terrible despair, as though if I let her down by refusing, some extraordinary calamity would descend upon us all. I turned away from that fearful thing. I was afraid to see more of it, so I accepted what she wanted. It was as though we worked together to keep a great, ferocious black bear locked into a dark cage where no one could see it; I saw it so little that I had no clear idea what it looked like, yet somehow I knew it was there, and that Mother knew it well. How badly I am expressing everything!'

'No, it is extraordinarily well expressed,' I answered quickly. 'I realise as you speak how little people ever allow themselves to talk about anything. How rare it is, for instance, for anyone to give a picture of their marriage which is anything other than perfectly rosy.'

'Rosy! I would have to lie, indeed, if I could give even the slightest tinge of rosiness to the two

179

years I spent with George. I didn't treat him well, I didn't, I couldn't. Oh, Vanessa – I can say it now – I couldn't bear him! I felt a terrible aversion to him, and he saw it clearly, although I never said it in words, of course. He was very angry – I believe that perhaps he even suffered, if only in his pride, but he was such a hard man, used to having his own way in everything, that I could never feel sorry for him. If only I could have, perhaps I would have changed. He never stopped exerting a great ceaseless pressure on me; that was the way he was in all things, in his life, in his business. He built slowly, without haste, pushing inexorably in the direction he wanted. It was unbearable to see him, sometimes. It's against nature to be so!'

'What did he exert pressure about?' I asked naïvely.

'To get what he wanted, always that. And from me, he wanted – oh, he wanted to own me,' she answered, blushing slightly, and fell silent. Then, after a pause, she continued, 'It was strange; he succeeded in everything sooner or later, and perhaps he would even have succeeded in that. I reasoned with myself that he probably would, sooner or later. And yet, somehow, he couldn't really touch me. I didn't have to resist him; I didn't need any strength of will, I was just myself, and somehow, that was enough. He said I was cold, but he was wrong. I'm not cold. But he repelled me. In the last months he was very angry with me, he even threatened me with things... I was frightened, and yet not really frightened. It was strange; I really felt that he couldn't touch me. And yet, perhaps he would have, in the end. It doesn't bear thinking about.'

'No,' I agreed, although in my mind, I wondered at Sylvia's natural preference not to think about whatever troubled her, rather than to make any attempt to master it. 'You did not deserve such a marriage, no one does. It was a great mistake to accept him – and for him, a great mistake not to see what made you accept.'

'Oh, he saw how things were; I never hid anything. But he believed he could overcome everything. Men always do.'

'Oh, Sylvia, I'm sure they don't, not always! All marriages are not like that! You are so young; you will fall in love, and marry again.'

'No!' she replied with emphasis. There was a strange light in her eyes. 'I'll never marry again, that's as certain as the fact that I'll die one day!'

I was taken aback by her vehemence.

'Once burned, twice shy? Surely you do not think that your experience is typical! I am not yet married, to be sure, but I have lived four years of such delight in my engagement that I cannot believe marriage will be anything other than a lovely continuation of it, with the added riches of children and a home of my own.'

'I don't want children, I don't care!' she said, her lower lip taking on its now familiar rounded, obstinate shape. 'I shall never marry because I – because I don't want to, I want to be free and – and – do as I like!'

'A husband who loves you would let you do as you liked,' I murmured, but gently, for I didn't want to argue with her; my words were more of a

181

quiet tribute to Arthur, destined for my own heart.

'Perhaps, but I don't care. I don't want a husband – never again! Anyway, I know what I want.'

'What is it, then?'

'I want to leave this place forever, leave England even, and live abroad, in Paris, and in the South of France, and in Italy, with...'

'With whom?'

'With enough money,' she said hastily.

'You must have spent a heavenly time when you were abroad,' I said, 'if it left you with the desire to spend the rest of your life so.'

'Oh, I did,' she said, a dreamy, enigmatic look coming into her eyes.

'What was it like? What did you do there?'

'Oh, nothing really. We – I – we just went out. To cafés, you know, and to the theatre. We made a lot of friends, we went dancing. We went to concerts – there's so much music in Paris! At midnight on the first of the year, we stood with half the city on the Pont Neuf and watched the fireworks against the moonlit sky. We visited the frightful tower that Mr Eiffel built for the Universal Exhibition three years ago – just think, he meant it as a joke and then it was to be pulled down, but they changed their minds and now they want to leave it up forever! We climbed the stone stairs of Montmartre at night, by the light of a hundred lanterns, and gazed at the Sacré Coeur; in the dark, under the stars, under the snow, it's like a sparkling fairyland. We walked for hours along the Seine, and took the boats. We stopped on the islands for ices. In Versailles, we learned everything that was ever known about Marie-Antoinette. We studied the French Revolution in the libraries and museums. We became fascinated by the Princesse de Lamballe. Did you know – she was murdered by a savage crowd, accused of – of–' Her voice broke off, and she glanced at me suddenly, as though seeking some response or knowledge in my eyes. Seeing that I was totally ignorant of everything concerning the Princesse de Lamballe, however, she continued more quietly, 'She was accused of crimes against the people. She was like our emblem, the Princesse de Lamballe. They carried her head on a pike under Marie-Antoinette's windows in the Temple, where she was a prisoner.'

'How horrible!' I exclaimed, shocked at Sylvia's gruesome fascination.

'Oh, no, it isn't. I mean, the crowd was horrible, but the fate of the princess is beautiful. She gave her life for ... for her friendship with the imprisoned Queen. I still daydream about that story.'

'But did she give her life willingly, poor lady?'

'She did, although she did not know how it would end. But she returned to the dangers of France when she could have remained safely abroad. She was resigned, and went where her gaolers led her, like all the other prisoners – like early Christian martyrs! What choice did they have? None, except to be resigned and accept death open-eyed when it came. The French Revolution was dreadful and frightful, but do you know – we often used to say that people *lived* during it – they drank life to the dregs, they knew fear and passion and loss of control. Loss of control! Do you ever think about that? Do you even have any idea what it means?'

'No,' I admitted. I must be a very simple creature, but I have a sort of cheerful appreciation of the natural, harmonious course of things, and the violence associated with loss of control does not appeal to me. I do not mean merely that I would not like to encounter it, for I believe most people love peace and are shocked in the presence of real violence. I mean that I am not even attracted by the study or the contemplation of it. My mind shies irresistibly away to sunnier regions. Still, I was oddly fascinated by this unsuspected dark side of Sylvia's personality. It awoke my curiosity about her secret, and reawakened my vague suspicions about some possible connection between the secret, and her life in Paris, and the murder of her husband; suspicions which Ellen's story had very nearly put out of my head.

'Were you much alone in Paris?' I asked.

'No,' she said, still with her dreamy smile. 'I hate to be alone. We were always together – Camilla and I, I mean.'

'And did you meet very charming people there?'

'Yes, heaps! People are so different there. If you only knew! The freedom that you feel, because others feel free, and also because nobody knows you! We were obliged to go visit friends of Mother – Mrs Clemming, you know, for old times' sake, and the Hardwicks at the Embassy whom she used to know quite well, but we tried to avoid it as much as we could, at least I did; Camilla quite liked Mrs Clemming's old professor friend who kept sending her to the library to read his books!' She laughed to herself a little, glancing downwards, and went on, 'But we met all kinds of other interesting people, and mostly frequented them.'

'Did you meet anybody really ... special?' I blushed at my own bluntness and lack of taste, but Sylvia seemed perfectly unconcerned, and I really do not think she was feigning, as she answered,

'They were all special! Writers, painters, artists, actors. Those are the kind of people that Camilla likes. She would like to be a writer.'

'Really? I had no idea! Has she written anything?'

'Well ... she started to write a novel.'

'How exciting! What about?'

'Love, of course,' and she laughed archly. 'Her father was not so happy about her leaving for more than a month, but she told him she needed to get local colour for her novel. And it was perfectly true, for she worked quite hard at it while we were there.'

'And what has become of it now?'

'She stopped writing it. She wrote only the beginning. She says that now that we're back in England, she doesn't know how to make it go on.'

'The inspiration is gone – is that it?'

'Oh, I don't know exactly why she stopped. She doesn't want to go on with it. It was in Paris, and we aren't there any more; it wouldn't ring true.'

'If one cannot write about a place without being there, then even less can one write about things one has not lived, or at least observed from the closest quarters,' I remarked. 'I wonder what Camilla based her novel on?' My question sounded more tactless than ever, and I hastened to qualify it by adding a little flattery. 'She is a fascinating person, really; so mysterious, and rather difficult to approach.'

'She is, isn't she,' agreed Sylvia, a little abruptly, and jumping to her feet, she began to gather up the picnic things which we had been unceremoniously nibbling directly from the basket as we spoke. 'Look how late it's getting – we must hurry back! Come, Vanessa,' and I found myself traipsing along behind her through the tall grasses in the yellow light of the lowering sun, and our talk was replaced by the whush of the breeze through the trees, and the buzz and hum of insects.

I wrote down everything I could remember of our conversation the very moment I returned to my room, and read it again and again. I do not find that I made much of my opportunity, yet at the same time, I cannot get rid of the feeling that she was trying to tell me something; that there was something she was holding back, dared not speak of, perhaps, and yet longed to. But I can't put my finger on it! She said so much, and yet not enough; between the lines, there is more. She didn't love her husband, she almost hated him, and she hardly tries to hide it. But what conclusion can be drawn from that? It isn't suspicious in itself ... yet something in the air is! Oh, Dora, I don't know if I'm on my head or my heels. Ellen? Sylvia? Somebody else entirely? Mrs Bryce-Fortescue herself, perhaps? Believe me, I have reflected upon the possibility! After all, she may have deeply resented the unpleasant behaviour of Mr Granger in making the whole world believe that he cared for her, and then publicly preferring her own daughter. And furthermore, if Mr Granger's money devolves to her daughter, then she would have a freer hand with her house than she would when he himself was the parsimonious administrator. Yes, I have certainly thought about her.

But I admit that I have dismissed the idea, for if I assume it, then I cannot understand what purpose she could have had in calling me in. To help in the rightful exculpation of her daughter, without which the inheritance would be lost? Impossible – it could not be done without discovering the truth. Can she wish, secretly, to be uncovered as the murderer? No, that is really too ridiculous. Why all the drama – it would be easy enough simply to confess! No, it is absurd; I cannot think it for a moment.

But I do not know *what* to think! Oh dear, I am not doing well at all. I am quite adrift – whatever shall I do?

Your dreadfully impatient to hear from you

Vanessa

Maidstone Hall, Tuesday, June 28, 1892

My dearest sister,

Finally – a letter from you!

I have read it a dozen times, trying to see whether I could not convince myself – of something, of *anything*. Oh Dora, I want to kiss you for your beautiful words, and hug you for your honesty, and appreciate you for your limpid soul. Of course you cannot believe anything of the kind – of course not! But why, why does everybody lie, why does everybody have secrets? So she told you about it – but only after you knew already. So she explained why she hid it – and I feel more indignant than ever at the description of Mr Granger's heartless attitude. And I can understand why a plea thus rejected may appear humiliating, before ever it is made, and a hundred times more afterwards. Yet the fact remains: she went, and she tried, and she failed. Yet she received confirmation that her child would benefit under Mr Granger's will – and just afterwards, he died!

And then there was no will. Or was there? Might he not have redacted a last will and testament with his own hand, without giving it to his lawyers? Perhaps he left everything to the child and nothing to Sylvia! Could she or her mother have found and destroyed such a will? Or – what if Sylvia found it, but instead of destroying it, she kept it – could *that* be her hidden secret? No, it is totally impossible. No one, but no one could be so foolish as to keep such a thing, when it would be enough to put it to a candle. And did she not say that she *could* not destroy it, whatever it was, because she cared too much about it? No, this theory is not convincing. In any case, it seems highly unlikely that a man of Mr Granger's type should make a will without the official stamp of his lawyer, the very man who is also his executor and who was a close and personal associate in all his business dealings. I am afraid that it is far more likely that he spoke of the will as an accomplished fact, when in fact it was merely an intention.

But Dora, the existence of the will is immaterial in what concerns Ellen, for *she herself* thought that it existed, that is clear! No, the real proof of her innocence lies in what you wrote to me.

Of course, when you say she is incapable of such an act, I believe you. But your description of her life, simple, hardworking and full of privation, all centred around her little boy, is even more convincing. I understand perfectly that she could not possibly leave her child alone for more than the briefest moment; you say that whenever she must be away from him even for a few hours, she leaves him with you. A little boy of six, not yet in school, knowing nothing but his home and his mother, a little boy whose greatest expedition is the much desired visit to Miss Dora (who can, I am certain, be counted upon to provide him with plenty of sweetmeats) – indeed, it does not seem possible that Ellen could leave him alone frequently enough, or long enough, to somehow arrange ... a murder, even by means of an accomplice.

Naturally, you wondered, as I did, whether she might not have left him on occasion with somebody else, or whether she had not, in spite of all appearances, become close to some man during the long period of her loneliness. But I find myself compelled to agree with you that she cannot have done so in total invisibility. If, truly, the neighbours know of no such thing, and if

189

little William himself does not, then it is false and must be discounted.

And the child is to be believed, of course. A child cannot lie, or even if he does, even if he has been ordered to do so, his sweet little face is sure to show some sign of it. You cannot have been misled about such a thing. No, I must resign myself, for the moment, to believe you absolutely.

Dora dear, you mustn't feel guilty about having questioned poor little William. It isn't wrong, wasn't wrong, cannot have been wrong! You speak of a betrayal – you speak of using the child to convict the mother – of forcing him to condemn her as the little Dauphin did poor Marie-Antoinette (about whom I have learned a great deal lately, in discussions with Sylvia and Camilla, who returned from Paris utterly fascinated by her history). But it was not so – surely nothing, nothing at all in the innocent question of whether he had ever spent a day alone at home, or with somebody else, or whether he would be frightened if he did so, could harm his innocent soul, or sow even the tiniest seed of suspicion against his mother in his tender mind. You say that if in some horrendous (and impossible, I now freely admit) manner she could have turned out nonetheless to be guilty, it would be as much of a crime to have her hung, or more, as it had been to shoot the odious Mr Granger. Perhaps you are right – and God alone knows what action we would have taken if that had been the case! I myself do not know, and neither can you. But it has not happened so, and as far as I can see, Ellen appears to be innocent of any connection with the fatal shot. An alibi discovered on the rosy lips of a six-year-old boy is not to be doubted for a single second, although were the police themselves to tread on that delicate and sacred ground in their heavy boots I cannot swear that they would believe this as fully as I – as the two of us – do. I promise you, they will learn nothing about Ellen from me, and I dearly hope that it will never even occur to Mrs Bryce-Fortescue to suspect her in any way, or to mention her to the police (whom she abhors), especially as doing so would reveal to the light of day a scandalous and horrid deed of her precious son-in-law, which she surely would wish to avoid at any cost. So Ellen is safe.

And yet, and yet, you who know me as you do yourself, must be able to guess that I am not completely and totally satisfied that we have learned everything there is to learn from her. You feel that your loyalties are sadly divided between Ellen and me – but it is not so! Do not forget that I am your twin, and it is difficult or impossible for me even to imagine my feelings truly differing from yours on a matter so important. Telling me what she told you is not a betrayal; you put no weapons into my hands, and if you did, I should not use them, certainly not without your full consent and agreement. But there are things you have not told me – very probably, because she has not told them to you. Yet they exist!

Why did she lie about her visit to Mr Granger? Simply because she was afraid, or ashamed, you will answer, and it may be the plain truth. Well, then, more intriguingly: what is the meaning of her strange attitude towards Sylvia? I noticed it

191

myself in her conversation with Mrs Bryce-Fortescue, and you say you have noticed it even much more strongly.

If it were merely her conviction, expressed in front of me, that Sylvia should never have married, one could attribute it (altogether wrongly, perhaps, but I am merely trying to be logical) to jealousy on the score of the man who after all was the father of her child. But why should she say that Sylvia will never make a good wife to any man? Sylvia herself said she would never marry again – but how could Ellen know that? Even if Sylvia used to say it as a young girl, it means nothing; half of all young, independent girls say so. Could a natural jealousy and anger over the course taken by events lead to such a remark? But you assure me that she is not jealous and freely avows that she never for one moment envisioned becoming Mrs Granger herself – that at least at first, she felt more grateful to Mr Granger for aiding her during the first terrible months than resentful about his abandonment. She could, of course, be lying – but there, I must trust to your instinct – and I do!

Yet she seems to hold a grudge of some kind against Sylvia, to speak thus of her. Either that, or to know some fundamental flaw in her character, something so serious as to make her unfit to marry and live normally! I cannot imagine any such thing ... unless it be that Ellen knows that Sylvia is capable of murder – but that's nonsense! Sylvia can hardly have been in the habit of murdering anyone as a child.

I cannot imagine what it could be, then. Might

Ellen have actually seen Sylvia during these last years, as she saw Mr Granger, and be hiding something about it? I must ask you, persuade you, beg you to help me once again, Dora – leave all notion of betrayal aside, and try to find out everything that Ellen knows about Sylvia, and what it can all possibly mean.

Sylvia – all paths lead strangely back to her, and yet none proves that she committed any crime. There is something that eludes me, and yet – there are moments when it appears so close, so clear, so transparent, like a butterfly fluttering nearby, that I can hardly believe it cannot be caught with a simple gesture. Surely, together, we will succeed in elucidating this at last!

Your loving

Vanessa

Cambridge, Thursday, June 30, 1892

My dearest Dora,

I am home again – something most important has happened!

Yesterday, I received a telegram from Arthur saying that Pat O'Sullivan told him he has a piece of information for me and I must come up to Cambridge at once. Between Ellen, Sylvia, and what I heard from old Martha, I have been so confused these last days that I was eager to hear any positive fact whatsoever (though I feared a little that whatever he had to tell me would merely add to the muddle). I hastened to inform Mrs Bryce-Fortescue of the new development, and arrange for Peter to take me up to Cambridge.

I telegraphed, and when I arrived, Arthur and Pat were waiting for me.

'Now they've found something worth knowing,' Pat cried eagerly the moment he saw me, without even waiting for the customary greetings, let alone the usual roundabout queries upon one's health and other topics which politeness generally requires upon such occasions. 'Already a couple of days ago, they'd managed to trace that fellow's trip to Haverhill all the way back from London. He came up from London, but yesterday, they discovered that he hadn't started his trip there – he'd come up in the boat train from *Dover* of all places! They're certain of it now, and they're down in Dover today, enquiring with the ferries. If they manage to trace him on a ferry over, then they'll be *certain!*'

'Certain of what,' I asked with tense reserve, wondering and not fully wanting to know what he was leading up to.

'Why, dead certain that he's some lover of Sylvia Granger's from Paris! Isn't it obvious? That's been their suspicion all along, hasn't it? And the gun being of French manufacture was a point in their favour. They're determined to find him; they've got several men at the port now, questioning everyone who worked on the ferries bound for England that morning! If he came over that way, they'll probably know it by tonight, or tomorrow at the latest.'

'And what will they do if that happens?'

'Ah, then, they'll be in a rare pickle, heh, heh. They can't go detecting in France – they'll have to turn the case over to the French police, and the French won't care so much about helping to detect an obscure murder over here when they've got so many of their own! And even if they could find and identify him, there'd be the problem of extradition. No, we've got a headstart on them there!'

'A headstart? What do you mean?'

'What do you mean, what do I mean?' said Pat, looking vexed at my obtuseness, which if not exactly deliberate, was certainly a consequence of my inner resistance to the police theory. 'Aren't you going to go detecting? Why, it can't possibly be so hard to identify the fellow, unofficially at least! If Sylvia had a lover, surely the people she frequented over there must have known all about it. And what about that girlfriend she was there with – girlfriends tell each other everything, don't they? Why don't you ask the girlfriend?'

'I have talked to her about Paris, but she has told me nothing of interest.'

'Of course she wouldn't, even less so if she has any notion of the danger her friend is in. But you ought to be able to surprise it out of her! And besides, those girls must have been all over the Paris scene together – they must have socialised with simply hordes of people! Go over there and ask questions, Vanessa! For Heaven's sake, what are you waiting for?'

'I – I don't know exactly,' I said hesitatingly. 'Perhaps I'm very stupid, and yet, at this point I'd have sworn that things can't be the way you're describing them.'

'Why ever not?'

'Well ... this sounds silly, but it doesn't correspond to the way Sylvia is behaving. She doesn't seem likely to have a lover. And even if she did, and even if he did come over and shoot her husband, you'd think she would guess it, even if she knew nothing about it and had nothing to do with the planning of it. But in fact, I don't believe any such idea has even crossed her mind. She'd show some signs of it – she couldn't possibly be *lighthearted* – as I assure you that she is, deep down inside her, beyond the level of present worry and fear, and the mourning and anguish.'

'Probably she thinks she'll get off scot free and finds it a cheering idea,' snarled Pat rather unpleasantly.

'Oh, no! She's not like that. It – no, I don't know. But something seems wrong.'

'Well, the police may have their knife into her, and maybe even a little too much, but you're all the other way! It's easy to see who hired *you*, and it may turn out in the end that you're doing a fine job of *not* looking for the murderer!'

'Oh dear, oh dear,' I sighed. 'Please don't be angry. I think your ideas about the murder must be wrong somehow, but I know that you're right about detecting. If the young man is really traced back on a ferry to the other side of the Channel, then that is where I must go and detect. I do, I really do see that if they find he came from there, it will be necessary to go, and I will most certainly do it. But it will be difficult; my French is not good enough for real detecting, even if Annabel *has* been teaching me for the last four years – and I could hardly go there all by myself!'

I looked at Arthur.

'Funnily enough,' he said, intervening in the conversation for the first time, 'Korneck has been pressing us lately – Charles and me, that is – to spend a couple of weeks in Paris. Charles Hermite is working over there on generalising Cayley and Sylvester's work on some of the same lines that we are, and it seems he's making some quite extraordinary discoveries. Well, our teaching has just come to an end, so – I suggest that we all go together. If you must go, I would much prefer to be near you.'

'Oh, Arthur – can it be possible?' I exclaimed. 'Oh, if it were not for this dreadful murder, it would be heavenly to travel to Paris with you! Still, I am worried that detecting in French will be too difficult for me.'

'How about if we take Annabel with us?' he suggested thoughtfully. 'Something tells me she would not refuse. It may be a little expensive, but we mathematicians may be subsidised by the Department, so if you can see with Mrs Bryce-Fortescue, it could be done.'

'Mrs Bryce-Fortescue! Arthur, I can't! I should have to explain to her about the Paris connection, and she will become perfectly terrified that Sylvia will be implicated,' I said. 'I know she firmly believes that Sylvia is innocent, but if it turns out that Sylvia had a lover in Paris who came over and killed her husband, it will cause an enormous scandal, even if Sylvia knew nothing about it! No – I can't, I daren't tell her, not now, not before I have been there and discovered what I can. Later, of course, it will probably be necessary to do so.'

'Are you sure?' said Arthur. 'She could help you with more than expenses; she could write you letters of introduction to her friends.'

'Arthur, she will not send me to Paris to investigate her daughter, and that is exactly what I will appear to be doing!' I said. 'Come – you do see that it is impossible! Yet Pat is right; the thing cannot stop now. No, I shall simply tell her that I am following up the clues concerning the young man, without saying where I am going. And I shall pay for myself, even if I use up all of my savings to do so. Depending on what we find out, I could always request expenses from Mrs Bryce-Fortescue later. But I will not think about that now. Let us just simply pay our way, and be off!'

'That's the attitude!' applauded Pat, smiling sunnily. 'But don't do anything until we know more. After all, it certainly sounds likely that he came over from France, since he took the boat train, but wait till they know for sure. I'll drop by my brother-in-law's later on to get the news.'

'Come to our place when you know,' said Arthur. 'You're right of course – the man may turn out to live in Dover, or to have come over from Oostende and be Dutch!'

'I'll let you know for sure. But if they find what I expect they will, you've got to go; that's my frank opinion, and I stick by it!' said Pat with emphasis, as though he suspected I might still change my mind, and he shook our hands and departed with his springy step.

'However shall we get through this evening without knowing,' I moaned.

'Oh, I forgot to tell you!' cried Arthur consolingly, taking my hand. 'We have an engagement for this evening – we're going to a concert! Do you remember your little pupil Rose?'

'Rose? Why, of course. How enchanting she was! She stopped coming to school ... a good two years ago, to devote herself to music. How old must she be now? My goodness, fifteen already – a real young lady! Is *she* to be playing in the concert?'

'Yes, she is,' he answered. 'I received an invitation from her mother, and I expect yours is waiting for you in your rooms.'

It was. When I opened the envelope, out fell a note, a program, and to my surprise, a ticket. I had somehow imagined that Rose would be playing in her home, but no; it was not a mere family affair, but was to take place in one of Cambridge's loveliest concert halls. The brief note, from her mother, informed me that this concert has been organised by her professor, as her farewell to Cambridge, for she will be leaving in a month to study in London.

Out of respect for an event of such importance, I put on my blue muslin with lace, redid my hair and sallied forth with shawl and hat to meet Arthur upon the front step. We walked together to the centre of town, almost in silence, but the most trusting and companionable silence imaginable. Every step we took together in the balmy summer breeze was like a prayer of thanks for such togetherness. Poor Sylvia – to have been married and never to have lived this.

The foyer was full of people milling about, preparatory to entering the hall. So many people come to listen to little Rose! I could hardly get over it, for even though I knew she was no longer a child, I was quite unable to imagine her any different from the fair-haired sprite who had attended my classes for three years. After taking a few moments to absorb the sociable yet hushed atmosphere which always precedes a concert, I looked about me, and perceived several acquaintances; there was Emily, beckoning to me furiously, and her mother, together with Rose's mother.

'We are so happy that you could come,' said the latter as I approached. 'Please do come backstage to see Rose after the concert; she will be absolutely delighted to see you again after so long! She knows she could have visited you often enough since she left school, but you know how children are – she's been too busy with her music ... and just with the process of growing up, little by little, into a young lady.'

'It's a good job she didn't drop *me*,' said Emily indignantly – 'and she probably would have, if I hadn't gone hunting her out every so often!'

'Oh no, not you, dear,' said Rose's mother soothingly. 'Young girls find their friends simply indispensable, as you well know! And Rose is an only child to boot.'

The warning bell rang, and the loose mass of people pressed towards the doors leading into the hall, broke loose again on the other side and edged between the rows of plush seats with a great deal of shifting about and arranging of stoles, hats and purses. Some ladies took off gloves, others took out fans, gentlemen opened programs with a rustle, and there was whispering and discussing. I seated myself next to Arthur, and enjoyed the slowly intensifying feeling of hushed waiting. The lights dimmed and darkened over the audience, while falling directly on the stage, which contained a beautifully burnished grand piano, a chair and a music stand with music ready upon it. There was complete silence for more than a minute, and then a door opened at the back of the stage and Rose appeared, followed by a dapper gentleman in tails, with a neatly waxed moustache, and a slender young man also in black, but not so elegant, who took his station humbly next to the grand piano on the side away from the audience, and prepared himself for the task of turning pages by anxiously licking his fingertips.

The clapping began and then swelled into a great clatter. Rose and her pianist smiled out over us and bowed slightly, then took their places. The pianist played a note, and Rose touched her bow lightly over the strings of her cello and tuned them softly. Then, suddenly, the music began in a great storm, piano and cello crying aloud together without warning!

Time appeared to stop. I felt suspended, motionless, in the rush of notes, and the young girl facing me on the stage, behind her great shining instrument, appeared to me at once like the Rose I had always known – the soft, tender, young lines of her cheek and chin, the great cascade of fair waves held back from her face by a wide ribbon, the childlike vigour of all her movements were exactly as before – and a new, mysterious Rose, whom I watched as from the other side of a great river, as with flushed cheeks and eyes dark with inward intensity, she seemed with ease and yet with effort to pitch the stream of notes upwards, so that they fell upon us like dashing raindrops. She played with authority – I can find no better word to express it – and that authority, and the extraordinary power of inwardness and concentration which she achieved as she sat facing such a crowd of people, and the beautiful dress of forest green silk relieved only by a narrow collar of cream-coloured lace, so different from the pink flounces she once favoured – all this made me feel much as though she had travelled over all the world since I last saw her, and become – more than a young lady, more even than an adult – she had become a consummate artist.

Grieg's Sonata came to an end suddenly. It seemed to me that no time at all had passed, so powerfully had I been under its spell. Applause surged around me, and I joined in, faintly because of my emotion. Rose stood up, smiled, bowed, left the stage, returned, left again, returned again. Arthur poked me, and laughed.

'You look mesmerised,' he said.

'I am mesmerised,' I answered. 'I remember notes like these under the bow of a little dancing elf, some four years ago – even then I was amazed, but now! There is something in her playing which defies any kind of judgement; something queenly, which is quite simply beyond commentary.'

Rose was returning, and the noise quieted down

to the merest rustle. She put the music stand aside, advanced her chair, and sat down alone. She remained for a long moment without moving, unaware of the waiting audience, capturing some inner mood. Then she shook back a strand of hair, set her bow on the strings, and began to play the second suite by Bach.

Now her playing appeared to me of devastating simplicity. I listened as the music developed itself onwards and forwards, moving inexorably, as it seemed, to its foregone and unavoidable conclusion. If such a thing were possible, I would have said that Rose's playing added nothing and subtracted nothing from the very soul of the notes themselves; I felt as though I were reading the music directly as Bach had written it, as if no arbitrary interpretation came between the notes and me. Movement followed movement in their right and prescribed order; Prelude, Allemande, Courante, then the bitter beauty of the Sarabande, the absurd cheer of the Gavotte and finally the strange irony of the Gigue, the natural gaiety of whose rhythm was belied by the weird agony of the melody.

The music stopped, followed by clapping, and there was a pause; many people got up and squeezed past my knees to go wander about outside. I believe even Arthur went, but I remained fixed in my seat, unwilling and indeed quite unable to return to a normal state of mind. I remained so, half hypnotised, mixed fragments of melodies running through my mind, until the bell rang again, the audience returned, the lights dimmed and Rose returned with her pianist, this time to launch directly into the passion of Beethoven's third Sonata. I followed the music as in a dream, and the dream continued; in fact I awoke to my senses quite suddenly by feeling my arm pulled unceremoniously. Arthur was tugging at it and saying,

'Everyone is leaving. Don't you want to go backstage and visit Rose?'

The music was over, the applause many times repeated had come and gone, and people were gathering up their wraps all around me and pouring out of the doors.

'Oh, please come with me!' I exclaimed, feeling almost dismayed at the idea of confronting the young crowned goddess I seemed to have been watching. He took my arm, and together we worked our way against the direction of the great majority of the crowd. I should not have known where to go, but eventually we went down some stairs and around a corridor, and there was a large room, and Rose was standing in it laughing, surrounded by several people, all of whom were kissing and congratulating her warmly.

'Oh, what *am* I doing here?' I exclaimed, overcome with shyness and the strong impression of not being in the same world as all these gaily dressed, cheerful people. 'Oh, do let's go!'

But before we could make a move toward the door, Rose spied me, and jumping towards me, she threw her arms around my neck and kissed me happily.

'Oh, I'm so glad you came!' she exclaimed, and my vision melted and disappeared, and there was Rose in front of me, exactly as she always had been; perhaps just a little taller, but really no different at all!

'I'm going away from Cambridge, did you know?' she told me eagerly. 'I'm going to study in London, at the Royal Academy! I *am* frightened – I'll be the worst student there, I just know it!'

'Nonsense,' I laughed with relief. 'Surely if they accepted you, they mustn't think so! How did it come about? Did you have to go there and play?'

'Oh, yes – it was *awful!*' she cried. 'I played for a professor who called me into his room. First I played my prepared pieces, and then he made me play scales and studies and horribly difficult exercises and things – they were much too difficult! He said "Do wat Ai do" and I had to try to imitate it all, and his hands are absolutely enormous – it wasn't at all fair! I thought he must be thinking how awful I was, but then he said "Eet ees good, you study wiz me." He's Italian – his name's Professor Pezze frrrrom Milano. Then I listened to his class and heard all his students. They're all wonderful – one of them is a girl, and she's even younger than I am! Her name is May Mukle. "Remember her name," he told me, "eet weel be famous some day!" Oh dear, oh dear.'

'I wish I could say "So will you",' I told her, 'but after hearing you play, I don't want to any more; it seems of no importance whether one is famous or not, when one can speak so with the voice of a wooden instrument. What matters is that voice. Never lose it, Rose! Don't let a teacher train it until it becomes unrecognisable!' I kissed her, and then turned away, for I felt near tears with emotion.

'Music tells everything, but everything,' I mused, as Arthur and I walked home through the quiet streets. 'I didn't think about Sylvia for a single second during the music, yet now that I remember her, I feel as though her whole story, and everything that must happen, and all that I must do was told there. The Sonata by Grieg told a story of mysterious passion, while the Bach suite described a kind of mathematically inexorable fate; then the Beethoven Sonata ended it all with a tale of intense suffering mellowing into unbearable sweetness. That's how the music says it will end, and I believe in such messages – at least, I pray that it may happen so!'

Arthur slipped his arm around my shoulders and squeezed hard, without speaking.

We arrived home, and were precisely in the process of kissing each other good night most tenderly – goodness, we *are* engaged! – when Mrs Fitzwilliam's door popped open and I nearly had a heart attack from dismay. I turned to her, sure that I was about to be the victim of serious remarks.

'You've received a telegram,' she said, 'I took it for you.' She handed it to me, and forgetting all about the kiss, I tore it open and read it together with Arthur. Its brief but powerful contents were as follows:

Your man was seen on six-fifteen ferry from Calais stop Pat

'We shall leave as soon as possible,' Arthur said simply. 'We'll arrange it tomorrow.'

So Pat was right. Oh, I do feel frightened of what I may find out in Paris. But there is nothing for it. It is clear that I must go.

Your deeply moved and worried

Vanessa

Paris, Sunday, July 3, 1892

My dearest sister,

Here we are in Paris – we arrived yesterday rather late and tired, booked into a hotel – *Le Grand Hôtel de Paris*, if you please, on the rue de Rivoli – and spent the evening trying not to make fools of ourselves while getting something to eat, and then walking along the indescribably beautiful moonlit banks of the Seine. The whole of today was devoted to exploring the city under the expert guidance of our ubiquitous friend Mr Korneck, who arrived separately (under more luxurious conditions, I have no doubt) but has made arrangements to join our party with alacrity.

I must write down these experiences while they are fresh in my mind, for I feel that if I do not, they will soon fade away and disappear. There is something so very unreal, so gossamer fragile, about all that is happening to me at this moment. I, Vanessa Duncan, ignorant and inexperienced schoolmistress from the country, taking a walk in Paris – why, one might as well take a climb up Mount Parnassus and meet the gods! The beauty and the history of the city make me feel simultaneously very humble and altogether euphoric, and I admit that for the space of one day, the purpose which brought me here slipped somewhat towards the back of my mind; but I shall turn my full attention to it again tomorrow.

The windows of our hotel rooms overlook the Tuileries where poor Marie-Antoinette, Sylvia's unhappy heroine, whiled away many miserable months before the axe of the Revolution finally descended upon her and her family.

I am armed, for detection, with the names of two of Mrs Bryce-Fortescue's friends in Paris whom Sylvia and Camilla frequented last winter; I retained them from our conversations. Indeed, I clearly remember her mentioning the Hardwicks of the Embassy – they should be easy enough to find, and then the Mrs Clemming with whom she was acquainted of old. Although Mrs Bryce-Fortescue would probably not have wished me to come here, she knows nothing of it, and I shall profit from this ignorance by making shameless use of her name in calling upon them, before they can find out the truth.

According to Sylvia, Mrs Clemming is a widow who is quite well off; constrained to live the simplest and soberest of proper lives during her husband's lifetime, she sold everything the moment he died and moved to Paris immediately, where she has lived ever since, having succeeded in establishing a rather chic *salon*, which means that writers and artists, with a seasoning of a few members of the minor aristocracy of various countries, frequent her house regularly once a week. It sounds rather fun – I only hope that she will think me fit to be invited there, as Sylvia was! As for the Hardwicks, I do not know what they are like, but I do know that Sylvia saw them when she was here, and that will be a starting point for my investigations. Tomorrow I will call at both their homes, and if they are not in, I shall leave notes; it should be cards, of course, but alas, I am not possessed of any!

Enough concerning my plans for tomorrow – I want to tell you everything we saw and did today. We began quite early by leaving the hotel to have our breakfast outside; *café crème* and *croissants*, namely, at a lovely sunny *terrasse de café*. If only Annabel would speak for us, all this would have been easy enough, but she would not, and obliged us all most severely to order for ourselves in French, saying that all our studies, and the many lessons she has given me, ought not to be wasted. I tried my best to overcome my shyness and remember much that I had carefully learned, and was quite pleased at the unexpectedly reasonable result. As for Arthur and Charles, they are unashamedly British. In fact, it makes very little difference whether the words they speak are French or English really, as they sound exactly the same in both languages. The *garçon de café* looked down his nose upon hearing them, and pretended not to understand, while simultaneously leering in Annabel and my direction.

'Bother the "confident and over-lusty French",' observed Arthur coldly, unconsciously touching his pocket.

'Hm,' I said as I made out the oblong flat shape

209

within it, 'I really don't think you should be using *Henry the Fifth* as your guide-book to France. Is that what you've been doing? I ought to confiscate it! You can't possibly learn to love the country with that as your inspiration!'

After this breakfast, we walked about the Louvre palace and the Tuileries gardens, and then purchased and consulted a map which we used to find our way to our prearranged meeting place with Mr Korneck.

'I tried to persuade him to meet us somewhere else,' said Charles with a guilty smile, 'but he *would* insist on meeting us in front of the Academy of Sciences. It's the epicentre of Paris as far as he's concerned, and he clearly can't think of anything more exciting than having a look around it. Girls, I promise you we won't talk shop – will we, Arthur?'

'No, no, we shall resist at all costs,' he laughed. 'I must admit that I'm longing to see the place myself, though, even just for a moment. It will make me feel less of a complete stranger here, to glimpse the place where so much of the history of mathematics has been made, and where we ourselves will spend most of our time for the next two weeks.'

After consulting our map, we crossed a delicate bridge arching over the Seine – a glorious great mass of water running between banks of royal stone, plied by large flat boats going seriously about their business; a true city river, so different from our secretive, lovely Cam, dotted with little pleasure crafts as it winds amongst the green fields and hedgerows. The famous Academy was not far;

it lies on the southern bank of the Seine, which they call the left bank, on the Quai de Conti. We had not yet arrived at the main entrance before we perceived our portly friend, puffing and looking about him with great impatience.

'Ah, what a pleasure, what a pleasure,' he said, shaking hands with an irrepressible air of pride and proprietorship. 'It is such a lovely day, we shall walk about Paris and see many sights. I promise these young ladies that we shall not dally too long within these illustrious walls, but let us walk inside briefly and see the main hall.'

We entered. The interior was cool and dim. Few people were present, a lone figure here and there crossed the hallway, loaded with books. Mr Korneck led us to an imposing round room with a podium and seats all around it.

'Here is where the meetings and announcements of the Members take place,' he pronounced respectfully. 'The history of this room, with all the events of importance that occurred here, is an astonishing one.'

'Has Fermat's mysterious theorem ever been discussed here?' I asked politely, seeing that he was longing to recount what he knew, but hesitating at the idea of boring us to tears with his pet topic.

'Indeed it has!' he replied with an air of delight. 'The terrible intellectual duel between Gabriel Lamé and Augustin Cauchy took place, week after week, in this very room!' He took a deep breath, assumed a special, dramatic expression, lowered his voice, and began to speak, stopping now and then to search for sufficiently impressive words.

'It was more than forty years ago, and at that time, my dear ladies, you should be aware that mathematics was a subject that was discussed and debated in the most elegant *salons* of Paris, and books were written expressly for young ladies to learn about it, so as not to appear ignorant when the theme arose naturally in conversation. The work of Sophie Germain had appeared so promising to the Academy that they established a glorious prize, to be awarded to anyone who could finally solve the mysterious theorem, and many of the most renowned mathematicians of the day were struggling for it, and dropping hints about their progress. And one fine day in the year 1847, during the regular Academy meeting, Gabriel Lamé arose and announced that he had solved the problem! At that time Lamé was one of the most illustrious mathematicians in all of France, and yet, it was an extraordinary thing for him to be interested in Fermat's theorem, for he was really more of a physicist than a mathematician, and deeply involved in designing and building the railroads that criss-cross France today. But his researches in physics had led him, a few years before, to study Fermat's beautiful equation $x^n + y^n = z^n$ when n is equal to the number 7, and he had succeeded in discovering a brilliant proof of the expected result that no solution to this equation can exist. This result had led him to new ideas, and he believed that he had solved the entire problem once and for all, and would soon become the winner of the newly established prize! He had not yet written his proof completely, but he was in the process of doing it, and expected to be finished within a few short weeks.

'No sooner had he finished making his announcement to the assembled company, who were stunned by the magnitude of the news, than another mathematician arose and pushed his way forward to the podium. It was Augustin-Louis Cauchy, devoted Catholic, ardent Royalist, unpleasant personage (if I may say so), but one of the most prolific mathematicians this country has ever known. Cauchy was a dangerous character; his understanding of mathematics was so gigantically vast, his ideas were so astoundingly varied and prolific, and his speed and eagerness so immense that he easily crushed any smaller or less influential person that crossed his path, and very possibly he never even noticed it. It had happened before and would happen again, and on this day, he could not endure Lamé's declaration, and the astonished and admiring faces of the audience, and their murmurs of approval. No sooner had Lamé returned to his seat, than Cauchy announced that he, too, had solved the problem, and that he, too, would have written down a full proof within the next few weeks. Look!'

Taking down one of the fat volumes of *Proceedings of the Academy* which lined one of the walls, he turned the pages and showed us a passage that I must admit I found more amusing and revealing than I would have thought possible for a dry scientific tome.

'You see – it was the first of March, 1847,' he said, showing us the date, 'and here is the report of Lamé in which he sketched out his proof. And

213

Cauchy could not bear to stand by and hear that! He could never endure someone else's making a discovery on anything to which he had already bent his fertile mind.

A la suite de la lecture faite par M. Lamé, M. CAUCHY prend aussi la parole et rappelle un Mémoire qu'il a présenté a l'Académie dans une précédente séance (19 octobre 1846), et qui a été paraphé, à cette époque. Dans ce Mémoire, M. Cauchy exposait une méthode et des formules qui étaient, en partie, relatives à la théorie des nombres, et qui lui avaient semblé pouvoir conduire à la démonstration du dernier théorème de Fermat. Détourné par d'autres travaux, M. Cauchy n'a pas eu le temps de s'assurer si cette conjecture était fondée. D'ailleurs, la méthode dont il s'agit était très-différente de celle que M. Lamé paraît avoir suivie, et pourra devenir l'objet d'un nouvel article.

'Monsieur Cauchy says that he had deposited a memoir – when was it? half-a-year earlier – in which he gave a method that he thought could also lead to a proof of Fermat,' translated Arthur. 'He had turned to other work and hadn't had time to check it, but his method was very different to Monsieur Lamé's, and would be the subject of a new article.'

'Doesn't he sound jealous!' exclaimed Charles. 'Just in the way it's written, you can almost imagine the stenographer thinking so.'

'He was jealous,' agreed Mr Korneck. 'After this, a race began between the two men. Lamé deposited a sealed envelope at the Academy, in case there should be some dispute over priority later on, and on the very same day, Cauchy did the same! Lamé published some small portions of his proof in these *Comptes-Rendus*, and Cauchy did the same. Each of the two claimed to be smoothing out the final details of their proofs. They continued to publish at regular intervals for two months – and then came the catastrophe, in the form of a letter from Germany! Ernst Kummer of Berlin had been reading the rival articles by Cauchy and Lamé as they appeared, and he soon recognised that both mathematicians had fallen into a trap that was perfectly familiar to him, for he had fallen into it himself not long before, but had subsequently realised the error of the method. When he read the announcements of the proofs, which I just showed you, he had his suspicions, and when he saw their subsequent articles, he became certain. He wrote a letter to Liouville, to be read out in front of the whole of the Academy, in which he detailed what he believed was their error. Kummer showed that there were two kinds of prime numbers, those called regular and those called irregular. The proofs Cauchy and Lamé were developing could only be applied to the regular primes – but Kummer himself had already understood how to deal with these many months earlier! As for the obstacle of the irregular primes, he felt that the methods proposed in the Academy publications could not succeed in vanquishing it.

'Cauchy could not endure to read Kummer's work – he reacted exactly as he had reacted to Lamé's announcement. Look here, what he wrote in May 1847,' and he turned several dozen pages in the same volume.

Dans la dernière séance, M. Liouville a parlé de travaux de M. Kummer, relatifs aux polynômes complexes. Le peu qu'il en a dit me persuade que les conclusions auxquelles M. Kummer est arrivé sont, au moins en partie, celles auxquelles je me trouve conduit moi-même par les considérations précédentes. Si M. Kummer a fait faire à la question quelques pas de plus, si même il était parvenu à lever tous les obstacles, j'applaudirais le premier au succès de ses efforts; car ce que nous devons surtout désirer, c'est que les travaux de tous les amis de la sciences concourent à faire connaître et a propager la vérité.

'What a hypocrite!' said Annabel. 'Just look – he says that Kummer appears to have found results which he himself had already discovered – but that *if* Kummer had done more than he had, then he would be the first to applaud! Why, he can't have been a good mathematician, can he? He sounds like he needed to attribute everybody else's work to himself!'

We all smiled.

'Yet he was very good, more than good; one of the great geniuses,' said Mr Korneck. 'It proves something, does it not? A man's satisfaction does not depend upon his abilities or accomplishments.'

'So how did the story end?' I wondered.

'After Kummer's letter was read, Lamé understood instantly that he had made an error. Cauchy continued stubbornly for several more months to insist on his success, publishing further morsels, but finally, under the guise of new interests, and without ever making a public retraction, he turned to other topics.

'This story represents the final flare of the history of Fermat's last theorem. Since Kummer's devastating result, no one has dared make another attempt at solving it.'

Mr Korneck fell silent and looked at us expectantly.

'It reminds me of the three-body problem,' I said doubtfully, 'these mathematical competitions really seem to do more harm than good. Did anybody ever win the prize?'

'Ten years later, Cauchy recommended that it be attributed to Kummer himself, for his remarkable discovery,' he responded. 'It was the closest he ever came to admitting he had made a mistake.'

'So Kummer won the prize for proving that it couldn't be done – more like the three-body problem than ever!'

'No, no, do not say that,' he answered, his heavy-featured face animated with passion. 'Kummer did not show that it could not be done, on the contrary; he showed that it *could* be done for regular primes, and developed a new and extraordinary notion in mathematics, even while explaining that the road adopted by Cauchy and Lamé was a bad one for the irregular primes. But it can be done in general, I am convinced of it – it can be done, and Fermat surely did it! My dream is to rediscover what he did. And I hope it is more than a dream.'

I glanced at Charles and Arthur, but they wore studied looks of expressionlessness. We followed the hallway to the main door and emerged once again into the glare of sunlight beating down on the stone buildings.

'Enough of mathematics for today,' said Mr Korneck kindly, but with a trace of wistfulness, 'let us now follow the traces of kings and queens. I shall take you to visit the Louvre.' And we spent the remainder of the afternoon and evening exploring and admiring many astonishing sights, with oases during which he guided us to his favourite restaurants, in which we tasted various dishes interestingly smothered in sauce. In the evening he took his leave of us (to return, no doubt, to a place of superior comfort and beauty), and we wandered back together along the quays, the river twinkling and purling below us, reflecting back the many lights which shone upon its wrinkled surface. Arthur and I soon fell behind the others, to offer ourselves the dreamy pleasure of walking hand in hand in the fresh evening air, and for a brief moment, I thought I was in heaven.

It has been a magical day. But tomorrow I must return to my business, and force myself to recall things which would be, perhaps, better forgotten...

Your loving sister,

Vanessa

Paris, Wednesday, July 6, 1892

My dearest Dora,

I have been very active, and I shall take advantage of writing to you to give a complete description of all that I have seen and done. To begin with, the day before yesterday, I left a small note with the concierge of Mrs Clemming's luxurious *immeuble*, whose address I was able to locate in the post office (there was no possibility of error, as there are no other Clemmings in Paris). You must imagine a solid and imposing, but most refined building made of heavy stone blocks, *pierre de taille* as they are called, with a giant wrought iron and glass door leading into an imposing tiled hallway, and a wide crimson-carpeted staircase leading upwards. The only room opening into this entrance belongs to the concierge, who peers out a little window to examine all comers and goers. She accepted my note together with the gift of a coin and grumbled something in French which I did not understand, but optimistically took to mean that the note would be duly delivered to '*Madame Clemming, la dame anglaise*' as I assiduously explained.

It must have succeeded, for the very next day I received a reply, in the form of a card printed with her name and the legend *At Home Wednesdays 4:30* in both French and English; underneath, she had written by hand 'Please do come and visit'.

Although I had mentioned my travelling comrades in my note to her, the card was addressed to me alone, so that I had not the reassurance of

219

bringing them with me. However, I imagined that this British lady would have many English speakers amongst her guests, and this, together with the idea that it was extremely likely that they should have encountered Sylvia during her winter visit, and could perhaps even share a great deal of information on her score, sufficed to put me into a state of great excitement. By three o'clock, I was already hovering over the clothes laid out upon my bed, hesitating because nothing seemed quite elegant enough for the occasion. Annabel watched me a little wistfully.

'I do wish you were coming with me!' I exclaimed warmly.

'Oh, it doesn't matter,' she said, smiling. 'I won't miss it. I am not so used to social occasions. After all, I am merely a governess.'

I glanced up in surprise. I had never thought that Annabel felt resentment about her place in society. On the contrary, since I had met her four years ago, I had frequently heard her express the sincerest gratitude towards Mrs Burke-Jones for having offered to a penniless orphan whose only accomplishment was an excellent education in a French convent, a position which in spite of being nominally inferior had all the charms of an authentic family life. As far as I could observe, Annabel had been treated with kindness and respect; on occasion, she was even invited to join Mrs Burke-Jones' guests for supper, to even out the numbers. It is true, I suppose, that there is no real equality in all of this, but I had never thought that Annabel felt it as a sting.

'You *were* a governess,' I observed, 'now you are

a schoolteacher, exactly as I am. I really see no difference, apart from the fact that you cannot claim the acquaintance of Mrs Bryce-Fortescue. But that means nothing.'

'Oh,' she answered, jumping up vigorously. 'I really didn't mean to hint that I wasn't invited because of my station; I just meant that I was used to missing out on social things because of it. But I don't care about *them* – not at all!'

'Well,' I said stoutly, 'as far as I am concerned, I'm proud of working for my living, and I love the work, and I'm proud of all the ideas I've had for it over these last years, and how well it is turning out. And so should you be! And to the D with high society!'

'Oh, I know you're right,' she sighed.

'But you are dreaming of something, nevertheless?' I looked at her closely, and a memory of something she had said recently came back to me, but I dared not mention it.

'Everybody dreams,' she said, and rising, she came to look at the clothes piled on my bed. Unhesitatingly she picked out a pretty afternoon dress in a deep grey shade and held it up against herself. 'Wear this one, it's lovely.'

'Everything looks lovely on you,' I said a little enviously, admiring the contrast between the shadowy hues of the dress and her thick fair hair with its golden reflections in the light, the fairness of her slender arm and the delicacy of her wrists as she turned the dress about to examine it. It struck me again, as it has occasionally over the last few years, what a lovely young woman she really is. Why is she still single, I wonder – can it really be due to her position in life? Is her position really inferior to mine? It doesn't feel so, and yet perhaps it is because of it that she meets few people other than those who come to Mrs Burke-Jones' house, and those are of a social class which... I thought of Arthur, and wondered if he would consider marrying a girl like Annabel. The thought was unexpectedly painful, but at the same time, it seemed clear to me that he would not hesitate if he loved her. But then, Arthur is in a special situation; he lost his parents young and has neither family nor fortune, so that there is no one who could really object to any idea of marriage he might have. Whereas most of the young men, mathematicians generally, who circulate around Charles in the home where Annabel lives are not likely to be equally free.

I was staring at her, lost in these thoughts, whilst she turned over my few things and looked amongst her own as well, choosing accessories, when a smart knock came upon the door, and I jumped.

'Yes?' I said, and almost immediately, the door opened and Charles thrust his friendly head inside.

'Are you girls almost ready?' he said cheerfully. 'It's past three-thirty now; if we're going to walk you down there, Vanessa, and then visit a museum as we said, we should be leaving fairly soon.'

'In just a few minutes,' said Annabel, thrusting the dress and shawl into my arms. 'Here, you should wear this pearl brooch with it, it's the only one light enough to stand out.'

Charles' head disappeared, and I put on the

222

dress and allowed Annabel to arrange my jewellery, hat and wrap in ways that I should not have thought of myself. She did not take any trouble to prepare herself, and indeed there was no need for her to do so; again I was struck by admiration of her fresh, neat looks and natural grace, and prettily flushed cheeks as we emerged from our room and joined Charles in the foyer.

'We really must go,' she said, looking about. 'Where is Arthur?'

'He's not coming,' said Charles a little too quickly, and then added lamely, 'What happened is, he suddenly had a good idea, and went rushing off to the Academy to look up a book there; he – he sends his excuses.'

Annabel's colour deepened and she looked confused. She glanced at me and said nothing. Charles looked straight ahead, and held the door for us as we stepped out of the hotel into the street. We set off in the direction of the great boulevards where Mrs Clemming resides, and both Annabel and Charles chatted to me quite intensively about the coming visit, so that it took me several minutes to notice – obtuse me – that they never addressed a single word to each other!

Ah, how foolish I have been, how blind. Oh dear, oh dear, I see now what I did not see before. Annabel's feelings have become as clear to me as if a radiant light were lit within her very soul.

But what about Charles? Thinking back over his remarkably frequent presence in the nursery, I wonder if he did not pack Arthur off to the Academy quite on purpose. I recall his words and tone on many occasions, but I cannot read in a man's mind as I can understand a young woman of my own age – I cannot guess what his feelings are. Oh, I do feel worried for Annabel.

Something of this was running through my mind already as we walked, but I put all such notions out of my head as soon as we reached the imposing building where Mrs Clemming resides, and taking leave of my companions, I entered alone, climbed the stairs to her door and rang timidly. A muffled murmur of guests reached me through the burnished wood, which was soon opened by a charming creature in black-and-white, who ushered me within and directed me towards the lady of the house, who was receiving in her vast parlour.

She sat enthroned in a large armchair, surrounded by tables loaded with *objets d'art* and tea things, and chairs and sofas upon which various ladies and gentlemen were perched, leaning towards her in animated discussion. Clearly I had entered a familiar little society in which friendliness reigned and from which the coldness or pomposity engendered by shyness was banished. Mrs Clemming raised her eyebrows upon seeing an unknown face, and then smiled.

'Ah, you must be Eleanor's young friend, Vanessa Duncan, is that it?' she said loudly but kindly. 'Well, I do hope you're enjoying your visit to Paris. Staying in a hotel, are you? Well, it's very kind of you to come and visit an old lady like me.'

'It's very kind of you to have me,' I smiled. 'I don't know anyone in Paris, except for the friends who are here with me.'

'Well, I hope you won't desert me as that little chit of a Sylvia did,' she said with a sniff. 'She came here just twice, with that tall silent friend of hers, and after that I didn't see hide nor hair of them for the whole two months they were here. They found other entertainment, so I heard, or Sylvia did, at least.'

'I imagine they must have made a great many friends after a while,' I said soothingly but secretly most interested.

'Indeed–' and Mrs Clemming glanced at the guests around her, who, interrupted in the conversation they had been having, were leaning forward and listening to ours with avid curiosity.

'Shocking, the way she went about alone, or worse than alone,' sniffed one British lady pointedly. 'My sister-in-law Victoire – my husband's sister, that is – and her husband saw her in the casino in Deauville with some gentleman, gambling and dancing until three o'clock in the morning!'

'My goodness, how fast,' I laughed. 'But she wasn't actually alone, was she? I mean, wasn't she with Camilla?'

'Camilla nothing!' interrupted Mrs Clemming with disapproval. 'Those girls have changed since I first met them four years ago at Sylvia's coming out. She was a dull little thing then, and Camilla was the strong, handsome one. Now here's Camilla still single, and never saying a word – even when she visited here she was off in the corner talking about fusty history with Gérard the whole time. And Sylvia behaved quite shockingly according to what I heard, and now she's a widow, and with a scandal, too.'

'A mystery more than a scandal,' I said, 'there is no shadow of any scandal associated with Sylvia.'

'Well, then she was better behaved in England than she was here, or took more trouble to cover her traces!' said the sniffy lady sharply. 'Out at all hours, Camilla nowhere to be seen – and appearing no better than she should be – dancing with the same gentleman all night, and wearing rouge, too – all in full view of everyone! If she'd done that kind of thing in England, she'd be in far worse trouble than she is now!'

'Perhaps Camilla was there and your sister-in-law didn't see her,' I said.

'Certainly not, Victoire asked after her particularly,' was the reply. 'Sylvia said that Camilla felt ill at the last moment and stayed in Paris. Do you know what I think, Alice?' she added thoughtfully. 'I think Camilla saw the way her friend was behaving, couldn't stop her, and decided to have no part in it.'

'Who was the man that Sylvia danced with all evening?' I asked lightly, but my heart thumped queerly. 'Did your sister-in-law know him?'

'Yes, who *was* it? Who could it have been, indeed?' interposed Alice Clemming. 'How shocking – what can she have been thinking of? You didn't tell me at the time, Jane, I would have written to her mother at once!'

'Victoire only mentioned it to me a little while ago,' replied Jane. 'She was in Deauville recently and it came back to her. I must ask her more about the young man. I believe she said she didn't know him, but saw Sylvia with him more than once. Disgusting.'

'Now, here you are standing while we talk about Sylvia,' said Mrs Clemming to me, unfortunately interrupting what I considered a most fascinating conversation. 'We must get you some tea. Gérard, Gérard, come and take care of Miss Duncan, do,' she called, turning and beckoning vigorously to an elderly gentleman who had been occupied all by himself in absorbing a pile of small iced cakes on a willow-pattern dish which he held in his hand.

'*Oui, oui, ma chérie,*' he said to her indulgently, pattering forward and peering at me through thick spectacles.

'This is Professeur Antugnac,' she told me, sitting solidly in her armchair and performing the necessary introductory gestures with her arms, while a plate remained balanced on her knee and a teacup on the fragile little table next to her. 'Miss Duncan from England, Gérard, a friend of Eleanor's. Like the two other girls who were here in the winter, remember? Find her a cup of something, will you?'

'Miss Duncan, ees it? A pleasure, a pleasure. I give you a cup of tea, yes?' He pottered cheerfully to the large silver urn and poured me out a cup, while still chattering vaguely. I glanced at the other occupants of the room; the guests were a mixture of English and French, mostly of an age with Mrs Clemming. The Professor appeared to enjoy a privileged position as 'special friend', almost even a secondary host to Mrs Clemming.

'You do not know anyone here?' he asked

227

worriedly, wrinkling his forehead. 'You have just arrived? You seek friends, yes?'

'Well, one is always delighted to meet new friends,' I smiled.

'There are no young people here,' he said, 'you will find it very boring, perhaps.'

'Why, no, of course not – I don't talk only to young people, you know! Quite the contrary; if anything, I think older people are much more interesting. They *know* so much more.'

'Know, know, it is perhaps the only thing which remains,' he said with a smile which was both sad and enchanting. I felt very fond of him, and as he seemed disposed to accept me into his solitary corner, and Mrs Clemming had returned to the animated conversation she had been having before I arrived, I felt inclined to follow him there. I thought that he was very probably the fusty historian who had so interested Camilla, and decided to sound him out.

'Anyway, it can't really be true that young people never come here,' I began. 'My friends Sylvia and Camilla were here last winter.'

'Ah yes, of course, of course. When the English matrons send their daughters, we receive them, naturally. But they do not stay. We play bridge, here, we talk politics, we talk about society and about the doings of our grown-up children, and they do not like it. Miss Wright, and little Mrs Granger, they came here in my corner also and we talked together. Twice or thrice, but not more often.'

'What did you talk about?' I asked with eager interest.

'Miss Wright was so very interested in my work,' he said with a shy smile. 'I thought perhaps times have changed – the young girls talk to the old professor about his studies, while the elderly ladies chat about parties and clothes and wrongdoing of those around them. It seems backwards from when I was a young man, yes? But perhaps the time, it has not changed, and Miss Wright is an unusual young lady, yes? After I spoke to her, she studied much and the second time she came, she knew a great deal more than the first time, and we spoke most interestingly. She wished to write a book, she told me. She went much to the library.'

'Really,' I said, a little surprised. 'I knew she was writing a book, but I thought it was a novel, a love story.'

'Did she tell you so?' he said, looking at me penetratingly.

'No, not she, Sylvia told me,' I replied, wondering if it was justified to be so extremely indiscreet.

'Ah, Sylvia told you so. Yes, Sylvia would see it that way, perhaps.'

'What do you mean? What was it she was writing about?' I asked, my curiosity now seriously piqued.

'I do not know what she was writing, but I know what she was studying, for it was I who led her to it,' he said with dreamy satisfaction. 'Marie-Antoinette, the fairy princess of France, the murdered child-queen. I have spent the whole of my professional life studying the fate of aristocrats during the French revolution, and have published several books on the subject – in French, of

229

course. Miss Wright read my books in the library while she was here, and came to talk to me about them. A very intelligent young lady. She was fascinated by the story and asked me a thousand questions; even her little friend became interested and listened to me as I told them of the uncontrolled luxury of her life as queen, which led her to mad decisions of buying and spending, and the terrible trials she underwent as a prisoner.'

'I quite understand their being interested,' I assured him, 'I am sadly ignorant but the little that I do know is fascinating. I do hope you will not find it boring to repeat to me some of what you told them. What interested them the most?'

'Ah, I remember that Miss Wright asked me again and again about the Princesse de Lamballe,' he said happily. 'I have spent much time and effort studying this lovely Italian princess, for many years the closest, most cherished friend of the unhappy queen. She remains a mysterious personage, of which not much is known, compared to the immense number of facts and details we possess about her more illustrious mistress. Indeed, from all the many letters and writings and testimonies left by those acquainted with Marie-Antoinette, it is possible to penetrate her psychology to some degree, to follow some of her thoughts and feelings, for few people have ever been so completely and entirely observed and described and documented throughout the whole of their lives. Marie-Antoinette was formed by her mother, and when she came to France, her mother sent people to observe and describe her every move, her every word, her every action. And from their letters, a stunningly accurate portrait can be drawn. But her constant companion, the Princesse de Lamballe, remains in shadow. Who was she? And what was the basis of her deep attachment to her Queen, which led directly to her arrest and death? What special role did she play in the queen's life, which was the cause of so much violent resentment and so many vulgar rhymes and songs, and which eventually caused the crowd to tear her from the courtroom and murder her on the streets, and promenade her head on a pike about the city?'

'Oh, the Princesse de Lamballe,' I cried in recognition – 'I remember now that Sylvia told me about her! She was fascinated by the story – so she learned of it from you?'

'Certainly,' he said with modest smugness. 'I would not, myself, have spoken to them about the details of my historical theory on the importance of the princess in the life of the queen, but I said something, and Miss Wright listened most intently, and then, the second time she came, she had read a great deal, and asked many profound and pointed questions. Aristocratic life before and during the French revolution is not an easy topic to discuss, especially in the presence of young ladies, and most particularly those from polite English society, where your Queen Victoria does not allow it.'

'Oh, come,' I smiled, 'certainly Queen Victoria is very strict, but I do not believe she actually forbids discussing the French Revolution!'

'But it is difficult to speak of it if one cannot speak of passion and crime and illicit love, which

231

we French know exist but English girls are brought up to believe does not.'

I laughed, and was about to assure him that English girls were not so goosey as he believed, Queen Victoria notwithstanding, but we were interrupted.

'Now, Gérard,' called Mrs Clemming suddenly, from the depths of her armchair, 'you're not boring the poor girl with Marie-Antoinette, are you? Dear me, the man simply can't keep off the subject!'

'It is a way of remaining young and fresh,' he said, pattering obediently towards her with a tender little smile. 'The heart stays young with the contemplation of grace and beauty, and is still capable of love after the passage of decades.' Unexpectedly, he took her pudgy hand and raised it to his lips with real affection. His eyes twinkled pleasingly, and I became aware that I was witnessing a silent declaration of love for the second time on the same day. It must be the influence of France.

Alas, I was prevented from learning anything further from the professor by having to join Mrs Clemming and her group, but it was not a total loss, for I made great friends with the lady with the sniff, whose claim to fame is that she is married to an elderly widower with a particle to his name; de la Brière, a minor aristocrat, in fact. This means that she moves simultaneously in two different circles of society; quite an elegant one, in which I fear she cuts but a poor figure as a mediocre specimen of a nationality which is, after all, that of France's ancient enemy, perfidious

232

Albion, and another, thoroughly British one, in which she is perfectly at home and is furthermore surrounded by a halo of glory due to the aristocratic names she is in the habit of letting fall in the course of the conversation.

At any rate, perceiving the deep impression made upon me by her mention of barons, counts and so on, she was graciously willing to invite me to her house, and by a miracle (consisting of serving up a great mixture of flattery and admiration) I succeeded in convincing her, in spite of many doubts and hesitations, to promise me to invite also the famous sister-in-law, who is apparently married, not merely to a minor aristocrat, but actually to a major one, the kind with a real title. Her desire to be admired for her high connections (I gather that Mrs Clemming's little society does not give her sufficient satisfaction on that score, as they are probably quite tired of hearing about it) finally vanquished the hesitations caused by her wish to keep her glorious acquaintances to herself (and also, perhaps, by the difficulties involved in persuading them to pay her a visit. But I must not be unkind).

She has promised to fix a day as soon as possible. In the meantime, I must go tomorrow to pay a call on Mrs Hardwick of the British Embassy. I consider that today has definitely not been wasted.

Your loving

Vanessa

Paris, Friday, July 8, 1892 (although it is already the 9th, really!)

My dearest sister,

It is extremely late, nearly one o'clock in the morning. I am very tired and feel I should go to bed at once, but then, if I do not throw my thoughts and impressions upon the paper, and share them with you as I always do while they are still imprinted fresh upon my mind, I am afraid that a long night of deep sleep will dull their sharpness and I shall forget most of what I saw and learned.

For I must confess to you before anything else that I have actually been to a party, and that at this party, there were a great many things to eat and particularly to drink; most delicious and succulent things the latter were, sugary and innocent seeming upon the tongue, but actually most unexpectedly treacherous, so that after several hours I found myself tottering instead of walking, and am not at all sure how I could have arrived home if Arthur had not held my arm and recalled the way. Now that I think of it, he cannot have been so very cool-headed himself, for he sang me a very lovely aria as we went along, which I thought nothing more of at the time than that I had never noticed him to sing so pleasantly, but find rather surprising now that I write it down.

The darkness is complete except in the little

circle glowing about my candle's flame. My eyelids feel alarmingly heavy, and Annabel is already sleeping deeply, so I feel I must hurry to write, and clear up the mass of confused impressions in my mind. Let me begin at the beginning, and tell you how I went yesterday to call upon Mrs Hardwick, whose husband is a diplomat, and who used to be quite a close friend of Mrs Bryce-Fortescue in her youth.

I found her in, but she was on the point of leaving, apparently to walk her dogs. Still, she welcomed me kindly, although a little as though she did not really know what she should do with me. She is very unlike Mrs Clemming, and does not seem to be interested in gossip, to the point that she seemed to make an effort to ask me even the simplest questions, and those were couched in the briefest of terms.

'So you're acquainted with Eleanor,' she said abruptly, upon hearing my name. 'In Paris alone, are you? No? With friends? Good, that. Not too lonely, then. Looking for something to do? People to meet? They all do. Can't stand parties myself. Have to go to far too many of them, that's the problem. Part of my work. And can't have my dogs here. Only real company, dogs.'

I was surprised at this remark, in view of the very large Saint-Bernard she held on a leash and the two sharp-voiced terriers, which bounded about her feet yapping unceasingly as we spoke. She caught my look.

'Those are not dogs,' she observed more telegraphically than ever. 'At least, they are dogs, I suppose, but not my pack. Hounds, I mean.

Best I can do here, living in a city.'

'Oh, I see!' I said, somewhat taken aback. 'You mean you cannot hunt here. But surely there are many compensations, living in Paris.'

'Awful place. Awful people. If you knew. But probably won't have time to find out. English here just as bad as the French. Worse, maybe.'

'Oh! And ... I suppose you are obliged to frequent a great many people?'

'Course, part of my job. Diplomat's wife – got to meet people all the time. Parties – far too many of 'em. Even worse when I have to organise them myself. Cook is wonderful – fortunately – but still, got to be there. We're hosting one this evening, round at the Embassy, rue du Faubourg St. Honoré. Come, why don't you? Come and bring your friends. How many? Four? I'll tell the maître d'. Eight o'clock, then. Nice to see some fresh faces.'

I felt these remarks to be in the nature of a dismissal, and accompanied Mrs Hardwick out the door and down the stairs in silence, as no conversation was possible above the pulling, tugging, dashing, leaping and yapping of the dogs in their eagerness to plunge into the fresh sunshine. I then hastened to my tea-time *rendez-vous* with my friends, eager to share the news about the evening's invitation.

Their reactions were most varied.

'It might be an awful bore, what?' said Charles doubtfully.

'Oh, how lovely, a real party here in Paris!' exclaimed Annabel with delight, at the same time.

236

'Yes, perhaps it'll be wonderful after all,' said Charles, exactly at the same time as Arthur said,

'But we were supposed to compute Hermitian matrices this evening.'

'Oh, come now,' I laughed, 'too much work and no play makes Jack a dull boy.'

'Do you think everybody will be very elegant?' worried Annabel.

'What does it matter if they are!' said Charles. 'Fresh cheeks are much prettier than pearls and diamonds any day.'

I looked at him in surprise, suddenly hearing him as though for the first time, and felt a tinge of worry. I must take Charles aside at the first opportunity and try, as tactfully as possible, to make him understand something very important.

We repaired to our rooms after tea; Annabel and I to prepare ourselves, while Charles and Arthur expressed the intention of packing as much calculation into the next two hours as possible in order to make up for the lost evening of work. I even heard them saying something about rising early in order to have something concrete to show at their meeting with M. Hermite tomorrow afternoon. (It seems a little unlikely, considering the aria and other behavioural phenomena observed this evening, but one never knows.) In any case, they disappeared into their room where they made a great rustling of paper and pencils, whilst Annabel and I once again laid out our prettiest items and I allowed her to compose and select for the two of us.

In spite of the ample amount of free time which lay before us, we were late, of course; a great deal

of inertia and confusion must necessarily be overcome before four people can be simultaneously
ready to depart (I admit, from long experience,
that it is generally much worse when some of
them are children). By the time we were all
arrayed neatly in our best and standing ready in
front of the main entrance of the hotel, tapping
impatiently because Arthur had dashed back
upstairs for a handkerchief, it was a quarter to
eight, and after walking along the Seine to the rue
du Faubourg St. Honoré, somewhat slowly so as
not to become hot and ruffled, it was nearing
eight-thirty. However, as it turned out, this was a
perfectly reasonable time to arrive; a great many
guests were present, but many others were not yet
come.

We were ushered in by the gentleman Mrs
Hardwick referred to as the maître d', whom I
would have called the butler. He bowed
courteously at the door, and asked for our names
in a humble murmur. He did, however, check
against a list which he had discreetly hidden
under a napkin, and cross off an entry marked
'Miss Duncan and friends'. The room he then
escorted us to was of noble proportions, spacious
and high-ceilinged. A grand piano stood in one
corner, its rich colour contrasting with the light
polish of the parquet. The wall contained numerous paintings, and heavy curtains draped the
enormous windows, not to shield the guests from
the looks of curious outsiders, for the windows
did not give directly onto the street, but perhaps
to increase the intimacy of the room by prevent-
ing the guests from seeing the outer reality.

Taller than almost anybody else, very regal in black silk and pearls, Mrs Hardwick stood in the middle of the vast salon, receiving. She may not have been gifted with many of the social graces, and certainly not with that of making easy conversation or flitting from group to group, but she appeared adequate enough in the role of queenly hostess, looking down her nose and offering her fingers to the arriving guests nearly as though they were supplicants – radiating British superiority the while, quite as though she had not made such uncharitable remarks earlier that very afternoon. She looked very cool and composed. The dogs, fortunately, were nowhere to be seen.

The guests were a motley mix of nationalities, all apparently from the diplomatic milieu. There were many British and French people there, but also an assistant to the Greek ambassador, a Turkish gentleman with a fez, a tall and very quiet American with spectacles and various other specimens of all flavours. Amongst them circulated graceful and silent young men and women, laden with trays. Some carried flutes of champagne, others tiny discs of bread, all different from each other, each containing an astonishing variety of tiny morsels piled upon it; a currant, a shred of Italian raw ham, a dice of cucumber and a microscopic sprig of parsley, or else a scrap of smoked salmon topped by a point of cream and a tiny wedge of lemon. We made our way across the room to Mrs Hardwick.

'So here you are,' she said, extending her hand to each of us in turn, and looking downwards upon us (not that she was really taller than the men, but she looked downwards at them anyway. An excellent tactic to master). 'Good to see you, good to see you,' she went on. 'A pleasure. Do any of you speak French? You do?' she said to Annabel. 'You'll be a real boon to me, my dear, if you will.' With an effortless gesture of the hand, she attracted the attention of a lonely gentleman holding a glass of champagne and standing at some distance from her, much as some people, blessed with the gift of authority, effortlessly attract the attention of waiters in restaurants while others are condemned to remain humbly unnoticed although they may gesture and wave their hand a dozen times in order to ask for more wine or for the bill to be brought.

'Now, you'll converse with Monsieur Olivier,' she said, the authoritarian ring in her voice quite audible although muted behind an air of jollity, as though she were proposing a great pleasure to all concerned. *'Venez, venez, Monsieur, rencontrer une charmante jeune amie anglaise,'* she added for the benefit of the approaching gentleman, fluently albeit with a strong British accent, and Annabel found herself accepting a *flûte de champagne* from Monsieur Olivier's hand, and chatting to him lightly as though she had no will of her own.

I was hoping to escape the same fate, but Mrs Hardwick had every intention of using her guests to neutralise each other to maximal effect. Charles, the next in line, was introduced to a dowager lady whose ample bosom was built up by stays to alarming proportions, so that her glorious emeralds lay upon it rather than hanging from her neck, while Arthur found himself speaking English at a snail's pace to a sallow-cheeked, black-haired and melancholy-eyed Spanish beauty. The very second Mrs Hardwick turned to deal with me, I took the bull by the horns.

'I should so like to meet anyone who is acquainted with Sylvia,' I said flutteringly – 'I *am* sorry, I am so very inexperienced in society, and it truly would help me to have a common friend to talk about.'

'Sylvia, Sylvia, what Sylvia is that? Oh, you mean Eleanor's daughter.'

'Yes, she was here last winter – surely she must have met many of the people here now,' I continued hopefully. Mrs Hardwick was too distracted to ignore my request and insist on something else; other guests were approaching and she wished to dispose of me quickly and without argument.

'Oh, certainly,' she said, glancing about her, a little at a loss. 'Here, you'd better ask my husband. He'll remember better,' and she directed me towards a diminutive gentleman whom I had absolutely not spotted until that very instant, although he was greeting guests assiduously at a mere arm's length from his wife.

I approached this gentleman quite timidly, but he seemed delighted to meet me, and I had immediately to revise my initial impression of an insignificant little man in the shadow of his wife. Small and slight though he was, Mr Hardwick was a consummate diplomat; suave to the point of liquidity, he greeted me as warmly as if I were exactly the person he had most desired to see at that precise moment, and I was quite carried away by the delight radiating in his sunny smile, the way he looked directly into my eyes, and the kind, familiar gesture with which he laid his hand upon my arm; only later did I notice him behaving similarly with nine out of ten of the other guests he greeted.

As he was so very welcoming, I decided to proceed to action at once.

'Mrs Hardwick would so like me to meet some of the people here, as I don't know anyone except my friends,' I began.

'Oh, now, we can surely remedy that very soon,' he smiled, and as though by a natural reflex, his eyes roved swiftly over the assembled crowd. I spoke quickly.

'I did hope to meet some people who were acquainted with Sylvia, my friend Sylvia Granger. Perhaps you remember her. She visited here last winter.'

'Naturally I remember Mrs Granger; I never forget anyone,' he said. I suppose it is due to a professional habit which must be quite useful and even indispensable – how awful to be introduced, in the home of the Prime Minister of some Republic, to some gentleman who says 'Of course we are already acquainted', and to have no idea whom he might be! I imagined, peculiarly, that my own face, form and name would be inscribed in the inscrutable and secret agenda hidden behind the friendly mask for all eternity – or at least until the man himself should have disappeared into the grave.

'A charming young lady,' he went on. 'She

242

attended at least two of our parties.'

'Who was she with?' I asked suddenly, as an idea started up in my mind. 'With your memory, perhaps you can tell me – I – she–'

I stopped, confused because of the abrupt oddity of my request, and hesitating between excusing myself on the grounds of shyness, or explaining untruthfully that Sylvia had spoken to me about so many of the kind guests at his excellent parties. But though he glanced at me with amusement, the echo of flattery in my words caused him to answer my question without any detours due to curiosity, and his words caused my hair to start up upon my neck.

'She came the first time with a lady friend, a very lovely girl, I remember, a real statue; tall and dark. I should remember her name. Yes, Camilla, of course. A perfect flower, a very suitable name. I quite enjoyed her company. My wife's friends do so often bring a breath of change to our familiar professional gatherings. I was very sorry not to see her again. The second time Sylvia attended a party here, she was accompanied by a gentleman.'

'Accompanied? Really accompanied? Or were they simply casual acquaintances of the evening?' I asked, hiding the excitement his words engendered within me.

'Oh, really accompanied!' he laughed. 'They were inseparable, and Katherine was in high dudgeon because they mixed so badly. A most interesting young gentleman – he would have been perfect for the old ladies, but Sylvia hardly let him speak to anyone.'

243

'Do you know who he was?' I asked, but I knew the answer would be negative before the words left my mouth.

'Not at all, never saw him again. I really don't know where she found him. He was the sensation of the evening among the old ladies, as a matter of fact. I can't recall what he said his name was, but it was something highly exotic, at any rate. Dear me, you had better circulate, hadn't you,' he added quickly, as a group of new arrivals, having paid court to Mrs Hardwick, bore down upon him. 'Here – come along,' and guiding me just a few steps towards the edge of the room, where chairs were lined up against the wall for those who were too elderly or tired to make continuous use of their legs, he presented me to a clump of ladies who sat there, gossiping and fanning themselves.

'Mrs Thurmond, Mrs Hilton, here's Miss Duncan, a friend of Sylvia Granger's, just arrived from England,' he said, pushing me forward slightly with his hand in the small of my back.

'You do remember Mrs Granger, of course; it was she who came here in ... January, was it? Yes of course – it was the New Year's celebration, for there were fireworks over the city at midnight. She came with an interesting young foreign gentleman – Miss Duncan is most interested to hear more about him. I thought you ladies would be sure to remember everything he said and did.' He slid away smoothly, leaving me in the hands of the dowagers, who shifted in their places, drew up a chair for me, and installing me in their midst, transformed me in a single gesture into

244

one of themselves: I felt myself to be rather aged and bodily weary, and perhaps even somewhat heavy; much decked out and tightly constricted in my stays, a little too warm but acutely interested in spite of all this, in the sayings and doings of every human being unlucky enough to stray into the radius of my small influence. As I sat, I spied Arthur, at some little distance, laughing wholeheartedly with the Spanish girl and bringing a melancholic smile to her lips. I felt a little twinge, as though my identity were slipping away from me.

However, I brought myself severely back to the matter at hand, and turned the conversation without the slightest difficulty onto the subject of my friendship with Sylvia and her fascinating masculine acquaintance, about whom I implied that she had told me many obscure and deeply intriguing facts.

'Oh, he was a *sensation*,' said the lady called Mrs Hilton, who wore a bonnet with an alarming amount of lace and appeared positively short of breath, whether from excitement or the tightness of her dress I could not be sure. 'He was so *very* romantic! A Russian prince, he was.'

'A Russian prince!' I was astonished at this unexpected piece of information, more worthy, seemingly, of a fairy tale than of bitter and sordid reality. But Mrs Hilton did not consider that being Russian was anything so very exotic.

'Paris is simply crawling with Russians,' she said. 'That's because the French lost the war in Russia eighty years ago; they've been swarming over here ever since. They learn French there as children, and then when they come here, they marry French girls as often as not and stay forever, living a life of parties and gambling.'

'Some of them are just here because they're diplomats,' observed another lady. 'We've a couple right here in this room, haven't we, dear?' and she turned to her friend Mrs Thurmond for confirmation.

'Why, certainly,' said this lady. 'There's Mr Grigoriev over there now, by the curtains; he's the gentleman petting the dog. He shouldn't do that,' she added as an afterthought. 'Katherine's dogs don't much like to be petted – there! He's snapped at his hand. I'm not in the least bit surprised.'

I fixed Mr Grigoriev with a fascinated gaze, and had to admit that although he wore pouches under his eyes, he bore no other noticeable resemblance to the image of a Russian gentleman which extensive reading had bred within me. He was not romantic, he did not fling himself to his knees nor challenge anyone to a duel, nor did he even wear a large fur hat. He did, however, according to my informants, possess a name and patronymic, and as a matter of fact, so did Sylvia's mysterious friend.'

'Vassily somethingvich, what was it?' fluttered Mrs Thurmond.

'Vassily Semionovich, prince Yousoupoff,' said Mrs Highsmith, with a sniff of superior knowledge. 'I have never understood exactly what is meant by a prince in Russia; they seem to have far too many of them.'

'Well, so do they here in France,' murmured

Mrs Thurmond. 'It seems to be something quite different from the sons of the King. I've never quite understood it.'

'Huh. Well, the title clearly does not carry the same weight in other countries as it does in England. Still, it is certainly a title, and Vassily Semionovich looked the part.'

'What was he like?' I enquired eagerly.

'Perfect manners, of course, but very reserved. He didn't speak much – and that little Mrs Granger never left his side. Her behaviour would have been positively shocking in London! But here in Paris we are used to seeing everything, and have lost all sense of surprise. At any rate, we exchanged only a few remarks, though I should certainly have liked to converse more with him. He wouldn't speak English with us, only French; he said his English was poor, although it was probably vanity disguised as modesty. He obviously came from a social class in which such things are learned as a matter of course. His French was delightful; the merest trace of an accent. He had been raised by a French governess, as so many of these young Russian nobles are.'

To my disappointment, this conversation essentially exhausted the ladies' store of information. I was eventually rescued by Mrs Hardwick from the dowagers' corner, and returned to Arthur's side; the Spanish girl had moved off to join a group of lugubrious-looking Spaniards dressed in black. Arthur was holding a glass of champagne; his third, as it appeared. He drew me close to him as I approached, and kissed my hair.

'Arthur!' I said, glancing around.

'Les dames et demoiselles pour être baisées devant leurs noces, il n'est pas la coutume de France?,' he began to quote teasingly, but snapped to attention as Mrs Hardwick bore down upon us. We were (a little grudgingly) allowed to remain together, but only on the unstated but clearly implied condition that we busy ourselves as much as possible with the gliding and sliding, fanning and circulating, and above all, chatting, chatting endlessly with an endless series of faces, all of which comes together to make a party end up being pronounced 'a great success'. I did try, while thus engaged, to bring up the subject of the mysterious Vassily Semionovich, prince Yousoupoff as often as I reasonably could, but few people possessed the accurate memory of Mr Hardwick, or the pointed interest in her fellow creatures of Mrs Hilton. I would have liked to approach the Russian diplomat, for I thought that he must have spoken to his countryman, but he had left early. The principal piece of information I obtained was a physical description several times confirmed; oh so vague, as a physical description of someone one has never seen must necessarily be, but still, a description which in no way contradicts that of the young man seen by Martha in Haverhill, and by other witnesses, no doubt, upon his way there. Of medium height, dark-haired, elegant and suave, he came here dressed in a billowing Russian blouse, clearly with a view to impress; exactly the kind of behaviour, in fact, which one would expect from the thumbnail sketch of the unknown young man in the vivid red cloak.

As the evening wore on, I confess that I thought progressively less and less about the romantic Russian prince. Indeed, I ceased to think at all after some time, and felt myself to be floating about the room, between the lights and candles, the *petits fours* and glasses of champagne on trays carried by silently gliding servants, and the unending swirl of conversation, followed later by music and dancing. After a certain hour, the more elderly members of the party appeared to have disappeared, and only those who had sufficient energy remained, but those had energy for twenty; speaking a medley of languages, dancing indefatigably and laughing a great deal, they made us feel quite gay and distracted, so that it was far after midnight before we finally took our leave. Mrs Hardwick shook my hand vigorously. I felt dizzy, exhausted and far too warm. She herself seemed absolutely unscathed by the evening's activities.

'Give my greetings to Eleanor and that silly daughter of hers,' were her last words as we took our departure.

There, I believe I have told you everything of importance; I hardly remember what I have written, but I shall read it all over carefully tomorrow morning before posting this. And now – I shall blow out this candle, and finally collapse into my bed!

Your most alarmingly tired

Vanessa

Paris, Sunday, July 10, 1892

My dearest sister,

My Russian prince appears to be evaporating, and I myself begin to feel lost in a quagmire of shifting sands! I must tell you what happened during my much-looked-forward-to visit with Mrs Clemming's friend Jane de la Brière.

As promised, I was introduced to her husband Monsieur de la Brière, his sister Victoire, and Victoire's husband, who bears the impressive title of le Baron de Vrille. I had no difficulty, after an ample dose of the usual society conversation on politics and the weather, in leading the two ladies around to the topic of Sylvia's shocking behaviour in the casino in Deauville, for Mrs de la Brière desired nothing more than to emit shocked criticism while listening to her sister-in-law recount the details of evenings spent in the casino. By her description, this casino is a place in which not only gambling takes place, but also dining, drinking, dancing and romantic promenades under false marble arches decorated with rather depressing palm trees in pots (in a desperate attempt to give an impression of being in Monte Carlo, even in the depths of winter – during which the palm trees are taken indoors).

The casino is frequented by all classes of society except the very poor, and even plays host to masked balls during which misbehaviour is a fully expected and recognised activity. On the night that Mme. de Vrille remembers encountering Sylvia, however, the casino had organised a public ball more classical in style, and she was not particularly surprised to encounter Sylvia; she knew her, for she had met her in Jane's drawing room, just as she was now meeting me. (I did wonder why this lady and her noble husband should deign to grace our humble society with their presence, which was obviously considered by all as something quite stellar, but eventually I was able to attribute this astonishing fact to something quite simple: the deep though quiet affection which unites Mme. de Vrille and her brother M. de la Brière, witnessed only by sundry small looks, smiles and gestures between the two.)

'I was not at all surprised to see little Mrs Granger at ze ball,' Mme. de Vrille told me with a very cosmopolitan smile, 'everybody goes zere, you should certainly visit eet yourself,' as though ladies travelling from England gravitated to the casino quite as a matter of course.

'Yet I heard that you found her behaviour surprising,' I said, with what I hoped was an easy smile denoting the complicity of extensive social experience, 'even you, who are used to the Parisian style of living.'

'Ah, her behaviour would have had nothing surprising in it for a lady of Paris!' she laughed. 'Many ladies of my acquaintance behave in quite the same way, yes, even married ones, and where ees the harm, if none ees meant? No, I was not *shocked*, as the British so often say. I was surprised, yes, I can certainly say I was surprised, not at the badness of her behaviour, thees makes me very much laugh, but because she seemed so different from the dull, quiet young lady I had met here in this house. She was quite a different person in Deauville.'

'Was she really? How did she seem, then?'

'Ah – she seemed so happy, so free. She danced and danced, her cheeks were flushed, her eyes were shining.'

I leaned forward, wondering how to justify the distressingly pointed questions I so longed to pose.

'And – is it true that she danced always with the same person?' I breathed, holding my fingers in front of my mouth, trying to look as though I had never heard of anything so shocking in my life, so as to stimulate her into more revelations calculated to horrify the staid English girl.

'Yes indeed, always with the same young man, and they took no pains to hide their deep interest in each other,' replied Mme. de Vrille, smiling at me benevolently, as though behind my (feigned) dismay, she detected a little envy, a longing to live such brilliant, exciting moments, and wished to satisfy me vicariously. 'When they were not dancing, I must admit it, they were always hand in hand.'

'Well I never,' said Mrs de la Brière with disgust. 'If I knew her mother as Alice Clemming does, I'd have written to her instantly. Such goings-on.'

'I heard that the young man was a Russian prince,' I said, directing my remarks confidentially to Mme. de Vrille. 'Do you know anything about him? Is it true?'

'A Russian prince?' she laughed, still with the same relaxed demeanour. 'I really do not think so! Certainly, the casino is full of Russians – what crazy people zey are, are zey not? Always gambling so madly. But I do not think that Sylvia's friend was a Russian (let alone a prince). Eet did not occur to me at the time. I spent an hour standing at the baccarat table, where he was playing between two Russians, and he spoke to them only in French. Indeed, I did believe zat he understood nothing of what they were saying, for zey appeared to be cheating mercilessly and he lost many times.'

I remained silent for several moments, confused, not sure what to think. Mme. de Vrille appeared to pity me, as she would a child who learns that fairies do not really exist.

'I really cannot believe he was a Russian prince,' she said. 'Yet who knows, my dear. Perhaps he was, and did not wish to show eet. Eet did not seem elegant, perhaps, to communicate with the cheaters at gambling. Perhaps he preferred only to speak to his beloved of wild steppes and sleighs drawn over the snow by white wolves,' she said. *'Après tout, ou est le mal?'*

'Well, she took him to another party where there were real Russians,' I said, thinking of Mr Grigoriev. I paused, recalling Mrs Hardwick's diplomatic party – could it be thought for a single instant that a young man announcing himself as Russian could have avoided being thrust together with Mr Grigoriev for forced conversation within two minutes of his arrival? No, they must have encountered each other there, and Mr Grigoriev

253

would know whether or not he was Russian. I made an urgent mental note to make an appointment with him, wondering why I had not thought of it before, and leaving the invention of the excuses I should have to make for such odd behaviour to a more propitious moment.

'What was his French like?' I asked. 'Sometimes one can recognise a person's nationality by his accent in a foreign language.'

'His French was excellent,' she answered. 'Yet I did notice a slight trace of something foreign, but eet was not a typically Russian accent. Eet was very faint; I could not identify it. But he told me that he had spent all his school years in France. Such a long time spent in the country during youth does much to erase the accent, does eet not? Indeed, a long time in a foreign country often has a strange effect on the mother tongue, I have noticed. Eet makes eet difficult, sometimes, to guess from where a person comes. Have you not noticed, for example, that Jane, for instance, bears a little trace of the French sound in her English?'

It was true, although I had not attributed her slight vocal peculiarity to the constant effect of a foreign language upon the ears, but (I admit) to a conscious effort to pose. However, it is undeniable that the ladies I have spoken to since I have been here all have some little oddities of language borrowed from the French, or at the very least, are heard to occasionally use English expressions which were the fashion of many years ago but which have been replaced by quite different terms since then.

'You did not catch the young man's name by any chance?' I asked, and then added, 'A name is certainly indicative of nationality, though of course it can be invented for the occasion!'

'No, the casino is not a place where people decline their identities,' she said. I smiled at the word 'decline', but I was most impressed by her English, really – if only my French were half as good!

Mme. de Vrille could not supply any further details about the anonymous young man; she had told me all she knew, and could not even suggest a source of further information. Indeed, she said that he had shown himself very reserved during the evening, concentrating most of his attention on Sylvia, and the remainder on the outcome of the baccarat.

I ruminated over her information in silence, wondering what I could do with it. I asked myself if I might not, daringly, confront Sylvia with all this and ask for an explanation, but it seemed premature; she would most probably answer that she had struck up a casual acquaintance with a young gentleman while in Paris and allowed him to accompany her hither and thither on occasion, nothing further.

And of course, this could also be the simple truth of the matter. Why is it that my mind is so firmly fixed on the idea that this man and no other is the author of Mr Granger's untimely death?

There is the matter of his description, which agrees with that of the murderer; then the matter of Sylvia's publicly observed behaviour with him, which goes far beyond a casual attachment. The main problem is now to find and identify him. I determined to pay a visit to Mr Grigoriev at the earliest opportunity, and applied myself to pushing my sulky frown to the inner depths of my being, and behaving as sociably as possible for the remainder of the visit, winning the good will of Mrs de la Brière in response to the respectful deference I displayed to the titled members of her family.

The visit over, I returned to the hotel with a heavy step, eager to talk with Arthur and ask his advice on what I had learned. It was a relief to pour out my heart, and a balm to feel the warm expression of his sympathy, in spite of the deep reservations I knew he held about the whole operation.

'Now, let's be methodical,' he said. 'After all, that's what one does in mathematics when one observes a surprising and seemingly inexplicable phenomenon. If one cannot find the explanation straightaway, one tries out examples, in order to show up either a contradiction or a general rule. Now, first of all, how can you be sure that there was only one young man? Perhaps there was a Russian one at the Hardwicks, and another one in Deauville.'

'Oh, no,' I cried, 'I cannot believe that! Sylvia is not so light – and the descriptions concur.'

'All right. Then let us temporarily make the assumption that there really was only one. The thing to do is to discover as many people as you can who saw them together, and ask them about him.'

'That is exactly what I have been doing,' I argued. 'But I am at something of a dead end. People describe him briefly, and then they know nothing further about him. I haven't even been able to find out whether or not he was really Russian – but I'm inclined to believe he can't have been, for those silly old ladies at the Hardwicks must have been very easy to take in by anyone who amused himself by posing with a fancy name like "Prince Yousoupoff", while the baroness is no fool. Still, Mr Grigoriev may hold the key to this question, although I hardly dare to hope.'

'You should be careful, Vanessa,' he said suddenly. 'What you are doing really could be dangerous. What if the man learns somehow that you are making enquiries about him?'

'How could he? Who would tell him? Nobody that I have spoken to appears to know him.'

'So far.'

'But you know, I don't really ask questions about him directly,' I said. 'I don't think it can really be so noticeable that I am trying to find out about him. I mean, I do always talk about ever so many other things all around it, and disguise my interest as mere curiosity about a friend.' (Dora, this is true, do believe me! I simply leave out all the nonsensical conversation about the weather and the state of the world, and the differences between the English and the French, when I write to you – for when I write to *you*, in a way, I am writing to myself also; organising my thoughts, reflecting, reasoning and clarifying. And asking for your help, also, of course, whenever you feel you have any to give me.) 'But still,' Arthur insisted, 'what if it gets back to Sylvia that you have heard about him, and she tells him?'

We were both silent for a moment.

'Let me go and see Mr Grigoriev for you,' said Arthur finally.

'Oh!' I said. 'But I must talk with him. I must at least come with you.'

'No,' he said. 'Believe me, I can find out what he knows. I would rather you didn't come. This way, if any news does get back to the fellow, it will be that a gentleman is asking about him, and your presence in the matter will not be known. You shall brief me, as they say, and tell me exactly what you would like me to ask him, and I shall do my best to succeed.'

'But you won't be able to tell me what he says properly,' I moaned. 'Men never can repeat a conversation.'

'Don't be so difficult,' he said, a little crossly, as though I were casting doubt upon his capacities. 'After all, your main point is just to learn whether or not he was really Russian, and whether Mr Grigoriev can give you any further information about his identity or whereabouts. Surely I can accomplish that task for you without needing to render it as a theatre play!'

I was compelled to be satisfied with this. Tomorrow Arthur will go to make an appointment with Mr Grigoriev, and as soon as he has been there, I shall tell you everything about it. I cannot deny that I am worried. Extremely worried. Sometimes I have the impression of discovering nothing at all – and at other moments, I feel as though a sinister net were closing in, whether on the murderer or on myself I cannot say.

Your loving twin,

Vanessa

Paris, Monday, July 11, 1892

Dearest Dora,

Annabel and I were awoken this morning by an unexpected commotion in the hall. Raising our sleepy heads from the pillow, we soon determined that a great knocking was going on, not at our door, but very nearby.

'Good Heavens, whatever can that be?' I said.

Without answer, Annabel slipped out of bed and padded across the floor to the door, which she opened a tiny crack.

'Why, it's Mr Korneck!' she exclaimed in surprise, shutting the door hastily and turning to face me.

'Oh my goodness, what time is it? What can he possibly want at this hour,' I gasped, reaching for my watch which lay on the bedside table. 'Oh me, it's eight o'clock. Where did the night go?'

'Whatever it is, I don't think he needs to see us girls about it,' said Annabel. 'Since we're awake, let us dress and go down for breakfast. Perhaps we'll see the others and find out what's happening. What a lovely day it is,' she added, drawing the curtains.

We dressed and descended together, and seated

ourselves in one corner of a table for four in the hotel's pretty breakfast salon. The windows of the large room look onto the rue de Rivoli below. A very few other guests were scattered about, and a young girl in black with a white apron was sweeping the floor and setting out dishes and cups upon the tables.

'*Oui mesdemoiselles? Qu'est-ce que je vous sers?*' she said, stopping abruptly in front of us.

'*Du café noir, s'il vous plaît, et des croissants,*' I replied. Dora dear, if I can be said to have learned a single French sentence during my stay here, but really learned, never to forget, this one is certainly it.

We poured out our coffee and began breakfast in silence. I wished very much to broach a certain subject with Annabel, but could not think how to begin, especially as she appeared lost in thought. She stirred, however, after some time, and smiled at me.

'Ah, I am beginning to feel awake,' she said. 'Let us make our plans for the day; do you have any more visits to make?'

'Only one today, but Arthur has said that he will take care of it for me, and it is merely to make an appointment, unless by chance the gentleman can receive him at once.'

'Really?' she said in surprise. 'Are you sending Arthur to keep the appointment for you? Oh, Vanessa – how *can* you involve him?' She stopped for a moment, then continued, speaking very low. 'Sometimes I wonder how you can even involve yourself in such a task. Oh, even though you never mention it to me, I know you are trying to find out who murdered that Mr Granger, and I think about it sometimes; a man who stood in front of another, pointing a gun, and pulled the trigger, and walked away, leaving him lying dead! It is such a frightful thing, I cannot even bear to think about it – and you are investigating it! I tell myself that what you are doing is surely right and necessary, but I cannot understand *why* you undertake it all – what makes you do it? Oh, how can you face it all? The risk, and the danger, and the horror of meeting a killer face to face!'

I said nothing. Meeting a killer face to face – it is a horrible image indeed! But for the moment, I find myself utterly unable to put a realistic face upon that anonymous killer, and literally imagine myself standing in front of him.

But there are other eyes ... Sylvia's, which I remember only too well looking into mine, filled with a mixture of naïveté and fear, troubled and confiding. She asked me for help with something of the absoluteness of a child, and I have no power within me to turn away from such a plea. All the more because Sylvia herself is but vaguely aware of the very real danger which threatens her; her innocence has cast a kind of veil in front of her eyes for which she only dimly perceives the inexorably approaching horrors of arrest, trial, noose... I do not know exactly why I undertook this investigation in the beginning, but I know why I am doing it now.

I found that I could not express these feelings and images to Annabel, and continued silent. Leaning towards me, she spoke again, urgently.

'Oh Vanessa, I feel certain that you should not

involve poor Arthur, whose only desire would be to remain distant from all such things. Something pure may be destroyed; should you not protect it?'

Her words strangely reflected my thoughts.

'Something pure may have to be destroyed in order to protect something else pure,' I said slowly. 'For what concerns Arthur, it is he who insisted on going; with distaste, I know it, but he wanted it this way, and I trust him. Perhaps it is true that he would prefer to remain distant from it all, and yet I believe that such a thing is impossible. What I am doing is not horrible – or perhaps it is, but in the same way as the human condition itself, the realities of life and death and mortal illness. Doctors and surgeons cannot avoid these things, and we are grateful enough that they exist. As for meeting the murderer, I do not feel a sense of intrinsic revulsion; he is a human being, with a black sin on his soul, but am I such an angel myself as to shudder away at the sight of him? I would certainly feel terrified if I believed that he was actively seeking to prevent me from investigating, but that is another question. At the moment, he seems such a hazy creature that I cannot convince myself that such a menace is a serious thing. No, there is something that troubles and disturbs me more deeply than I can say, but it is not that; it is the idea that were I truly to discover and identify the murderer, and deliver him to the police – then, then I should then be responsible for his fate, and that would be a dreadful weight to bear. That is what torments me the most, Annabel! I do not know how to face up to it, and can only continue on the optimistic assumption that the case may never occur.'

'Never occur? But surely you do not expect to fail!'

'I do not feel at all confident of success. I have been singularly useless up to now, I find. But there are other possibilities; the police may discover the solution soon, the murderer may give himself up; it may also happen that I somehow believe I have discovered the truth and yet have no proofs that would allow the police to act. It is not desirable, yet it might happen. I do not want to send anyone to the gallows, Annabel! My situation is like that of an unwilling witness to a crime, who must, perhaps, then testify. And I know that a person who has killed successfully once may well kill again, and if I kept silent, I should be partly guilty of those other deaths.'

'The task is so difficult that it cannot be done to anyone's satisfaction,' said Annabel with a little sigh. 'I do not know how you can undertake it – but then, I have so few capacities myself that I can certainly not give anyone lessons on how to behave. If I could only use the miserable talents I possess to advantage, that is all I would ask.'

My ears perked up, and I hastened to distance myself from the previous topic, which evokes murky movements deep within a black, viscous pool.

'What would you like to do, then, in your life?' I asked quickly.

'Oh, you will think it very stupid – you have so many ideas and are always so busy; I envy you, but all I really want is a home with, with someone

I love heart and soul, and children to raise.'

'That is what I want, too,' I said, smiling. 'It may be banal, but it is beautiful, isn't it? Everything else I do is just to while away the time of waiting.' Even as I spoke, I knew that I was not convinced of what I was saying. Annabel pounced on it.

'Oh, you may think that, but I know it isn't true!' she said. 'You'll be engaged in a hundred things all your life, teaching and planning and investigating and travelling! You put vital energy into what you do – that's why I can't believe it's just whiling the time away. And even if it is, at least you have only a certain amount of time to while away – you know your future – you know that you will eventually possess what you want. Whereas I...'

'You know what you want, but not whether you will ever have it,' I heard myself announce suddenly and quite unexpectedly. She glanced up at me quickly.

'Yes, that is true,' she said simply.

'I know it now,' I murmured, 'but it took me a long time to realise it. Now, Annabel, tell me: what are you going to do about it?'

'Nothing,' she said, with something of Sylvia's stubborn passivity in her tone.

'No! That's not a recipe for success!' I countered energetically.

'Oh, success, do you think I hope for success?' she said. 'I cannot stretch out my hand to grasp for that which resists.'

'But are you sure it resists?' I asked, remembering how Charles' face lit up at the sight of her.

'It does not come of itself,' she said simply.

Oh, how impatient I feel with such people! I felt greatly tempted to argue at length, but knew that it would be useless if not counterproductive, so I resolved instead to speak to Charles at the first opportunity, and at least try to detect whether it was worth Annabel entertaining any hope at all, or whether it would be better for her to renounce all at once, and start afresh.

Just as I was pondering upon this, and trying to imagine how I could raise the subject with him, I heard his cheery voice raised in the hall, and he entered the breakfast room with Arthur and Mr Korneck in tow.

They joined us at the table, pulling up an extra chair, and Charles ordered a new pot of coffee, but Mr Korneck interrupted him to ask the young girl to bring out a pitcher of freshly pressed juice, eggs for everyone, a large piece of cheese and an assortment of varied Viennese pastries. Radiant with delight, he beamed upon us all around.

'Just look at the man,' said Charles, sitting comfortably in one of the wicker chairs, and serving himself generously of all that the waitress provided. 'He's beyond himself with glee, girls – he claims to have proved the great result! Can you believe it?'

'Is it true?' I gasped, dumbfounded. Indeed, I realised only at that moment that in spite of all his optimism, I had lent no credence at all to the idea that Korneck was on his way to a true and valid proof of the famous theorem!

'I can't tell you,' responded Charles gaily. 'He won't show it to us – he's keeping it all a secret!

I haven't seen a line of it, and he's submitted it formally to the Academy already; he sprung the *fait accompli* on us this morning, fresh from the post office!'

'I still think it might have been better to let simple folks like us have a look at it, before sending it off to Mount Parnassus,' mumbled Arthur through a *pain au chocolat*.

'But I have checked each and every line of it – I am certain of success!' beamed Mr Korneck. 'It is not difficult, my friends; I have done nothing, nothing that Fermat or Germain themselves could not have done. It is long, yes, I will admit that it is long.'

'How long?' I enquired with interest.

'One hundred pages or so,' he said with a sigh. 'I wish it could have been shorter. I did not imagine Fermat's proof to have been so long. But each step appears to be necessary, and I took the time to explain as fully as possible, perhaps too fully; perhaps I wrote too many trivial things.'

'Well, at a hundred pages, it certainly was not likely to have fit within a margin,' I exclaimed.

'The proof Fermat had in his head must surely have been shorter. But perhaps the main ideas were the same, and there are shortcuts I did not see. Or, perhaps, if he had written his entire proof down with care, it would have become quite long. But Fermat almost never wrote things down completely. He very much preferred to give hints and riddles, and he wrote many letters to his colleagues with – how do you say *pari* – with a bet that they would be unable to prove the results he had discovered in secret. Must it not have been very terrible for them?'

'I do hope he hasn't bungled,' whispered Charles discreetly into my ear. 'One doesn't like to insist on seeing the thing, you know – it'd look so like one wanted to make off with it or something. Still, it would have been better...' Catching Mr Korneck's eye, he continued in a normal voice,

'So it will be read by some reviewers now, and then discussed in front of the Academy. That's glory for you!'

Mr Korneck was glowing with sheer happiness, and insisted on taking us all off for the afternoon on a remarkable sight-seeing tour, the last part of which consisted of a heartstoppingly beautiful boat-ride down the Seine on a floating restaurant. We dined in luxury upon duck with orange sauce, with a delicious wine selected after interminable discussion with the obsequiously polite waiter, and followed by a *charlotte aux fraises* which melted upon the tongue. The lights over our heads twinkled up at us from the water's rippled surface, and the sky was shot with magical hues of pink moving continuously into the deepest blue. I had never been in any place so utterly romantic, and I saw the reflection of my own quivering heart in the eyes of three of my four companions, while Mr Korneck radiated a satisfaction and pleasure delightful to bask in.

It was a lovely, lovely day. I shall never forget it.

Your very own,

Vanessa

PS. In the heat of all this, I forgot to tell you that Arthur managed to make a brief stop at the Imperial Russian Embassy, in the rue de Grenelle, while we waited for him below – Annabel biting her fingernails nervously while I studiedly pretended to ignore it – and he has obtained an appointment with Mr Grigoriev for tomorrow. Perhaps, oh perhaps we shall finally discover something worthwhile.

Paris, Tuesday, July 12, 1892

My dearest sister,

'The man exists!' were Arthur's first words, upon returning from his meeting with Mr Grigoriev and knocking on the door of my hotel room – from which I had not budged an inch during the whole time of anxiously awaiting him.

'What do you mean? Who exists?' I exclaimed, jumping to my feet.

'Why, that Prince Yousoupoff. He is a real person after all; Mr Grigoriev knows him. He even provided me with his personal address. He lives with a whole Russian household of servants, at an *hôtel particulier* privately rented from an aristocratic family in dire financial straits, in the rue de Varenne.'

I stared at Arthur, dumbfounded, and digested this totally unexpected piece of information in silence. I could not think what to make of it. A rich and distinguished Russian prince, living in the heart of aristocratic Paris, rushing across the

Channel to shoot a wealthy middle-aged businessman for love of Sylvia? It sounded perfectly absurd – yet on the other hand, do not Russians constantly murder each other for love? To be sure, Mme. de Vrille had told me that she was hardly sure the young man was Russian, let alone a rich, distinguished and well-known prince – but perhaps she was quite simply mistaken. Impulsively, I gathered my things together.

'What are you doing?' said Arthur suspiciously. 'Not intending to rush off to the rue de Varenne, are you?'

'Well, yes,' I said, 'at least–'

'No, Vanessa, you are not going to go and converse with a murderer, and certainly not without careful reflection beforehand. I would like to know what you intend to ask him. How do you mean to begin?'

'Oh, well – I wouldn't speak to him, I think. I would like to see the house; perhaps he would go in or come out, and then, one might say something to the servants...' I said feebly.

'Certainly not alone,' he said firmly. 'But before you go rushing off so hot-headedly, don't you want me to tell you about my meeting with Mr Grigoriev?'

'Yes, of course,' I said, sitting down again and berating myself secretly.

'The really important thing I have to tell you is that Mr Grigoriev was not at Mr Hardwick's party that famous night,' he began.

'Oh!' I said, taken aback. 'Then how–'

'Why, I told him the name, quite simply,' Arthur told me. 'I said his name was Vassily

269

Semionovich Yousoupoff, and he said "Yousoupoff, why of course, Vassily Trofimovich, not
Semionovich, actually". He is acquainted with
him, he said, though he never encountered him
at Mr Hardwick's. But he said that it is certainly
not impossible that he accompanied a young lady
there. He is a single man and very rich; he also
travels regularly to Deauville. So perhaps the lady
who told you Sylvia's friend didn't seem Russian
was wrong after all.'

'Oh, Arthur, what shall we *do?* What if we do
manage to see this prince – then what?'

'Then we would need to identify him as the
person who accompanied Sylvia,' he said.

'We could ask Mme. de Vrille, though it might
be a little awkward,' I said. 'We might have to. But
there is someone else who might be useful. Mr
Grigoriev told me that as he cannot always attend
all the diplomatic *soirées* he is invited to, he has a
colleague who acts as his deputy on occasion, and
it is most likely that his colleague was there on the
night we are talking about, and saw the prince. I
have his name, too: Michael Oblonsky, to be
contacted at the Russian Embassy as well, right
there in the rue de Grenelle.'

'Oh Arthur, I do hate to ask you to accompany
me, but I *must* go and see both the prince and
this Mr Oblonsky, and I know you won't want
me to go alone!' I said anxiously, dying with
impatience to be off.

'Of course I shall come with you,' he said, 'and
I want you to remain as invisible as possible when
we observe Yousoupoff's home. Shall we go there
first?'

I consulted my map of Paris hastily.

'Yes, let us – rue de Varenne is not a long walk from here,' I said. 'We need to cross the Seine – do let us go now!'

'He may be out, or it may be simply impossible to enter his place or talk with anyone,' he said. 'Let us not expect too much from all this. And even if we saw him, there is not a lot we could conclude at once. He will not look like a murderer, I take it, and in any case we had better not jump to conclusions. Yes, yes, I am coming,' and he held the door for me just as I was about to swing it open myself with a gesture indicative of my nervous state of mind.

The walk to the rue de Varenne was a silent one. I held Arthur's arm closely and reflected upon a great number of things that are really not worth the retelling. When we arrived in the rue de Varenne, Arthur stopped to look about.

'Look at these homes,' he said, 'all these gracious buildings belonging to aristocratic families; no poor people ever set foot here, I'll wager, unless it be the servants.'

We stopped at the house which, according to Mr Grigoriev, was the one presently rented by Prince Yousoupoff, and peered through the *porte cochère*, the great arched opening, large enough to admit a coach and four, which was the only means by which the house gave onto the street. Through it, we perceived a paved or cobbled courtyard, surrounded by the three wings of a stone building of fair proportions, pierced with enormous arched windows. Nobody appeared to be about. We edged a small way in, but Arthur

271

appeared nervous.

'What shall we do?' he whispered.

'We can hardly simply go up and knock at the door, at least not without some story,' I said. 'Shall we wait a while and see if anybody comes out?'

'Well, let us walk down the street,' he said. 'We'll try to stay in sight of the place, but we could also keep an eye out for the nearest café and ask some questions there.'

We walked down the street very slowly, and rounded the corner. There, we came upon an awning stretched over the wide sidewalk, underneath which a tiny lane formed by large green trees in pots led up to the glass door of a restaurant called *Chez Victor*.

'Here's a place,' said Arthur.

'Yes, but it isn't a café,' I said, 'it's a very chic restaurant. Good heavens, they must serve a lovely supper. No, don't!' I added, as Arthur walked up to the glass door and pressed his forehead against it, shading his eyes to avoid the reflection and peering indiscreetly within. The door opened immediately, and a young boy in livery popped out his head.

'*Le restaurant est fermé, Monsieur,*' he said courteously.

'Of course,' said Arthur hastily.

'Ah, you are Engleesh. Can I inform you?' the youth said, his face lighting up with pleasure at the opportunity to practice his linguistic talents. 'I have worked in London some months. Eet ees very beautiful.'

'Indeed, yes,' replied Arthur with alacrity. 'Paris

is very beautiful too. We like this street.'

'Very important people live here, and dine here,' said the boy proudly, giving us exactly the entry we most desired.

'Yes, indeed they must! We heard about a Russian prince.'

'*Oui, oui,* a Russian prince there is with many, many servants, all Russian, and two white dogs, very big.'

'Does he also dine here?' Arthur said.

'Certainly, on occasion.'

'What does he look like?'

'The Russian monsieur is very distinguished, very tall, very elegant.'

I tapped my toes impatiently on the sidewalk and burst in, 'Black hair?'

He glanced up at me, surprised at my sudden intervention, but seemed just about to answer, when alas, a sharp cry of *'Jacquot! Eh, Jacquot!'* was heard from within the restaurant, and he turned to flee. I gave a little yelp of annoyance, but at that precise moment, the sound of smartly trotting hooves became audible, and a carriage came down the street toward us and turned the corner into the rue de Varenne. Jacques glanced back.

'Ah – zat ees he, zat ees ze prince!' he said. 'Please – enjoy your stay in Paris very much!' and he disappeared into the dark interior and closed the door behind him.

'Quick!' said Arthur, snatching my hand, and we half walked, half trotted as quickly as our legs would carry us around the corner and back towards the Yousoupoff residence. The carriage had already pulled up in front of the *porte cochère* and the footman had jumped down and was in the process of opening the door. We slowed to a snail's pace as we approached and Arthur's hand tightened on mine. I thought – are we going to set eyes on a murderer? but I felt no sense of reality. The footman gave his arm to the occupant of the carriage, and slowly, a leg emerged, followed by a hand with a cane, and finally the whole gentleman appeared and stood straight and noble upon the sidewalk.

'*Spasibo*, Ivan,' he said. Arthur and I remained staring at him in blank amazement. Although certainly tall, elegant and distinguished, the gentleman who stood in front of us also possessed a shock of white hair and bristling, beetling eyebrows over sharp, deep-set black eyes. Still on the arm of his footman, and leaning upon his cane, he turned and walked slowly under the archway and into the courtyard.

'Why, he's an old man!' I gasped.

'It's the wrong person,' said Arthur.

'It must be, if it really is the prince – but perhaps it's someone else. Couldn't it be?'

With impressive daring, Arthur darted up to the coachman, who was turning the carriage preparatory to guiding it through the arch after the prince.

'Prince Yousoupoff?' he asked him, pointing in.

Instead of answering, the coachman leaned under the arch and shouted something in Russian after the disappearing backs; it sounded like '*Vashe velitchestvo, vashe velitchestvo!*' They turned back toward him, and he pointed to Arthur and

274

gabbled in Russian. It was horribly unexpected and most embarrassing. I cringed secretly, and Arthur must surely have cringed as well. He showed no sign, however, and smiled engagingly as the prince returned towards him with a look of distinguished annoyance in the sharp eyes under their bristling brushes.

'I am so very sorry to trouble you,' said Arthur, reverting to English and inventing rapidly. 'I – I am a British journalist, and I am writing a report on – on the Russian community in Paris. I have spoken to Mr Grigoriev from the Imperial Russian Embassy; he told me that Prince Yousoupoff lived here, and I wished to humbly request an interview.'

'I am prince Yousoupoff,' said the gentleman with extreme coldness and excellent English, 'and I am not interested. I beg you will depart and leave me in peace at once.'

'Oh, ah!' said Arthur. 'But – please do excuse my rudeness – I must have made a mistake. Mr Grigoriev thought he was sending me to visit someone who would be interested in an interview, but – perhaps I have got the name wrong – the description he gave me did not seem to correspond to you at all. He spoke to me of a young man with black hair. Would you know of such a person with a name similar to yours? Your son, perhaps?'

'There is no such person,' said Prince Yousoupoff with contempt. 'Please cease to trouble me.' He turned away and, leaning on his cane, returned a second time to the interior courtyard, crossed it, and entered the building without a backward look. The coachman threw us a glance of disgust and trotted in after him. Arthur joined me with a sigh.

'What a fool I feel,' he said grumpily.

'What lies you told about Mr Grigoriev,' I said. 'I do hope they do not get him into trouble.'

'Bah, even if they do, we will be long gone,' he said.

'Well, but what if this awful prince has him recalled to Russia in disgrace?'

We looked at each other in dismay.

'Well, let us not be pessimistic,' I said finally. 'That unpleasant old gentleman has probably forgotten about us already. But Arthur – he is obviously not the right person! What can it mean?'

'Well, we still have one more hope; we must go to see Mr Grigoriev's colleague Michael Oblonsky. Come along, we are not too far from the rue de Grenelle now.'

We walked there, but it was not really so very near, and we found the doors locked and barred upon our arrival.

'Bother!' said Arthur. 'We'll come back tomorrow. Let's have supper.'

'*Chez Victor?*' I proposed hopefully.

'Certainly not! Please, Vanessa, do let's stop hunting non-existent Russian princes for the remainder of the evening.'

I was about to protest indignantly – I am really too tenacious and single-minded – when I noticed his brown eyes fixed intensely upon me, and I was suddenly seized with a desire to forget it all, as he said – to slip away, and join him in his dreamy world where ideas count for so much more than deeds, poetry than facts, and symbols than words.

'Then you take me somewhere,' I said softly, putting his arm around my shoulder. The rest of the evening bears no relation whatsoever to the mystery I am supposed to be attempting to elucidate.

But tomorrow – tomorrow we shall return to our task!

Your loving twin,

Vanessa

Paris, Wednesday, July 13, 1892

Dear Dora,

Let me waste no time, but recount the result of our visit to the Russian Embassy at once.

We arose and proceeded there quite early, and found the doors unlocked and the place bustling with business, but we were told that Mr Oblonsky would not arrive until shortly before midday. I was about to turn away, but Arthur leaned over the burnished desk behind which a charming blonde girl called Natalia was shuffling papers, and smiling at her, he said,

'We will wait for him. But perhaps you could help us with some information in the meantime.'

'*Ya ne ponimayu, je ne comprends pas bien l'anglais,*' she said hesitatingly.

Arthur attempted a strange mixture of French

and English.

'Do you know Prince Yousoupoff? *Le Prince Yousoupoff?*' he began.

'Ah yes yes. I know,' she said, smiling with the pleasure of being able to comprehend and communicate.

'Is he a young man? *Jeune?* With black hair? *Noir?*' he added, pointing to his own head as the word for hair escaped him.

'Ah no no no,' said Natalia, with a big smile. '*C'est un vieux monsieur,* he very old.'

'He does not have a son?'

'Son?' she said blankly. 'Sun?'

'*Un fils,*' I intervened awkwardly, wishing that Annabel were with us.

'*Non, non.* He has no family; he is alone.'

'Do you know a young man called Vassily Semionovich?'

'Vassily Semionovich?' Her face lit up with delight. 'Yes, yes, Vassily Semionovich. Come, come.' Arising from her chair, Natalia led us down a corridor and before we could emit the slightest objection, she knocked smartly upon a door, and opening it, she proceeded to direct a flow of Russian at the gentleman within. He emerged to greet us. Fortunately, his English was a great deal better than hers.

Arthur and I stared at him with some doubt. Certainly he was a young man, and his hair was very dark and curly, but without being fat, it must be admitted that he was rather plump and somewhat short. His name, written neatly on a card pinned to the door, appeared to be Vassily Semionovich Kropoff.

'Can I help you?' he enquired politely. The moment was awkward, although not so bad as with Prince Yousoupoff. Still, it was quite difficult to think of what to say. Even Arthur appeared to be at a loss.

'We are looking for a friend of a friend of mine in England,' I said. 'His name is Vassily Semionovich, but unfortunately, we simply cannot remember his last name.'

'I do not believe I have friends in England,' he remarked. 'What is the name of your friend?'

Arthur trod heavily on my toe, but it seemed too late to change tactic.

'Sylvia Granger,' I said, moving my foot out of his reach. 'She visited Paris last winter and spoke to us of her charming Russian friend.'

His face remained absolutely blank.

'I am so very sorry,' he said. 'I am not familiar with this name.'

'Her friend accompanied her to a party given by Mr and Mr Hardwick of the British Embassy,' I said.

'Ah, how nice. But it was not I,' he answered. 'I have not the duty to attend the British parties. That would be Grigoriev or Oblonsky. My duties are the smaller countries. I attend the parties of the embassies of Belgium and Denmark and Luxemburg.'

It seemed pointless to continue, so we excused ourselves for our error and bid him goodbye. As soon as we rounded the corner of the corridor, Arthur turned upon me furiously.

'V-V-V-Vanessa,' he said, speaking with difficulty, so upset was he, 'are you absolutely out of your mind? What if he is the one! You c-can't just go around mentioning Sylvia that way! If he killed Granger, he'll know what's up at once, and we'll be in horrendous trouble!'

His words stabbed a little dart of fear inside me. I hadn't thought–

'It isn't he, I'm sure of it,' I said quickly. 'He's too fat, don't you think? Nobody mentioned that to me. In fact that old lady at Mr Hardwick's party said he was romantic-looking and a sensation.'

'That doesn't mean a thing! A f-fake title and smooth manners can go a very long way to cover up a p-p-potbelly, especially for some foolish old lady with nothing to do! Or maybe he became fat since.'

I took Arthur's hand, and found to my surprise that it was shaking.

'Arthur! You don't seriously think... You do!' I cried in disbelief.

'Vanessa, it might be.'

I was about to state the obvious, viz. that Sylvia could not possibly have fallen in love with a young fellow who was short, chubby and somewhat moon-faced, and that all the ladies who had described him to us would not have failed to mention those particulars if they had existed. But it crossed my mind that women have adored far uglier men than poor Mr Kropoff, and I began to wonder ... in the glamorous atmosphere of a party or a casino, dressed differently...

The foolishness of the step I had taken was borne in upon me. I was about to say that it was all Arthur's fault for having broached the whole subject so abruptly with Natalia to begin with, but it seemed to be the wrong moment for mutual accusations. Instead, I said feebly,

'He surely has no idea who we are. Oh, Arthur, perhaps we had better just leave at once.'

'We can leave, but we *must* come back. Oblonsky may know something that can solve the problem once and for all,' he replied, but he took my arm and we slipped quickly out of the main door of the building onto the street. Suddenly, he hesitated, poked his head quickly back inside, and addressed himself to Natalia, who was calmly seated behind her desk again.

'Monsieur Oblonsky, what is he like?' he asked her.

'Is like?'

'Big, small, young, old, *grand, petit, jeune?*'

'Ah! *Pas vieux, pas jeune. Pas de cheveux,*' she said, passing her hand over her own thick blonde braids. 'Nothing here.' She smiled hopefully.

'All right. Thank you *so* much,' said Arthur, as he shut the door hastily behind us and darted down the stairs. He glanced up anxiously at the windows of the embassy and then pulled me into a café across the street.

'We'll keep an eye on everyone going in,' he said, 'and try to catch him outside. That Kropoff fellow's windows don't look out this way. Surely Oblonsky will arrive within the next hour; it's eleven now.'

We sat down at a small table near the window and ordered *café crème*. These having arrived, we stirred them (I enjoyed mine in spite of everything, I am not so sure about Arthur) and waited, watching the door across the street. A few people went in or came out, but for some time we saw no one who appeared sufficiently bald to be our man. However, after more than an hour, when we were almost ready either to give up altogether or to return inside and question Natalia, a likely prospect suddenly appeared upon the steps leading up to the door! I scampered outside quick as lightning to stop him before he entered the building.

'Excuse me,' I said breathlessly, chasing him up the stairs. He turned around with some surprise.

'Are you Mr Oblonsky?' I asked, trying not to breathe noisily; my sudden lack of air was surely more a consequence of emotion than of running.

'Yes I am,' he replied politely. 'And you are?'

Another awkward moment! Should I give my name, only to have Kropoff eventually find it out and pursue me? I gulped.

'My name is Miss Case,' I said using the first word that came into my head. 'I am so sorry to disturb you, and do hope you are not in a hurry. I should be most grateful for just a few minutes private conversation with you in the café across the street, where I have been waiting for you with a friend. Mr Grigoriev advised us to speak with you,' I added, seeing his face grow dark with suspicion and surprise.

'What is this about?' he enquired, without moving.

'Oh, it is just a little thing,' I said with my most winning smile. 'We are trying to locate a young man whom we have reason to believe that you once encountered at a party given by a friend of ours.'

'His name?'

'I would really rather talk about it in the café,' I insisted, a little fearfully. At that moment something most awful happened. The main door of the Embassy flew open cheerfully, and the man who emerged was no other than Vassily Semionovich Kropoff himself. My heart lurched as he stopped to greet me, with a smile that may or may not have contained a leer.

'What is the name of the man you seek?' insisted Oblonsky.

'Ah, you are still looking for him?' smiled Kropoff with a friendly air. 'They are looking for someone called Vassily Semionovich, can you imagine? Natalia brought them to me, but I cannot give satisfaction, I am afraid. It is I who told them to address themselves to you,' he added, turning to Oblonsky and speaking to him in English for my benefit. 'The man they want attended one of the Hardwick parties.'

It seemed more and more inconceivable to me that this man could be the murderer, and my heartbeat slowed down considerably.

'Grigoriev goes to most of those, I haven't been to one for months,' said Oblonsky.

At this point, Arthur, who had spotted what was going on from the café window and hastily paid for the coffee, joined us and put his hand protectively upon my shoulder.

'This was a party last January or February,' I told him, abandoning all pretence at discretion. 'We already asked Mr Grigoriev and he doesn't seem to have attended that particular party, so he supposed you must have been there. What happened there is that a friend of mine, an English girl called Sylvia Granger, came to the party unexpectedly with a young man who called himself Vassily Semionovich Yousoupoff and claimed to be a prince. We thought that surely, as a Russian, he would have been introduced to you.'

'Ah, of course! The Russian prince! Yes, indeed – I remember him perfectly,' cried Mr Oblonsky, throwing back his head and laughing loudly. Arthur glanced at me and I saw that like mine, his suspicion of Kropoff had just gone up in smoke. Somewhere, this may have been a disappointment, but I assure you, Dora dear, that it was first and foremost an immense relief!

'Well, I did say I would keep the secret,' smiled Oblonsky, 'but I suppose it doesn't matter now. Yes, there was a young man at Mr Hardwick's party. Nobody knew who he was, nobody had ever seen him before, and he was enjoying himself greatly posing as a Russian prince and impressing all the old ladies, while the pretty English girl on his arm could not take her eyes from him. And then all of a sudden – the bother! Mr Hardwick, who never allows her guests to relax but always puts them to work making the conversation with each other, sends him to me. "Oh, look, prince Yousoupoff, here is our Russian diplomat, Mr Oblonsky! He comes from Moscow as well. You two will surely have so much to talk about." I look at this young man and he looks at me, and he draws me into a corner, where I greet him politely in Russian, and ask him what branch of the Yousoupoff family he belongs to. He does not understand a single word, but not one word! The young man is no more Russian than you are. It is all just a ridiculous piece of theatre playing!'

'So that was it after all, as Mme. de Vrille thought,' I said, half to myself, half to Arthur. Turning back to Mr Oblonsky, I began to explain. 'We are trying to find him, and it is quite difficult, because we know neither his name nor even his nationality – the name Vassily Semionovich was probably a complete invention along with the rest of it.'

'Oh, very likely,' he agreed. 'How amusing that he took the same name and patronymic as Kropoff here; I hadn't noticed it.' He laughed, clumping his colleague on the shoulder. 'So you came here to try and hunt him down? How very amusing!'

Arthur and I did not find it at all amusing, but then, Mr Oblonsky could have no idea of the true nature of our investigation, so we forced ourselves to chuckle complacently.

'Still, Mr Oblonsky,' I asked, hoping against hope to obtain at least one morsel of additional information from him, 'is there anything that you can tell us about him? Do you know anything about who he really was?'

'No, I am very sorry. He did not say. He simply said he was acting the Russian role as a practical joke.'

'Or to impress the young lady who was with him, perhaps,' I suggested.

'Oh no, certainly not. The young lady was in on the joke; she was standing with us when he told me, she was with him all the time.'

'Ah!' I said, quickly putting this piece of information away for future reference. 'Do you at least know, or can you guess, his real nationality?'

'Oh, I think he was British! Out of politeness to Mr Hardwick, I insisted in speaking to him in that language, although I believe he would have preferred to speak French (part of his play-acting, I suppose), but I should say there is almost no question about it. He was not a native French speaker. He had a slight trace of foreign accent in that language. But in English, though he spoke little and quite low, he had no accent at all, quite the opposite. His speech was very elegant and natural. Now,' he added, looking at his watch, 'I am very sorry, I must leave you. I am sorry I cannot tell you anything further about the man you seek. Why do you not enquire with your young lady friend?'

'She has lost him – she did not really know who he was,' I stammered.

'I see. A mystery man,' he said, and winked. 'Perhaps she wishes to find him again, and you are helping her, is that it? I am very sorry I cannot do more for you. My best wishes in your quest,' he said, shaking hands vigorously with me, then with Arthur. We bid him goodbye, and accepting also the friendliest salutations from our erstwhile suspect Kropoff, we turned away together down the street.

Oh, Dora, I don't know what to think any more! All my ideas must be revised. If I am to believe Mr Oblonsky – and it corroborates what Mme. de Vrille believed – then the young man we are seeking for was quite simply British, and

Sylvia certainly knew it. What could he have been doing here in Paris? And where is he now? Perhaps he is still here, since he came from France when he went to murder Mr Granger. But he could equally well be in England, or anywhere else, for that matter. I cannot imagine what my next step should be.

There always remains the final possibility, which is almost certain to turn into a necessity; I shall have to go home and corner Sylvia. Yet I fear that this final, drastic step may not prove very definitive. What shall I do if she simply speaks to me of a casual acquaintance with whom she played the fool for a few weeks, without even knowing his real name, perhaps? As for the idea that this person could possibly have anything to do with the murder of her husband, it seems clear, unless I understand nothing of Sylvia, that it has not occurred to her for an instant.

Yet – I cannot get around the fact that she lied. Yes, she lied; she told me she had not met anyone special in Paris – and even if her foolish behaviour, observed by so many, constituted nothing of emotional importance to her, she took care to hide it nevertheless. Unquestionably, there is a mystery associated with Sylvia and her behaviour, and the point will come when I shall *have* to elucidate it!

Yours ever,

Vanessa

Paris, Thursday, July 14, 1892

My dearest twin,

After I wrote to you yesterday, Arthur and I returned to the hotel; our visit to the Russian Embassy had left us feeling foolish, gloomy and at a loss which the dimness of the evening did nothing to dispel. However, as we stopped at the front desk of the hotel to ask for our keys, the young employee plunged his hand into my pigeonhole and extracted not only a key, but also a white envelope.

'*Un télégramme pour vous, Mademoiselle,*' he said respectfully, handing it over.

I tore it open at once.

'It's from Pat!' I cried, and Arthur and I read it together. Pat had expressed himself without heed to expense.

French police have totally failed to trace subject stop first recorded observation on gangplank leading up onto Dover-bound ferry stop appears to have materialised there by magic stop interviews of dozens of sailors, workers, passengers etc. have given no result stop nobody observed this person's arrival at the port stop he was not observed on any train destination Calais and did not take cab in Calais stop French police terminating investigation stop what can this mean stop look in yesterday's newspaper stop Pat

'How strange,' I said, struck by this message and forgetting my troubles. 'Arthur, look what it says. It is peculiar that they can't find any trace of him.

After all, no matter who the mysterious young man is, surely he *must* have arrived in Calais somehow!'

'It probably just means that the French police are not putting a lot of energy into it,' he replied, reading over the telegram glumly. 'And even if they are, don't you think it must be practically impossible to find anyone who can remember one particular person in such a large crowd of people as the passengers who take the ferry every day?'

I reflected for a moment.

'Well, I don't know. There are all kinds of people working around a boat; someone must have sold him the ticket, there are people loading luggage, someone welcomes the passengers on board, and he was noticed *on* the boat, after all, so why not on the way there?'

'But the people on the boat are shut in with this person for a certain length of time. Even if the boat is rather large, it makes sense that several of them remember seeing him. But in the port, on the quay, you're looking for someone who caught sight of him as he walked past for a brief moment. That seems much harder.'

'Well, but he was observed by many people on the train in England, and the English police traced him up from Dover easily enough.'

'True,' he said. 'But one will remember one's fellow passengers in a train just as one does in a boat. At most, assuming the police have done their work correctly, it's fair to conclude that he did not arrive in Calais by train.'

'How then? By balloon? On horseback? Not by cab – he can hardly have taken a cab from another city!'

'Perhaps he was already in Calais. Or he drove here in a friend's carriage,' he said, thinking aloud.

'But a person cannot descend from a carriage directly onto the gangplank! He must necessarily have had to walk some distance along the quay, and how could he not be observed then, with that red cloak of his?'

'Ah, the cloak – I had forgotten about that. Why, that's the reason he was so amply observed everywhere he went. That makes it simple, Vanessa! He arrived at the boat carrying the cloak over his arm or something; it's probably a different colour on the inside. And then once he was in the boat, he slipped it over his shoulders.'

'But why?'

'Well, that cloak business sounds awfully like he wanted to be observed, don't you think?'

'Yes, it really does! But Arthur, why *should* he want to be observed? It sounds mad, impossible! Would *you* want to be observed on your way to commit a murder? Why – everyone knows exactly where he came from because of it!'

'No, that's not true at all. We don't know where he came from.'

'Well, you know what I mean. We know he came over from France. And why would he want anybody to know even that?'

'I don't know,' he said thoughtfully. 'It would help, maybe, if we knew more about the exact moment he was first observed. Then perhaps we could guess why he wanted to be observed in that particular place.'

I glanced down at the telegram. 'Oh, Arthur, do let us go out and see if we can buy the newspaper! Pat must have written an article about this.'

'You think he means the *Cambridge Evening News?*'

'Oh – well, I assume so! That's his newspaper.'

'You're right. I thought he just meant the British newspapers had somehow gotten wind of the mystery and were writing about it.'

'Well, let us buy several,' I said anxiously, and handing our keys back to the surprised bellhop, we returned out into the streets.

We walked some distance before locating a kiosk with sufficiently international tendencies to carry newspapers of several nationalities, but eventually we discovered one, in the vicinity of Gustave Eiffel's metallic pointed tower, under whose gigantic spreading feet tourists of all nationalities congregate like flies. The editions were of course those of the day before, but that was just what we wanted. We selected three, and carrying them away, we sat down on a bench to peruse them.

'There's nothing about it in these,' said Arthur at length. 'Well, at any rate, here is Pat's article,' I answered, folding back the pages of the *Cambridge Evening News* to show it to him.

French police stymied by problem of mysterious stranger in Granger murder case

The police enquiry into the identity and where-abouts of the mysterious young man seen lurking about the village of Haverhill on the day of the murder of respected citizen George Burton Granger has run into an inexplicable difficulty. Indeed, although diligent and detailed enquiry has succeeded in producing an accurate account of each and every step of the young man's trip to Haverhill from the time he embarked on the Dover-bound ferry in the French port of Calais, it has proved entirely impossible, even with the close collaboration of the French police, to determine where he had come from before that moment.

At first glance, it may seem an impossible task to determine the trajectory of a single individual, to, from, and within a bustling port such as Calais, crowded with passengers and travellers of every description. But in fact, the police have powerful methods at their disposal; they have combed the town, enquired with every cab driver, every mode of transportation, checked with the young man's description at every hotel in the town and outlying villages, and questioned dozens upon dozens of merchants and workers whose jobs lead them to remain stationary for long hours at locations in and around the docking pier of the Dover ferry.

Because the young man's clothing and appearance, as described by the large number of witnesses who noticed him during his journey to Haverhill, were particularly striking and unusual, the British police were able to pinpoint that he was definitely observed at the moment of boarding the boat and handing his ticket to the ticket-taker. Some witnesses have also been found who testify to his having stood in line and mounted the gangplank near them. Thus, he was certainly perceived just at the moment of embarkation. Yet no single person can be found who noticed anyone resembling him prior to that moment, even under the natural assumption that he must have arrived carrying rather than wearing the red cloak subsequently mentioned by so many of the witnesses. The chief detective inspector of the Calais police, M. Lemaire, states that he is terminating his researches at least until further information is forthcoming. The mystery remains complete.

'What can the meaning of it be?' I said thoughtfully, as Arthur finished reading over my shoulder.

'I still can't believe it means much,' he answered with a deprecatory wave of his hand. 'So nobody noticed an ordinary-looking fellow walking past at an ordinary pace, in the middle of a large crowd of people milling around. I probably wouldn't have noticed a thing myself.'

'But you're a mathematician!' I exclaimed. 'You never do notice anything, when you're thinking about some problem. If he was really in the middle of a crowd, then he was surrounded by dozens of people who are *not* mathematicians, and who *might* therefore have spotted him. How is it possible that no one has?'

'The police cannot really have tracked down and questioned most of those people, can they?'

'I don't know. There must be a great many people who are not just passing by, but work there around the boats and are there every day. Oh, Arthur – do you know what we should do?

293

We should go and talk to this Monsieur Lemaire and find out exactly how seriously they really did search! We mustn't miss the opportunity – we're taking the boat back Sunday – we could go to Calais on Saturday!'

'But how could we persuade the certainly very busy Monsieur Lemaire to receive us?' he said.

I thought for a moment.

'I know! We'll wire him and say we have important information about the young man. Either he or some other high-ranking person *must* receive us then! And we'll pump him.'

'He'll pump us, more likely. What if he starts by asking for your information?'

'Oh dear – well, we'll set him off on a wrong tangent with some story about Prince Yousoupoff. That can't be so very bad, can it? The worst that can happen is that they go and see him, and make fools of themselves with him, and he gets even redder and more annoyed than he was with us, and shakes his stick at them.'

Arthur sighed.

'I'll come with you, Vanessa, but I leave it to you to do the talking and pumping,' he said. 'You might be persuasive enough to find out what you want, although I can hardly see what that could be. I must say – we've been here nearly two weeks and I can't see that we've made any progress at all on finding out anything whatsoever.'

'Oh, I do feel grateful when you say "we",' I cried. 'No, we haven't failed completely, really we haven't. We know that Sylvia was going about with *someone*, and that person still has a good chance of being the one we're looking for. If no one else can identify him for us, she still can, and if push comes to shove, she must be made to.'

'It isn't completely certain that even Sylvia is aware of his real identity, is it? And furthermore, if we draw her attention to him, she will certainly realise (even if she has not yet wanted to think about it or admit it to herself) that he is either guilty or at the very least, in danger.'

'That's why questioning her is a last recourse. But it could be tried, I think, with enough tact – and Camilla should be questioned, too. She *must* know something, and she would be more inclined to understand the reality of Sylvia's own danger than Sylvia herself would. Still, it would have been so infinitely much better to have been able to find out more here! Whether or not she knows who he is, it is bound to be horrible for her; can you imagine? Feeling that it was her fault, not wanting to betray ... yet, a murderer!'

'It is fishy,' mused Arthur. 'I mean, if she knows who he is and remained in contact with him, then how could she not suspect? Can she, after all, be shielding him as the police believe? But if she lost contact with him and it never has never occurred to her that he may be the murderer, then how can she have been important enough to him to make him murder someone for her? What a muddle. Well, we will be back in England on Monday and can think about all this then,' he added, taking my hand. 'Let us content ourselves with planning our next step, purchasing our tickets to Calais and wiring Monsieur Lemaire. That makes tomorrow our last day here in Paris, then. Are you sad to leave?'

'No! Oh, Arthur, I want to go home! I haven't been here for my pleasure, and even the pleasure I did get from admiring all the beauties of this splendid city cannot be compared to what I feel when I'm surrounded by the small things of England – the ancient stones, the cathedral spires, the wild flowers, the fresh breezes and the little birds, the flavour and savour of it all. I miss home.'

'So do I,' he said very softly, kissing my hair.

'Really, Arthur? And you, are you not sorry to leave? For the mathematics, at least?'

'Not at all. We've done some glorious work, but I think we have plenty to go on with for the moment. We have to think things out and let them develop; it will take time. The ideas have got to be nurtured slowly, and that can only be done in peace and quiet. No, I want to go home, but I want you near me, and safe.'

We rose and walked together to the telegraph office. I did not answer Arthur's last remark. Oh dear, I am rather afraid that it is not merely a brief visit to the tempestuous City of Lights that has not proved conducive to an atmosphere of peace and quiet, but rather something to do with my own activities. But what can I do? Nothing, except try to finish as quickly as I can with this dreadful story.

Your very own,

Vanessa

Calais, Saturday, July 16, 1892

My dear twin,

I am writing to you in the evening, from a little hotel in Calais, which is modest enough yet incomparably more pleasant than the miserable tenement in which I stayed with Emily and little Robert four years ago. Ah, how I remember my anguish and terror then, and how different my life is now; how lovely altogether, except for my single-minded obsession with discovering the identity of Mr Granger's murderer.

Having arrived here by train early on, the main effort of our day was to meet with M. Lemaire, which we duly did. He received us graciously enough, considering that (as it soon transpired) he was very near to the point of dismissing the whole story of the murderer's having arrived in England from Calais as a perfect fiction. Still, he showed himself willing to listen to the ridiculous tale of Russian princes and casinos which I poured out to him as a preliminary condition to asking him questions. He paid careful attention to each detail. I skipped over the embarrassing interludes concerning Mr Vassily Semionovich Kropoff and the elderly prince himself, confining myself to recounting hearsay. When I had finished what I hoped sounded like a convincing demonstration that we were well on the way to discovering the identity of the criminal, and that a little help from the police was all that would be needed to complete the task, he said,

'But Mademoiselle, as you may know, our

police have excluded the possibility that the person who was supposedly observed on the ferry to Dover and subsequently on the train to this town, what is it called, where the murder took place, could have come from Paris, or from any other town, or even from Calais itself.'

'But, Monsieur,' I responded politely, 'that is very hard to believe. How can you be sure of it?'

'We have questioned an enormous number of people around the docks at the time of the departure of the ferry,' he replied. 'This man was observed on the boat and on the train in England. Why was he not observed coming to the boat? Something is wrong.'

'Well,' I said hesitantly, glancing at Arthur, 'we thought that perhaps he was observed so frequently after he put on the red cloak that has been mentioned in all the newspapers, and perhaps he arrived near the boat without wearing it.'

He laughed.

'You take the police for children, Mademoiselle! Do you think we went about asking people if they had observed a young man in a bright red cloak?'

'But supposing he was not really such a noticeable kind of person,' I persisted, 'how can you be sure that he would have been observed at all? Perhaps he was already living in Calais, or simply arrived here in a friend's carriage, and then walked to the boat, and nobody noticed him.'

He smiled indulgently.

'Mademoiselle, we have considered every possibility, including the ones you now raise. We wished to see if a person could cross the port and accede to the ferry without being noticed at all. You will, I suppose, admit that the young man must have done so, according to the British theory at least. So we devised a little test, and sent one of our agents, dressed in the most normal way possible, walking quietly across the quay to board the same ferry as our unknown gentleman. We then waited some days, and then proceeded to question as many as possible of the people who were present at the time he went.' Pausing, he reached for a sheaf of papers and shuffled them. 'Here are the statements of the witnesses. I will not lie to you; of sixty people that we interviewed, only seven claimed to have seen the person we described, and of those, only three were finally able to identify our agent from a group of similar young men. One of them is an old woman who sits in the sunshine near the quay for most of every day, selling nuts and crumbs of old bread to feed the pigeons. When we questioned her about our agent, she said that she had seen a young man of his description and described his clothing. We were not completely convinced as the description was somewhat vague and could conceivably have corresponded to a different person, but she then picked him out among ten others.' Selecting a paper from the pile, he continued, 'The same woman is one of our main witnesses in the question of the young man in the red cloak, and the other is the mother of a family of small children. Of everyone we questioned, only these two are of any interest whatsoever. Let me translate the first statement for you.

'"*I watched the passengers walking up the ...* (how

do you call it?) *gangplank. I saw a young man with dark hair, wearing a red cloak standing on the gangplank, moving up among the people there. He was standing next to some children. I do not know where he came from. I had not seen him before I noticed him on the gangplank. He definitely did not walk past me going there. Not even without his cloak. I would have noticed him. He had a handsome, youthful face and his hair was noticeable, thick and very dark with waves or curls."*

'Now, here is the other statement, from the mother of the children just mentioned.

'*"We had just reached the foot of the gangplank and were about to walk up it onto the boat when my little son said to me 'Maman, look at the lovely cape.' A young man came out in front of us wearing a red silk cape like I have never seen. He smiled and said a word or two to my son. Not much, something like 'ça te plaît?' He walked up in front of us and gave his ticket to the man. We saw him later on the boat. We would certainly recognise him if we saw him again. But we had definitely not seen him before then, as we were walking up towards the boat."*

'*"When you first saw him, why do you say he came out in front of you?"* we asked her.

'*"He came out from the other side of a pile like that one."* She pointed to a large heap of barrels and crates which were being stocked on the boat.'

M. Lemaire put down the paper. 'Certainly, there are such piles of merchandise in front of the boat, being loaded, every day,' he said. 'So what she described is natural enough. But where did he come from before being there? We do not know.'

'What do you conclude?' I asked, rather at a loss.

'Our first thought was of a disguise. One could ask whether he was disguised before taking the boat or on the boat. Now, as I just told you, there are always great piles of crates or barrels being loaded or unloaded on the docks around the boats, and he could certainly have hidden briefly behind one of them. But people pass there all the time. It is not a hiding place. Nothing prevents passengers going to the boat from walking behind the heaps, and the dockworkers come to take them. So if he went there before coming out in his red cloak, it is more likely that he quickly removed a disguise than that he actually put something particular on, apart from the cloak itself, of course.'

'That makes sense,' I agreed. 'It is a very good idea – it *must* be right.'

'But it has a great flaw in it. Do you not see it?'

'No,' I replied, feeling stupid.

'What about the disguise, Mademoiselle? The disguise!' he exclaimed. 'Where is it? We expected to find something – some package of clothing, some abandoned objects! We searched the entire area, questioned dozens of people, put up notices. We went to the office of found objects, and carefully inspected everything that had been given in there. There are many, many things in that place – you cannot imagine!' He pulled out a list and scanned it with annoyance. 'A child's coat – ah, children! They always lose things. Children's toys – a doll. Several scarves for the neck, of both men and women. A lady's hat. A shoe – bah! How can

301

a person lose one shoe? A cane. We were very interested in the cane. We asked our pigeon lady and other people if they had spotted a man *with a cane* – even an old man, stooping, with white hair. But it gave no result. There were men with canes, to be sure, but they all seemed to be accounted for.'

'We-ell,' I said, considering the list, 'he must have carried the disguise off with him.'

'But none of the witnesses say he was carrying any kind of a bundle.'

'The disguise must have consisted of something quite small.'

'Such as?'

I stopped to reflect, trying to visualise the situation.

'Suppose – suppose that he quickly wiped off grease-paint from his face with a handkerchief, and brushed up his hair which had been slicked down with oil, or covered with a hat or cap which he then stuffed into a pocket. Maybe he was wearing something noticeable – one of those scarves around his neck, for instance – which he took off and dropped there. Then he would just wrap himself up in the cloak he'd been carrying rolled up over his arm.'

'Mademoiselle, what you say is possible, but believe me, it is not very likely. A man wearing sufficient grease-paint to really hide his features would be very noticeable on a sunny day; you may not realise it is there when you see an actor upon the stage, but outdoors it is completely different. He would look like a clown. We heard no hint of anything so strange. We are stymied, as you English say. I do not see what further researches we can now do here. I could contact my colleagues in Paris and Deauville in order to attempt to identify the young man you speak of, but it is unfortunate that we have no element at all linking him either to the crime or even to a trip to Calais. It is difficult to undertake a serious investigation on these grounds. It would be much better for the British police to simply find out his identity from the woman you told me about, the wife of the murdered man. Then his background could be checked and we might get somewhere.'

M. Lemaire rang a bell as he spoke, and instructed the young man who poked in his head respectfully to escort us out.

'He was really very kind, don't you think?' I asked Arthur, as we reached the street.

'I don't much appreciate being dismissed that way,' he said. 'But he was nice enough, I suppose. Still, it is all dashed unhelpful. We seem to be at a dead end once again.'

'Yes,' I sighed. 'He's right about the grease-paint, I'm afraid. And yet, there must be something in the disguise idea. There isn't anything else that could explain it!'

'I still think it could be explained by the simple fact that he was there and nobody noticed him,' he grumbled.

'No. I believe him. There really are too many people standing around the boat all the time; that old pigeon lady was sure of herself. Oh, he must have done something quite special to just appear there so suddenly, all ready and dressed up – and if he did it, we can find it! I must think.'

Indeed, I must think. Oh, Dora, it is so strange. There is something in the back of my mind – something I have heard recently which has some bearing on this absurd conundrum. Is it something to do with disguising? Have I had any discussions about disguising lately? I cannot remember any. Have you noticed anything of the sort in my letters?

Your greatly puzzled

Vanessa

Cambridge, Sunday, July 17, 1892

Dearest Dora,

How lovely it feels to be home again! Everything is wonderfully the same, and yet strangely unfamiliar at the same time.

Your letter was waiting for me here when I arrived. I shall come to visit immediately – I shall leave tomorrow, and arrive very nearly at the same time as this very letter! Oh, Dora, what *can* be on Ellen's mind? You say she has been letting strange hints fall – and that she seems certain that Sylvia cannot have had a lover ever. Yet we know that she did have one, or at the very least, a suitor or a flirt, however innocent it may really have been! What makes Ellen so stubbornly sure of herself? What can she possibly know about it?

Alas, if you have not been able to persuade her to tell you what she means, then it is not likely that I shall succeed either. Yet I can argue that it is for Sylvia's defence. It could be that deep down, she really wishes or needs to speak, and something, some fear perhaps, is restraining her. I shall see what my utmost tact can accomplish – but Dora, I have never, ever had even half the tact that you have – so I am not as optimistic as I might otherwise be!

It does not seem worth my writing much, as I shall see you tomorrow or the next day – only I simply *must* tell you what happened on the boat back. After my talk with Annabel in which my foolish blind eyes were unsealed, I determined that I must corner Charles and beard him, for I am dearly fond of Annabel and quite see that her present situation is untenable. I did hope, over the last several days, that as Arthur has spent a great deal of time with me, and we even came away to Calais together one day before the others, perhaps there would be some development between the two of them, but as soon as we met at the ticket office, I knew that nothing had happened, for Annabel's face was all downcast, whereas Charles was exactly his usual cheerful self, which he would surely not have been if some explanation had occurred, either pleasant or unpleasant.

On our way to the boat, I determined that I would tackle him on board, but I very nearly forgot, for Arthur and I had other things on our mind. Indeed, we tried a little last minute detecting as we approached the ferry; we surveyed the area with care and occupied a few minutes with a couple of minor experiments. First, we saw the old lady sitting behind her little stand of bird food. Mingling with the groups of people milling about, Arthur walked past her, behaving as normal as possible, and disappeared around a corner. A few minutes later, I hastened up to her, looking upset, and asked her in a tone of urgency if she had seen a young man with brown hair and a light brown topcoat pass by, as I had lost him. She glanced up at me and then gestured with her chin in the direction he had disappeared. 'He passed three, four minutes ago,' she said with a nod. I rushed after him, and soon discovered him and hauled him back. She winked at me as she saw us pass.

'Arthur, she remembered you instantly! It's amazing,' I said breathlessly.

'Bah,' he said, 'five minutes is not the same as five days.'

As a second experiment, I tried to imagine that I was disguised and needed to transform myself before boarding the boat. I slipped behind one of the large mounds of crates and trunks which were in the process of being loaded onto the boat we were travelling by, but I had been there less than half a minute when I was elbowed aside by a burly Frenchman in overalls, who snatched up the very box I was pressed against and heaved it up on his shoulders. Indeed, I must agree with M. Lemaire that anyone trying to don or doff a decent disguise would be taking a great risk to do it in such a place, where one cannot be sure of being alone for any time at all! How could one change one's appearance within a few seconds? Yet I see no other possibility; that is what *must* have happened.

I was still puzzling over this problem as we boarded the boat, and it made me absent-minded for some little time, but as we pulled away from the shore, and I found myself hanging next to Charles over the rail on the port side of the deck, watching the coast of France distance itself slowly, I suddenly remembered my purpose with respect to him. I glanced around, but Annabel was nowhere to be seen, and Arthur was leaning on the railing some distance farther down. I turned to Charles, and raised my voice to be heard over the various roaring and churning noises of the engine and the slap of the waves. For an effect of greater severity, I planted my hands upon my hips. However, before I had pronounced a single word, he turned a glum face in my direction and said,

'I simply can't believe that by tonight, we'll be back in the usual grind again. It really was a heavenly two weeks, wasn't it?'

'Ha,' I said, seizing the occasion, and wondering if hints would not succeed where I had intended to employ more brutal means. 'And why should you return to the old grind, just as before? Can some essential element of the delight you felt during your stay not accompany you back home?'

'I wish it could,' he smiled uncomprehendingly. 'What could such an element be? The exotic nature of it all – that is what I would choose, followed by a cuisine containing snails. But I don't see how I could carry that home in my pockets. Do you?'

'Are you sure it's really France and snails which

made your stay so wonderful?' I said, wondering if he were very dense, or if on the contrary he fully realised my purpose, but was parrying it expertly in order not to find himself in a highly embarrassing situation. I began to ask myself if I were doing the right thing in attempting to bring him to a realisation of Annabel's feelings. For if he were aware of it but reticent, it would be a cruelty to force the statement out into the open. Yet I found it hard to believe that such was the case. No one, seeing him in Paris, could have thought it for a moment – and he certainly is not a flirt. I decided to persist, and flung delicacy to the winds.

'What about Annabel?' I said. 'Why, Arthur and I were perfectly convinced that your radiant mood was due to all the time you spent with her, as much if not more than to the architecture and historical landmarks of Paris!'

'Annabel?' he repeated, sincerely surprised. 'Of course it was lovely going about with her. It's ever so much nicer than being alone!'

'Well, why stop then, when you are back in England?'

'Why – why – it's not in our habits, to go walking together, when we're at home.'

I looked straight into his eyes, determined to gauge his feelings.

'Would it not give you the same pleasure?' I said.

'I – why yes – no–' he began awkwardly, flushing a little. 'I guess it *would* be nice – I guess it would be wonderful, really, to take tea with Annabel on the grass, or in Grantchester, sometimes, as you do with Arthur. In fact, now that you mention it,

I can hardly think of any prospect which would please me more! Funny, I never thought of it before.' He stopped, thoughtfully, and then added, 'But Annabel won't want to, I expect. And it wouldn't really do, you know.'

'Why not? And why wouldn't she want to?' I asked firmly.

'Well, it's obvious, isn't it?'

'By no means. Charles – Annabel is very fond of you and in fact she is rather unhappy. It's wrong to tell you this, I suppose. But I think you should know it so that you can react one way or another. Any way you wish, as long as it is not just ignoring the situation, whether consciously or unconsciously. Because that is what is troubling her, and Annabel is my friend, and it saddens me to see her sad.'

Charles looked amazed.

'Annabel sad? I can't believe that, Vanessa! Why, she laughed all the time we were together!'

'Well,' I said.

'Oh,' he said. 'I see. What should I do?'

'It all depends on what you feel,' I told him, suppressing the words *you idiot* which rose spontaneously to my lips. 'I do not wish to pry into your feelings; I am not asking you what they are. I am just telling you to determine them and to make them clear in a kind and generous way. Do you understand what I mean?'

'Of course, of course,' he said quickly, then added, 'I mean I really do see what you mean. One doesn't want to be dishonourable, does one?'

'No. And if you don't feel anything other than light-hearted friendship for Annabel, then I really think that she ought to leave your house, and probably leave Cambridge altogether. For it is not an easy situation.'

'Oh!' he said, very much struck. 'Oh, I should hate it if she left. That would be awful! No, no. She mustn't leave! I – why, that would be–'

He stopped, and we looked at each other. A multitude of expressions passed over his face.

'Look here, Vanessa,' he said after a while. 'What can I do?. I want Annabel to be there. And now that you mention it, I would like to see more of her, as we did in Paris. But in a way, wouldn't that be just as bad?'

'If it were not to go any farther, yes,' I said pitilessly.

'Farther? But I can't! My sister would be furious! How could I? Annabel ... Annabel is an orphan – and she's the governess of Constance's children! After what happened with my sister's husband and the previous governess, she would never be able to accept such a thing! It's awful, Vanessa. What can I do?'

'Before you think about your sister, think about yourself,' I said quietly. 'Do you want to marry?'

'Not the girls Constance keeps introducing me to, I'll say that!' he said. 'And I get tired of being alone. Very tired; it's too much to bear, sometimes. But I haven't found the perfect... I mean...Well, yes. I should like to marry Annabel! Why, I've just realised it. How could you have seen it before I did, Vanessa? So you think that Annabel cares? Really?' He looked at me eagerly and I had to laugh. But his face fell.

'It's no good,' he said, fingering his small moustache doubtfully. 'It's not possible. I really don't see how I can do it, Vanessa. I know that when I get home and have to think about announcing it, I'll go all limp.'

'I am not going to press you,' I said. 'Don't expect me to force you into any decision! You must decide yourself. I wish only to influence you into doing so openly, clearly and soon, for reasons which you must understand now.'

'I hate deciding,' he muttered with an aggrieved look, but I was already turning away, fearful of pushing him too hard into saying things he might afterwards regret and feel obliged to retract. I joined Arthur, and we made no further reference to the affair; when we all came together upon descending from the boat, Charles appeared to be altogether his usual self, and gave his arm to Annabel in a natural and comfortable manner, without any undue eagerness. I have sown a seed, Dora – I do not know what will come of it, but the look in Annabel's eyes as we sat across from each other over breakfast is not one that I can easily forget. What will be, will be.

Till tomorrow, my dear!

Vanessa

Cambridge, Tuesday, July 19, 1892

My dearest sister,

How wonderful it was to see you, and to talk

311

everything over with you so carefully! How lovely, to sit up late at night in the room we used to share, talking for hours on everything under the sun! I meant to discuss the case with you in detail, but I cannot regret the fact that we did nothing of the kind. It was too lovely to leave it all behind for a moment – and to live for a little while in your private world instead of mine. When I think how naturally young Mr Edwards of long ago has transformed himself, over the last four years, into 'Dora's John' – and that the end of all the long years of waiting may finally be within sight, and he will be able, with equal smoothness, to transform himself into 'Dora's husband'! Poor man. He is miserable in Ceylon, and you are miserable here without him, and only one little element is missing to restore harmony to all concerned: a posting to some diplomatic office in England, such as are offered to young Cambridge and Oxford graduates every day! It is but a small thing; surely it cannot elude him much longer, especially if he himself has begun to hear positive rumours. How wonderful it will be, when the rhythm of your daily life is no longer measured by the arrival of letters, and by the too-rare, too-short visits which leave almost more pain behind them than they bring joy whilst they last. Oh, Dora, I wish for his return and for your marriage almost as ardently as I wish for mine!

The importance of all these questions entirely outshadowed my investigation, which in the end we had no time to discuss. Yet, Dora, if you would do as you promised; re-read all my letters, let the story they tell take shape and form within you, and write to me what you think of it all, I know that it would be of infinite help to me. Your mind is so calm, so logical compared to mine, which always seems to be darting hither and thither like a silly rabbit! When you sum up a situation, then and only then does it begin to seem clear and coherent to me.

Now, I must tell you what you are surely longing to know; namely, about the talk I had with Ellen this morning, before catching my train back here. Unfortunately, it was as uninformative as my worst fears had led me to suspect it would be (otherwise, I should certainly have begun this letter by speaking of it!) I arrived at her cottage bearing a pretty gift for her little boy. William is really a delightful child. His country upbringing has made him a straightforward, good-hearted little creature without much complexity and he was immediately delighted with the train I had produced for him (as similar a one as I could find to that which we bought for a miserable, trembling little boy in Calais four years ago, which brought such a colour into his little cheeks), and with the milk and buns he was served for tea, and the unusual opportunity to discuss his affairs with a lady who was obviously both familiar with and deeply interested in all the most cherished concerns of small boys of six. After I had admired his caterpillar, which he was going to tame and teach to do tricks, and his vegetable patch, from whose muddy depths the family sustenance was soon to emerge, and a tattered ABC of which his mother had begun to show him the initial pages, he led me into his diminutive bedroom and opening a drawer, he took out a framed photo-graph showing a young, vigorous man of twenty-five or thirty, who bore a remarkable resemblance to the child himself.

'That's my dad,' he announced with pride.

'I can see that it is,' I said, staring at the photograph in amazement.

'William – put that away at once!' said Ellen, who had entered after us, taking it from him and thrusting it back into the drawer. And much to his annoyance, she dispatched him forthwith to collect a great bunch of flowers in my honour, and we began to talk.

Of course I began in the most circuitous fash-ion, and conversation went easily upon the subjects of her work, her child, her difficulties, the problem of his schooling.

'It isn't easy. A boy needs a father, especially a boy like mine, so strong and active.'

'He loves his father's picture,' I said gently.

'He shouldn't have shown you that!' she exclaimed. 'It's a secret between us, he knows it! But what does it matter,' she added more calmly. 'You know who his father is well enough, Miss. I saw you up in the gallery that day when I told Mrs Bryce-Fortescue all about it. I'd have been out of myself if it had been anybody else, but you are Miss Dora's sister, and so like her; I trust you like I trust her. I know you know, and what of it?'

'But – that picture is of Mr Granger, then?' I said in surprise.

'Yes, it is a picture of him when he was young,' she said. 'He'd given it to Mrs Bryce-Fortescue, and I stole it when I left – yes, it's the only thing

I ever stole. I took it to give my child a father, and I don't regret it.'

It took me both time and tact to lead the conversation around to Sylvia, but I finally succeeded in doing so. I was not sure how best to approach the issue, but finally decided to let Ellen understand that Sylvia was actually in danger. I was not sure exactly how much her loyalty to Sylvia might make her rise in her defence, so I also hinted at the obvious consequence that Sylvia's inheritance from her husband might be a matter of doubt, which would bode ill for the realisation of Mrs Bryce-Fortescue's kind promises.

'Miss Sylvia in danger,' she said, 'surely not? Why, as the police have not arrested her, I thought they had made up their minds she couldn't have done it.'

'They believe her guilty none the less,' I said, 'if not of the actual shooting itself – for which she has an alibi, although the police profess to be unconvinced even by that – but of conspiracy with an accomplice.'

'An accomplice? Who could have done such a thing for her?'

'Well, the police ... well, it has been discovered that during her visit to Paris, she seems to have gone about accompanied by a young man whom no one appears able to identify, and as she and this young man were observed to behave in public exactly like lovers, they are very eager to identify him, and quite suppose that he may be the murderer. Sylvia has never mentioned any such person, and unless she is really a consummate actress, she really does not appear to have

315

thought of such a thing at all. I do not know what to think.'

Ellen did not answer my remarks at once, but looked extremely sceptical.

'Of course, you have not seen Sylvia for so long, that you must have no idea about all this,' I said encouragingly, wondering why she wore a knowing look underneath her doubting expression.

'No, I know nothing about it,' she said. There was a pause, and then she added in a rush,

'It sounds very unlikely to me, though perhaps I am all wrong.'

'What exactly is unlikely?' I asked with interest. 'I know that there was a time when you knew Sylvia far better than anyone else could, perhaps even better than her own mother. No one knows a child like her nurse. So even though she was young then and may have changed, still, your instincts must certainly be revealing. What appears unlikely to you?'

She writhed on her seat, sipped her tea and hesitated.

'Miss Sylvia wasn't that way,' she said at length, but very uncomfortably.

'Wasn't what way?' I persisted.

'She wouldn't have had a lover in Paris. It doesn't sound like her.'

I remembered asking Sylvia *Did you meet anyone really special?* and her casual, spontaneous answer, *They were all special!* And yet ... we knew that she had!

'But Ellen,' I said finally, 'surely there are many girls of fifteen who do not want lovers, but that usually changes by the time they are twenty-two, as Sylvia is now. It would be strange indeed, if it did *not* change!'

'Not girls like Sylvia,' she said. 'If Sylvia had a lover in Paris, then...' She glanced up at me suddenly, as if an idea had suddenly struck her, and a look of fear flashed through her eyes. She stopped speaking and looked down into her teacup. I stared at her in complete disarray.

'Please, do tell me what you mean,' I begged. 'What about girls like Sylvia? What if she had a lover in Paris? What was it about her?'

A stubborn look crept onto her face.

'I can't say,' she said finally. 'She was a strange girl, that's all. A strange girl, and it's a strange story. The police are barking up the wrong tree, maybe.'

Dora, no persuasion would extract even a single further grain of information from her. How stupid I do feel! What on earth can she mean by it? Oh, her words must somehow contain the key to the mystery! Why can I not guess it? Can you think of anything? Do, do come to my aid! I am at my wits' end and really do not know what to think!

Your loving

Vanessa

Maidstone Hall, Thursday, July 21, 1892

Oh, Dora – you will never guess what has happened!

I have news, Dora, marvellous, astonishing, long-awaited and yet utterly unexpected news!

It came, yesterday afternoon, just upon the heels of something very serious; a telegram from Pat, which I was holding in my hand.

Police unable identify traveller stop trail ends in Calais stop had enough stop Mrs Granger almost certain to be arrested within days stop Pat

Blank with dismay, I had barely time to digest this information and congratulate myself that my rushed visit to Maidstone Hall was already planned for that very evening, when I heard a vigorous knock at my door. Upon opening it, I was utterly taken aback to see Arthur of all people – flushed with excitement and shining with delight!

'Arthur, what is happening?' I asked in some alarm. For all response, he took me suddenly and tightly in his arms, and kissed me resoundingly. Mrs Fitzwilliam's door across the hall opened slightly and she peered out.

'Mrs Fitzwilliam, I have some wonderful, wonderful news,' said Arthur, turning towards her with a totally irrepressible grin painted upon his features, and brandishing a letter which I had not yet had time even to glimpse. 'We are going to be married! As soon as possible, I mean. Look, Vanessa! They've made me a Lecturer! I can marry now, and what's more, we'll have enough to live on!'

'Now, that's very nice for you,' said Mrs

Fitzwilliam, looking slightly mollified. 'I've no married couples in my rooms, of course.'

'Oh, I'm so sorry about your rooms,' he rejoined hastily. 'We shall be giving you notice, of course. Vanessa and I are going to have a house of our own, aren't we? Only something modest to start with; outside of Cambridge. In Newnham, perhaps. The right house for you,' he added, considering me tenderly. 'With jasmine and honeysuckle and things all over the front door.'

I remained stunned for a moment, unable to respond – it was all so unexpected and so sudden! And yet, I have been so impatient, and waited so long for this.

'Oh, Arthur, when?' I finally managed to say.

'It depends on what kind of a marriage you want, and if you want to find a house beforehand,' he answered, looking at me hungrily, as though he would be more than willing to marry me tomorrow and hang the rest.

'Oh, I do want it to be soon, and yet – I need time to get used to it!' I exclaimed. 'Let us begin to search for a house, and choose a date and make a little plan, nothing grandiose! But Dora and my family must come, and all our friends from here.' I glanced at Mrs Fitzwilliam, who nodded sagely. Arthur unwound his arms from around my waist reluctantly.

'Come outside,' he said, 'come for a walk with me. Let us go and enquire about how two independent and consenting adults go about getting married. There must be some formalities, and we shall stop at the church also. And then this evening, I shall write a letter to your father.

Shall I do that, Vanessa?'

I smiled up at him.

'You shall. But don't forget that I am returning to Maidstone Hall this evening. Charles is coming to drive me down at five.'

His face changed.

'Blast the place,' he said. 'I'd forgotten all about it. Oh, Vanessa, I do wish you weren't mixed up in this whole awful story. I wish it were over. I feel like a fresh start.'

'I shan't stay there long, I promise. Arthur, I have no reason to remain there. I am at my wits' end about this mystery and my only hope is to speak to Sylvia so severely that she grasps that she must tell me the truth. If she chooses to say nothing, then there is nothing more that I can do to prevent her being arrested. Look at this telegram from Pat! Even if, as I suppose, she has managed not to realise that her friend from Paris appears to be the murderer of her husband, she must be made to realise it now. And if she will not, then my work is over.'

Arthur was not really listening.

'How long will you go for?' he asked anxiously.

'I don't know exactly,' I said. 'I just wired Mrs Bryce-Fortescue this morning, and she has not answered yet. I thought she would have by now. Still, I don't think it would be of any use to me to stay longer than one or two days. If I don't find out what I need to know by then, I am afraid that more time will not help.'

Arthur looked glum. He cheered up a little during our walk, but his long face returned as we reached home and I looked at my watch.

'You have no idea how much I wish you were well out of this,' he said. 'Or at the very least, that I could go down with you. But I cannot simply arrive without warning.'

'I only hope that Mrs Bryce-Fortescue has received my wire, and is expecting me!' I said. 'Well, at worst, if I find the house all boarded up and everybody gone, Charles shall drive me straight back here and you will be happy.'

Charles appeared at that very moment, looking very smart in newly tailored clothing. I smiled up at him, looking him over with surprised appreciation.

'Ah, it's nice to get back to one's clothes after spending two weeks living out of a suitcase, however well garnished,' he said, responding to my glance. A little colour rose in his cheeks and he added,

'Hum, ha. Ahem.'

He was about to speak but in my impatience I could not resist bursting out with our own news first.

'Charles, Charles, just think! Arthur has been made a Lecturer, and we will finally be able to be married,' I told him, jumping onto the carriage step. 'Oh, it's been so long – it will be so wonderful! I can hardly believe it yet.'

'Re-e-e-ally,' he said, his eyes widening with surprise. 'So they gave you a real job,' he added, turning to Arthur with merriment. 'It was that last paper of yours that did the trick, no doubt – the normal forms one. Well, what we just did in Paris will make that one look like child's play, old fellow, won't it? Perhaps even I won't go on being

321

a Research Fellow forever.' He stepped onto the sidewalk and clumped Arthur unceremoniously on the shoulder.

'So you'll be able to get married now, congratulations, congratulations to the happy couple! We'll have to organise a grand fiesta for you, shan't we? And when is the happy event to take place?'

'We don't know yet – but soon,' I said, kissing Arthur and quickly climbing up onto the box to sit next to Charles. We drove along the streets of Cambridge – I felt a little pang at leaving my lovely town already, when I have just barely come back to it, but I know that is very silly – and took the country road at a smart trot. Charles appeared to have something on his mind; once I was able to detach my mind from selfish contemplation of my own fascinating affairs, this was slowly borne in upon me.

'Ahem,' he said after quite a long silence, during which I absorbed the rays of the slowly sinking sun with the intense concentration of a cat.

'Yes? Do tell me,' I said encouragingly.

'You know ... what you told me and all?' he said, blushing.

'Of course! Well? What about it?' I said, a bit sharply now, for I was pricked by a little needle of worry.

'Well, it's done,' he said in a rush.

'Done, what is done, what do you mean done? What *are* you trying to tell me, Charles? Express yourself, do!'

'All right. I've asked Annabel to marry me.

After I talked with you – after you talked with me, I should say – I saw things differently. How stupid it all is, isn't it? The way life runs, with all these considerations about whether or no and worry about the future and what other people think. When happiness is right there and you just have to stretch out your hand and grasp it. It's interesting,' he added after a slight pause. 'You're a useful friend to have; I've learned a few things from you. It's a funny thing how I've a tendency to avoid thinking by myself sometimes. It's so remarkably easy to let people think for you, and they're so awfully eager to do it most of the time!'

'They are!' I concurred, feeling myself turn slightly pink, partly as a reaction to his compliment, partly out of an embarrassing suspicion that the last words might also be directed at me. 'But it usually just annoys me and makes me feel stubborn,' I added, deciding to pretend that we were in agreement about referring to third parties.

'It must be tiring, sometimes, to be you,' he answered, laughing. 'Yet it warms the heart to watch you, the way you move through life, just doing what you want when you want it, turning the world on its head in a small way. You've got to know what you want, in order to be that way. But I don't always really know just what it is I want.'

'Don't you? Aren't you just avoiding it, often, so as not to make a stir?' I said accusingly.

'Perhaps; but then, you could say that not wanting to make a stir is an honest form of wanting, too. Yet everything does seem much clearer to me now. It seems positively amazing to me, that I could spend all those evenings strolling all over Paris in the twilight with Annabel in perfect happiness, and not have it cross my mind one single time that what I really wanted was to go on doing the same thing forever. I think the idea of how my sister would react simply drowned out the rest.'

'Well, that was one of your fears, certainly,' I smiled, 'although the fear of engaging oneself to settle down may well have been even stronger. But if that second problem has now solved itself for you, the first still remains, I take it. Have you decided what to do?'

'Better; I've done it already,' he said proudly. 'I shouldn't have told you about it if I hadn't. I told Constance fair and square, and soon realised that in worrying about her reaction, I hadn't given sufficient credit to the stiffness of her upper lip. I won't pretend she rejoiced; it obviously came as a shock to her. But if she resented the fact that her governesses appear to make a rule of pairing off with the men of the house (little Edmund will be next to go, at this rate), she didn't show it. Nor did I hear even a single word about the advantageous marriage she had often expressed the hope that I would make to restore the family fortunes, which, if not disastrous, are a little depressed at the moment. Poor Constance. She's had to put up with a lot of things she didn't like over the last several years. This is just another of the series, I guess.'

'I don't think it's as bad or as sad as you make it out to be,' I said. 'There were difficult moments; I remember how reluctant she was at first to adopt the little boy her husband left behind when he died, and she was reluctant to let Edmund leave boarding school – and for that matter also to allow Emily to attend Girton. But I think that in the end she has drawn pride and joy from each of these events. And the same will probably be true, eventually, of your marriage to Annabel. I hope so! But do tell me what Annabel said when you spoke to her.'

'Oh, bother Annabel,' he said, laughing heartily. 'She said all kinds of nonsense. First, that she couldn't possibly dream of marrying me, ruining my chances in society and all sorts of rubbish, true rubbish perhaps, but rubbish nevertheless. Then she said that she had loved me for years and if she hadn't married me, she would never have married anyone else. But then she said that I was a happy creature and she was a weeping willow, and started all over again on how bad it would be for me to marry her, and that she couldn't possibly. I had to threaten to storm out and get a marriage license then and there to make her stop. She did insist on a longish engagement, though. I'm in a tearing hurry to marry, now that I've decided on it, but she says we have to see how the knowledge of it will work on our feelings. On mine, that is. Hers are unchanging forever, she swore, and gave me a little ring which I keep on my bedside table, as it's much too small for any of my fingers.' He laughed again with a sound of bells, and I settled comfortably into my seat, in beatific contentment. We spent the next hour discoursing upon churches and gowns and services, guests and bridesmaids.

We had reached the point of discussing the names of the babies we were soon to have, when the shadows began to lengthen, and the distance to Maidstone Hall to shorten considerably.

'We're arriving,' said Charles, as we approached the house. 'I do hope she got your wire and is expecting you.'

'Someone is home, at any rate,' I said, seeing that the candles were lit in the front room, even though it was not yet dark out. Our carriage drew up smartly in front of the door, and the horses champed and shifted their hooves on the wide path, as Charles descended and came around to help me alight.

Before we had time to reach the front door, it flew open of itself, and Mrs Bryce-Fortescue stood framed within it, lit from behind. She looked extremely young and flushed, and raising her two hands to her cheeks, she cried out,

'Oh my goodness, my goodness, how stupid I have been! My dear Miss Duncan, I am so very sorry – I received your wire and meant to wire you back this afternoon, but I absolutely and completely forgot! Oh, I am so stupid!' She added in some confusion, 'As a matter of fact, I – I meant to tell you that you should put off your visit. The girls are not here at the moment; they have gone off to Severingham, Camilla's place, you know. Of course, now that you are here, you must certainly spend the night.'

She was fluttering and incoherent, which quite surprised me.

'Do come in, do come in,' she continued,

taking me by the hand. 'Tell Peter to put away the horses, Mr Morrison. You'll find him over by the stables. I – I have a surprise for you – you will be most surprised, both of you. A friend of yours is here!'

Charles and I glanced at each other. Who *could* she mean? He darted quickly over towards the stables, obviously eager to come into the cosy house and discover the secret which was revealed to me one instant later, as I entered the parlour.

There, holding a glass of tawny port and deeply and contentedly embedded in a large and becushioned armchair, sat Mr Korneck.

He stood up as I came in, and came towards me with his warm, friendly smile, stretching out his hand. We spoke simultaneously.

'So you are here, and Charles too!' he exclaimed. 'This is a great surprise – I had not thought to meet any acquaintance here, indeed.'

'What *are* you doing here?' I cried, astounded to see him there, when we had left him happily installed in Paris.

'I am here for consolation,' he replied. 'Ah, I have had bad luck, very bad luck and a sad, sad thing has happened to me after you left Paris. I was most sorrowful and devastated, I can assure you, and I wished very much to travel to a place of happiness for repairing of my wounded heart. I thought at first I would return to Poznània to visit the horses, but then I had the idea of a visit to this beautiful house and wrote a letter to this dear lady, who answered me so very kindly. I arrived here only this morning.'

Charles entered the room at this moment, and

stopped short, staring with eyes even rounder than mine.

'Well, of all things!' he exclaimed, shaking Mr Korneck's hand vigorously. 'You here – I wouldn't have guessed it in a thousand years! You do get about, don't you? We said goodbye to you on the other side of the Channel just a few days ago!'

'Alas, alas, I had nothing more to do on the other side of the Channel, after my great discomfiture,' said poor Mr Korneck, a wave of dismay flowing over his features.

'What discomfiture? What happened to you? Is it your proof?' said Charles quickly.

'Alas, you have guessed it. It is the proof.' Stooping, Mr Korneck opened the leather case in which he carried his documents and mathematical papers, and extracted something which he handed gloomily and a little reluctantly to Charles.

'I had no thought, when I sent in my manuscript, that it would be discussed at the very next meeting,' he said lugubriously. 'I thought it must wait until the following one at least, for time would be needed to read through the many pages. Alas, it seems that Monsieur Henri Poincaré does not need any time to read through such a manuscript. He put his finger immediately upon an error, a grievous error, contained deep in the heart of the method. I have thought long and hard about it, but what can I say? He is right, and I was wrong. I cannot see how to make it work.'

Poor Mr Korneck, his face was so very long. He lifted the glass of port to his lips and took a sip.

Mr Bryce-Fortescue quickly replenished it, and while Charles and I bent over the fascicle, she drew him into another part of the room and began, in a trusting tone, to ask him a great many questions upon what sounded like business matters.

We opened the paper he had handed us. It was the formal report of the last weekly meeting of the Academy of Sciences, which had taken place some days before. On the first page, where the order of the day was inscribed, we perceived the notice:

MEMOIRES PRESENTES

*M. **G. Korneck**, de Kempen (Posnanie), adresse un Mémoire contenant une démonstratian du théorème de Fermat.*

(Commissaires: MM. Picard, Poincaré).

Charles turned over the pages to find where the subject of Mr Korneck's unfortunate paper was discussed in the course of the meeting, and located it easily enough a few pages later on. Even I could see that it was, indeed, a disappointment.

RAPPORTS

ANALYSE MATHEMATIQUE. – *Rapport verbal concernant une démonstration du théorème de Fermat sur l'impossibilité de l'equation $x^n + y^n = z^n$ adressée par* M. G. Korneck.

(Commissaires: MM. Picard, Poincaré, rapporteur.)

La demonstration proposée par M. Korneck ne peut être acceptée. Elle s'appuie, en effet, sur le lemme suivant:

Soient les deux nombres n et k dont n est supposé impair, premiers entre eux et non divisibles par un carré; si l'on a en nombres entiers

$$nx^2 + ky^2 = z^n,$$

x sera divisible par n.

Ce lemme est inexact, car on peut faire par exemple:

$$N=3, k=1, x=y=z=4,$$
$$n=5, k=3, x=1, y=3, z=2,$$
$$n=7, k=65, x=3, y=1, z=2.$$

'Oh, for Heaven's sake,' murmured Charles into my ear. 'Do you see that, Vanessa? Look – they say old Korneck's proof is impossible because he went and put this silly lemma into the middle of it–' He stopped and glanced around quickly, but Mr Bryce-Fortescue was still talking to Mr Korneck. 'Why on earth didn't he show us his proof? We'd never have let a thing like this get past us; you don't have to be Poincaré to see that this can't work! Why, he went and said that if you've got numbers that make this formula $nx^2 + ky^2 = z^n$ work, then n has to divide x – and they came up with all these examples where the formula works but n doesn't divide x at all! Oh, my goodness gracious. Why *didn't* he show us his proof?'

'Perhaps it wouldn't have been so easy to find the mistake,' I said. 'Wasn't it a very long proof?'

'Oh, yes,' said Mr Korneck, overhearing my words, and coming over to where we stood. 'It was nearly one hundred pages. A needle in a haystack, this little lemma lost inside it. And yet he is right, Poincaré. It was the heart of the proof, the absolute necessary little pin holding everything else together, without which nothing of the rest can work. And it was on page sixty-nine. Ah, he is a genius. Perhaps I wasted the time of a genius, but still, I have the honour of saying that I was read by him. Until page sixty-nine, at least.'

He took back the report and locked it up in his leather case.

'Sophie Germain must be turning over in her grave,' he said sadly. 'I do not like to think about it. Ah, the great Sophie, she had to overcome so many obstacles, just to persuade anyone to read her wonderful discoveries, while I, who have had every advantage and have the honour to be read by the greatest genius of the day by simple virtue of submitting a manuscript, I make a fool of myself. I shall cease to pursue Fermat's theorem this very day, and devote myself to things I can do better: to questions of business and investment. Yes, I have taken this resolution. I no longer believe that Fermat had a proof of his own theorem – there is no use in searching for it!'

He smiled suddenly, and raised his glass in a toast.

'To the future!' he cried with so admirable an

331

effort at good humour that all three of us echoed him with the greatest goodwill you can imagine!

We had supper, and no further mention was made of the sad tale of Mr Korneck's proof. Instead, we talked about the successes of his horse farm in Prussia (without ostentation, without boasting and without apparent effort, he caused us to become aware that the farm was a highly profitable venture) and how happy it would make him to keep up two beautiful establishments, one in Prussia and one in England, one for horses and one for the pleasures of domesticity.

'For the English understand the pleasures of domestic life better than any nation on Earth,' he exclaimed, poking his fork into the excellent roast of lamb provided by Mr Firmin, as if to prove his point. 'Perhaps the cooking is not the most sophisticated in Europe, but it is so healthy, so ample – and then, only in England does one have tea-time, and they put cream on the scones instead of butter!'

We dined so long and so late that Charles had to rush for his horses afterwards, and make a hasty departure; not, however, before taking me briefly aside and putting on a scolding expression.

'What have you been doing to the groom, Vanessa,' he whispered. 'He watched us drive up together, and his face looked pretty stormy – and he asked me if I was your fiancé! Of course I said no, your fiancé had remained in Cambridge, and he said "is that so?" and I said "yes, but what business is it of yours, my man?" and he looked annoyed, I mean to say extremely annoyed, and mumbled something to the effect that women were all the same everywhere and who could be surprised?'

'Oh dear,' I moaned, feeling most embarrassed.

'So you have been up to something,' he said disapprovingly. 'Well, get out of it. You'd better clear things up pretty sharply and pretty soon, that's what I say.'

He left, frowning, and Mr Bryce-Fortescue accompanied me up to my room. I followed her quietly. I mean to rise early and make my way to Severingham as quickly as I can tomorrow morning, arriving if possible without warning, but thought it better not to mention these plans, nor, for the moment, Pat's telegram. I have decided to take no step, no step at all, until I have talked to Sylvia.

In the meantime, I am writing this letter before going to bed. As late as it is, I can still make out the murmur of voices downstairs. I do hope that everything will turn out all right after all, so that poor Mr Korneck can find a little happiness, without the very thing he has turned to for consolation collapsing immediately!

Oh, if only Sylvia were here. If only I could make out, once and for all, the exact degree of her involvement! I came here to talk to her, to question her, to confront the problem as directly as possible, and I am unable to do it; I feel extremely frustrated. I am compelled to inactivity, at least for the moment. I can do nothing but think.

Dora, I know so many facts – I hold so many clues to this mystery! Surely I no longer need to rush about trying to find out more. If I could just understand all that I have learned, resolve the seeming contradictions, and see how everything fits together into a whole, then, I believe, the answer would stand out clear and obvious.

Oh, well. I shall sleep on it, and tomorrow concentrate on nothing else.

Goodnight, my dearest twin

Vanessa

Maidstone Hall, Friday, July 22, 1892 (although really, it is the 23rd already)

My dearest sister,

It is very late at night, but I cannot sleep.

I wrote you yesterday night, thinking that today I would leave this place today in the early morning, to try to find Sylvia and talk to her. But as it happens, I did not leave. Indeed, after having finished breakfast, I informed Mrs Bryce-Fortescue of my intentions, and asked if Peter could bring me to the train station. But instead of acquiescing, she leaned towards me, staring at me intently with her eagliest expression, and said penetratingly,

'Have you come to some conclusion about my son-in-law's murder?'

'I certainly have some important information,' I answered carefully, 'but before I speak of it at all, I really must talk to Sylvia.'

'But I am your client,' she said, 'and as such, I think you should inform me of exactly what is going on.'

I felt trapped; she was not wrong, yet instinct told me not to reveal anything yet.

'I believe that Sylvia holds an important piece of information which may identify the murderer,' I said finally, 'but it seems possible that she does not realise it herself. That is why I absolutely must talk to her. And in fact, it is extremely urgent,' and pulling Pat's telegram from my pocket, I spread it out in front of her. She read it and blanched.

'I will wire for her to return immediately,' she said. 'Whatever is to happen, I would much prefer that it happen here and not at some distant place where I can be of no help to her. I beg of you to remain until she arrives. The trip is a rather complicated one as Severingham is very out of the way, but she will surely arrive by this evening at the latest.'

Thus, Dora, I found myself once again unexpectedly unoccupied for the space of an entire day. Time dragged endlessly, and it was still too early to think of expecting Sylvia; I worried and fidgeted and was unable to reflect tranquilly. It was your letter, which was laid at my place at luncheon (together with one from Arthur exhorting me to put a speedy end to my stay), which finally released me from the terrible tension in which I was trapped. It spurred me to a depth of concentration during which I forgot everything else. And I spent the rest of the afternoon wandering alone through fields and groves, forcing my mind to think over the facts again and again, but alas, feeling it constantly twisting aside as though to avoid the course of reasoning I wished

335

to impose upon it.

In the end, exhausted, I retired to my room not long after dinner. There was still no sign of Sylvia, and Mrs Bryce-Fortescue was visibly unnerved. I myself felt unreasoningly afraid that she had perhaps been arrested during the course of the day, yet it seemed that this could not possibly have happened without our somehow being apprised of the fact. I closed my door and sat down on my bed, then lay down and fell into a strange doze from sheer mental exhaustion, although it was not late. The thoughts that had been writhing unformed in my mind all day turned themselves into strange dreams, shaping into vague images and dissolving away again until I woke up from sheer torment, my forehead damp. I seemed to feel a sense of impending doom, and my body was cramped with tension, so I arose and looked at the time. My dear, I had slept for hours, it was – is – two o'clock in the morning! I lit my candle and sat down at the desk to write this letter; surely, surely, this gentle activity will, as always, soothe my feverish brain and clarify my racing thoughts.

I seem to feel exactly what the mathematicians describe, when they have puzzled for weeks and months over some difficult theory, and suddenly they realise that they are on the very brink of the solution, and that the fog is lifting, and the whole landscape is forming clear and sunlit in front of their wondering eyes.

And my mind has been shying away from what it is beginning to perceive, just as they have often told me happens at the moment of discovery.

That precise moment – when one becomes aware that the course of thought will lead inexorably and very soon to total certainty – that is the moment when the mathematician drops his pen and rushes out to take a long walk in the city, or drink a cup of tea which lasts for hours. And so I have done today. Things are coming to a head, and discovery can no longer be avoided; I must do what I can to ensure that the innocent are spared. This means that now, I must apply myself to my task with no more detours. Yes, I shall follow the advice contained in your extraordinary letter, and try to set down on paper, in orderly form, the list of those facts and contradictions that must be resolved. So many things that don't fit – they must be examined, one by one, and *made* to fit!

1. It seems certain that Sylvia had a lover while in Paris. Yet, this contradicts all of Ellen's instincts, though she will not say why. It also contradicts Sylvia's own inclinations, which she expressed to me in what I believed to be complete spontaneity. Of course, Ellen could be mistaken as she has not seen Sylvia for so many years, and Sylvia could be lying. Yet it does not seem so to me ... it *must* mean something.

2. The following three people are, it appears to me, unquestionably to be identified as a single person: Sylvia's friend mentioned above, seen with her in Paris and Deauville, then the young man observed on the boat and in the train to Haverhill, and finally Mr Granger's murderer.

What do we know about him? After various mistaken assumptions, the information most likely to be correct is that he is English, although he was certainly in France last winter, and he certainly took the boat over from there on the day of the murder. Yet it is not necessarily in France that he must be sought.

3. No one appears to be able to discover where he came from just before taking the boat. It seems that the only way in which he could have done what he did is by wearing a disguise, a disguise both very effective, consisting of very few and small elements (as nothing seemed to have been left behind) and incredibly quick to put on or off – off probably being much faster as the French inspector pointed out.

4. I heard something this evening – I feel certain that it was something Mr Korneck mentioned – which rang a bell inside me. At the moment he said it, it was as though a little voice said *Note that – that reminds me of something important!* But I paid no attention, I was so concerned by the sad fate of his proof. And now I cannot figure out what it was – yet it seems as though it were on the very tip of my tongue!

I have just glanced over your letter again, and my eye fell upon your remarkable observations about mathematics. Are you clairvoyant, Dora? Does it really all mean something?

What a strange parallel can be erected between the

story of Fermat's lost theorem, and the problem you are investigating. An equation that is surely true – a murder which really happened! A proof sought by many and not yet understood, and a hopeful optimist who does not give up the search. A young woman who holds the key to a fundamental piece of knowledge, but who is prevented from speaking out frankly by the rigid social constraints of her time. And the margin, the margin which is always too narrow; a margin of paper too narrow to allow the proof to fully unfold – a margin of time too short to allow a change of disguise – a seemingly invisible margin of space through which someone slipped onto a boat – and a margin of error too tight to allow any haphazard explanation to fit the facts.

Dora – *OF COURSE!* I remember now what it is that Mr Korneck talked about! Your words have just reminded me; but how, how could you possibly have guessed it? He said–
   Wait!
   It is very strange – I seem to hear some faint sounds coming from next door, from the large vacant room onto which mine gives. Someone is moving around in there, lightly, softly. Oh! what can it be? I feel unreasonably afraid – terrified! What shall I do? I must stop writing – I will take my candle, unshoot the bolt and fling the door open to face whatever is there.

In haste –

V.

Maidstone Hall, early morning, Saturday, July 23, 1892

My dearest, dearest and only, unique twin,

I am in a sorry state, as I write this note to you, before I hasten, at the very first crack of dawn, to quit this house forever. Dawn is barely breaking over the sky, and my previous letter, written just a few hours ago, lies on the desk before me, barely dry. This one is an addendum to it, and yet it is much more. For during the long hours of this fatal night, I have passed the barrier to the other side.

Oh, I did not realise, when I began this investigation, that the solving of it could perturb me so deeply, could tear such rifts into what I thought, hitherto, was a natural, healthy and straight-forward moral sense. Wrong, right, and responsibility – nothing is clear to me any more! Yes, something *is* clear. The truth has been revealed to me beyond the need for proof – and if proof were needed, it would be easy to come by now.

I left you last night, when I wiped my pen and put it down next to the letter I had just finished writing. I stood by the desk, momentarily para-lysed, straining my ears for the soft rustling noises from next door, and running my eyes, at the same time, over the list of points I had taken such pains to write just moments before – I will send you that letter, dear, with this one, although it seems so foolish and blind now! I was reading over the sentences you wrote me, when suddenly, in an instantaneous flash, in infinitely less time than it takes to read this, and even while my heart was knocking in fear at the sly little movements I could still make out next door, something hit me which had not hit me before.

Sophie Germain – the genius mathematician, Mr Korneck's idol – *she had to pretend to be a man!* Charles had told us all about her story, and Mr Korneck's mention of her had lit a sudden spark in my mind, in connection with all our talk about disguises; hasty disguises that must be put on and off in a moment behind a pile of crates.

A woman – disguised as a man! What could be easier? A tall woman with a long stride, and thick dark hair controlled by a net and combed severely back into a heavy knot, a woman who is able to sew the most sophisticated dresses for herself and her friend... If such a woman were to pass quietly along the quay, wearing a long, ample skirt of some modestly coloured stuff and a hat upon her head – if her hair were in fact cut short like a man's, and her knot of black hair were a false one, attached with pins – if the skirt should in fact be fastened down the front with nothing more difficult than buttons or ribbons, and lined, invisibly, with brightly coloured silk – if it were worn over a pair of men's trousers and boots – if this woman should, then, slip behind a mountain of waiting luggage, snatch off her *lady's hat* and fling it to the ground, to be picked up later by some stray passenger or by a dock-worker after the loading was finished, and handed to the office of lost objects – if she were then to remove the net and the knot and thrust them into a pocket, ruffle up her mass of hair into curls, and unbinding her skirt, transform it into a vivid cape with a single swish?

If this same woman amused herself, months earlier, by donning her masculine guise in public, and accompanying her friend about the city in the role of a lover?

Dora – what if this woman planned a murder, and planned it carefully, travelling to Dover and crossing to France in her female clothing, descending from the boat onto the quay, and turning herself into a young man in just a few swift gestures, leaving no trace at all behind her (except, perhaps, a lost hat)? And if she boarded the boat again, her ticket of course purchased beforehand, and travelled back to England as noticeably as possible in her scarlet silk cape, and went about her terrible business there? And then quietly, in a washroom on the return train to London, resumed her woman's garb, took a different seat, and descended at the terminal, undetected and undetectable (except, perhaps, by a vague, wandering old woman who had seen her, upon occasion, visiting Haverhill manor)?

Camilla!

These thoughts, or rather, these images flashed through my mind within a single second, together with the startled question – but *why? Why?* Why would Camilla hate Sylvia's husband enough to murder him?

And one who murders once can murder again, I thought, gripping my candle and staring at the door of my room with horror. I heard again slight sounds of movement, and even something that sounded, faintly, like the rustling of paper. Stepping silently to the door, with one brusque, sharp gesture, I kicked aside the little dressing table which stood in front of it, pushed the bolt, flung it open, and stretched my arm with its candle into the total darkness that confronted me.

I perceived no one, yet I still felt afraid. My candle shed a little circle of light which did not reach into the farthest corner of the large space, and it was well stocked with old furniture and boxes behind which a person could be hiding. Yet I would not have thought that a person could have had enough warning of my approach to hide, so quick had I been. I stood for a moment, wavering.

Then I saw another movement, like a streak. The large orange cat whom I had already encountered in this same room leapt down suddenly from the top of a high old closet where he had been perched, landing with a soft, heavy plunk, and trotted over to me with a meow. I heaved a tremulous sigh of relief, then jumped as I heard a rustling noise; something, disturbed, slipped from the top of the closet after the cat and fell, bumping, to the ground. It was a little sheaf of papers, which he had probably been investigating, as cats will, if they find anything unusual in their familiar domain. I stepped over to it with care and picked it up, my heart pounding uncontrollably.

This little packet, folded tightly and tied with a string, was undoubtedly what Sylvia had been hiding in her jewel box, that object which had subsequently disappeared.

Dora, I hardly know how to comment on such

a document. I do not know what to do with it, where to put it; it burns my fingers. I will send it to you, Dora; keep it for me. I think it contains more explanations, and of a deeper kind, than any other kind of proof ever could, no matter how factual.

Truth

A poem-novel, a novel-poem, a raving novel, an impossible attempt

I. Madness

This book contains the truth about Camilla: Camilla is mad. Her madness has a source, a wellspring, a catalyst that shoots it forth like jets of flame pouring from the cannon's mouth, and when the fire dies down, it leaves only white ashes like death.

Camilla's madness is invisible to all about her. She walks upright, she walks tall and straight, her eyes are calm, her words are plain. Sometimes she sneers, but only slightly.

Camilla's life, and her madness, are divided into three. When the source is far and the need is small, the madness rolls like a ball, curls like a ball, and remains dense and thick and quiet in a deep place. When the source is near, and the inflamed thirst is constantly slaked, the madness lurks within like a ravening animal just after food: satisfied for the present, yet infinitely wary,

344

infinitely tense. But when ferocious demand wells up uncontrollably and finds no satisfaction, meets only silence, that is when Camilla's madness swells into a giant and all-consuming roar that drowns out, in her ears, every pleasant sound of the world around her; birdcalls and running water and the echo of distant conversations. All are lost; only the screaming roar remains.

In that swirling darkness all becomes possible, all becomes necessary, all becomes inexorable for all eternity, for the raving monster is stronger than any barrier the world can raise against it. As Mohammed moved the mountain, Camilla feels that she will heave gigantic, unknown weights and tear apart the very fabric of existence, if she lifts her hand to do so.

The wild beast is invisible. Camilla herself cannot see it.

In these moments, she rises slowly and walks, step by step, to the mirror. Carefully, as though she needs an effort to recall the simplest gestures. Step by step, to the mirror, and there, she stops and stares at herself.

Black eyes stare back: tormented. Black hair smoothed back, drawn back, forced back, pulled back. The creature with its slavering fangs is nowhere to be seen, and yet she feels it gnawing and gnashing within.

She stares in the mirror for many long minutes.

Without knowing it, she is rocking back and forth, slowly, intently, and her gaze is becoming fixed. She presses her fingers to her temples, hard, strong hard sensitive fingertips pressing against the delicate place, then forces them slowly upwards into the hair, into the very roots of the hair where it springs forth, a heavy mass controlled, a wild thing tamed. Deep into the roots the fingers force their path until they are buried entirely, and she grasps the hair, grasps it in a frenzy, wrenches and twists it, pulls it loose from its binding, and as it falls in a tangled web on her shoulders, she is crying, rocking back and forth, crying, twisting the hair as though to tear it out altogether, staring at herself in the mirror, rocking and crying, devoured from within by the monster, destroyed and devoured by the monster, and she stares at the girl in the mirror, no longer a girl, a banshee, keening and wailing, suffering and desire forbidden, and therefore mad. And she whispers again and again to the abandoned creature in the mirror,

'Is it possible? Can it be? Were I a man, this madness would be love?'

II. Stonehenge

Great rocks embedded in the earth, thrusting toward the sky. Gigantic and immobile and silent; mere stones, yet radiating the still power of pagan gods. The air is thick beneath them, thick with tension, heavy with their eternal past, silent echoes of the formless, hypnotic thoughts of those

346

who built and worshipped them. They move not, they speak not, yet they stand, shrouded in meaning, inaccessible to time and effort, monuments to eternal, expressionless existence.

That same eternal monument is the cornerstone of Sylvia's soul; silent, inscrutable, invisible, powerful.

'She's just a slip of a girl.' That is what they say of her.

A slip of a girl, a flower perhaps, but merely a small and insignificant one. Yes, that describes her quite well.

She sits at the window, staring outside. Her hands are idle, her body motionless. It is early evening, and the room is filled with people, the air is crossed by a multitude of sounds. Yet the girl at the window is alone. She is at a party, yet she sits, and stares out the window, at the dusk slowly gathering over the stone urns bordering the terrace. She is not absent, not irritated, not disturbed, not bored, not anxious, not hopeful. Her profile, the profile of a very young girl, is sharply outlined in white against the darkening window. Camilla stands watching her. The party swirls around her, and she stands, watching the girl at the window and trying to fathom what she sees, what she feels. The power of the presence of the unknown girl is such that the party fades into mist, and her silent world becomes the only truth. To be so motionless (her hands and feet so totally still) – how is it possible when Camilla's whole being twitches with restlessness, when interest, annoyance, surprise, pleasure and boredom alternate so rapidly within her that she hardly knows what it is that she feels? Her first season; at times she feels like a queen, at others, hatefully, on display. Sometimes she dances (she has danced a great deal lately), sometimes she watches and her thoughts are tinged with irony and malice. The parties seem like giant games of chess; each piece moving according to preconceived rules, no infractions tolerated. Camilla plays her role, but sometimes the thoughts within her run wild.

The girl at the window is not playing the game, is not aware of any game; has never, perhaps, heard that one must hide one's thoughts; has, perhaps, no thoughts to hide, but contents herself with existing, with the quiet inexorable strength of being which defies reason and effort and purpose.

The lilies of the field toll not, neither do they spin.

Why struggle, why hope and strain and worry, why weary oneself with vain attempts? Why play the cosmic game?

'Camilla, Camilla, what are you doing, dear? They're beginning to dance, won't you go?'

She awakens, startled, out of her reverie, and transfers her gaze with difficulty to her hostess, standing in front of her. It is a moment where nothing but truth is possible.

'I was wondering who the girl at the window is,' she says, so directly that her hostess raises her eyebrows, but she turns and glances.

'Oh, her. That's Sylvia Bryce-Fortescue, the daughter of an old school friend of mine. Now look at her; what is she doing? Isn't she impossible! I shall fetch her at once.'

Camilla gazes fascinated, her heart pinched. Will the idol fall, smashed? Will the girl stand up, unfold her fan, laugh, dance, blink up into her partner's face? Mrs Clemming is blind; all people are alike to her. Cogs in her large, well-oiled machine, they must be made to behave. She is talking to Sylvia, smiling and beckoning, but her tone is cross. Sylvia turns her face from the gathering darkness to the glittering room. Camilla cannot hear the words. The scene passes silently in front of her, and she is afraid, afraid of losing what she has just found. The unknown girl will not, cannot possibly resist the order to come, to move, to dance, to mingle, to talk, to eat an ice. She is rising, she is following her hostess. They are approaching the place where Camilla is still standing.

'Here's Camilla Wright. She was asking about you,' says Mrs Clemming brightly, thrusting Sylvia forward. 'Camilla, this is Sylvia, the daughter of an old friend of mine, as I told you, just up from the country for the season. I'm sure you two girls will be friends. You're the same age, aren't you? Both eighteen, like my Helen. Camilla, see that Sylvia spends a nice evening, show her about, will you, dear? She's a little lost here tonight.'

And she moves away, leaving Camilla in front of her lily, her idol, whose whole expression and demeanour are exactly as before; even now, as she stands and moves and speaks, she is surrounded by an aura of silent stillness. Her smiles and words are not those of other people, masks in front of their true faces; her smiles and words spring unconsciously and directly from the inner source of still power. And Camilla takes her arm, and searches for expression, and speaks it slowly.

'You were looking at the terrace. It is very pretty in the moonlight. Would you like to take a turn?'

III. Obsession

Camilla cannot think about anything else. The colours of the days of this season, this social season during which Camilla was to come out, to enter into the great world, to see and be seen, to marry and be married, are now determined exclusively by a single factor. The days where she is not to see Sylvia are dove grey, wrapped in felt. They have their beauty, those empty days; they have the quietness of waiting and the secret excitement of using them to build the self into something greater than before, something that can charm and conquer her. Yet the mystery is how to set about it, how to be worthy of Sylvia, for Sylvia does not care about worth; not moral worth, nor riches, nor sparkling intelligence, nor beauty. What, then, does she want? She wants nothing, is content, is not even content, but quite simply, is. And so Camilla spends the empty days seeking the words and gestures with which she can transmit this most fragile and delicate of all notions: love, that which reaches and enfolds and protects without spoiling or crushing even the tiniest petal.

Then there are the diamond days, when she knows that this evening, she will enter, somewhere, some house, and search in the crowded room until her eyes, irresistibly attracted, locate the slender figure, who, with the passing of time, has become less solitary; indeed she is always surrounded by young men and dances nearly all the dances, yet she has not lost an iota of her original quietness. On those days, from early in the morning, Camilla watches herself, observes herself like an outsider, bursting with verve and laughing too much, eating nothing and looking constantly in the mirror; hears herself saying eagerly,

'Oh, tonight's party is *sure* to be wonderful! The Mannings are such marvellous hosts!' –

– and doesn't know whether to be annoyed or amused.

Worst are the black days where Camilla must go to some party, some fête, some ball, not knowing whether Sylvia will be there or not. On those

351

days, Camilla frets and counts the hours in spite of herself. She hates it, stamps her foot alone in her room, argues to herself that such frenzy can have no good effect, is merely foolish, wearying and wasteful, snatches up a book and glares at the pages, walks with great strides up and down the avenues, buys white flowers for her dark hair, and finally, lies on her bed, dreaming, dreaming the hours away, until finally she is late, not yet dressed, and her body seems heavy as lead. The effort of rising, dressing and crossing the streets of the city seems beyond human strength. And sometimes, the hope of seeing Sylvia pushes her through these gestures like a rusty automaton, rewarded by the gift of life if Sylvia is present after all, whereas on certain other days she pleads a headache and falls asleep, a heavy sleep, tormented with strange dreams like lush tropical flowers, which seize her like a prisoner until morning, leaving her wearier than when she lay down.

If she could only penetrate Sylvia's opacity. But Sylvia does not seek to understand the minds of others any more than a flower does, as it stands in its spot, spreading its green leaves in the sunshine.

'There's a soirée at the Kinnocks the day after tomorrow,' Camilla says to her tentatively. 'You know them, don't you? So I expect you'll be there.'

'I don't know,' Sylvia answers, and her answer gives no sign: *I don't know* – it can mean a thousand things, hint a thousand desires, hide or reveal an infinity of thoughts, be garnished, like a dish, with smiles or frowns, dimples or eyelashes. But Sylvia's words are as plain as school cooking; quite literally, she does not know, and there is nothing further to be said.

'How can you not know? Haven't you an agenda?'

'Mrs Clemming arranges everything for me,' she says, and again, one could seek in vain the meaning behind her words; is she annoyed, does she find it silly, or on the contrary, does the arrangement suit her perfectly?

'Can't you ask her? I'll only come if you do,' the words are on the tip of Camilla's tongue, poised, ready to slip off; and yet no, it is impossible. One does not speak to Sylvia in hints. So Camilla goes to see Mrs Clemming, sitting in her corner, following her daughter Helen with her eyes.

'The Kinnocks, yes of course. Why, naturally. Oh, Sylvia, I don't know, I really don't! She's such a very *difficult* girl, changes her mind without notice, has no idea how annoying it can be. I wash my hands of her. She can come or not, as she likes. But Helen will be there.' And she watches her daughter intently, and Camilla follows her gaze, staring uncomfortably at the hefty girl standing alone at the refreshment table, while Sylvia cannot get away from three young men who clamour for the next dance and seem not at all put out by her inability to banter, quite the contrary. So Camilla remains in the same position as before, thinking of the following Thursday, knowing that she will suffer, not knowing how to avoid it, tormented by the desire to exert pressure on Sylvia, to exact a promise from her, yet knowing that it would serve no purpose at all, that her promises would slip away from her as innocently as clouds floating across the sky.

For promises are binding, and Sylvia cannot be bound.

IV. The Kiss

Camilla no longer knows exactly when the idea first took shape within her, exactly how it eventually came to take her psyche prisoner. When she thinks back, she perceives a myriad of fragmented origins.

She is standing quite far from Sylvia; she still hardly knows her, but she watches her across the heads and shoulders of a cheerfully swirling crowd. A young man is talking to Sylvia, earnestly, intensely. Camilla is far too distant to be able to hear or even guess at what he is saying. Sylvia listens quietly, motionlessly. The young man leans towards her a little more, then suddenly bends so that his face approaches hers. Camilla is transfixed.

'If he kisses her, I'll strangle him.'

The thought flashes through her mind so quickly she has no time to note it. Already the young man has straightened up. He is shaking Sylvia's hand cordially, he seems to be taking his leave. He is walking away, he is gone. Camilla feels suddenly safe and yet fustigates herself for such ridiculousness.

Camilla is walking alone under the trees, on the lane which runs along the little, sparkling stream. The place is absurdly right for lovers, and indeed, all the other occupants of the lane seem to be grouped in pairs; gloved hands linked under arms, parasols hanging from wrists. Only Camilla is alone. She has given herself a task: she will walk a mile up the stream, and a mile back down, and she will count the minutes it takes her, walking slowly. As slowly as possible, for the goal of the game is to cheat time, to make it move along, to push it faster than its present crawl. She advances slowly, and crosses couples passing in the other direction. Look at this young girl coming towards her now. Slender and pale, she could be Sylvia, but is not; she is with a young man, she is hanging on his arm, her face is turned up to his. He looks down at her patronisingly.

'You'll see then, sweet,' he is saying as they pass Camilla, 'by this time next year we'll be married and you'll be the mistress of your own home.' The girl simpers, and Camilla wants to scream. Look at him – all the charm of feminine youth clinging to his arm, and he talks to her as though to some tame pet. Ah, if Camilla were in his place, she

355

could tear through clothes and flesh with her breath, with her eyes, and there would be no room for idle talk within the flame of her passion. She would not speak in words, she would speak in kisses. And her body feels tense with the strain of passing, turning her head away, and continuing her walk, slowly, in rhythm, one step after another, under the arching willow branches which dangle their tips, loose and abandoned, into the endless lapping caresses of the water.

Or they are walking together, arm in arm, during one of those moments stolen from the duties imposed upon them; those duties which consist, essentially, in displaying the self like merchandise for sale, to best advantage. They have slipped out, as they quite often manage to do, sometimes for just a few minutes, sometimes for the better part of the evening. They are strolling across the garden tinged with moonlight, and everything seems abnormally beautiful to Camilla, as grass and trees, sky and stars breathe their magic headily forth. Sylvia's face glows softly in the darkness, a pale dim vision, yet its warm life radiates and Camilla knows that she is going to stop everything, stop the world in its tracks, seize that face between her hands and drown it in the kisses that have been restrained for so long – she knows she will do it, except for this one obstacle: she knows she will not do it. The fear of frightening away forever something as wild and uncontrollable as a fawn, of sending it scampering back eternally into the shadows of outer darkness – is stronger than even such desire.

Or so she tells herself, as the days slip by, until, without her being at first aware of it, new little thoughts begin to emerge, like droplets forming on a cold surface. For she sees Sylvia differently now, sees more deeply into her nature, begins to understand the ineffable femininity of her. She is the slender creature for whom great stags battle in duels, crashing their antlers together until one of them lopes away, defeated. She is the Sabine seized by the desperate Roman in his thirst for woman, the trophy awarded to the conquering hero, seated unresisting within the circle of his arm. Sylvia need not be conquered nor persuaded nor convinced. She is there for the taking, like a glass of sweet wine.

If I don't take her, someone else will.

And the evening comes when Camilla prepares her mind, her dress, her words, her gestures, reflects for hours on the very nature of what she is about to do, hesitates between the endless languor of something infinitely long and warm, or a lightning stroke, brutal and blinding.

And in the end it is so simple.

Sylvia melts in her arms with a small, secret smile. She is not angry, not shocked, not even surprised, yet neither is she worldly-wise, nor had she expected anything. She is just flowerlike Sylvia, preserving her quiet mystery intact in spite of the snatching and seizing and plucking and bruising.

The ultimate possession, ultimately unpossessable.

V. Marriage

And now, just as she thought she had reached the haven of security, Camilla finds herself more storm-tossed than ever. Mad with desire, obsessed with discoveries renewed every day, seeking endlessly to penetrate Sylvia's secret, leaving no stone unturned, no place untouched, like a drinker of vinegar, never quenched, only inflamed.

And she is invaded by nameless doubts. Sylvia is like a landscape of shifting sands, she thinks, and tries to tear reassurance from her with words. Her light-heartedness is torture.

'I wish I could marry you, Sylvia.'

'What for?'

'Because I want you for myself for ever and ever.'

'Marriage has nothing to do with that.'

'If I married you I would keep you prisoner and tie you up and lock you in and visit you every night.'

'Do it anyway.'

But Camilla can't. It has something to do with the eyes of the world.

Marriage looms thick in the air that Mrs Clemming breathes.

'Sylvia, they're trying to marry you off!'

'Of course. They're trying to marry you off, too.'

'I'll never marry.'

'It's easy for you. You've a castle of your own and something to live on. I don't.'

Camilla doesn't dare to tell her that she doesn't have a castle, not really. Not forever.

'But you don't want to marry, do you?'

'I don't want to, but what I want doesn't matter at all, it never has.'

'It matters to me! I want you to do what you want.'

'I don't know what I want.'

'Ah, because you haven't lived yet. Come – let me show you, and then you'll know what you want forever and ever.'

It is hopeless. Nothing will bind Sylvia, not even her own desires. Abandoned in Camilla's arms, a secret little half-smile on her lips, she says as though the previous conversation had never been interrupted,

'Yes, but Mother won't agree. If I don't marry, we'll have nothing to live on, and Mother will have to give up the house.'

'You traitress – you want to get married, don't you?'

'No, I don't. I don't care.'

'Sylvia, don't you understand – if you had a husband, he would want to take – what's mine, *only mine*.'

She merely shrugs.

'I'd never let a husband do anything I didn't want to.'

'Oh, heavens,' Camilla says, staring up at the sky.

VI. Absence

The branches of the trees are darker grey against the grey sky, and the new leaves tremble colourlessly. Camilla sits on the tow path staring at them, counting the passing seconds, the passing minutes, the slowly shifting and passing clouds.

Sylvia has left London. She had enough of parties, enough of balls, enough of coming out, enough of Helen, so she went home. Quite simply went home, Mrs Clemming said, with mingled resentment and satisfaction.

Elle n'en fait qu'a sa tête, Camilla says. She is right, and I am wrong. If she wants to do a thing, she does it. If she doesn't like it, she drops it. She can no more force herself than a plant – and why should she?

Her mind wanders over the subject, trying to dull pain by curiosity. Why do we insist, labour, struggle, so stupidly? We want the end and dislike the means – is that it? Yet no. Camilla does not desire the end which looms before her.

Then what do I want?

She wants Sylvia, nothing else. Her arms ache with absence, with emptiness. And if it were just the secret union of their souls, of their lips, of their hands... But she knows already that it would not be enough. Ah, she wants more, she wants to walk in the streets, her head high, Sylvia on her arm – she wants a banner to proclaim her possession, a burning brand to mark her publicly.

Why? It's stupid, she thinks. Why offend everyone? Why not be satisfied with the sweetness of clandestinity? Why long for public recognition? She grinds her teeth.

I don't know what I want, and when I do know, I don't know why I want it.

It should be so simple, as it is for Sylvia. If I want her, then I should go and find her. And why don't I do it? What keeps me from her, when she is separated from me by nothing more than a few hours in the train?

Now we come to the heart of the matter, the bitter syllogism.

Sylvia has gone.

Sylvia does what she wants.

Therefore, she wanted to go. And not to stay, not here, where I am. She fled from me, not from the rest. I will not pursue her.

The world with its gay ribbons winds and tangles around Camilla from morning till night, and she feels fixed in the central point of the milling throng; she feels unmoving, rigid, stuck. And after a while, nausea and fever. She lies in bed without moving and stares out the window at the buildings across the way. Like a tiny, tiny fresh breeze, she glimpses a vision of trees and fields and sky, but it is only in her memory. Camilla decides, like Sylvia, to go home.

VII. Severingham

When Camilla was a little girl, she used to think that the walk from her bedroom to the breakfast room was immensely long.

When she was still tiny, she had to follow her governess there, and it seemed a long time before she actually knew the way. When she was a little older, she went by herself. Down the corridor past ten doors. Around the corner, up the stone stairs. The short cut across the roof to the other turret, back down. Halfway down the main stairway leading to the ground floor with its ballrooms and dining rooms. Around the balcony overhanging the foyer. Here is the breakfast room, inundated with the morning light. Here is Mother, standing at the sideboard to cut the child's bread herself, a little thinner, as she likes it. There is father, grumbling because he has already poured out the last drop of coffee, looking around for the maid. The sun shines in and the groom is walking Camilla's pony outside: after breakfast, she will ride. Camilla's riding habit has already been the subject of a number of quarrels.

She opens her eyes suddenly, stares hard at the sideboard. That was fifteen years ago. Miss Winston is gone, Mother is dead, the pony also. Father is sitting at the table as of old, if greyer, but he does not speak more now than he did then. She pours out the coffee for him without being asked, gives him the last drops.

'I'll go riding after breakfast,' she says. And she rides, canters madly all over the grounds, hears her voice laughing as she leaps the muddy stream; you can never be sure.

One hour, two hours. What shall I do this afternoon? I'll read over all my old books, garden maybe. What is my life for? Just surviving. Can I snatch a little comfort from this, the cradle of the time when I was carefree? The trouble is, it's difficult to stop thinking, stop the burning images from rushing through the mind. I'll talk with Father. I wonder whom he talks to nowadays?

The sun is high and Camilla brings her horse around to the stables.

'No, I'll brush him,' she tells the boy, lifting the saddle off and hanging it on a nail.

'Hoo, where've you been with 'im?' he says, looking at the muddy hooves. Camilla takes a scraper, lifts the front leg and holding the hoof firmly against her thigh, digs it into the clotted mud. Clump! It drops down into the hay. She drops the hoof, slaps the horse gently, and takes another. Four hooves to scrape, and then brush, brush the dusty coat. The horse looks at her lazily, gleaming and pleased.

Luncheon will soon be served. Camilla goes into the house, past all the doors and corridors, up to her room, and takes off her riding habit – the one she made for herself specially, to ride at home with, for real, not sidesaddle. The sense of freedom she had only just begun to achieve slips away as she binds herself into blouse and skirt. The walk down to the dining room is slower and wearier than the way in. She opens the door. Father is already seated at the table.

'The mail has come in, dear,' he says in his voice grown a little peevish from monotony and loneliness. 'You've got a letter.'

There is a letter by Camilla's dish. Blank side up.

She sits at the table and stares at the white square until it grows and fills up the whole room, the horizon. She has no strength to pick it up and turn it over, and face the abyss. The room seems to whirl.

'What's yours?' says her father with interest. His life is so empty now.

Like a machine. Say nothing, show nothing. Reach out and take it. Turn it over. Sit tight, don't move.

The letter is from Sylvia.

This is ridiculous, thinks Camilla to herself. Stop it at once. She rips the envelope quietly, lifts her eyes from it to smile at her father, takes out the little sheet and unfolds it.

A mere glance suffices to read it. It speaks with Sylvia's voice.

Dear Camilla,

I hated it so in London that I decided to come away. I'm home now. Won't you come visit? Mother and I would love to have you. Do write and let me know.

Love, Sylvia

Quite quietly, the world stops spinning. Camilla turns to her father.

'It's just a note from a friend I got to know in London,' she says. 'Perhaps I'll go visit her.'

'So soon? You only just came,' he says softly.

'I shan't leave right away,' she answers, holding the letter.

It is like a shield, protecting her. What more does one need? Now she can sleep at night, and occupy herself during the day. Tend the flowers, play cards with her father, canter around the property – see friends, even, perhaps. The prison doors have opened in front of her, and they will remain open. She need not rush to leave, now. The joy of expectant waiting is one of the most intense.

Like a flow of water into an empty place, meaning has returned to the rhythm of the days.

VIII. Betrayal

Like a person in delirium, Camilla has analysed the nature of her pain a thousand and again a thousand times; like the swirls on the wallpaper, it is always the same and inescapable. She has confronted herself, she has exercised her self-control, clenched her teeth, stared severely at the distraught girl in the mirror and spoken aloud to her, in a voice harsh with misery.

'And what, exactly, are you finding so very hard to bear?'

There are too many answers. There is no answer. Periods of peace still as forest pools are interrupted, too often, by shocks so severe that Camilla spends the nights walking up and down her room, faster and faster, gnawing her fist and watching the colour of the sky change slowly from black to blue to pink. A pain so intense cannot last for hours, yet it does.

Sylvia is going to be married; she told Camilla about it quite lightly, brushing aside her stammered objections, ignoring the horror in her eyes.

'Camilla, it won't change anything – nothing at all. Except that I'll be freer. You'll come down and visit – I'll come up and visit you. Why should you mind?'

She has no idea, no idea of anything; no more idea of other people's feelings than a buzzing bee who dips for honey or stings. For a fleeting moment, Camilla feels acutely sorry for Sylvia's future husband, a sharp point of pity piercing the shield of hatred she holds up against him. Hours go by before she asks the only question.

'But do you love him?'

'What nonsense! Have you seen him? Camilla – he's old and rich. I thought he wanted to marry

Mother all this time. Mother thought so too, I'm sure. But now he's asked for me instead.'

'But why in heaven's name don't you refuse?'

'Oh, Camilla, I have to marry; Mother wants me to. She needs the money; we've nothing here, less than nothing, only debts. And what do I care who it is? If not him, it would just be someone else.'

'But shan't you hate him touching you?'

Sylvia's eyes blazed like a cat's for just an instant.

'He won't.'

'Are you stupid, Sylvia?'

'You don't know me.'

And perhaps she is right. She is stupid and ignorant, thoughtless, and yet she is absolute. And Camilla wants to believe her, so desperately.

'If he touches you I'll–'

'If he touches me I'll–'

Their voices, simultaneously, die away because there is no need.

XI. The Princesse de Lamballe

It is in Paris, beautiful Paris, that Camilla learns

about the princess. And the night is lit by a thousand shooting stars.

How could she not have known?

Marie Thérèse Louise de Savoie-Carignan, Princesse de Lamballe.

Lamballe, a name of infinitely many resonances. Lamballe, ball – the days of her glory and her love, sparkling before all the court. Lamballe, lamb – a lamb, led to the slaughter. Lamballe, *lamelle* – the shreds of her flesh torn to pieces by the raging crowd.

It is the little professor who opens, for Camilla, the door to a new existence. He flutters.

'My researches are so very fascinating, so very fascinating, but it is most difficult to discuss them with the English,' he says. 'The English ... your Queen ... so very prudish. English girls...'

'Oh, we are not really like that,' says Camilla engagingly. And learns far more than she ever dreamed. Learns, above all, that she is not alone, has never been alone, has belonged, forever, to a sorority whose glory and beauty was sung, recognised, celebrated for centuries, before being forced into shame and oblivion by the forbidding decrees of Christianity.

The professor speaks and speaks; timidly at first, then freely, and even passionately.

'The rabble of the streets grew to hate Marie-Antoinette for her lightheartedness, the flamboyant display of her riches, her life of pleasure, her disregard of duty. And they directed their fearsome hatred to the princess, her closest, her dearest friend, whom she tenderly loved for so many years. And the princess became, in the mouths of the rabble, the sign and symbol of unspeakable dissolution and debauchery.

'Safe in England in 1791, she returned to France to join the desperate Queen and the rest of the royal family who, confined to the Tuileries palace, daily suffered the increased power of the Assembly led by the monster Robespierre, and the screams and insults of the crowd under their windows.

'All were arrested there together on the 10th of August, 1792: Marie-Antoinette and Louis XVI, their two surviving children, the Princesse de Lamballe and also the Princesse Elisabeth, sister of the king; the entire family was imprisoned together in the Temple. But the day came on which the Princesse de Lamballe was sent, alone, to public judgement.

'Her trial was one of those many sickening farces which the Revolution has bequeathed us. She would not take the oath against the King, and for this, she was condemned and sent forth from the tribunal, in the full knowledge that the ravening crowd was waiting outside to snatch her from the hands of her guards and tear her limb from limb then and there, in the very courtyard of the prison – you can see the place today, if you wish; it is in the rue du Roi de Sicile. The prison itself is gone, of course, but the stones still bear the memory of her blood.

'The violent destruction of her body, the promenading of her head upon a pike under the very windows of the Temple where the poor Queen was confined, the lewd screams and shouts and the accusations of the bloodthirsty crowd – all of these things have been described and documented again and again. My work as a historian, which I have written down in books that you can certainly find in the library if you are really interested, has been to try to determine, from the surface film of envy and revenge and violence that drove the populace into a wild medley of accusations, expressed in all manner of speeches, pamphlets, drawings and jingles – what, in all these accusations, can be taken as the true reflection of a deep, intimate and secret reality. I have spent many years studying every known aspect and detail of the relationship between the two women; I have read the memoirs of their family members and of the ladies-in-waiting who attended them, and I have tried to read between the lines without ever betraying the search for truth. And I came, many years ago, to the conclusion that the love which bound these two women together was–' (here the professor, who had delivered the whole of this lecture to his hands, which, fragile and veined, lay before him upon the table, glances quickly up and then down again) '–what we call a Sapphic love, a love of passion, that kind of love which, ceding to irresistible impulses defying all rational behaviour, can often lead to terrible disaster. Had the princess not returned from England, or had she accepted the many possibilities of escape which presented themselves to her while she remained with the beleaguered royal family in the Tuileries palace, she would not merely have been safe and well, but she could even have worked, from a distance, at their rescue. Had she not forgiven the Queen for her betrayal, in transferring for a long time her affections and favours to the Princesse de Polignac; had this distanced her from the Queen, she might then have been saved. But as I believe it, her love for the Queen defied all such measure. Having once become bound to her in the flesh, she could never again endure the test of physical separation; she must needs be near her, even when the poor Queen, in her despair, no longer had any mind or inclination for pleasure. It is just as in many marriages, which lead to the binding together of husband and wife in body and soul more deeply than ever, once the fire of youth has died into glowing embers. Of course, the true nature of the relationship between these two extraordinary women will never be known; all this is theory, based on the multitude of clues that history has left us. But I, for one, am as convinced that it was what I say as if I were personally acquainted with the protagonists.'

'Even if one were personally acquainted with the

protagonists, how could one know such a thing?' says Camilla, teasing yet afraid of the old man's perspicacity. Again he looks up at her, again that quick glance of flame.

'Who can ever know?' he says, quizzically, and quietly. 'Who can ever know?'

X. Sappho

That man seems to me peer of gods, who sits in thy presence, and hears close to him thy sweet speech and lovely laughter; that indeed makes my heart flutter in my bosom. For when I see thee but a little, I have no utterance left, my tongue is broken down, and straightway a subtle fire has run under my skin, with my eyes I have no sight, my ears ring, sweat pours down, and a trembling seizes all my body; I am paler than grass, and seem in my madness little better than one dead. But I must dare all, since one so poor...

XI. Birth

Camilla leaves the library and finds that her legs are trembling underneath her, will barely carry her. She sits down on a bench underneath a chestnut tree, whose large, lush green leaves shade and veil the flushed confusion and amazement that she cannot hide. Camilla has begun to exist; she herself, the person that she is. The flush of shame as she feels this new existence as a birth. A birth is a passage from the womb to the world.

Before, she was hidden, or believed she was; a

non-being. It was a torture akin to sequestration. Yet it was safe.

Now, she feels exposed.

'Nothing has changed,' she tells herself. 'It's only I, I who didn't know. It was all there, all in the books. There is no difference, no difference at all.'

But she feels public.

XII. Wearing trousers

'Why do you care, Camilla? Why? What does it matter, what other people see and think and believe and gossip about?'

'I don't know. I care. The eyes of others are like a ... a mirror in which you can see yourself being. Can you imagine standing in front of a mirror and seeing nothing facing back at you? I want to *be* there! I want to be myself, with my flame and all complete, and see it reflected back in the mirror of their eyes. I want the impossible – I want to walk down the Champs Elysées with you on my arm and stare, head high, at all I cross. I cannot live in secrecy – I'm not a clandestine being. I hate it – I hate it! I need sunlight.'

Sylvia looks at her wonderingly. It is clear that she cannot understand.

'I like secrecy,' she says thoughtfully. 'Looking

violates the thing inside. I want to preserve it pure.'

Camilla is still preoccupied by her discovery.

'Sylvia,' she says suddenly. 'How did you learn – how did you know about yourself? Being *this* way, I mean? When did you realise it?'

Sylvia reflects for a moment, stirring the long spoon in her glass.

'I never realised it, because I always knew it,' she says finally. 'There was never any discovery, any break, for me.' She smiles, remembering. 'Even when I was a child... You know, I used to have a governess; she was very beautiful. As far back as I can remember, I adored her because she was so tall and dark and noble. I loved her, and loving her, I wanted to touch her all the time. I was constantly in her lap ... and even when I was older, I still always wanted to sit on her lap and press myself against her breasts.'

'And what did she do? What did she say?'

'Nothing. She let me do it. Now, I think that perhaps she didn't know how to say something without hurting me or shaming me or making a scandal; perhaps she would have, some day, but she left when I was fifteen. She was always very reserved; she never really responded to me, yet she never rejected me: never. I used to kiss her and kiss her...'

375

Sylvia's voice trails away into memories. Camilla thinks with pain: no wonder she was able to become what she is: so natural, so free from inner conflict. And she thinks of the soft breasts and tender arms of the governess.

They sit in silence, together, next to each other – cool drinks – tall glasses – little round marble-topped table – wide sidewalk – broad boulevard – arching chestnut trees ... and Camilla champs inwardly and desperately over her inner contradiction, while Sylvia turns her glass calmly between her fingers; condensed moisture is dripping down the outside of it. The tips of Sylvia's fingers are cold and wet, as she touches Camilla's wrist very lightly, with a little smile.

'You know,' she says, 'you could have your wish, and I mine.'

'I never can,' says Camilla gloomily.

'It depends on what you want,' says Sylvia, looking at her friend intently. 'And on how daring you are. Why don't you dress like a man?'

Her words strike Camilla's fevered brain like a powerful blow, causing her thoughts to shatter into shards like a smashed glass. Kaleidoscope images tumble in her mind.

Why not?

How could she have never thought of it before?

Could it be done? Is it feasible?

Why not?

Sylvia leans forward, murmurs in her ear, so close that her lips brush a bit of hair. Her voice is warm, contains a vibrating laugh underneath its quiet tones.

'Let's do it,' she says. 'We can shop tomorrow – for your brother, we'll pretend. And cut your hair. Oh, Camilla – what an adventure!'

XIII. Free

Camilla cannot believe the change which occurs in her the very moment she pulls on the unfamiliar garments, the curtains drawn over the sunny window, her dress, as though it contained her very personality, flung limp and abandoned over the bed; left, temporarily, behind. She stares in the mirror, holds up her arms to hide her too-familiar head, watches her long legs encased in trousers, planted well apart, buttons the stiff jacket over the firm, even surface she has created by binding a cloth tightly over her small breasts, as she has heard that the Japanese ladies do. She feels like leaping and shouting; she whirls about, laughing, to face Sylvia, whose subjugated expression provokes a burning wave. She practices throwing herself onto a chair, long-legged and free. She drapes one leg casually over the arm.

'Pity about the hair,' she says, letting it down. 'I can't go out like this.'

She puts on her dress reluctantly, but her impatience drives her.

Sylvia takes her to a hairdresser's shop on a little side street. Without undue shame, Camilla explains what she wants.

'Short like a man, and a chignon made from the cuttings.'

'Oui, Madame.' Used to every absurd folly, no questions asked. He washes the hair, combs it out, cuts quickly and surely. Sylvia is sitting nearby, watching. The long locks fall to the ground; Camilla thought she would feel some regret, but instead feels only lighter and freer as the thick short waves lift and come to life, unencumbered by the weight that always pulled them down. The switch will be ready only the next day. Camilla returns home timidly, wearing a large hat.

'I can't go to the dining room like this,' she says, removing it in front of the mirror, ruffling the hair, staring at herself, entranced, amazed.

'Silly,' says Sylvia, handing her the trousers.

And now it is true. Camilla is transformed; Camilla, in fact, is gone.

'Gone to the library!' smirks Sylvia insanely.

A young man stares back at her, takes her arm.

'We're going out,' he says, his voice quiet and low. And together, excited, tense, fearful and adventurous, they brave the streets.

Nothing happens. No one notices anything. And that, in itself, is the most exciting and extraordinary thing of all. Camilla increases in bravery; she stops staring at the ground, stands tall, strides long, laughs.

'We're going to have supper in a restaurant,' she says. And they do.

When they return to the hotel, she is inflamed as never before.

XIV. The Party

They go out together every evening.

After a *verre d'absinthe*, they begin to invent wild plans.

'Let's elope and live together on a Greek island,' whispers Camilla. 'Let's go to a church and get married. Let's hunt antelope together in the savannah.'

But Sylvia, as usual, dazzles her with the infinitely higher degree of daring contained in her perfectly feasible, down-to-earth projects. After all, she is the one who said *Dress like a man*. And now she says,

'Let's go to a party together.'

'A party? What party?'

'We're invited to the Hardwicks' this evening. Let's go there.'

'Sylvia! *Camilla* is invited there with you – there are people we *know!* It'll never work.'

After another absinthe, they decide to go. Camilla will speak only French, and introduce herself as a Russian prince.

'This is mad,' she says. She is terrified. Sylvia is crazy with laughing.

'When I do something silly, this is what I always say to myself,' she gasps, 'what is the worst thing that can possibly happen?'

'"Camilla, what *do* you mean by that ridiculous get-up?"' says Camilla, mimicking being recognised instantly by their high-nosed hostess.

'"Dear Eleanor, Sylvia has been behaving most peculiarly,"' chokes Sylvia, mimicking a letter being addressed to her mother by a well-meaning blue-haired busybody. They are laughing so much they can hardly breathe.

But when they arrive at the party, after the first minute of sheer terror, Camilla realises that nobody recognises her; it is not so surprising, after all. She has only encountered their hostess once before, and that briefly. She stops wanting to burst into nervous laughter and begins to live her part; to live her life, she thinks. Camilla is a part.

'Where is Camilla?'

The words break on her ear like a wave, she looks up, startled. But Mr Hardwick is addressing Sylvia.

'She couldn't come, I'm so sorry,' Sylvia is saying with impressive self-composure. 'She – she had to go to the library!' Camilla loves her madly. Her face burns as she hooks her arm over Sylvia's and draws her away.

She adopts her role so completely that she feels Slavic to the soul.

'This is my friend, Vassily Semionovich, Prince Yousoupoff,' says Sylvia inanely to a bunch of old ladies who fan themselves, fluttering, and Camilla becomes the Russian prince, advances a leg and swings her arm over the back of a chair in a pose of casual mastery.

Oh, the moment of exquisite panic and beauty when Mr Hardwick suddenly takes it into her stupid head to introduce the Russian prince to a Russian diplomat! Within five seconds, he has grasped that the impostor in front of him is no Russian at all – *but the real imposition in front of his very eyes – of that, he sees nothing!* Flooded, blinded by euphoria, Camilla recounts a ridiculous tale of a joke and binds him to the secret – and he merely laughs, and promises.

'Do you mind, sometimes,' Sylvia asks her later, 'that you do after all need to disguise? Does it mar your pleasure in being able to behave openly?'

'No!' answers Camilla, so sharply she surprises herself. 'This is the openness that I wanted. This is it; I have it. I don't need the other Camilla, the one in the dress. She can disappear, she can–'

'–go to the library!' finishes Sylvia with a giggle.

XV. The farm

Marie-Antoinette had it built for her entertainment; a frivolous, artificial but ravishingly beautiful plaything. Sylvia and Camilla walk through it, through the little dilapidated buildings: stable, dairy, farmhouse. Their thatched rooves are half eaten away and their yellowish colour is dirty, yet it is easy to see how dainty they must have been when they were fresh and new. A toy for a princess.

'It cost a fortune to have it all built,' said Camilla.

'Even the lake is artificial. And look at the little houses around it; she had a whole tiny toy village built next to her farm.'

Enormous branches of wisteria twine around the half-collapsed balconies, covered in light green leaves; the flowers are gone already. A pigeon-house, a bee-garden, a vegetable patch. Camilla can only shake her head in disbelief. It is the tangible sign of a cosmic effort to play at life.

'What does it mean to play at life?' wonders Sylvia, unconvinced.

'To engage yourself in something ... but not deeply. Not for real. Just for fun, or for show.'

'Like me marrying,' she says then. 'Perhaps I meant to play at it.'

'You did,' says Camilla.

'But George didn't,' she answers. Camilla whirls, turns on her.

'Sylvia – have you – has he–'

'No,' she says, a little wrinkle of worry appearing between her eyes, belying her unconcerned voice. 'Camilla, you know I never will. I don't want to, and anyway, I couldn't. I should go mad. But then, I am destined to go mad anyway, I suppose. In fact, I am already mad.'

'Nonsense, Sylvia, what are you saying? Sylvia – if it's becoming very bad, you should leave him!'

'Oh, Camilla, I can't leave him any more. I didn't want to tell you. He's got a certificate from a doctor friend of his, that says I'm quite mad. Really he does. He made him write it because he did the doctor a favour. He told me if I make him, he'll use it to have me locked up in a madhouse.'

Camilla stares at her in blank shock.

'Sylvia, how can you bear to go on with it?'

'Oh, he won't really do it, I suppose,' says Sylvia, smoothing out her forehead with her fingers. 'At least I hope not. Anyway, I'm here now.'

She has a magic ability, which Camilla totally lacks, to remain carefree under such a menace, as long as she is momentarily far away from it. But Camilla is cramped with terror. Sylvia twines her arms around her neck with kisses.

'Perhaps I'll never go back,' she says. 'Let's just stay here forever.'

Reality has no power over her.

XVI. Escape

'We know too many people in Paris. Let's leave.'

Camilla has slipped so entirely into the skin of a young man that the feel of the lace ruffle on her fingers confuses her when she buttons her blouse, and the swish of the long skirt swinging around her legs feels awkward, like a disguise, like an obstacle. She puts them on, hating it, when they must visit Sylvia's friends.

'Your clothes are so lovely, Camilla – it's almost a pity!'

'I never want to see them again. I'll still make things for you.'

And they leave Paris altogether and take a train up to Deauville, and live in the night altogether; dancing, gambling, walking on the waterfront wrapped in greatcoats, kissing on the beach under the winking stars, sleeping until the afternoon. Moonlight is their time – moonlight is the time for secrets. Deauville is their place – a nocturnal town where phantom people dripping with phantom diamonds fling phantom money, laughing, to the winds.

When they run out, Sylvia says they must return to Paris and wire.

'You wire your father for money, and I'll wire George and say we're staying on here. I wonder what he'll say,' she suggests. 'Perhaps he'll come and get me, and lock me up in a madhouse after all.' She laughs, half-bitterly, half-lightly. And Camilla spends another night of agony, trying to pierce the blackness out of the window, trying to pierce the blackness of the future, while Sylvia lies in bed, her naked limbs abandoned in sleep, and incomprehensibly, perfectly tranquil.

The manuscript broke off suddenly at this point. My candle had grown small as I read, and now, as I remained still and trembling, it guttered and went out. I sat in the dark, clutching the bundle of papers, pictures whirling in my brain, unable to think or act. A long time passed, I believe, before I finally rose and tried to feel my way quietly, in the pitch darkness, back to my room. It was only a few feet away, but objects were littered about the place, and I soon knocked something over – it fell with a crash and I gasped into the darkness.

A match scraped nearby and I heard the sound of a bolt, and simultaneously, saw a line of light form underneath the door leading into Sylvia's room. It opened, and she stood in the doorway, framed in the square of light. She stared at me, and it seemed to me that on her face, in her wide eyes, was imprinted a strange look of horror that I had never seen there before. Her eyes fell upon the papers in my hand, and she raised them in a quick glance to the top of the closet, then to my face.

'So you know,' she said quietly.

'Yes. I know now. Did you know?' I answered. I spoke low, but could not whisper, for it was too ghostly in that dark room, shivering with spirits of the dead.

'Only today, when Mother's wire came. She only wrote that you had come back, and wanted to see me. I thought it quite ordinary, but Camilla panicked. I didn't understand at first, when she said you must have realised everything. She said you were looking for George's murderer, she knew it. She said that that lady in Paris, Mrs Clemming, had written to Mother while you were over there. Camila saw the letter arrive, though Mother never mentioned it. I thought that stupid lady just wanted to scold Mother for my bad behaviour in Paris, but Camilla was sure that it was because you were investigating over there. She was so upset this morning, when the wire came. I couldn't understand it. *Don't you see? She knows. She knows it was me*, she said. I stared at her. It took me a long time to understand. *You'd better leave. Go back home*, she said. *I'll write to you.* So I left. It seemed like such a long way back. I arrived after you had gone up, so I went to bed, but I couldn't sleep. Then I heard something fall in here, and knew it was you.' She paused for a moment.

'I feel numb,' she continued. 'I don't seem to be able to feel anything. Camilla is gone. She's gone forever, I think. Maybe to Russia, maybe to Africa. And I can't feel what she did, I can't feel that she's gone. I feel dead.'

'It's shock,' I said gently, going to her.

'People thought it was for the money!' she said, with a strange giggle. 'The money – George's money! What'll happen to it now? I don't want it – I'll never touch it, even if they give it to me, after all. Oh, it isn't mine – if I had my way, I'd –

387

I'd make it all over to Ellen's little boy.' She was speaking a little feverishly, her eyes strange, her breath short. 'If only – if only there was some way they could prove he was really George's son.'

'I think it could be proven,' I said softly, remembering the photograph. I approached her, worried about the echo of madness in her voice, and held out the manuscript, I don't know why. But she pushed my hand away.

'Oh no, not that!' she cried. 'I don't want it, I never want to see it again! Oh God, I'm afraid of it – it means death ... yet it means love. It's too beautiful to destroy.' She paused, and added softly, 'Do you think Camilla will write to me? I don't know what I'll do if she does. Burn the letter, maybe. Or follow her to the ends of the earth. I don't know. I don't know.'

She reached out a finger and lightly touched the manuscript I held, then turned away and returned to her room, silently.

The dawn was just beginning to flush the sky with pink streaks. I closed my door behind me and tried to lie down upon my bed, but I could not rest at all; it seemed to hold a secret horror for me. I rose and dressed instead, packed my small bag, thrusting Camilla's manuscript deep into it amongst my things, and now I am writing to you until it should be late enough for Peter to be about his work. Oh, Dora, I cannot face Mrs Bryce-Fortescue and tell her these things – I cannot! I mean to slip away to Cambridge as soon as I can get Peter to take me to the station. I need to go home, I need to see Arthur. I shall write or telegraph from there – but only God knows what I shall say...

Your desperately upset

Vanessa

Cambridge, Sunday, July 24, 1892

My dearest sister,

All is over; I am here, and safe. I am worn out with it all. Only this morning, awakening with the sun, I suddenly remembered that the fresh breeze blowing the curtains and the shrill birdsong outside signified, perhaps, the beginning of a new chapter in my life.

Yesterday after I finished writing to you, I picked up my bag and went out to the stable. I thought it might still be too early, but I found Peter there already, employed in waxing saddles.

'Peter, I need you to take me to the station,' I said miserably.

'So you're leaving,' he said tonelessly, putting down his work.

'Yes, I am leaving,' I said. He stood up, and began the complex work of leading out the horses and hitching them up without speaking or looking at me.

'Oh, Peter,' I said, climbing up on the box beside him, 'I do feel terrible that I never told you I was engaged. It was awful of me. I am so sorry. Please forgive me. But I never thought you would

389

care at all – I thought it was all just...'

I stopped, for why should I add another lie to all the harm I had already done? I had seen well enough that he was growing fond of me.

'It doesn't matter, Miss Vanessa,' he said with a ghostly smile. 'It was all just... That's all it was. All I want now is to get away from this place and this family and start off afresh.'

'That is all I want, as well,' I said with heartfelt sincerity. He glanced up at me in quick surprise, but said nothing until we reached the little country station in the nearest village. Only then, as he reached my bag down and helped me alight, did he speak again, but then it was with a kinder expression in his eyes.

'Goodbye, then,' he said with the hint of a smile. 'Folks like you and me will always fall on their feet, I think. So it's all right. Good luck!' He turned away abruptly, and heaving a sigh of mingled guilt and relief, I stepped onto the quay, sat down upon a sunny and dilapidated wooden bench, and waited for the first train of the day.

It took me far too long to reach home; changing trains, and waiting, alone, on platforms in tiny stations overgrown with vines, in villages with enchanting names. It was afternoon already when I reached Mrs Fitzwilliam's house. I rushed upstairs at once, and knocked on Arthur's door, terrified that he would not be in. But he opened it at once, took one look at me and collected me in his arms.

'Oh, Arthur,' I cried. 'You didn't want me to shake hands with a murderer...'

It took me a long time to steel myself to tell Arthur everything; much longer, in fact, than it took for the actual telling. He listened, white, and wanted to rush to the police at once.

'Wait just a moment,' I said. 'There is something I must show you.'

Not sure I was doing the right thing, not sure what to do at all, I slowly dug Camilla's manuscript out from among my tumbled things and handed it to him. He read through it attentively; it took him some time. After he finished it, he put it down upon the table and remained silent for a while; when he spoke, it was to quote the words of Rosalind.

Were it not better
Because that I am more than common tall,
That I did suit me all points like a man?
A gallant curtle-axe upon my thigh,
A boar spear in my hand; and – in my heart
Lie there what hidden woman's fear there will –
We'll have a swashing and a martial outside,
As many other mannish cowards have
That do outface it with their semblances.

He paused, and then, taking my hand, he said, 'I think we must go to the p-p-p-; to the police. Now.'

I hesitated; it felt wrong and yet I felt it must be inexorably the only thing to do. I was afraid of Camilla's being arrested and also afraid that she would be long gone. Above all, I felt that I no longer had any will at all in the matter. Dora, I felt quite simply too tired, bone-tired. I followed Arthur wordlessly outside.

We were proceeding down the path to the gate

when it swung open vigorously, and Pat O'Sulli-van walked up towards us with his springiest step.

'So you're back!' he exclaimed eagerly, rushing towards me. 'Well? Have you found everything out?' He stopped short, taking in the expression on our faces.

'What is it?' he said. 'You two look about as cheerful as gravestones. Is it something to do with the murder? What's going on?'

I turned to Arthur, unable to answer. But he was not looking at me nor even at Pat; he was looking down the path to the gate. A young boy was standing in front of it, studying it. He put his hand out and pushed it open, but remained peering in hesitantly.

'What are you looking for?' Arthur called out to him.

He consulted something white he held in his hand.

'Does Miss Vanessa Duncan live here?' he enquired.

'I am she,' I said, leaving go of Arthur's hand and hastening down the path.

'Letter for you, Miss,' he said, giving it to me. 'Hand delivery. Lady gave it to me yesterday afternoon to be delivered after twenty-four hours, she said.'

Half consciously I saw Arthur thanking the boy and handing him a bit of coin. I knew who the letter was from before I tore open the envelope which bore my name. I extracted the sheets it contained, and read them; leaning over my shoulder, Pat and Arthur read them too.

Dear Vanessa,

You will most surely not wish to receive a letter from such a person as I am, and for this reason I will remain brief considering myself lucky enough if you will only consent to open it.

Your sudden appearance, your subsequent trip to Paris, the anxiety of Sylvia's mother – all these things finally caused me to understand your true purpose among us, and that for my own safety, as worthless and unjustified as that may be now that I belong to the abhorred portion of humanity which shares the brand of Cain, I am better far away.

Yet I cringe at the idea that any blame for anything that has happened should fall on any head but my own, and for this reason, I have written a confession, after a great deal of reflection on how to best achieve my purpose. It is addressed directly to the police; I humbly beg that you will transmit it to them without delay.

Yours sincerely,

Camilla Wright

The letter to the police was written on a loose sheet of paper; I pulled it out and read it over, Pat breathing heavily in my ear.

To the British Police,

I the undersigned, Camilla Wright, hereby admit and

confess to the murder of Mr George Burton Granger of Haverhill Manor, Haverhill. I shot Mr Granger because he betrayed me. Unsatisfied by his wife, he turned to me for solace and declared that his passion for me was such that he had never felt anything like it, that his marriage was an error, that he would have it annulled and that we would be married as soon as possible. Although Mrs Granger was one of my closest friends, I naturally kept this affair entirely secret from her.

Recently, by a strange coincidence, I discovered that Mr Granger had had a mistress by whom he had a son. I taxed him with it, and during the scene that ensued, he changed completely; he told me that he had had and continued to have many mistresses, that I was merely one of them and had never been anything more to him than a passing whim; that far from annulling his marriage, he now intended to consummate it and ensure himself of a legitimate heir.

In the early afternoon of the fifth of June of this year 1892, I shot Mr Granger in the chest with my own personal weapon, purchased in France several months earlier. In order to avoid detection, I travelled up to Dover and crossed over to Calais, then came back from there disguised as a man with a red cape, hoping to be noticed and remembered by a number of people; it was an easy matter to remove my disguise in the train back to London. I hoped to escape suspicion entirely, but I see now that what I have done is bringing undeserved fear and accusation to innocent people. I write my confession for this reason: I, and I alone, am responsible for Mr Granger's death.

394

Dona nobis pacem.

Camilla Wright

I had barely had time to take in what I was reading before Pat was off, setting the bell on the gate a-jangle as he swung through.

'Police won't see the press before tomorrow morning at the earliest,' he called back over his shoulder. 'Maybe I can make the evening paper with this! Yes!'

'Oh, Arthur, how awful,' I murmured, hiding my face against his coat. 'I shouldn't have let him see it.'

'Murder is awful,' he answered. 'It doesn't matter, Vanessa. Pat can't make any difference now. Camilla left yesterday morning, didn't she? She must be halfway across Europe by this time. Whether they find her or not is a matter of chance at this point; it doesn't depend on what Pat does, or even on what we do. For the moment at least, she seems to have escaped by a narrow margin.'

'Maybe too narrow,' I answered, turning resolutely towards the gate.

Mathematical History in *Flowers Stained with Moonlight*

The main events concerning the story of Fermat's Last Theorem occurred as recounted in this book. Pierre de Fermat (1601-1665), professional magistrate, and amateur but brilliant mathematician, wrote exactly the famous claim quoted by Korneck in the margin of his copy of *Diophantus*; it is now commonly believed that his proof must have contained an error which he quite possibly later noticed himself. He was not immune to errors; he did claim to have proved his theorem for the exponent $n=3$, but there is a gap in his proof which was repaired only a century later by the astoundingly prolific Swiss mathematician Leonhard Euler (1707-1783) – at least, there appears to be a gap in Euler's proof as well, but that one has been convincingly plugged since then.

The young Sophie Germain (1776-1831) was indeed forced to assume a male identity both to study (by correspondence) at the Ecole Polytechnique and to address herself to the great Carl Friedrich Gauss (1777-1855), who, upon discovering her true identity as described, wrote her the letter quoted in the text.

The public rivalry between Augustin Cauchy (1789-1857) and Gabriel Lamé (1795-1870), who deposited sealed manuscripts at the

Academy of Sciences and published successive portions of their 'proofs' until the breakthrough described in the letter by Ernst Kummer (1810-1893) was publicly read out in front of all the members, really existed; it is documented by the reports of the weekly meetings published in the *Comptes-Rendus de l'Académie des Sciences,* and the two passages concerning Cauchy are cited verbatim. These old *Comptes-Rendus,* containing reports on every kind of scientific progress, and sundry remarks upon the behaviour of the members, make remarkably interesting reading.

The record of the submission of an attempted proof of Fermat's theorem by a certain G. Korneck of Kempen, Poznània, and the brief report on it by Henri Poincaré (1854-1912) are reproduced here exactly as they were published in the *Comptes-Rendus,* although they actually appeared a little later, in 1894. Apart from this unfortunate effort, G. Korneck has left no other detectable trace; the depiction of his character in this book is entirely fictional.

A most informative popular rendering of the story of Fermat's Last Theorem from its inception until its final proof by Andrew Wiles in 1994, can be found in the book *Fermat's Last Theorem* by Simon Singh (Fourth Estate, London, 1997). A very complete website containing the biographies of hundreds of mathematicians can be found on the Internet at the address

http://www-gap.dcs.st-and.ac.uk/~history/ BiogIndex.html

Although not mathematical, it is worth noting that the facts concerning the Princesse de Lamballe recounted in the novel are also entirely historical, including the contemporary accusations linking her with Marie-Antoinette. The ultimate truth on this matter, of course, is unlikely ever to be known.

The publishers hope that this book has given you enjoyable reading. Large Print Books are especially designed to be as easy to see and hold as possible. If you wish a complete list of our books please ask at your local library or write directly to:

Magna Large Print Books
Magna House, Long Preston,
Skipton, North Yorkshire.
BD23 4ND